"So when were you going to tell me that you were pregnant?" Kruz demanded.

"You seem more concerned about my faults than our child. There were so many times when I wanted to tell you…. I don't want to argue with you about this, Kruz. I want to discuss what has happened while we've got the chance. For God's sake, Kruz, what's wrong with you? Anyone would think you were trying to drive me away—taking your child with me."

"You'll stay here until I tell you to go," he said, snatching hold of her arm.

"Let me go!" Romy cried furiously.

"There's nowhere for you to go. There's just thousands of miles of nothing out there."

"I'm leaving Argentina—"

"And then what?" he demanded.

"And then I make a life for me and our baby—the baby you don't care to acknowledge."

Was that a flicker of something human in his eyes? Had she got through to him at last? His grip had relaxed on her arm.

Dear Reader,

We know how much you love Harlequin®Presents®, so this month we wanted to treat you to something extra special—a second classic story by the same author for free!

Once you have finished reading *Taming the Last Acosta*, just turn the page for another powerful working together story from Susan Stephens.

This month, indulge yourself with double the reading pleasure!

With love,

The Presents Editors

Susan Stephens

TAMING THE LAST ACOSTA

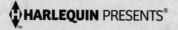

ISBN-13: 978-0-373-13132-7

TAMING THE LAST ACOSTA

Copyright © 2013 by Harlequin Books S.A.

The publisher acknowledges the copyright holder of the individual works as follows:

TAMING THE LAST ACOSTA
Copyright © 2013 by Susan Stephens

ITALIAN BOSS, PROUD MISS PRIM
Copyright © 2009 by Susan Stephens

Recycling programs for this product may not exist in your area.

Printed in U.S.A.

www.Harlequin.com

CONTENTS

All about the author...
Susan Stephens

SUSAN STEPHENS was a professional singer before meeting her husband on the tiny Mediterranean island of Malta. In true Presents style they met on Monday, became engaged on Friday and were married three months later. Almost thirty years and three children later they are still in love. (Susan does not advise her children to return home one day with a similar story, as she may not take the news with the same fortitude as her own mother!)

Susan had written several nonfiction books when fate took a hand. At a charity costume ball there was an after-dinner auction. One of the lots, "Spend a Day with an Author," had been donated by Presents author Penny Jordan. Susan's husband bought this lot, and Penny was to become not just a great friend, but a wonderful mentor who encouraged Susan to write romance.

Susan loves her family, her pets, her friends and her writing. She enjoys entertaining, travel and going to the theatre. She reads, cooks and plays the piano to relax, and can occasionally be found throwing herself off mountains on a pair of skis or galloping through the countryside.

Visit Susan's website: www.susanstephens.net. She loves to hear from her readers all around the world!

Other titles by Susan Stephens available in ebook:

Harlequin Presents®

TAMING THE LAST ACOSTA

For Joanne, who holds my hand when
I'm in the dentist's chair.

CHAPTER ONE

TWO PEOPLE IN the glittering wedding marquee appeared distanced from the celebrations. One was a photojournalist, known as Romy Winner, for whom detachment was part of her job. Kruz Acosta, the brother of the groom, had no excuse. With his wild dark looks, barely mellowed by formal wedding attire, Romily—who preferred to call herself no-nonsense Romy—thought Kruz perfectly suited to the harsh, unforgiving pampas in Argentina where this wedding was taking place.

Trying to slip deeper into the shadows, she stole some more shots of him. Immune to feeling when she was working, this time she felt excitement grip her. Not just because every photo editor in the world would pay a fortune to get their hands on her shots of Kruz Acosta, the most elusive of the notorious Acosta brothers, but because Kruz stirred her in some dark, atavistic way, involving a violently raised heartbeat and a lot of ill-timed appreciation below the belt.

Perhaps it was his air of menace, or maybe it was his hard-edged warrior look, but whatever it was she was enjoying it.

All four Acosta brothers were big, powerful men, but rumours abounded where Kruz was concerned, which made him all the more intriguing. A veteran of Special Forces, educated in both Europe and America, Kruz was believed to work for two governments now, though no one really knew anything about him other than his success in business and his prowess on the polo field.

She was getting to know him through her camera lens at this wedding of Kruz's older brother, Nacho, to his beautiful blind bride, Grace. What she had learned so far was less than reassuring: Kruz missed nothing. She ducked out of sight as he scanned the sumptuously decorated wedding venue, no doubt looking for unwanted visitors like her.

It was time to forget Kruz Acosta and concentrate on work, Romy told herself sternly, even if he *was* compelling viewing to someone who made her living out of stand-out shots. It would take more than a froth of tulle and a family reunion to soften Kruz Acosta, Romy guessed, as she ran off another series of images she knew Ronald, her editor at *ROCK!*, would happily give his eye teeth for.

Just one or two more and then she'd make herself scarce…

Maybe sooner rather than later, Romy concluded as Kruz glanced her way. This job would have been a pleasure if she'd had an official press pass, but *ROCK!* was considered a scandal sheet by many, so no one from *ROCK!* had received an invitation to the wedding. Romy was attending on secret business for the bride, on the understanding that she could use some of the shots for other purposes.

Romy's fame as a photographer had reached Grace through Holly Acosta, one of Romy's colleagues at *ROCK!* The three women had been having secret meetings over the past few months, culminating in Grace declaring that she would trust no one but Romy to make a photographic record of her wedding for her husband, Nacho, and for any children they might have. Inspired by the blind bride's courage, Romy had agreed. Grace was fast becoming a friend rather than just another client, and this was a chance in a million for Romy to see the

Acostas at play—though she doubted Kruz would be as accommodating as the bride if he caught her.

So he mustn't catch her, Romy determined, shivering with awareness as she focused her lens on the one man in the marquee her camera loved above all others. He had a special sort of energy that seemed to reach her across the crowded tent, and the menace he threw out was alarming. The more shots she took of him, the more she couldn't imagine that much got in his way. It was easy to picture Kruz as a rebellious youth who had gone on to win medals for gallantry in the Special Forces. All the bespoke tailoring in the world couldn't hide the fact that Kruz Acosta was a weapon in disguise. He now ran a formidably successful security company, which placed him firmly in charge of security at this wedding.

A flush of alarm scorched her as Kruz's gaze swept over her like a searchlight and moved on. He must have seen her. The question was: would he do anything about it? She hadn't come halfway across the world in order to return home to London empty-handed.

Or to let down the bride, Romy concluded as she moved deeper into the crowd. This commission for Grace was more of a sacred charge than a job, and she had no intention of being distracted by one of the most alarming-looking men it had ever been her pleasure to photograph. Running off a blizzard of shots, she realised Kruz couldn't have stood in starker contrast to the bride. Grace's gentle beauty had never seemed more pronounced than at this moment, when she was standing beneath a flower-bedecked canopy between her husband and Kruz.

Romy drew a swift breath when the man in question stared straight at her. Lowering her camera, she glanced around, searching for a better hiding place, but shadows were in short supply in the brilliantly lit tent. One of the few things Grace could still detect after a virus had stolen her sight was light, so the dress code for the wedding was 'sparkle' and every corner of the giant marquee was floodlit by fabulous Venetian chandeliers.

Mingling with the guests, Romy kept her head down. The crowd was moving towards the receiving line, where all the Acostas were standing. There was a murmur of anticipation in the queue—and no wonder. The Acostas were an incredibly good-looking family. Nacho, the oldest brother, was clearly besotted by his beautiful new bride, while the sparks flying between Diego and his wedding planner wife Maxie could have ignited a fire. The supremely cool Ruiz Acosta clearly couldn't wait to get his firebrand wife, Romy's friend and colleague Holly, into bed, judging by the looks they were exchanging, while Lucia Acosta, the only girl in this family of four outrageously good-looking brothers, was flirting with her husband Luke Forster, the ridiculously photogenic American polo player.

Which left Kruz...

The only unmarried brother. So what? Her camera loved him, but that didn't mean *she* had to like him—though she would take full advantage of his distraction as he greeted his guests.

Those scars... That grim expression... She snapped away, knowing that everything about Kruz Acosta should put her off, but instead she was spellbound.

From a safe distance, Romy amended sensibly, as a pulse of arousal ripped through her.

And then he really did surprise her. As Kruz turned to say something to the bride his expression softened momentarily. That was the money shot, as it was known in the trade. It was the type of unexpected photograph that Romy was so good at capturing and had built her reputation on.

She was so busy congratulating herself she almost missed Kruz swinging round to stare at her again. Now she knew how a rabbit trapped in headlights felt. When he moved she moved too. Grabbing her kitbag, she stowed the camera. Her hands were trembling as panic mounted inside her. She hurried towards the exit, knowing this was unlike her. She was a seasoned pro, not some cub reporter—a thick skin came with the job. And why such breathless excitement at the thought of being chased by him? She was hardly an innocent abroad where men were concerned.

Because Kruz was the stuff of heated erotic dreams and her body liked the idea of being chased by him. Next question.

Before she made herself scarce there were a few more shots she wanted to take for Grace. Squeezing herself into a small gap behind a pillar, she took some close-ups of flowers and trimmings—richly scented white roses and lush fat peonies in softest pink, secured with white satin ribbon and tiny silver bells. The ceiling was draped like a Bedouin tent, white and silver chiffon lavishly decorated with scented flowers, crystal beads and fiery diamanté. Though Grace couldn't see these details the wedding planner had ensured she would enjoy a scent sensation, while Romy was equally determined to make a photographic record of the day with detailed descriptions in Braille alongside each image.

'Hello, Romy.'

She nearly jumped out of her skin, but it was only a famous celebrity touching her arm, in the hope of a photograph. Romy's editor at *ROCK!* loved those shots, so she had to make time for it. Shots like these brought in the money Romy so badly needed, though what she really longed to do was to tell the story of ordinary people in extraordinary situations through her photographs. One day she'd do that, she vowed

stepping forward to take the shot, leaving herself dangerously exposed.

The queue of guests at the receiving line was thinning as
people moved on to their tables for the wedding feast, and
an icy warning was trickling down her spine before she even
had a chance to say goodbye to the celebrity. She didn't need
to check to know she was being watched. She usually managed to blend in with the crowd, with or without an official
press pass, but there was nothing usual in any situation when
Kruz Acosta was in town.

As soon as the celebrity moved on she found another hiding place behind some elaborate table decorations. From here
she could observe Kruz to her heart's content. She settled
down to enjoy the play of muscle beneath his tailored jacket
and imagined him stripped to the buff.

Nice...

The only downside was Grace had mentioned that although
Kruz felt at home on the pampas he was going to open an office in London—'Just around the corner from *ROCK!*,' Grace
had said, as if it were a good thing.

Now she'd seen him, Romy was sure Kruz Acosta was
nothing but trouble.

But attractive... He was off-the-scale *hot*.

But she wasn't here to play make-believe with one of the
lead characters at this wedding. She had got what she needed
and she was out of here.

Glancing over her shoulder, she noticed that Kruz was no
longer in the receiving line.

So where the hell was he?

She scanned the marquee, but there was no sign of Kruz
anywhere. There were quite a few exits from the tent—he
could have used any one of them. She wasn't going to take

any chances, and would head straight for the press coach to send off her copy. Thank goodness Holly had given her a key.

The press coach wasn't too far. She could see its twinkling lights. She quickened her step, fixing her gaze on them, feeling that same sense of being hunted—though why was she worried? She could look after herself. Growing up small and plain had ruled out girlie pursuits, so she had taken up kick-boxing instead. Anyone who thought they could take her camera was in for a big surprise.

He had recognised the girl heading towards the exit. There was no chance he would let her get away. Having signed off the press passes personally, he knew Romy Winner didn't appear on any of them.

Romy Winner was said to be ruthless in pursuit of a story, but she was no more ruthless than he was. Her work was reputed to be cutting-edge and insightful—he'd even heard it said that as a photojournalist Romy Winner had no equal—but that didn't excuse her trespass here.

She had disappointed him, Kruz reflected as he closed in on her. Renowned for lodging herself in the most ingenious of nooks, he might have expected to find Ms Winner hanging from the roof trusses, or masquerading as a waitress, rather than skulking in the shadows like some rent-a-punk oddity, with her pale face, thin body, huge kohl-ringed eyes and that coal-black, gel-spiked, red-tipped hair, for all the wedding guests to stare at and comment on.

So Romy could catch guests off-guard and snap away at her leisure?

Maybe she wasn't so dumb after all. She must have captured some great shots. He was impressed by her cunning, but far less impressed by Señorita Winner's brazen attempt to gate-crash his brother's wedding. He would make her pay.

He just hadn't decided what currency he was accepting today. That would depend on his mood when he caught up with her.

Romy hurried on into the darkness. She couldn't shake the feeling she was being followed, though she doubted it was Kruz. Surely he had more important things to do?

Crunching her way along a cinder path, she reasoned that with all the Acosta siblings having been raised by Nacho, after their parents had been killed in a flood, Kruz had enjoyed no softening influence from a mother—which accounted for the air of danger surrounding him. It was no more than that. Her overworked imagination could take a rest. Pausing at a crossroads, she picked up the lights and followed them. She couldn't afford to lose her nerve now. She had to get her copy away. The money Romy earned from her photographs kept her mother well cared for in the nursing home where she had lived since Romy's father had beaten her half to death.

When Romy had first become a photojournalist it hadn't taken her long to realise that pretty pictures earned pennies, while sensational images sold almost as well as sex. Her success in the field had been forged in stone on the day she was told that her mother would need full-time care for the rest of her life. From that day on Romy had been determined that her mother would have the best of care and Romy would provide it for her.

A gust of wind sweeping down from the Andes made her shudder violently. She wondered if she had ever felt more out of place than she did now. She lived in London, amidst constant bustle and noise. Here in the shadow of a gigantic mountain range everything turned sinister at night and her chest tightened as she quickened her step. The ghostly shape of the wedding tent was far behind her now, and ahead was just a vast emptiness, dotted with faint lights from the *haci-*

enda. There were no landmarks on the pampas and no stars to guide her. The Acosta brothers were giants amongst men, and the land they came from was on the same impressive scale. There were no boundaries here, there was only space, and the Acostas owned most of it.

Rounding a corner, she caught sight of the press coach again and began to jog. Her breath hitched in her throat as she stopped to listen. Was that a twig snapping behind her? Her heart was hammering so violently it was hard to tell. Focusing her gaze on the press coach, with its halo of aerials and satellite dishes, she fumbled for the key, wanting to have it ready in her hand—and cried out with shock as a man's hand seized her wrist.

His other hand snatched hold of her camera. Reacting purely on instinct, she launched a stinging roundhouse kick—only to have her ankle captured in an iron grip.

'Good, but not good enough,' Kruz Acosta ground out.

Rammed up hard against the motorcoach, with Kruz's head in her face, it was hard for Romy to disagree. In the unforgiving flesh, Kruz made the evidence of her camera lens seem pallid and insubstantial. He was hard like rock, and so close she could see the flecks of gold in his fierce black eyes, as well as the cynical twist on his mouth. While their gazes were locked he brought her camera strap down, inch by taunting inch, until finally he removed it from her arm and placed it on the ground behind him.

'No,' he said softly when she glanced at it.

She still made a lunge, which he countered effortlessly. Flipping her to the ground, he stood back. Rolling away, she sprang up, assuming a defensive position with her hands clenched into angry fists, and demanded that he give it up.

Kruz Acosta merely raised a brow.

'I said—'

'I heard what you said,' he said quietly.

He was even more devastating at short range. She rubbed her arm as she stared balefully. He hadn't hurt her. He had branded her with his touch.

A shocked cry sprang from her lips when he seized hold of her again. His reach was phenomenal. His grip like steel. He made no allowance for the fact that she was half his size, so now every inch of her was rammed up tight against him, and when she fought him he just laughed, saying, 'Is that all you've got?'

She staggered as Kruz thrust her away. She felt humiliated as well as angry. Now he'd had a chance to take a better look at her he wasn't impressed. And why would he be?

'How does a member of the paparazzi get in here?'

Kruz was playing with her, she suspected. 'I'm not paparazzi. I'm on the staff at *ROCK!*'

'My apologies.' He made her a mocking bow. 'So you're a fully paid-up member of the paparazzi. With your own executive office, I presume?'

'I have a very nice office, as it happens,' she lied. He was making her feel hot and self-conscious. She was used to being in control. It was going too far to say that amongst photojournalists she was accorded a certain respect, but she certainly wasn't used to being talked down to by men.

'So as well as being an infamous photojournalist *and* an executive at *ROCK!* magazine,' Kruz mocked, 'I now discover that the infamous Romy Winner is an expert kick-boxer.'

Her cheeks flushed red. Not so expert, since he'd blocked her first move.

'I suppose kick-boxing is a useful skill when it comes to gate-crashing events you haven't been invited to?' Kruz suggested.

'It's one of my interests—and just as well with men like you around—'

'Men like me?' he said, holding her angry stare. 'Perhaps you and I should get on the mat in the gym sometime.'

'Over my dead body,' she fired back.

His look suggested he expected her to blink, or flinch, or even lower her gaze in submission. She did none of those things, though she did find herself staring at his lips. Kruz had the most amazing mouth—hard, yet sensual—and she couldn't help wondering what it would feel like to be kissed by him, though she had a pretty good idea...

An idea that was ridiculous! It wouldn't happen this side of hell. Kruz was one of the beautiful people—the type she liked to look at through her lens much as a wildlife photographer might observe a tiger, without having the slightest intention of touching it. Instead of drooling over him like some lovesick teenager it was time to put him straight.

'Kick-boxing is great for fending off unwanted advances—'

'Don't flatter yourself, Romy.'

Kruz's eyes had turned cold and she shivered involuntarily. There was no chance of getting her camera back now. He was good, economical with his movements, and he was fast.

Who knew what he was like as a lover...?

Thankfully she would never find out. All that mattered now was getting her camera back.

Darting round him, she tried to snatch it—and was totally unprepared for Kruz whipping the leather jacket from her shoulders. Underneath it she was wearing a simple white vest. No bra. She hardly needed one. Her cheeks fired up when he took full inventory of her chest. She could imagine the kind of breasts Kruz liked, and perversely wished she had big bouncing breasts to thrust in his face—if only to make a better job of showing her contempt than her embarrassingly desperate nipples were doing right now, poking through her flimsy top to signal their sheer, agonising frustration.

'Still want to take me on?' he drawled provocatively.

'I'm sure I could make some sort of dent in your ego,' she countered, crossing her arms over her chest. She circled round him. 'All I want is my property back.' She glanced at the camera, lying just a tantalising distance away.

'So what's on this camera that you're so keen for me not to see?' He picked it up. 'You can collect it in the morning, when I've had a chance to evaluate your photographs.'

'It's my work, and *I* need to edit it—'

'Your unauthorised work,' he corrected her.

There was no point trying to reason with this man. Action was the only option.

One moment she was diving for the camera, and the next Kruz had tumbled her to the ground.

'Now, what shall I do with you?' he murmured, his warm, minty breath brushing her face.

With Kruz pinning her to the ground, one powerful thigh planted either side of her body, her options were limited— until he yanked her onto a soft bed of grass at the side of the cinder path. Then they became boundless. The grass felt like damp ribbons beneath her skin, and she could smell the rising sap where she had crushed it. Overlaying that was the heat of a powerful, highly sexed, highly aroused man.

She should try to escape. She should put up some sort of token struggle, at least. She should remember her martial arts training and search for a weakness in Kruz to exploit.

She did none of those things. And as for that potential weakness—as it turned out it was one they shared.

As she reached up to push him away Kruz swooped down. Ravishing her mouth was a purposeful exercise, and one at which he excelled. For a moment she was too stunned to do anything, and then the sensation of being possessed, entered, controlled and plundered, even if it was only her mouth, by a man with whom she had been having fantasy sex for quite a few hours, sent her wild with excitement. She even groaned a complaint when he pulled away, and was relieved to find it was only to remove his jacket.

For such a big man Kruz went about his business with purpose and speed. His natural athleticism, she supposed, feeling her body heat, pulse and melt at the thought of being thoroughly pleasured by him. Growing up with a pillow over her head to shut out the violence at home had left her a stranger to romance and tenderness. Given a choice, she preferred to observe life through her camera lens, but when an opportunity for pleasure presented itself she seized it, enjoyed it, and moved on. She wasn't about to turn down *this* opportunity.

Pleasure with no curb or reason? Pleasure without thought of consequence?

Correct, she informed her inner critic firmly. Even the leisurely way Kruz was folding his jacket and putting it aside was like foreplay. He was so sexy. His powerful body was sexy—his hands were sexy—the wide spread of his shoulders was sexy—his shadowy face was sexy.

Kruz's confidence in her unquestioning acceptance of everything that was about to happen was so damn sexy she could lose control right now.

A life spent living vicariously through a camera lens was ultimately unsatisfactory, while this unexpected encounter was proving to be anything but. A rush of lust and longing gripped her as he held her stare. The look they exchanged spoke about need and fulfilment. It was explicit and potent. She broke the moment of stillness. Ripping off his shirt, she sent buttons flying everywhere. Yanking the fabric from the waistband of his pants, she tossed it away, exclaiming with happy shock as bespoke tailoring yielded to hard, tanned flesh. This was everything she had ever dreamed of and more. Liberally embellished with tattoos and scars, Kruz's torso was outstanding. She could hardly breathe for excitement when he found the button on her jeans and quickly dealt with it. He quickly got them down. In comparison, her own fingers felt fat and useless as she struggled with the buckle on his belt.

'Let me help you.'

Kruz held her gaze with a mocking look as he made this suggestion. It was all the aphrodisiac she needed. She cried out with excitement when his thumbs slipped beneath the elastic on her flimsy briefs to ease them down her hips. His big hands blazed a trail of fire everywhere they touched. She couldn't bear the wait when he paused to protect them both, but it was a badly needed wake-up call. The fact that this man had thought of it before she had went some way to reminding her how far she'd travelled from the safe shores she called home.

Her body overruled the last-minute qualms. Her body was one hundred per cent in favour of what was coming. Even her tiny breasts felt swollen and heavy, while her nipples were cheekily pert and obscenely hard, and the carnal pulse throbbing insistently between her legs demanded satisfaction.

Kruz had awakened such an appetite inside her she wouldn't be human if she didn't want to discover what sex could be like with someone who really knew what he was doing. She was about to find out. When Kruz stretched his length against her she could feel his huge erection, heavy and hard against her leg. And that look in his eyes—that slumberous, confident look. It told her exactly what he intended to do with her and just how much she was going to enjoy it. And, in case she was in any doubt, he now spelled out his intentions in a few succinct words.

She gasped with excitement. With hardly any experience of dating, and even less of foreplay, she was happy to hear that nothing was about to change.

CHAPTER TWO

SHE EXCLAIMED WITH shock when Kruz eased inside her. She was ready. That wasn't the problem. Kruz was the problem. He was huge.

Built to scale.

She should have known.

Her breath came in short, shocked whimpers, pain and pleasure combined. It was a relief when he took his time and didn't rush her. She began to relax.

This was good... Yes, better than good...

Releasing the shaking breath from her lungs, she silently thanked him for giving her the chance to explore such incredible sensation at her leisure. Leisure? The brief plateau lasted no more than a few seconds, then she was clambering all over him as a force swept them into a world where moving deeper, harder, rougher, fast and furious, was more than an imperative: it was essential to life.

'You okay?' Kruz asked, coming down briefly to register concern as she screamed wildly and let go.

It seemed for ever before she could answer him, and then she wasn't sure she said anything that made sense.

'A little better, at least?' he suggested with amusement when she quietened.

'Not that much better,' she argued, blatantly asking for more.

Taking his weight on his arms, Kruz stared down at her.

It didn't get much better than this, Romy registered groggily, lost in pleasure the instant he began to move. She loved his hard, confident mouth. She loved the feeling of being full and ready to be sated. She even loved her grassy bed, complete with night sounds: cicadas chirruping and an owl somewhere in the distance hooting softly. Kruz's clean, musky scent was in her nostrils, and when she turned her head, groaning in extremes of pleasure, her bed of grass added a piquant tang to an already intoxicating mix. She was floating on sensation, hardly daring to move in case she fell too soon. She didn't want it to end, but Kruz was too experienced and made it really hard to hold on. Moving persuasively from side to side, he pushed her little by little, closer to the edge.

'Good?' he said, staring down, mocking her with his confident smile.

'Very good,' she managed on a shaking breath.

And then he did something that lifted her onto an even higher plane of sensation. Slowly withdrawing, he left her trembling and uncertain, before slowly thrusting into her again. Whatever she had imagined before was eclipsed by this intensity of feeling. It was like the first time all over again, except now she was so much more receptive and aroused. She couldn't hold back, and shrieked as she fell, shouting his name as powerful spasms gripped her.

When she finally relaxed what she realised was her pincer grip on Kruz's arms, she realised she had probably bruised him. He was holding her just as firmly, but with more care. She loved his firm grip on her buttocks, his slightly callused hands rough on her soft skin.

'I can't,' she protested as he began to move again . 'I truly can't.'

'There's no such word as *can't*,' he whispered.

Incredibly, he was right. It didn't seem possible that she had anything left, but when Kruz stared deep into her eyes it was as if he was instructing her that she must give herself up to sensation. There was no reason to disobey and she tumbled promptly, laughing and crying with surprise as she fell again.

It turned out to be just the start of her lessons in advanced lovemaking. Pressing her knees back, Kruz stared down. Now she discovered that she loved to watch him watching her. Lifting herself up, she folded her arms behind her head so she had a better view. Nothing existed outside this extreme pleasure. Kruz had placed himself at her disposal, and to reward him she pressed her legs as wide as they would go. He demanded all her concentration as he worked steadily and effectively on the task in hand.

'You really should try holding on once in a while,' he said, smiling against her mouth.

'Why?' she whispered back.

'Try it and you'll find out,' he said.

'Will you teach me?' Her heart drummed at the thought.

'Perhaps,' Kruz murmured.

He wasn't joking, Romy discovered as Kruz led her through a lengthy session of tease and withdraw until her body was screaming for release.

'Greedy girl,' he murmured with approval. 'Again?' he suggested, when finally he allowed her to let go.

Bracing her hands against his chest, she smiled into his eyes. For a hectic hook-up this was turning into a lengthy encounter, and she hadn't got a single complaint. Kruz was addictive. The pleasure he conjured was amazing. But—

'What?' he said as she turned her head away from him.

'Nothing.' She dismissed the niggle hiding deep in her subconscious.

'You think too much,' he said.

'Agreed,' she replied, dragging in a fast breath as he began to move again.

Kruz didn't need to ask if she wanted more; the answer was obvious to both of them. Gripping his iron buttocks, she urged him on as he set up a drugging beat. Tightening her legs around his waist, she moved with him—harder—faster—giving as good as she got, and through it all Kruz maintained eye contact, which was probably the biggest turn-on of all, because he could see where she was so quickly going. Holding her firmly in place, he kept her in position beneath him, and when the storm rose he judged each thrust to perfection. Pushing her knees apart, he made sure they both had an excellent view, and now even he was unable to hold on, and roared with pleasure as he gave in to violent release.

She went with him, falling gratefully into a vortex of sensation from which there was no escape. It was only when she came to that she realised fantasy had in no way prepared her for reality—her fantasies were wholly selfish, and Kruz had woken something inside her that made her care for him just a little bit. It was a shame he didn't feel the same. Now he was sated she sensed a core of ice growing around him. It frightened her, because she was feeling emotional for the first time with a man. And now he was pulling back—emotionally, physically.

No wonder that niggle of unease had gripped her, Romy reflected. She was playing well out of her league. As if to prove this, Kruz was already on his feet, pulling on his clothes. He buckled his belt as if it were just another day at the office. She might have laughed under other circumstances when he was forced to tug the edges of his shirt together where she had ripped the buttons off. He did no more than hide the evidence of her desperation beneath his tie. How could he be so chillingly unfazed by all this? Her unease grew at the thought that what had just happened between them had made a dangerously strong impression on her, while it appeared to have washed over Kruz.

And why not? What happened was freely given and freely taken by both of you.

'Are you okay?' he said, glancing down when she remained immobile.

'Of course I am,' she said in a casual tone. Inwardly she was screaming. Was she really so stupid she had imagined she would come out of something like this unscathed?

Even inward reasoning didn't help—she was still waiting for him to say something encouraging. How pathetic was that? She had never felt like this before, and had no way of dealing with the feelings, so, gathering up her clothes, she lost herself in mundane matters—shaking the grass off her jacket, pulling on her jeans, sorting her hair out, then smoothing her hands over her face, hoping that by the time she removed them she would appear cool and detached.

Wrong. She felt as if she'd come out the wrong end of a spin dry.

Her thoughts turned at last to her camera. It was still lying on the bank, temptingly close. She had learned her lesson where lunging for it was concerned, but felt confident that Kruz would give it to her now. It was the least he could do.

Fortunately Kruz appeared to be oblivious both to her and to her camera. He was on the phone, telling his security operatives that he was patrolling the grounds.

She eased her neck, as if that would ease the other aches, most of which had taken up residence in her heart.

Hadn't she learned anything from the past? Had Kruz made her forget her father's rages and her mother's dependency on a violent man?

Kruz hadn't been in any way violent towards her—but he

was strong, commanding, and detached from emotion. All
the things she had learned to avoid.

She was safe in that, unlike her mother, she had learned
to avoid the pitfalls of attachment by switching off her emotions. In that she wasn't so dissimilar from Kruz. This was
just a brief interlude of fun for both of them and now it was
over. Neither of them was capable of love.

Love?

He swung round as she made a wry sound. Love was a
long road to nowhere, with a punch in the teeth at the end. So,
yes, if she was in any doubt at all about the protocol between
two strangers who'd just had sex on a grassy bank, she'd go
with cool and detached every time.

'Right,' he said, ending the call, 'I need to get back.'

'Of course,' she said off-handedly. 'But I'd like my camera first.'

He frowned, as if they were two strangers at odds with
each other. 'You've had your fun and now you're on your
way,' he said.

She'd asked for that, Romy concluded. 'Well, I'm not going
anywhere without it,' she said stubbornly. It was true. The
camera was more than a tool of her trade, it was a fifth limb.
It was an extension of her body, of her mind. It was the only
way she knew how to make the money she needed to support
herself and her mother.

'I've told you already. You'll get it back when I've checked
it,' he said coldly, hoisting the camera over his shoulder.

'You're my censor now?' she said, chasing after him. 'I
don't think so.'

The look Kruz gave her made her stomach clench with
alarm.

'You can sleep in the bunkhouse,' he said, 'along with the

rest of the press crew. Pick up your camera in the morning from my staff.'

She blinked. He'd said it as if they hadn't touched each other, pleasured each other.

They'd had sex and that was all.

Except for the slap in the face she got from realising that he saw it as no reason to give up her camera. 'By morning it will be too late—I need it now.'

'For what?' he said.

'I have to edit the photographs and then catch the news desk.' It was a lie of desperation, but she would do anything to recover her camera. 'There is another reason,' she added, waiting for a thunderclap to strike her down. This idea had only just occurred to her. 'I need to work on the shots I'm donating to your charity.'

As if he'd guessed, Kruz's eyes narrowed. 'The Acosta charity?'

'Yes.' She had a lot of shots in the can, Romy reasoned, quickly running through them in her mind. She had more than enough to pay for her mother's care and to keep herself off the breadline. She had taken a lot of shots specifically for Grace's album, and he couldn't have those, but there were more—plenty more.

Had she bought herself a reprieve? Romy wondered as she stared at Kruz. 'I've identified a good opportunity for the charity,' she said, as the germ of an idea sprouted wings.

'Tell me,' Kruz said impatiently.

'My editor at *ROCK!* is thinking about making a feature on the Acostas and your charity.' Or at least she would make sure he was thinking about it by the time she got back. 'Think of how that would raise the charity's profile,' she said, dangling a carrot she hoped no Acosta in his right mind could refuse.

'So why didn't Grace or Holly tell me about this?' Kruz

probed, staring at her keenly. 'If either of them had mentioned it I would have made sure you were issued with an official pass.'

'I *am* here on a mission for Grace,' Romy admitted, 'which is how I got in. Grace asked me not to say anything, and I haven't. It's crucial that Nacho doesn't learn about Grace's special surprise. I hope you'll respect that.' Kruz remained silent as she went on. 'I'm sure Grace and Holly were just too wrapped up in the wedding to remember to tell you,' she said, not wanting to get either of her friends into trouble.

Kruz paused. And now she could only wait.

'I suppose Grace could confirm this if I asked her?'

'If you feel like interrogating a bride on her wedding day, I'm sure she would.'

One ebony brow lifted. Whether Kruz believed her or not, for the moment she had him firmly in check.

'The solution to this,' he remarked, 'is that *I* take a look at the shots and *I* decide.'

As he strode away she ran after him. Dodging in front of him, she forced him to stop.

He studied Romy's elfin features with a practised eye. He interpreted the nervous hand running distractedly through her disordered hair. The camera meant everything to her, and if there was one thing that could really throw Ms Winner he had it swinging from his shoulder now. She was terrified he was going to disappear with her camera. She worked with it every day. It was her family, her income stream, her life. He almost felt sorry for her, and then stamped the feeling out. What was Romy Winner to *him?*

Actually, she was a lot more than he wanted her to be. She had got to him in a way he hadn't quite fathomed yet. 'Is there some reason why I shouldn't see these shots?' he asked, teasing her by lifting the camera to Romy's eye level.

'None whatsoever,' she said firmly, but her face softened in response to his mocking expression and she almost smiled.

Testing Romy was fun, he discovered, and fun and he were strangers. With such a jaundiced palette as his, any novelty was a prize. But he wouldn't taunt her any longer. He wasn't a bully, and wouldn't intentionally try to increase that look of concern in her eyes. 'Shall we?' he invited, glancing at the press coach.

She eyed him suspiciously, perhaps wondering if she was being set up. She knew there was nothing she could do about it, if that were the case. She strode ahead of him, head down, mouth set in a stubborn line, no doubt planning her next move. And then she really did throw him.

'So, what have you got to hide?' she asked him, swinging round at the door

'Me?' he demanded.

Tilting her head to one side, she studied his face. 'People with something to hide are generally wary of me and my camera, so I wondered what *you* had to hide...'

'You think that's why I confiscated it?'

'Maybe,' she said, not flinching from his stare.

That direct look of hers asked a lot of questions about a man who could have such prolonged and spectacular sex with a woman he didn't know. It was a look that suggested Romy was asking herself the same question.

'Are you worried that I might have taken some compromising pictures of you?' she said. There was a tug of humour at one corner of her mouth.

'Worried?' He shook his head. But the truth was he had never been so reckless with a woman. He sure as hell wouldn't be so reckless again.

'Kruz?' she prompted.

His name sounded soft on her lips. That had to be a first. He smiled. 'What?'

'Just checking you know I'm still here.'

He gave her a wry look and felt a surge of heat when she tossed one back. He wasn't an animal. He was still capable of feeling. His brother Nacho had made him believe that when Kruz had been discharged from the army hospital. It was Nacho who had persuaded him to channel his particular talents into a security company, saying Kruz must need and feel and care before he could really start living again. Nacho was right. The more he looked at Romy, the more human he felt.

Did Kruz *have* to stare at her lips like that? Here she was, trying to forget her body was still thrilling from his touch, and he wasn't making it easy. She was a professional woman, trying to persuade herself she would soon get over tonight— yet all he had to do was look at her for her to long for him to take hold of her and draw her into an embrace that was neither sexual nor mocking. She had never wanted to share and trust and rest awhile quite so badly.

And she wasn't about to fall into that trap now.

'Shall we take a look?'

She looked at Kruz and frowned.

'The pictures?' he prompted, and she realised that he had not only removed the key to the press coach from her hand, but had opened the door and was holding it for her.

That yearning feeling inside...?

It wasn't helpful. Women who felt the urge to nurture men would end up like her mother: battered, withdrawn, and helpless in a nursing home.

She led the way into the coach. Her manner was cold. They were both cold, and that suited her fine.

Romy's mood now was a slap in the face to him after what they'd experienced together, but he had to concede she was only as detached as he was. He was just surprised, he supposed, that those much vaunted attributes of tenderness and sensitivity, which women were supposed to possess in abundance, appeared to have bypassed her completely. He should be pleased about that, but he wasn't. He was offended. Romy was the first woman who hadn't clung to him possessively after sex. And bizarrely, for the first time in his life, some primitive part of him had wanted her to.

'Are you coming in?' she said, when he stood at the entrance at the top of the steps.

His senses surged as he brushed past her. However unlikely it seemed to him, this whip-thin fighting girl stirred him like no other. He wanted more. So did she, judging by than quick intake of breath. He could feel her sexual hunger in the energy firing between them. But Romy wanted more that he could give her. He wanted more of Romy, but all he wanted was sex.

CHAPTER THREE

SHE MADE HER way down the aisle towards the area at the rear of the coach set aside for desks and equipment. Her small, slender shape, dressed all in black, quickly became part of the shadows.

'I know there's a light switch in here somewhere,' she said.

Her voice was a little shaky now the door was closed, and the tension rocketed between them. He could feel her anticipation as she waited for his next move. He could taste it in the air. He could detect her arousal. He was a hunter through and through.

'Here,' he said, pressing a switch that illuminated the coach and set some unseen power source humming.

'Thank you,' she said, with her back to him as she sat down at a desk.

'You'll need this,' he said, handing over the camera.

She thanked him and hugged it to her as if it contained gold bars rather than her shots.

He had more time than he needed while she logged on. He used it to reflect on what had happened over the past hour or so. Ejecting Romy from the wedding feast should have been straightforward. She should have been on her way to Buenos Aires by now, then back to London. Instead his head was still full of her, and his body still wanted her. He could still hear her moaning and writhing beneath him and feel her beneath his hands. He could still taste her on his mouth, and he could remember the smell of her soap-fresh skin. He smiled in the shadows, remembering her attacking him, that tiny frame surprisingly strong, yet so undeniably feminine. Why did Romy Winner hide herself away behind the lens of a camera?

A blaze of colour hit the screen as she began to work. What he saw answered his question. Romy Winner was quite simply a genius with a camera. Images assailed his senses. The scenery was incredible, the wildlife exotic. Her pictures of the Criolla ponies were extraordinary. She had captured some amusing shots of the wedding guests, but nothing cruel, though she *had* caught out some of the most pompous in less than flattering moments. She'd taken a lot of pictures of the staff too, and it was those shots that really told a story. Perhaps because more expression could be shown on faces that hadn't been stitched into place, he reflected dryly as Romy continued to sort and select her images.

She'd made him smile. Another first, he mused as she turned to him.

'Well?' she said. 'Do you like what you see?'

'I like them,' he confirmed. 'Show me what else you've got.'

'There's about a thousand more.'

'I'm in no hurry.' For maybe the first time in his life.

'Why don't you pull up a chair?' she suggested. 'Just let me know if there any images you don't feel are suitable for the charity.'

'So I'm your editor now?' he remarked, with some amusement after her earlier comment about censorship.

'No,' she said mildly. 'You're a client I want to please.'

He inclined his head in acknowledgement of this. He could think of a million ways she could please him. When she turned back to her work he thought the nape of her neck extremely vulnerable and appealing, just for starters. He considered dropping a kiss on the peachy flesh, and then decided no. Once he'd tasted her...

'What do you think of these?' she said, distracting him.

'Grace is very beautiful,' he said as he stared at Romy's shots of the bride. He could see that his new sister-in-law was exquisite, like some beautifully fashioned piece of china. But did Grace move him? Did she make his blood race? He admired Grace as he might admire some priceless *objet d'art*, but it was Romy who heated his blood.

'She is beautiful, isn't she?' Romy agreed, with a warmth in her voice he had never noticed before. She certainly didn't use that voice when she spoke to him.

And why should he care?

Because for the first time in his life he found himself missing the attentions of a woman, and perhaps because he was still stung, after Romy's enthusiastic response to their lovemaking, that she wasn't telling him how she thrilled and throbbed, and all the other things his partners were usually at such pains to tell him. Had Romy Winner simply feasted on him and moved on? If she had, it would be the first time any woman had turned the tables on him.

'This is the sort of shot my editor loves,' she said as she brought a picture of him up on the screen.

'Why is that?'

'Because you're so elusive,' she explained. 'You're hardly ever photographed. I'll make a lot from this,' she added with a pleased note in her voice.

Was he nothing but a commodity?

'Though what I'd *like* to do,' she explained, 'is give it to the charity. So, much as I'd like to make some money out of you, you can have this one *gratis*.'

As she turned to him he felt like laughing. She was so honest, he felt…uncomfortable. 'Thank you,' he said with a guarded expression. 'If you've just taken a couple of shots of me you can keep the rest. '

'What makes you think I'd want to take more than one?'

Youch.

What, indeed? He shrugged and even managed to smile at that.

Romy Winner intrigued him. He had grown up with women telling him he was the best and that they couldn't get enough of him. He'd grown up fighting for approval as the youngest of four highly skilled, highly intelligent brothers. When he couldn't beat Nacho as a youth he had turned to darker pursuits—in which, naturally, he had excelled—until Nacho had finally knocked some sense into him. Then Harvard had beckoned, encouraging him to stretch what Nacho referred to as the most important muscle in his body: the brain. After college he had found the ideal outlet for his energy and tirelessly competitive nature in the army.

'There,' Romy said, jolting him back from these musings. 'You're finished.'

'I wouldn't be too sure of that,' he said, leaning in close to study her edited version. He noticed again how lithe and strong she was, and how easy it would be to pull her into his arms.

'I have a deadline,' she said, getting back to work.

'Go right ahead.' He settled back to watch her.

The huge press coach was closing in on her, and all the tiny hairs on the back of her neck were standing erect at the thought of Kruz just a short distance away. She could hear him breathing. She could smell his warm, sexy scent. Some very interesting clenching of her interior muscles suggested she was going to have to concentrate really hard if she was going to get any work done.

'Could you pass me that kitbag?' she said, without risking turning round. She needed a new memory card and didn't want to brush past him.

Her breath hitched as their fingers touched and that touch wiped all sensible thought from her head. All she could think about now was what they had done and what they could do again.

Work!

She pulled herself back to attention with difficulty, but even as she worked she dreamed, while her body throbbed and yearned, setting up a nagging ache that distracted her.

'Shall I put this other memory card in the pocket for you?' Kruz suggested.

She realised then that she had clenched her hand over it. 'Yes—thank you.'

His fingers were firm as they brushed hers again, and that set up more distracting twinges and delicious little aftershocks. Would she ever be able to live normally again?

Not if she kept remembering what Kruz had done—and so expertly.

Her mind was in turmoil. Every nerve-ending in her body felt as if it had been jangled. And all he'd done was brush her hand!

Somehow she got through to the end of the editing process and was ready to show him what she'd got. She ran through the images, giving a commentary like one stranger informing another about this work, and even while Kruz seemed genuinely interested and even impressed she felt his aloofness. Perhaps he thought she was a heartless bitch after enjoying him so fully and so vigorously. Perhaps he thought she took *what* she wanted *when* she wanted. Perhaps he was right. Perhaps they deserved each other.

So why this yearning ache inside her?

Because she wanted things she couldn't have, Romy reasoned, bringing up a group photograph of the Acostas on the screen. They were such a tight-knit family...

'Are you sure you want to give me all these shots?'

'Concerned, Kruz?' she said, staring at him wryly. 'Don't worry about me. I've kept more than enough shots back.'

'I'd better see the ones you're giving me again.'

'Okay. No problem.' She ran through them again, just for the dangerous pleasure of having Kruz lean in close. She had never felt like this before—so aware, alert and aroused. It was like being hunted by the hunter she would most like to be caught by.

'These are excellent,' Kruz commented. 'I'm sure Grace can only be thrilled when she hears the reaction of people to these photographs.'

'Thank you. I hope so,' she said, concentrating on the screen. Grace's wedding was the first romantic project she had worked on. Romy was better known as a scandal queen. And that was one of the more polite epithets she'd heard tossed her way.

'This one I can't take,' Kruz insisted when she flashed up another image on the screen. 'You have to make *some* money,' he reminded her.

Was this a test? Was he paying her off? Or was that her insecurity speaking? He might just be making a kindly gesture, and she maybe should let him.

She shook her head. 'I can't sell this one,' she said quietly. 'I want you to have it.'

The picture in question showed Kruz sharing a smile with his sister, Lucia. It was a rare and special moment between siblings, and it belonged to them alone—not the general public. It was a moment in time that told a story about Nacho's success at bringing up his brothers and sister while he was still very young. They would see that when they studied it, just as she had. She wouldn't dream of selling something like that.

'Frame it and you'll always have a reminder of what a wonderful family you have.'

Why was she doing this for him? Kruz wondered suspiciously. He eased his shoulders restlessly, realising that Romy had stirred feelings in him he hadn't experienced since his parents were alive. He stared at her, trying to work out why. She was fierce and passionate one moment, aloof and withdrawn the next. He might even call her cold. He couldn't pretend he understood her, but he'd like to—and that was definitely a first.

'Thank you,' he said, accepting the gift. 'I appreciate it.'

'I'll make a copy for Lucia as well,' she offered, getting back to work.

'I know my sister will appreciate that.' After Lucia had picked herself off the floor because he'd given her a gift outside of her birthday or Christmas.

The tension between them had subsided with this return to business. He was Romy's client and she was his photographer—an excellent photographer. Her photographs revealed so much about other people, while the woman behind the lens guarded her inner self like a sphinx.

DAMN. She was going to cry if she didn't stop looking at images of Grace and Nacho. So that was what love looked like…

'Shall we move on?' she said briskly, because Kruz seemed in no hurry to bring the viewing session to an end. She was deeply affected by some of the shots she had captured of the bridal couple, and that wasn't helpful right now. Since she was a child she had felt the need to protect her inner self. Drawing a big, thick safety curtain around herself rather than staring at an impossible dream on the screen would be her action of choice right now.

'That was a heavy sigh,' Kruz commented.

She shrugged, neither wanting nor able to confide in him. 'I just need to do a little more work,' she said. 'That's if you'll let me stay to do it?' she added, turning to face him, knowing it could only be a matter of minutes before they went their separate ways.

This was the moment she had been dreading and yet she needed him to go, Romy realised. Staring at those photographs of Grace and Nacho had only underlined the fact that her own life was going nowhere.

'Here,' she said, handing over the memory stick. 'These are for you and for the charity. You *will* keep that special shot?' she said, her chest tightening at the thought that Kruz might think nothing of it.

'So I can stare at myself?' he suggested, slanting her a half-smile.

'So you can look at your family,' she corrected him, 'and feel their love.'

Did he *have* to stare at her so intently? She wished he wouldn't. It made her uncomfortable. She didn't know what Kruz expected from her.

'What?' she said, when he continued to stare.

'I never took you for an emotional woman,' he said.

'Because I'm not,' she countered, but her breath caught in her throat, calling her a liar. The French called this a *coup de foudre*—a thunderbolt. She had no explanation for the longing inside her except to say Kruz had turned her life inside out. It made no sense. They hardly knew each other outside of sex. They didn't know if they could trust each other, and they had no shared history. They had everything to learn about each other and no time to do so. And why would Kruz *want* to know more about her?

They could be friends, maybe...

Friends? She almost laughed out loud at this naïve suggestion from a subconscious that hadn't learned much in her twenty-four years of life. Romy Winner and Kruz Acosta? Ms Frost and Señor Ice? Taking time out to get to know each other? To *really* get to know each other? The idea was so preposterous she wasn't going to waste another second on it. She'd settle for maintaining a truce between them long enough for her to leave Argentina in one piece with her camera.

'Thanks for this,' Kruz said, angling his stubble-shaded chin as he slipped the memory stick into his pocket.

She felt lost when he turned to go—something else she would have to get used to. She had to get over him. She'd leave love at first sight to those who believed in it. As far as she was concerned love at first sight was a load of bull. Lust at first sight, maybe. Lack of self-control, certainly.

Her throat squeezed tight when he reached the door and turned to look at her.

'How are you planning to get back to England, Romy?'

'The same way I arrived, I guess,' she said wryly.

'Did you bring much luggage with you?'

'Just the essentials.' She glanced at her kitbag, where everything she'd brought to Argentina was stashed. 'Why do you ask?'

'My jet's flying to London tomorrow and there are still a few spare places, if you're stuck.'

Did he mean stuck as in unprepared? Did he think she was so irresponsible? Maybe he thought she was an opportunist who seized the moment and thought nothing more about it?

'I bought a return ticket,' she said, just short of tongue in cheek. 'But thanks for the offer.'

Kruz shrugged, but as he was about to go through the door he paused. 'You're passing up the chance to take some exclusive shots of the young royals—'

'So be it,' she said. 'I wouldn't dream of intruding on their privacy.'

'Romy Winner passing up a scoop?'

'What you're suggesting sounds more like a cheap thrill for an amateur,' she retorted, stung by his poor opinion of her. 'When celebrities or royals are out in public it's a different matter.'

Kruz made a calming motion with his hands.

'I *am* calm,' she said, raging with frustration at the thought that they had shared so much yet knew so little about each other. Kruz had tagged her with the label paparazzi the first moment he'd caught sight of her—as someone who would do anything it took to get her shots. Even have sex with Kruz Acosta, presumably, if that was what was required.

'Romy—'

'What?' she flashed defensively.

'You seem…angry?' Kruz suggested dryly.

She huffed, as if she didn't care what he thought, but even so her gaze was drawn to his mouth. 'I just wonder what type of photographer you think I am,' she said, shaking her head.

'A very good one, from what I've seen today, Señorita Winner,' Kruz said softly, completely disarming her.

'*Gracias*,' she said, firming her jaw as they stared at each other.

And now Kruz should leave. And she should stay where she was—at the back of the coach, as far away from him as possible, with a desk, a chair and most of the coach seats between them.

She waited for him to go, to close the door behind him and bring this madness to an end.

He didn't go.

Leaning over the driver's seat, Kruz hit the master switch and the lights dimmed, and then he walked down the aisle towards her.

CHAPTER FOUR

THEY COLLIDED SOMEWHERE in the middle and there was a tangle of arms and moans and tongues and heated breathing.

She kicked off her boots as Kruz slipped his fingers beneath the waistband of her jeans. The button sprang free and the zipper was down, the fabric skimming over her hips like silk, so that now she was wearing only her jacket, the white vest and her ridiculously insubstantial briefs. Kruz ripped them off. Somehow the fact that she was partly clothed made what was happening even more erotic. There was only one area that needed attention and they both knew it.

Her breathing had grown frantic, and it became even more hectic when she heard foil rip. She was working hectically on Kruz's belt and could feel his erection pressing thick and hard against her hand. She gasped with relief as she released him. She was getting better at this, she registered dazedly, though her brain was still scrambled and she was gasping for breath. Kruz, on the other hand, was breathing steadily, like a man who knew exactly where he was going and how to get there. His control turned her on. He was a rock-solid promise of release and satisfaction, delivered in the most efficient way

'Wrap your legs around me, Romy,' he commanded as he lifted her.

Kruz's movements were measured and certain, while she

was a wild, feverish mess. She did as he said, and as she clung to him he whipped his hand across the desk, clearing a space for her. She groaned with anticipation as he moved between her legs. The sensation was building to an incredible pitch. She cried out encouragement as he positioned her, his rough hands firm on her buttocks just the way she liked them. Pressing her knees back, he stared into her eyes. Pleasure guaranteed, she thought, reaching up to lace her fingers through his hair, binding him to her.

This time...this one last time. And then never again.

She was so ready for him, so hungry. As Kruz sank deep, shock, pleasure, relief, eagerness, all combined to help her reach the goal. Thrusting firmly, he seemed to feel the same urgency, but then he found his control and began to tease her. Withdrawing slowly, he entered her again in the way she loved. The sensation was incredible and she couldn't hold on. She fell violently, noisily, conscious only of her own pleasure until the waves had subsided a little, when she was finally able to remember that this was for both of them. Tightening her muscles, she left Kruz in no doubt that she wasn't a silent partner but a full participant.

He smiled into her eyes and pressed her back against the desk. Wherever she took him he took her one level higher. Pinning her hands above her head, he held her hips firmly in place with his other hand as he took her hard and fast. There was no finesse and only one required outcome, and understanding the power she had over him excited her. Grabbing his arms, she rocked with him, welcoming each thrust as Kruz encouraged her in his own language. Within moments she was flying high in a galaxy composed entirely of light, with only Kruz's strong embrace to keep her safe.

It was afterwards that was awkward, Romy realised as she pulled on her jeans. When they were together they were as close as two people could be—trusting, caring, encouraging, pleasuring. But now they were apart all that evaporated, disappeared almost immediately. Kruz had already sorted out his clothes and was heading for the door. They could have been two strangers who, having fallen to earth, had landed in a place neither of them recognised.

'The seat on the jet is still available if you need it,' he said, pausing at the door.

She worked harder than ever to appear nonchalant. If she looked at Kruz, really looked at him, she would want him to stay and might even say so.

'I won't be stuck,' she said, assuming an air of confidence. 'But thanks again for the offer. And don't forget I'm only an e-mail away if you ever need any more shots from the wedding.'

'And only round the corner when I get to London,' he said opening the door.

What the hell...? She pretended not to understand. Say anything at all and her cool façade would shatter into a million pieces. When tears threatened she bit them back. She wasn't going to ask Kruz if they would meet up in London. This wasn't a date. It was a heated encounter in the press coach. And now it was nothing.

'I'll put the lights on for you,' he said, killing her yearning for one last meaningful look from Kruz.

'That would be great. Thank you.' She was proud of herself for saying this without expression. She was proud of remaining cool and detached. 'I've got quite a bit of work left to do.'

'I'll leave you to it, then,' he said. 'It's been a pleasure, Romy.'

Her head shot up. Was he mocking her?

Kruz was mocking both of them, Romy realised, seeing the tug at one corner of his mouth.

'Me too,' she called casually. After all, this was just another day in the life of a South American playboy. It didn't matter how much her heart ached because Kruz had gone, leaving her with just the flickering images of him on a computer screen for company.

Glancing back, he saw Romy through the window of the coach. She was poring over the monitor screen as if nothing had happened. She certainly wasn't watching him go. She was no clinging vine. It irked him. His male ego had taken a severe hit. He was used to women trying to pin him down, asking him when they'd meet again—if he'd call them—could they have his number? Romy didn't seem remotely bothered.

The wedding party was still in full swing as he approached the marquee. He rounded up his team, heard their reports and supervised the change-over for the next shift. All of these were measurable activities, which were a blessed relief after his encounter with the impossible-to-classify woman he'd left working in the press coach.

The woman he still wanted

Yeah, that one, he thought.

The noise coming from the marquee was boisterous, joyous, celebratory. Shadows flitted to and fro across the gently billowing tent, silhouettes jouncing crazily from side to side as the music rose and fell.

And Romy was on her own in the press coach.

So what? She was safe there. He'd get someone to check up on her later.

Stopping dead in his tracks, he swung round to look back the way he'd come. He'd send one of the men to make sure she made it to the bunkhouse safely.

Really?

Okay, so maybe he'd do that himself.

* * *

Romy shot up. Hearing a sound in the darkness, she was instantly awake. Reaching for the light on the nightstand, she switched it on. And breathed a sigh of relief.

'Sorry if I woke you,' the other girl said, stumbling over the end of the bed as she tried to kick off her shoes, unzip her dress and tumble onto the bed all at the same time. 'Jane Harlot, foreign correspondent for *Frenzy* magazine—pleased to meet you.'

'Romy Winner for *ROCK!*'

Jane stretched out a hand and missed completely. 'Brilliant—I love your pictures. Harlot's not my real name,' Jane managed, before slamming a hand over her mouth. 'Sorry—too much to drink. Never could resist a challenge, even when it comes from a group of old men who look as if they have pickled their bodies in alcohol to preserve them.'

'Here, let me help you,' Romy offered, recognising a disaster in the making. Swinging her legs over the side of the bed, she quickly unzipped her new roomie's dress. 'Did you have a good time?'

'Too good,' Jane confessed, shimmying out of the red silk clingy number. 'Those gauchos really know how to drink. But they're chivalrous too. One of them insisted on accompanying me to the press coach and actually waited outside while I sent my copy so he could escort me back here.'

'He waited for you outside the press coach?'

'Of course outside,' Jane said, laughing. 'He was about ninety. And, anyway, it didn't take me long to send my stuff. What I write is basically a comic strip. You know the sort of thing—scandal, slebs, stinking rich people. I only got a look-in because my dad used to work with one of the reporters who got an official invitation and he brought me in as his assistant.'

Looking alarmed at this point, Jane waved a hand, keeping the other hand firmly clamped over her mouth.

Jane had landed a big scoop, and Romy was hardly in a position to criticise the other girl's methods. This wasn't a profession for shrinking violets. The Acostas had nothing to worry about, but some of their guests definitely did, she reflected, remembering those prominent personalities she had noticed attending the wedding with the wrong partner.

'Are you sure you're okay?' she asked with concern as Jane got up and staggered in the general direction of the bathroom.

'Fine…I'll sleep it off on the plane going home. The gauchos said their boss has places going spare on his private jet tomorrow, so I'll be travelling with the young royals, no less. And I'll be collected from here and taken to the airstrip in a limo. I'll be in the lap of luxury one minute and my crummy old office the next.'

'That's great—enjoy it while you can,' Romy called out, trying to convince herself that this was a good thing, that she was in fact *Saint* Romy and thoroughly thrilled for Jane, and didn't mind at all that the man she'd had sex with hadn't even bothered to see her back to the bunkhouse safely.

He stayed on post until the lights went out in the bunkhouse and he was satisfied Romy was safely tucked up in bed. Pulling away from the fencepost, it occurred to him that against the odds his caring instinct seemed to have survived. But before he could read too much into that he factored his security business into the mix. Plus he had a sister. Before Lucia had got together with Luke he had always hoped someone would keep an eye on her when he wasn't around. Why should he be any different where a girl like Romy was concerned?

London. Monday morning. The office. Grey skies. Cold. Bleak. Dark-clad people racing back and forth across the rainswept street outside her window, heads down, shoulders hunched against the bitter wind.

It might as well be raining inside, Romy thought, shivering convulsively in her tiny cupboard of an office. It was so cold.

She was cold inside and out, Romy reflected, hugging herself. She was back at work, which normally she loved, but today she couldn't settle, because all she could think about was Kruz. And what was the point in that? She should do something worthwhile to make her forget him.

Something like *this*, Romy thought some time later, poring over the finished version of Grace Acosta's wedding journal. She had added a Braille commentary beside each photograph, so that Grace could explain each picture as she shared the journal. Romy had worried about the space the Braille might take up at first but, putting herself in Grace's place, had known it was the right thing to do.

Sitting back, she smiled. She had been looking forward to this moment for so long—the moment when she could hand over the finished journal to Grace. She wasn't completely freelance yet, though this tiny office at *ROCK!* had housed many notable freelance photographers at the start of their careers and Romy dreamed of following in their footsteps. She hoped this first, really important commission for Grace would be the key to helping her on her way, and that she could make a business out of telling stories with pictures instead of pandering to the insatiable appetite for scandal. Maybe she could tell real stories about real people with her photographs—family celebrations, local news, romance—

Romance?

Yes. Romance, Romy thought, setting her mouth in a stubborn line.

Excuse me for asking the obvious, but what exactly do you know about romance?

As her inner critic didn't seem to know when to be quiet, she answered firmly: *In the absence of romance in my own life, my mind is a blank sheet upon which I will be able to record the happy moments in other people's lives.*

Gathering up her work, Romy headed for the editing suite run by the magazine's reining emperor of visuals: Ronald Smith. *ROCK!* relied on photographs for impact, which made the editor one of the most influential people in the building.

'Ronald,' Romy said, acknowledging her boss as she walked into his hushed and perfumed sanctum.

'Well? What have you got for me, princess?' Ronald demanded, lowering his *faux*-tortoiseshell of-the-moment spectacles down his surgically enhanced nose.

'Some images to blow your socks off,' she said mildly.

'Show me,' Ronald ordered.

Romy stalled as she arranged her images on the viewing table. There was no variety. Why hadn't she seen that before?

Possibly because she had given the best images to Kruz?

Ronald was understandably disappointed. 'This seems to be a series of shots of the waiting staff,' he said, raising his head to pin her with a questioning stare.

'They had the most interesting faces.'

'I hope our readers agree,' Ronald said wearily, returning to studying the images Romy had set out for him. 'It seems to me you've creamed off the best shots for yourself, and that's not like you, Romy.'

A rising sense of dread hit her as Ronald removed his glasses to pinch the bridge of his nose. She needed this job. She needed the financial security and she hated letting Ronald down.

'I can't believe,' he began, 'that I send you to Argentina and you return with nothing more than half a dozen shots I can use—and not one of them of the newly married couple in the bridal suite.'

Romy huffed with frustration. Ronald really had gone too far this time. 'What did you expect? Was I supposed to swing in through their window on a vine?'

'You do whatever it takes,' he insisted. 'You do what you're famous for, Romy.'

Intruding where she wasn't wanted? Was that to be her mark on history?

'It was you who assured me you had an in to this wedding,' Ronald went on. 'When *ROCK!* was refused representation at the ceremony I felt confident that you would capture something special for us. I can't believe you've let us down. I wouldn't have given you time off for this adventure if I had known you would return with precisely nothing. You're not freelance yet, Romy,' he said, echoing her own troubled thoughts. 'But the way you're heading you'll be freelancing sooner than you want to be.'

She was only as good as her last assignment, and Ronald wouldn't forget this. She had to try and make things right. 'I must have missed something,' she said, her brain racing to find a solution. 'Let me go back and check my computer again—'

'I think you better had,' Ronald agreed. 'But not now. You look all in.'

Sympathy from Ronald was the last thing she had expected and guilty tears stung her eyes. She didn't deserve Ronald's concern. 'You're right,' she said, pulling herself together. 'Jet-lag has wiped me out. I should have waited until tomorrow. I'm sorry I've wasted your time.'

'You haven't wasted my time,' Ronald insisted. 'You just haven't shown me anything commercial—anything I can use.'

'I'm confident I can get hold of some more shots. Just give me chance to look. I don't want to disappoint you.'

'It would be the first time that you have,' Romy's editor pointed out. 'But first I want you to promise that you'll leave early today and try to get some rest.'

'I will,' she said, feeling worse than ever when she saw the expression on Ronald's face.

Actually, she did feel a bit under the weather. And to put the cap on her day she had grown a nice crop of spots. 'I won't let you down,' she said, turning at the door.

'Oh, I almost forgot,' Ronald said, glancing up from the viewing table. 'There's someone waiting for you in your office.'

Some hopeful intern, Romy guessed, no doubt waiting in breathless anticipation for a few words of encouragement from the once notorious and now about to be sacked Romy Winner. She pinned a smile to her face. No matter that she felt like a wrung-out rag and her only specialism today was projecting misery and failure, she would find those words of encouragement whatever it took.

Hurrying along the corridors of power on the fifth floor, she headed for the elevators and her lowly cupboard in the basement. She could spare Ronald some shots from Grace's folder. Crisis averted. She just had to sort them out. She should have sorted them out long before now.

But she hadn't because her head was full of Kruz.

'Thank you,' she muttered as her inner voice stated the obvious. Actually, the real reason was because she was still jet-lagged. She hadn't travelled home in a luxurious private jet but in cattle class, with her knees on her chin in an aging commercial plane.

And whose fault was that?

'Oh, shut up,' Romy said out loud, to the consternation of her fellow travellers in the elevator.

The steel doors slid open on a different world. Gone were the cutting edge bleached oak floors of the executive level, the pale ecru paint, the state-of-the-art lighting specifically designed to draw attention to the carefully hung covers of *ROCK!* In the place of artwork, on this lowly, worker bee level was a spaghetti tangle of exposed pipework that had nothing to do with minimalist design and everything to do with neglect. A narrow avenue of peeling paint, graffiti and lino led to the door of her trash tip of a cupboard.

Stop! Breathe deeply. Pin smile to face. Open door to greet lowly, hopeful intern—

Or not!

'Language, Romy,' Kruz cautioned.

Had she said a bad word? Had she even spoken? 'Sorry,' she said with an awkward gesture. 'I'm just surprised to see you.' *To put it mildly.*

It took her a moment to rejig her thoughts. She had been wearing her most encouraging smile, anticipating an intern waiting eagerly where she had once stood, hoping for a word of encouragement to send her on her way. Romy had been lucky enough to get that word, and had been determined that whoever wanted to see her today would receive some encouragement too. She doubted Kruz needed any.

So forget the encouraging word.

Okay, then.

Standing by the chipped and shabby table that passed for her desk, Kruz Acosta, in all his business-suited magnificence, accessorised with a stone-faced stare and an over-abundance of muscle, was toying with some discarded images she had printed out, scrunched up and had been meaning to toss.

They were all of him.

CHAPTER FIVE

OKAY, SHE COULD handle this. She had to handle this. Whatever Kruz was here for *it wasn't her.*

She had to make sure he didn't leave with the impression
that he had intimidated her.

*And how was she going to achieve that with her heart rac-
ing off the scale?*

She was going to remain calm, hold her head up high and
meet him on equal ground.

'I like your office, Romy,' he murmured, in the sexy,
faintly mocking voice she remembered only too well. 'Do
all the executives at *ROCK!* get quite so much space?'

'Okay, okay,' she said, closing this down before he could
get started. 'So space is at a premium in the city.'

The smile crept from Kruz's mouth to his eyes, which had
a corresponding effect on her own expression. That was half
the trouble—it was hard to remain angry with him for long.
She guessed Kruz probably had the top floor of a skyscraper
to himself, with a helipad as the cherry on top.

'What can I do for you, Kruz?' she said, proud of how
cool she sounded.

So many things. Which was why he'd decided to call by.
His office was just around the corner. And he'd needed to…
to take a look at some more photographs, he remembered,
jolting his mind back into gear.

'Those shots you gave me for the charity,' he said, producing the memory stick Romy had given him back in Argentina.

'What about them?' she said.

She had backed herself into the furthest corner of the room, with the desk between them like a shield. In a room as small as this he could still reach her, but he was content just to look at her. She smelled so good, so young and fresh, and she looked great. 'The shots you gave me are fantastic,' he admitted. 'So much so I'd like to see what else you've got.'

'Oh,' she said.

Was she blinking with relief? Romy could act nonchalant all she liked, but he had a sister and he knew all about acting. He took in her working outfit—the clinging leggings, flat fur boots, the long tee—and as she approached the desk and sat down he concluded that she didn't need to try hard to look great. Romy Winner was one hell of a woman. Was she ready for him now? he wondered as she bit down on her lip.

'We've decided the charity should have a calendar,' he said, 'and we thought you could help. What you've given me so far are mostly people shots, which are great—but there are too many celebrities. And the royals... Great shots, but they're not what we need.'

'What do you want?' she said.

'Those character studies of people who've worked on the *estancia* for most of their lives. Group shots used to be taken in the old days, as well as individual portraits, and that's a tradition I'd like to revive. You make everyone look like members of the same family, which is how I've always seen it.'

'Team Acosta?' she suggested, the shadow of a smile creeping onto her lips.

'Exactly,' he agreed. He was glad he didn't have to spell it out to her. On reflection, he didn't have to spell anything out for Romy. She *got* him.

'What about scenery, wildlife—that sort of thing?' she said, turning to her screen.

'Perfect. I think we're going to make one hell of a calendar,' he enthused as she brought up some amazing images.

Hallelujah! She could hardly believe her luck. This was incredible. She wouldn't lose her job after all. Of course a charity would want vistas and wildlife images, while Ronald wanted all the shots Kruz wanted to discard. She hadn't been thinking straight in Argentina—*for some reason*—and had loaded pictures into files without thinking things through.

'So you don't mind if I have the people shots back?' she confirmed, wondering if it was possible to overdose on Kruz's drugging scent.

'Not at all,' he said, in the low, sexy drawl that made her wish she'd bothered to put some make-up on this morning, gelled her hair and covered her spots.

'You look tired, Romy,' he added as she started loading images onto a clean memory stick. 'You don't have to do this now. I can come back later.'

'Better you stay so you're sure you get what you want,' she said.

'Okay, I will,' he said, hiding his wry smile. 'Thanks for doing this at such short notice.'

She couldn't deny she was puzzled. He was happy to stay? Either Kruz wanted this calendar really badly, or he was… what? Checking up on her? Checking her out?

Not the latter, Romy concluded. Kruz could have anyone he wanted, and London was chock-a-block full of beautiful women. Hard luck for her, when she still wanted him and felt connected to him in a way she couldn't explain.

Fact: what happened in the press coach is history. Get used to it.

With a sigh she lifted her shoulders and dropped them

again in response to her oh, so sensible inner voice. Wiping a hand across her forehead, she wondered if it was hot in here.

'Are you okay?' Kruz asked with concern.

No. She felt faint. Another first. 'Of course,' she said brightly, getting back to her work.

The tiny room was buzzing with Kruz's energy, she thought—which was the only reason her head was spinning. She stopped to take a swig of water from the plastic bottle on her desk, but she still didn't feel that great.

'Will you excuse me for a moment?' she said shakily, blundering to her feet.

She didn't wait to hear Kruz's answer. Rushing from the desk, she just made it to the rest room in time to be heartily sick.

It was just a reaction at having her underground bunker invaded by Kruz Acosta, Romy reasoned as she studied the green sheen on her face. Swilling her face with cold water, she took a drink and several deep breaths before heading back to her room—and she only did that when she was absolutely certain that the brief moment of weakness had been and gone.

He was worried about Romy. She looked pale.

'No… No, I'm fine,' she said when he asked her if she was all right as she breezed back into the room. 'Must have been something I ate. Sorry. You don't need to hear that.'

He shrugged. 'I was brought up on a farm. I'm not as rarefied as you seem to think.'

'Not rarefied at all,' she said, flashing him a glance that jolted him back to a grassy bank and a blue-black sky.

'It's hot in here,' he observed. No wonder she felt faint. Opening the door, he stuck a chair in the way. Not that it did much good. The basement air was stale. He hated the claustrophobic surroundings.

'Why don't you sit and relax while I do this?' she suggested, without turning from the screen.

'It won't take long, will it?'

She shook her head.

'Then I'll stand, thank you.'

In the tiny room that meant he was standing close behind her. He was close enough to watch Romy's neck flush as pink as her cheeks.

With arousal? With awareness of him?

He doubted it was a response to the images she was bringing up on the screen.

He felt a matching surge of interest. Even under the harsh strip-light Romy's skin looked as temptingly soft as a peach. And her birdwing-black hair, which she hadn't bothered to gel today, was enticingly thick and silky. A cluster of fat, glossy curls caressed her neck and softened her un-made-up face…

She was lovely.

She felt better, so there was no reason for this raised heartbeat apart from Kruz. Normally she could lose herself in work, but not today. He was such a presence in the small, dingy room—such a presence in her life. Shaking her head, she gave a wry smile.

'Is something amusing you?' he said.

'No,' she said, leaning closer to the screen, as if the answer to her amusement lay there. There was nothing amusing about her thoughts. She should be ashamed, not smiling asininely as it occurred to her that she had never seen Kruz close up in the light other than through her camera. Of course she knew to her cost that close up he was an incredible force. She was feeling something of that now. She could liken it to being close to a soft-pawed predator, never being quite sure when it would pounce and somehow—insanely—longing for that moment.

'There. All done,' she said in a brisk tone, swinging round to face him.

It was a shock to find him staring at her as if his thoughts hadn't all been of business. Confusion flooded her. Confusion wasn't something she was familiar with—except when Kruz was around. The expression in his eyes didn't help her to regain her composure. Kruz had the most incredible eyes. They were dark and compelling, and he had the longest eyelashes she'd ever seen.

'These are excellent,' he said, distracting her. 'When you've copied them to a memory stick you'll keep copies on your computer, I presume?'

'Yes, of course,' she said, struggling to put her mind in gear and match him with her business plan going forward. 'They're all in a file, so if you want more, or you lose them, just ask me.' *For anything,* she thought.

'And you can supply whatever I need?'

She hesitated before answering, and turning back to the screen flicked through the images one more time. 'Are you pleased?'

'I'm very pleased,' Kruz confirmed.

Even now he'd pulled back he couldn't get that far away, and he was close enough to make her ears tingle. She kept her gaze on the monitor, not trusting herself to look round. This was not Romy Winner, thick-skinned photojournalist, but someone who felt as self-conscious as a teenager on her first date. But she wasn't a kid, and this wasn't a date. This was the man she'd had sex with after knowing him for around half an hour. When thousands of miles divided them she could just about live with that, but when Kruz was here in her office—

'Your compositions are really good, Romy.'

She exhaled shakily, wondering if it was only she who could feel the electricity between them.

'These shots are perfect for the calendar,' he went on, apparently immune to all the things she was feeling.

She logged off, wanting him to go now, so her wounded heart would get half a chance to heal.

'And on behalf of the family,' Kruz was saying. 'I'm asking you to handle this project for us.'

She swung round. Wiping a hand across her face, she wondered what she'd missed.

'That's if you've got time?' Kruz said, seeming faintly amused as he stared down at her. 'And don't worry—my office is just around the corner, so I'll be your liaison in London.'

Don't worry?

Her heart was thundering as he went on.

'I'd like to see a mock-up of the calendar when you've completed it. I don't foresee any problems, just so long as you remember that quality is all-important when it comes to the Acosta charity.'

Her head was reeling. Was she hearing straight? The Acosta family was giving her the break she had longed for? She couldn't think straight for all the emotion bursting inside her. She had to concentrate really hard to take in everything Kruz was telling her. A commission for the Acosta family? What better start could she have?

Something that didn't potentially tie her in to Kruz?

She mustn't think about that now. She just had to say yes before she lost it completely.

'No,' she blurted, as the consequences of seeing Kruz again and again and again sank in. 'I'd love to do it, but—'

'But what?' he said with surprise.

Answering his question meant looking into that amazing face. And she could do that. But to keep on seeing Kruz day after day, knowing she meant nothing to him... That would be too demoralising even to contemplate. 'I'd love to do it,' she said honestly, feeling her spirit sag as she began to destroy her chances of doing so, 'but I don't have time. I'm really sorry, Kruz, but I'm just too tied up here—'

'Enjoying the security that comes with working for one of the top magazines?' he interrupted, glancing round. 'I can see it would take guts to take time out from *this*.'

She wasn't in the mood for his mockery.

'No worries,' he said, smiling faintly as he moved towards the door. 'I'll just tell Grace you can't find the time to do it.'

'Grace?' she said.

'Grace is our new patron. It was Grace who suggested I approach you—but I'm sure there are plenty of other photographers who can do the job.'

Ouch!

'Wait—'

Kruz paused with his hand on the door. She remembered those hands from the grassy bank and from the press coach, and she remembered what they were capable of. Shivering with longing, she folded her arms around her waist and hugged herself tight.

'Well?' Kruz prompted. 'What am I going to say to Grace? Do you have a message for her, Romy?'

How could she let Grace down? Grace was trying to help her. They had had a long talk when Romy had first arrived in Argentina. Grace had been so easy to talk to that Romy had found herself pouring out her hopes and dreams for the future. She had never done that with anyone before, but somehow her words came easily when she was with Grace. Maybe Grace's gentle nature had allowed her to lower her guard for once.

'I'll do it,' she said quietly.

'Good,' Kruz confirmed, as if he had known she would all along.

She should be imagining her relief when he closed the door

behind him rather than wishing he would stay so they could discuss this some more—so she could keep him here until they shared more than just memories of hot sex on someone else's wedding day.

'Romy? You don't seem as pleased about this work as I expected you to be.'

She flushed as Kruz's gaze skimmed over her body. 'Of course I'm pleased.'

'So I can tell Grace you'll do this for her?'

'I'd rather tell her myself.'

Kruz's powerful shoulders eased in a shrug. 'As you wish.'

There was still nothing for her on that stony face, but she was hardly known for shows of emotion herself. Like Kruz, she preferred to be the one in control. A further idea chilled her as they locked stares. Romy's control came from childhood, when showing emotion would only have made things worse for her mother. When her father was in one of his rages she'd just had to wait quietly until he was out of the way before she could go to look after her mother, or he'd go for her too, and then she'd be in no state to help. Control was just as important to Kruz, which prompted the question: what dark secret was he hiding?

Romy worked off her passions at the gym in the kick-boxing ring, where she found the discipline integral to martial arts steadying. Maybe Kruz found the same. His instinctive and measured response to her roundhouse kick pointed to someone for whom keeping his feelings in check was a way of life.

The only time she had lost it was in Argentina, Romy reflected, when something inside her had snapped. *The Kruz effect?* All those years of training and learning how to govern her emotions had been lost in one passionate encounter.

She covered this disturbing thought with the blandest of questions. 'Is that everything?'

'For now.'

Ice meets ice—today. In Argentina they had been on fire for each other. But theirs was a business relationship now, Romy reminded herself as Kruz prepared to leave. She had to stop thinking about being crushed against his hard body, the minty taste of his sexy mouth, or the sweet, nagging ache that had decided to lodge itself for the duration of his visit at the apex of her thighs. If he knew about that she'd be in real trouble.

'It's been good to see you again,' she said, as if to test her conviction that she was capable of keeping up this cool act.

'Romy,' Kruz said, acknowledging her with a dip of his head and just the slightest glint of humour in his eyes.

The Acosta brothers weren't exactly known for being monks. Kruz was simply being polite and friendly. 'It will be good to be in regular contact with Grace,' she said, moving off her chair to show him out.

'Talking of which…' He paused outside her door.

'Yes?' She tried to appear nonchalant, but she felt faint again.

'We're holding a benefit on Saturday night for the charity, at one of the London hotels. Grace will be there, and I thought it would be a great opportunity for you two to get together and for you to meet my family so you can understand what the charity means to us. That's if you're interested?' he said wryly.

She stared into Kruz's eyes, trying to work out his motive for asking her. Was it purely business, or something else…?

His weary sigh jolted her back to the present. 'When you're ready?' he prompted, staring pointedly at his watch.

'Saturday…?'

'Yes or no?'

He said it with about as much enthusiasm as if he were booking the local plumber to sort out a blocked drain. 'Thank you,' she said formally. 'As you say, it's too good a chance to miss—seeing Grace and the rest of your family.'

'I'm glad to hear it. There may be more work coming your way if the calendar is a success. A newsletter, for example.'

'That's a great idea. Shall I bring my camera?'

'Leave it behind this time,' Kruz suggested, his dark glance flickering over her as he named the hotel where they were to meet.

She couldn't pretend not to be impressed.

'Dress up,' he said.

She gave him a look that said no one told her what to wear. But on this occasion it wasn't about her. This was for Grace. She still felt a bit mulish—if only because Kruz was the type of man she guessed liked his women served up fancy, with all the trimmings. Elusive as he was, she'd seen a couple of shots of him with society beauties, and though he had looked bored on each occasion the girls had been immaculately groomed. But, in fairness to the women, the only time she'd seen Kruz animated was in the throes of passion.

'Something funny?' he said.

'I'll wear my best party dress,' she promised him with a straight face.

'Saturday,' he said, straightening up to his full imposing height. 'I'll pick you up your place at eight.'

Her eyes widened. She had thought he'd meet her at the hotel. Was she Kruz's *date?*

No, stupid. He's just making sure you don't change your mind and let The Family down.

'That's fine by me,' she confirmed. 'Before you go I'll jot my address down for you.'

He almost cracked a smile. 'Have you forgotten what business I'm in?'

Okay, Señor Control-Freak-Security-Supremo. Point taken.

Her address was no secret anyway, Romy reasoned, telling herself to calm down. 'Eight o' clock,' she said, holding Kruz's mocking stare in a steady beam.

'Until Saturday, Romy.'

'Kruz.'

She only realised when she'd closed the door behind him and her legs almost gave way that she was shaking. Leaning back against the peeling paintwork, she waited until Kruz's footsteps had died away and there was nothing to disrupt the silence apart from the hum of the fluorescent light.

This was ridiculous, she told herself some time later. She was being everything she had sworn never to be. She had allowed herself to become a victim of her own overstretched heart.

There was only one cure for this, Romy decided, and she would find it when she worked out her frustrations in the ring at the gym tonight. Meanwhile she would lose herself in work. Maybe tonight she would be better giving the punch-bag a workout rather than taking on a sparring partner. She didn't trust herself with a living, breathing opponent in her present mood. And she needed the gym. She needed to rebalance her confidence levels before Saturday. She wanted to feel her strength and rejoice in it—her strength of will, in particular. She had to remember that she was strong and successful and independent and safe—and she planned to keep it that way. She especially had to remember that on Saturday.

Saturday!

What the hell was she going to wear?

CHAPTER SIX

'LOOKING HOT,' ONE of the guys said in passing, throwing a wry smile her way as Romy finished her final set of blows on the punch-bag.

The bag must have taken worse in its time, but it had surely never taken a longer or more fearsomely sustained attack from a small angry woman with more frustration to burn off than she could handle. Romy nodded her head in acknowledgement of the praise. This gym wasn't a place for designer-clad bunnies to scope each other out. This was a serious working gym, where many of the individuals went on to have successful careers in their chosen sport.

'What's eating you, Romy?' demanded the grizzled old coach who ran the place, showing more insight into Romy's bruised and battered psyche than her fellow athlete as Romy rested, panting, with her still gloved hands braced on her knees. 'Man trouble?'

You know me too well, she thought, though she denied it. 'You know me, Charlie,' she said, straightening up. 'Have camera, will travel. No man gets in the way of that.'

'I bet that camera's cosy to snuggle up to on a cold night,' Charlie murmured in an undertone as he moved on to oversee the action in another part of his kingdom.

What did Charlie know? What did *anyone* know? Romy

scowled as she caught sight of herself in one of the gym's full-length mirrors. What man in his right mind would want a sweating firebrand with more energy than sense? *Kruz wouldn't.* With her bandaged hands, bitten nails, boy's shorts and clinging, unflattering vest, she looked about as appealing as a wet Sunday. She probably smelled great too. Taking a step back, she nodded her thanks as another athlete offered to help her with the gloves.

'Looking fierce,' he said.

'Ain't that the truth?' Romy murmured. She was a proper princess, complete with grubby sweatband holding her electro-static hair off her surly, sweaty face.

He saw her the moment he walked into the gym. Or rather something drew his stare to her. She felt him too. Even with her back turned he saw a quiver of awareness ripple down her spine. And now she was swinging slowly round, as if she had to confirm her hunch was correct.

We have to stop meeting like this, he thought as they stared at each other. He nodded curtly. Romy nodded back. Yet again rather than looking at him, like other women, Romy Winner was staring at him as if she was trying to psych him out before they entered the ring.

That could be arranged too, he reflected.

They were still giving each other the hard stare when the elderly owner of the gym came up to him. 'Hey, Charlie.' He turned, throwing his towel round his neck so he could extend a hand to greet an old friend warmly.

'You've spotted our lady champion, I see,' Charlie commented.

Kruz turned back to stare at Romy. 'I've seen her.'

Romy had finished her routine. He was about to start his. She looked terrific. It would be rude not to speak to her.

* * *

Oh... Argh! What the...?

Romy blenched. For goodness' sake, how could anyone look *that* good? Kruz was ridiculously handsome. And what the hell was he doing in *her* gym? Wasn't there somewhere billionaire health freaks could hang out together and leave lesser mortals alone to feel good about themselves a few times a week?

Even with the unforgiving lights of the workmanlike sports hall blazing down on him Kruz looked hot. Tall, tanned and broader than the other men sharing his space, he drew attention like nothing else. And he was coming over—oh, *good.* Even a warrior woman needed to shower occasionally, and Kruz was as fresh as a daisy.

Gym kit suited him, she decided as he advanced. With his confident stroll and those scars and tattoos showing beneath his skimpy top he was a fine sight. She wanted him all over again. If she'd never met him before she'd want him. And, inconveniently, she wanted him twice as much as she ever had. A quick glance around reassured Romy that she wasn't the only one staring. She couldn't blame the gym members for that. Muscles bunched beneath his ripped and faded top, and the casual training pants hung off his hips. Silently, she whimpered.

And Kruz didn't walk, he prowled, Romy reflected, holding her ground as he closed the distance between them. His pace was unhurried but remorseless and, brave as she was, she felt her throat dry—it was about the only part of her that was.

'We meet again,' he said with some amusement, stopping tantalisingly within touching distance.

'I didn't expect it to be so soon,' she said off-handedly, reaching for a towel just as someone else picked it up.

'Here—have this. I can always grab another.'

'I couldn't possibly—'

Kruz tossed his towel around her neck. Taking the edges, she wrapped it round her shoulders like a cloak. It still held his warmth.

'So you're really serious about the gym?' he said.

'I like to break sweat,' she agreed, shooting him a level stare as if daring him to find fault with that. 'Why haven't I seen you here before?' she said as an afterthought. 'You slumming it?'

'Please,' Kruz murmured. 'My office is only round the corner.'

'And you don't have a gym?' she said, opening her eyes wide with mock surprise.

'It's under construction,' he said, giving her the cynical look he was so good at.

'I'm impressed,' she said.

'You should be.'

If only that crease in his cheek wasn't so attractive. 'Maybe I'll come and take a look at it when it's finished.'

'I might hold you to that.'

Please. 'I'm very busy,' she said dryly, still holding the dark, compelling stare. 'I have a very demanding private client.'

Kruz's eyes narrowed as he held her gaze. 'I hope I know him.'

'I think you do. So, how do you know Charlie?' she said, seizing on the first thing that came to mind to break the stare-off between them.

'Charlie's an old friend,' Kruz explained, pulling back.

'Were you both in the army?' she asked on a hunch.

'Same regiment,' Kruz confirmed, but then he went quiet and the smile died in his eyes. 'I'd better get started,' he said.

'And I'd better go take my shower,' she agreed as they parted.

'Don't miss the fun,' Charlie called after her.

'What fun?'

'Don't miss Kruz in the ring.'

She turned to look at him.

'Why don't you come in the ring with me?' Kruz suggested. 'You could be my second.'

'Sorry. I don't do second.'

He laughed. 'Or you could fight me,' he suggested.

'Do I look stupid? Don't answer that,' she said quickly, holding up her hands as Kruz shot her a look.

This was actually turning out better than she had thought when she'd first seen Kruz walk into the gym. They were sparring in good way—verbally teasing each other—and she liked that. It made her feel warm inside.

Charlie caught up with her on the way to the changing rooms. 'Don't be too hard on him, Romy.'

'Who are we talking about? Kruz?'

'You know who we're talking about,' the old pro said, glancing around to make sure they weren't being overheard. 'Believe me, Romy, you have no idea what that man's been through.'

'No, I don't,' she agreed. 'I don't know anything about him. Why would I?'

Did Charlie know anything? Had Kruz said something? Her antennae were twitching on full alert.

'You should know what he's done for his friends,' Charlie went on, speaking out of the corner of his mouth. 'The lives he's saved—the things he's seen.'

The guarded expression left her face. This was the longest speech she had ever heard Charlie make. There was no doubt in her mind Charlie was sincere, and she felt reassured that

Kruz hadn't said anything about their encounter to him. 'I don't think Kruz wants anyone to go easy on him,' she said thoughtfully, 'but I'll certainly bear in mind what you've said.'

Charlie shook his head in mock disapproval. 'You're a hard woman, Romy Winner. You two deserve each other.'

'Now, that's something I have to disagree with,' Romy said, lightening up. 'You just don't know your clientele, Charlie. Shame on you.' She smiled as she gave Charlie a wink.

'I know them better than you think,' Charlie muttered beneath his breath as Romy shouldered her way into the women's changing room. 'Go take that shower, then join me ringside,' he called after her.

Romy rushed through her shower, emptying a whole bottle of shower gel over her glowing body before lathering her hair with a half a bottle of shampoo. The white tiled floor in the utilitarian shower block was like a skating rink by the time she had finished. Thank goodness her hair was short, she reflected, frantically towelling down. She didn't want to miss a second of this bout. She stared at herself in the mirror. Make-up? Her eyes were bright enough with excitement and her cheeks were flushed. Tugging on her leggings, her flat boots and grey hoodie, she swung her gym bag on to her shoulder and went to join the crowd assembling around the ring at the far end of the gym.

The scent of clean sweat mingled with anticipation came to greet her. This was her sort of party.

'Quite a crowd,' she remarked to Charlie, feeling her heart lurch as Kruz vaulted the ropes into the ring. When he turned to look at her, her heart went crazy. Naked to the waist, Kruz was so hot her body couldn't wait to remind her about getting up close and personal with him. She pressed her thighs together, willing the feeling to subside. No such luck. As

Kruz turned his back and she saw his muscles flex the pulse only grew stronger.

'It's not often we get two champions in the ring—even here at my gym,' Charlie said, his scratchy voice tense with anticipation.

The other kick-boxer was a visitor from the north of England called Heath Stamp. He'd been a bad boy too, according to rumour, and Romy knew him by reputation as a formidable fighter. But Heath was nothing compared to Kruz in her eyes. Kruz's hard, bronzed body gleamed with energy beneath the lights. He was a man in the peak of health, just approaching his prime.

A man with the potential to happily service a harem of women.

'Stop,' she said out loud, in the hope of silencing her inner voice.

'Did you say something, Romy?' Charlie enquired politely, cupping his ear.

'No—just a reminder to myself,' she said dryly.

'There's no one else the champ can spar with,' Charlie confided, without allowing his attention to be deflected for a second from the ring.

'Lucky Kruz came along, then.'

'I'm talking about Kruz,' Charlie rebuked her. 'Kruz is the champ. I should know. I trained him in the army.'

She turned to stare at the rapt face of the elderly man standing next to her. He knew more about Kruz than she did. And he would be reluctant to part with a single shred of information unless it was general info like Kruz's exploits in the gym. What *was* it with Charlie today? She'd never seen him so animated. She'd never seen such fierce loyalty in his eyes or heard it in his voice. It made her want to know all those things Kruz kept secret—for he did keep secrets. Of that much she was certain.

So some men were as complex as women, Romy reasoned, telling herself not to make a big deal out of it as the referee brought the two combatants together in the centre of the ring. Kruz was entitled to his privacy as much as she was, and he was lucky to have a loyal friend like Charlie.

As the bout got under way and the onlookers started cheering Romy only had eyes for one man. The skill level was intense, but there was something about Kruz that transcended skill and made him a master. Being a fighter herself, she suspected that he was holding back. She wondered about this, knowing Kruz could have ended the match in Round One if he had wanted to. Instead he chose to see it through until his opponent began to flag, when Kruz called a halt. Proclaiming the match a draw, he bumped the glove of his opponent, raising Heath Stamp's arm high in the air before the referee could say a word about it.

'That's one of the benefits of having a special attachment to this gym,' Kruz explained, laughing when she pulled him up on it as he vaulted the ropes to land at her side.

'A special attachment?' she probed.

'I used to own it,' he revealed casually, his voice muffled as he rubbed his face on a towel.

'You used to own this gym?'

'That's right,' Kruz confirmed, pulling the towel down.

She glanced round, frowning. Charlie was busy consoling the other fighter. She'd known Charlie for a number of years and had always assumed *he* owned the gym. 'I had no idea you were in the leisure industry,' she said, turning back to Kruz.

'Amongst other things.' Grabbing a water bottle from his

second, Kruz drank deeply before pouring the rest over his head. 'I own a lot of gyms, Romy.'

'News to me.'

'My apologies,' he said with a wry look. 'I'll make sure my PA puts you on my "needs to know" list right away.'

'See that you do,' she said, with a mock-fierce stare. Were they getting on? Were they *really* getting on?

'So, what are you doing next?' Kruz asked her.

'Going home.'

'What about food?'

'What about it? I'm not hungry.'

'Surely you're over your sickness now?'

'Yes, of course I am.' Actually, she *had* felt queasy again earlier on.

'Hang on while I take a shower,' he said. 'I'll see you in Reception in ten.'

'But—'

That was all she had time for before Kruz headed off. Raking her short hair with frustration, she was left to watch him run the gauntlet of admirers on his way to the men's changing room. Why did he want to eat with her? Or was food not on the menu? Her heart lurched alarmingly at the thought that it might not be. She wasn't about to fall into ever-ready mode. Just because she enjoyed sex with a certain man it did *not* mean Kruz had a supply on tap.

In all probability he just wanted to talk about the charity project, her sensible self reassured her.

And if he didn't want to chat...?

They'd be in a café somewhere. What was the worst that could happen?

They'd leave the food and run?

Clearly the bout had put Kruz in a good mood, Romy

concluded as he came through the inner doors into the reception area.

'Ready to go?' he said, holding the door for her.

So far so good. Brownie points for good manners duly awarded.

'There's a place just around the corner,' he said, 'where we can get something to eat.'

'I know it.' He was referring to the café they all called the Greasy Spoon—though nothing could be further from the truth. True enough, it was a no-nonsense feeding station, with bright lights, Formica tables, hard chairs, but there was a really good cook on the grill who served up high-quality ingredients for impatient athletes with colossal appetites.

They found a table in the window. There wasn't much of a view as it was all steamed up. The air-conditioning was an open door at the back of the kitchen.

'Okay here?' Kruz said when they were settled.

'Fine. Thank you.' She refused to be overawed by him—but that wasn't easy when her mind insisted on undressing him.

She was working for the Acosta family now, Romy reminded herself, and she had to concentrate on that. It was just a bit odd, having had the most amazing sex with this man and having to pretend they had not. Kruz seemed to have forgotten all about it—or maybe it was just one more appetite to slake, she reflected as the waitress came to take their order.

'Do you mind if I take a photo of you?' she said, pulling out her phone.

'Why?' Kruz said suspiciously.

'Why the phone? I don't have my camera.'

'Why the photograph?'

'Because you look half human—because this is a great setting—because everyone thinks of the Acostas as rarefied beings who live on a different planet to them. I just want to show people that you do normal things too.'

'Steak and chips?' Kruz suggested wryly, tugging off his heavy jacket.

'Steak and chips,' she agreed, returning his smile. Oh, boy, how that smile of his heated her up. 'You'd better not be laughing at me,' she warned, running off a series of shots.

'Let me see,' he said, holding out his hand for her phone.

'Me first,' she argued. *Wow.* She blew out a slow, controlled breath as she studied the shot. Kruz's thick, slightly too long hair waved and gleamed like mahogany beneath the lights. The way it caught on his sideburns and stubble was...

'Romy?' he said

'Not yet,' she teased. 'You'll have to wait for the newsletter.' *To see those powerful shoulders clad in the softest air-force blue cashmere and those well-packed worn and faded jeans...*

'Romy?' Kruz said, sounding concerned when she went off into her own little dreamworld.

Snap! Snap!

'There. That should do it,' she said, passing the phone across the table.

'Not bad,' Kruz admitted grudgingly. 'You've reminded me I need to shave.'

'Glad to be of service,' she said, blushing furiously half a beat later. Being that type of service was not what she meant, she assured herself sternly as Kruz pushed the phone back to her side of the table.

Fortunately their food arrived, letting her off the hook. She had ordered a Caesar salad with prawn, while Kruz had ordered steak and fries. Both meals were huge. And every bit as delicious as expected.

'This is a great place,' she said, tucking in. As Kruz murmured agreement she made the mistake of glancing at his mouth. Fork suspended, she stared until she realised he was looking at her mouth too. 'Yours good?' she murmured distractedly. Kruz had a really sexy mouth. And an Olympian appetite, she registered as he called for a side of mushrooms, onion rings and a salad to add to his order.

'Something wrong with your meal, Romy?'

'No. It's delicious.' She stared intently at her salad, determined not to be distracted by him again.

Food was a great ice-breaker. It oiled the wheels of conversation better than anything she knew. 'So, tell me more about Charlie's gym. I've been going there for years and I had no idea you used to own it.'

Kruz frowned. 'What do you want to know?'

'I always thought Charlie owned it. Not that it matters,' she said.

'He does own it.' And, when she continued to urge him on with a look of interest, Kruz offered cryptically, 'Things change over time, Romy.'

'Right.' The conversation seemed to have gone the same way as their empty plates. 'Charlie never stopped talking about you,' she said to open it up again. 'He admires you so much, Kruz.'

Personal comments were definitely a no-no, she concluded as Kruz gave her a flat black look. 'Do you want coffee?' He was already reaching for his wallet. This down-time was over.

'No. I'm fine. Let me get this.'

For once in her life she managed not to fumble and got out a couple of twenties to hand to the waitress before Kruz had a chance to disagree.

He did not look pleased. 'You should not have done that,' he said.

'Why not? Because you're rich and I'm not?'

'Don't be so touchy, Romy.'

She was touchy? 'I'm not touchy,' she protested, standing up. 'Aren't you the guy who's taking me to some swish event on Saturday?' She shrugged. 'The least I can do is buy you dinner.'

'You will be a guest of the family on Saturday,' he said.

Heaven forfend she should mistake it for a date.

'And where Charlie's concerned I'd prefer you don't say anything about the gym to him,' Kruz added. 'That man is not and never has been in my debt. If anything, I'm in his.'

She hadn't anticipated such a speech, and wondered what lay behind it—especially in light of Charlie's words about Kruz. *The plot thickens,* she thought. But as it showed no sign of being solved any time soon she followed Kruz to the door.

'Until Saturday,' he said, barely turning to look at her as he spoke.

Someone was touchy when it came to questions about his past. 'I'll meet you at the hotel,' she said briskly, deciding she really did not want him at her place. She was surprised when he didn't argue.

She watched Kruz thread his way through the congested traffic with easy grace—talking of which, for Grace's sake she would find something other than sweats or leggings to wear on Saturday night. She wanted to do the family proud. She didn't want to stand out for all the wrong reasons. Khalifa's department store was on her way home, so she had no excuse.

In the sale she picked out an understated column of deep blue silk that came somewhere just above her knees. It was quite flattering. The rich blue made her hair seem shinier and brought out the colour of her eyes. No gel or red tips on Saturday, she thought, viewing herself in the mirror. She normally dressed to please herself, but she didn't want to let

Grace down. And, okay, maybe she *did* want strut her stuff just a little bit in front of Kruz. This was one occasion when being 'wiry', as Charlie frequently and so unflatteringly referred to her, was actually an advantage. The sale stuff was all in tiny sizes. She even tried on a pair of killer heels—samples, the salesgirl told her.

'That's why they're in the sale,' the girl explained. 'You're the first person who can get her feet into them. They're size Tinkerbell.'

Romy slanted her a smile. 'Tinkerbell suits me fine. I always did like to create a bit of mayhem.'

They both laughed as they took Romy's haul to the till.

'You'll have men flocking,' the girl told her as she rang up Romy's purchases.

'Yeah, right.' And the one man she would like to come flocking would be totally unmoved. 'Thanks for all your help,' Romy said, flashing a goodbye smile as she picked up the bag.

CHAPTER SEVEN

SOMETHING PROPELLED HIM to his feet. Romy had just entered the sumptuously dressed ballroom. He might have known. Animal instinct had driven him to his feet, he acknowledged wryly as that same instinct transferred to his groin. Romy had taken his hint to dress for the occasion, expanding his thoughts as to what she might wear beyond his wildest dreams. Hunger pounded in his eyes as her slanting navy blue gaze found his. Nothing could have prepared him for this level of transformation, or for the way she made him feel. He acted nonchalant as she began to weave her way through the other guests, heading for their table, but with that short blue-black hair, elfin face and the understated silk dress she was easily the most desirable woman in the room.

'Kruz...'

'Romy,' he murmured as she drew to a halt in front of him.

'Allow me introduce you around,' he said, eventually remembering his manners.

His family smiled at Romy and then glanced at him. He was careful to remain stonily impassive. His PA had arranged the place cards so that Romy was seated on the opposite side of the table to him, where he could observe her without the need to engage her in conversation. He had thought he would prefer it that way, but when he saw the way his hot-blooded brothers reacted to her he wasn't so sure.

It was only when it came to the pudding course and Grace suggested they should all change places that he could breathe easily again.

'So,' he said, settling down in the chair next to Romy, 'what did you and Grace decide about the charity?' The two women hadn't stopped talking all evening and had made an arresting sight, Grace with her refined blond beauty and Romy the cute little gamine at her side.

'We discussed the possibility of a regular newsletter, with lots of photographs to show what we do.'

'We?' he queried.

'Do you want me to own this or not?' Romy parried with a shrewd stare.

'Of course I do. It's important to me that everyone involved feels fully committed to the project.' Surprisingly, he found Romy's business persona incredibly sexy. 'That's how I've found employees like it in the past.'

'I'm not your employee. I work for myself, Kruz.'

'Of course you do,' he said, holding her gaze until her cheeks pinked up.

She was all business now—talking about anything but personal matters. That was what he expected of Romy in this new guise, but it didn't mean he had to like it.

'We also talked about a range of greetings cards to complement the calendar—Kruz, are you listening to me?'

'It sounds as if you and Grace have made a good start,' he said, leaning back in his chair.

The urge to sit with Romy and monopolise her conversation wasn't so much a case of being polite as a hunting imperative. His brothers were still sitting annoyingly close to her, though in fairness she didn't seem to notice them.

She was so aroused she was finding it embarrassing. Her cheeks were flushed and she didn't even dare to look down to see if her ever-ready nipples were trying to thrust their way through the flimsy silk. She couldn't breathe properly while she was sitting this close to Kruz—she couldn't think. She could only feel. And there was a lot of feeling going on. Her lips felt full, her eyes felt sultry. Her breasts felt heavy. And her nipples were outrageously erect. *There.* She knew she shouldn't have looked. Her breathing was super-fast, and she felt swollen and needy and—

'More wine, madam?'

'No, thank you,' she managed to squeak out. She'd hardly touched the first glass. Who needed stimulus when Kruz Acosta was sitting next to her?

'Would you like to dance?'

She gaped at the question and Kruz raised a brow.

'It's quite a simple question,' he pointed out, 'and all you have to say is yes or no.'

For once in her life she couldn't say anything at all. The table was emptying around them. Everyone was on their feet, dirty-dancing to a heady South American beat. The dance floor was packed. Kruz was only being polite, she reasoned. And she could hardly refuse him without appearing rude.

'Okay,' she said, trying for off-hand as she left the table.

There was only one problem here—her legs felt like jelly and sensation had gathered where it shouldn't, rivalling the music with a compelling pulse. Worse, Kruz was staring knowingly into her eyes. He didn't need to say a word. She was already remembering a grassy bank beneath a night sky in Argentina and a press coach rocking. His touch on her back was all the more frustrating for being light. They had around six inches of dance floor to play in and Kruz seemed determined they would use only half those inches. Pressed up hard against him, she was left wondering if she could lose control right here, right now. The way sensation was mounting inside her made that seem not only possible but extremely probable.

'Are you all right, Romy?' Kruz asked.

She heard the strand of amusement in his voice. He knew, damn him! 'Depends what you mean by all right?' she said.

Somehow she managed to get through the rest of the dance without incident, and neither of them spoke a word on their way back to the table. The palm of Kruz's hand felt warm on her back, and maybe that soothed her into a dream state, for the next thing she knew he had led her on past the table, through the exit and on towards the elevators.

They stood without explanation, movement or speech as the small, luxuriously upholstered cabin rose swiftly towards one of the higher floors. She didn't mean to stare at it, but there was a cosy-looking banquette built into one side of the restricted space. She guessed it was a thoughtful gesture by the hotel for some of its older guests. Generously padded and upholstered in crimson velvet, the banquette was exerting a strangely hypnotic effect on her—that and the mirror on the opposite side.

She sucked in a swift, shocked breath as Kruz stopped the elevator between floors.

'No…' she breathed.

'Too much of a cliché?' he suggested, with that wicked grin she loved curving his mouth.

They came together like a force of nature. It took all he'd got to hold Romy off long enough for him to protect them both. Remembering the last time, when she had wrenched the shirt from his pants, he kept her hands pinned above her head as he kissed her, pressing her hard against the wall. She tasted fresh and clean and young and perfect—all the things he was not. His stubble scraped her as he buried his face in her neck and her lips were already bruised. Inhaling deeply, he kissed her below the ear for the sheer pleasure of feeling tremors course through her body. His hands moved quickly to cup the sweet remembered swell of her buttocks.

This was everything he remembered, only better. Her skin was silky-smooth. His rough hands were full of her. In spite of being so tiny she had curves in all the right places and she fitted him perfectly. Lodging one thigh between her legs, he moved her dress up to her waist and brought her lacy underwear down. 'Wrap your legs around me, Romy,' he ordered, positioning her on the very edge of the banquette.

Pressing her knees back, he stared down as he tested that she was ready. This was the first time he had seen her—really seen her—and she was more than ready. Those tremors had travelled due south and were gripping her insistently now.

'Oh, please,' she gasped, holding her thighs wide for him.

She alternated her pleas to him with glances in the mirror, where he knew the sight of him ready and more than willing to do what both of them needed so badly really turned her on. He obliged by running the tip of his straining erection against her. She panted and mewled as she tried to thrust her hips towards him to capture more. He had her in a firm grasp, and though he was equally hungry it pleased him to make her wait.

'What do you want?' he murmured against her mouth, teasing her with his tongue.

He should have known Romy Winner would tell him, in no uncertain language. With a laugh he sank deep, and rested a moment while she uttered a series of panting cries.

'Good?' he enquired softly.

Her answer was to groan as she threw her head back. Withdrawing slowly, he sank again—slowly and to the hilt on this occasion. Some time during that steady assault she turned again to look into the mirror. He did too.

'More,' she whispered, her stare fixed on their reflection.

A couple of firm thrusts and she was there, shrieking as the spasms gripped her, almost bouncing her off the banquette. The mirror was great for some things, but when it came to this only staring into Romy's eyes did it for him. But even that wasn't enough for them. It wasn't nearly enough, he concluded as Romy clung to him, her inner muscles clenching violently around him. Picking her up, he maintained a steady rhythm as he pressed her back against the wall.

'More,' he agreed, thrusting into her to a steady beat.

'Again,' she demanded, falling almost immediately.

'You're very greedy,' he observed with satisfaction, taking care to sustain her enjoyment for as long as she could take it.

'Your turn now,' she managed fiercely.

'If you insist,' he murmured, determined to bring her with him.

Romy was a challenge no man could resist and he had not the slightest intention of trying. She was hypersensitive and ultra-needy. She was a willing mate and when he was badly in need of someone who could halfway keep up. Romy could more than keep up.

This was special. This was amazing. Kruz was so considerate, so caring. And she had thought the worst of him. She had badly misjudged him, Romy decided as Kruz steadied her on her feet when they had taken their fill of each other. For now.

'Okay?' he murmured.

Pulling her dress down, she nodded. Feeling increasingly self-conscious, she rescued her briefs and pulled them on.

'I'll take you upstairs to freshen up,' Kruz reassured her as she glanced at her hair in the mirror and grimaced.

Kruz was misunderstood, she decided, leaning on him.

Yes, he was hard, but only because he'd had to be. But he could be caring too—under the right circumstances.

'Thanks,' she said, feeling the blush of approval spreading to her ears. 'I'd appreciate a bit of tidy-up before I return to the ballroom.'

She had a reputation for being a hard nut too, but not with Kruz…never with Kruz, she mused, staring up at him through the soft filter of afterglow. Maybe after all this time her heart was alive again. Maybe she was actually learning to trust someone…

They exited the elevator and she quickly realised that the Acostas had taken over the whole floor. There were security guards standing ready to open doors for them, but what she presumed must be Kruz's suite turned out to be an office.

'The bathroom's over there,' he said briskly, pointing in the direction as his attention was claimed by a pretty blond woman who was keen to show him something on her screen.

This wasn't embarrassing, Romy thought as people shot covert glances as her as she made her way between the line of desks.

And if she would insist on playing with fire…

Locking herself in the bathroom, she took a deep, steadying breath. When would she ever learn that this was nothing more than sex for Kruz, and that she was nothing more than a feeding station for him? And it was too late to worry about what anyone thought.

Running the shower, she stripped off. Stepping under the steaming water felt like soothing balm. She would wash every trace of Kruz Acosta away and harden her resolve towards him as she did so. But nothing helped to ease the ache inside her. It wasn't sexual frustration eating away at her now. It was something far worse. It was as if a seed had been planted the first time they met, and that seed had not only survived but had grown into love.

Love?

Love. What else would you call this certain feeling? And no wonder she had fallen so hard, Romy reasoned, cutting herself some slack as she stepped out of the shower. Kruz was a force of nature. She'd never met anyone like him before.

She was a grown woman who should have known better than to fall for the charms of a man like Kruz—a man who was in no way going to fall at her feet just because she willed it so.

And maybe this grown woman should have checked that there was a towel in the bathroom before she took a shower?

Romy stared around the smart bathroom in disbelief. There was a hand-dryer and that was it. Of course… The hotel had let this as an office, not a bedroom with *en-suite* bathroom. Wasn't that great? How much better could things get?

'Are you ready to go yet?' Kruz bellowed as he hammered on the door.

Fantastic. So now she was the centre of attention of everyone in the office as they waited for her to come out of the bathroom.

'Almost,' she called out brightly, in her most business-like voice.

Almost? She was standing naked, shivering and dripping all over the floor.

'Couple of minutes,' she added optimistically.

Angling her body beneath a grudging stream of barely warm air wasn't going so well. But there was a grunt from the other side of the door, and retreating footsteps, which she took for a reprieve. Giving up, she called it a day. Slipping on her dress, she ran tense fingers through her mercifully short hair and realised that would have to do. Now all that was left was the walk of shame. Drawing a deep breath, she tilted her chin and opened the door.

Everyone in the office made a point of looking away. *Oh...* She swayed as a wave of faintness washed over her. This was ridiculous. She had never fainted in her life.

'Are you all right, Romy?' Kruz was at her side in an instant with a supporting arm around her shoulders. 'Sit here,' he said, guiding her to a chair when all she longed for was to leave the curious glances far behind. 'I'll get you a glass of water.'

It was a relief when the buzz in the office started up again. She tried to reason away her moment of frailty. She'd hardly drunk anything at the dinner. Had she eaten something earlier that had disagreed with her?

'I'm fine, honestly,' she insisted as Kruz handed her a plastic cup.

'You're clearly not fine,' he argued firmly, 'and I'm going to call you a cab to take you home.'

'But—'

'In fact, I'm going to take you home,' he amended. 'I can't risk you fainting on the doorstep.'

He was going to take her to the tiny terrace she shared with three other girls in a rundown part of town?

Things really couldn't get any better, could they?

She didn't want Kruz to see where she lived. Her aim was one day to live in a tranquil, picturesque area of London by the canal, but for now it was enough to have a roof over her head. She didn't want to start explaining all this to Kruz, or to reveal where her money went. Her mother's privacy was sacrosanct.

She expected Kruz to frown when he saw where she lived. He had just turned his big off-roader into the 'no-go zone', as some of the cabbies called the area surrounding Romy's lodgings. She sometimes had to let them drop her off a couple of streets away, where it was safer for them, and she'd walk the rest of the way home. She wasn't worried about it. She could look after herself. This might look bad to Kruz, but it was home for her as it was for a lot of people.

'What are you doing living here, Romy?'

Here we go. 'Something wrong with it?' she challenged.

Kruz didn't answer. He didn't need to. His face said it all—which was too bad for him. She didn't have to explain herself. She didn't want Kruz Acosta—or anyone else, for that matter—feeling sorry for her. This was something she had chosen to do—*had* to do—took pride in doing. If she couldn't look after her family, what was left?

Stopping the car, Kruz prepared to get out.

'No,' she said. 'I'm fine from here. We're right outside the front door.'

'I'm seeing you in,' he said, and before she could argue with this he was out of the car and slamming the door behind him. Opening her door, he stood waiting. 'This isn't up for discussion,' he growled when she hesitated.

Was anything where Kruz was concerned?

CHAPTER EIGHT

ROMY HAD GOT to him when no one else could.

So why Romy Winner?

Good question, Kruz reflected as he turned the wheel to leave the street where Romy lived. As he joined the wide, brilliantly lit road that led back to the glitter of Park Lane, one of London's classiest addresses, he thought about his office back at the hotel and wondered why he hadn't asked one of his staff to drive her home.

Because Romy was his responsibility. Why make any more of it?

Because seeing her safely through her front door had been vital for him.

Finding out where she lived had been quite a shock. He might have expected her to live in a bohemian area, or even an area on the up, but in the backstreets of a nowhere riddled with crime…?

He was more worried than ever about her now. In spite of Romy's protestations she had still looked pale and faint to him. The kick-ass girl had seemed vulnerable suddenly. The pint-sized warrior wasn't as tough as she thought she was. Which made him feel like a klutz for seducing her in the elevator—even if, to be fair, he had been as much seduced as seducer.

Forgetting sex—*if he could for a moment*—why did Romy live on the wrong side of the tracks when she must make plenty of money? She was one of the most successful photo-journalists of her generation. So what was she doing with all the money she earned?

And now, in spite of all his good intentions, as he drew the off-roader to a halt outside the hotel's grandiose pillared entrance, all he could think about was Romy, and how she had left him hungry for more.

She was a free spirit, like him, so why not?

Handing over his keys to the hotel valet, he reasoned that neither of them was interested in emotional ties, but seeing Romy on a more regular basis, as Grace had suggested, would certainly add a little spice to his time in London. His senses went on the rampage at this thought. If Romy hadn't been under par this evening he wouldn't be coming back here on his own now.

She was sick on Monday morning. Violently, sickeningly sick. Crawling back into bed, she pulled the covers over her head and closed her eyes, willing the nausea to go away. She had cleaned her teeth and swilled with mouthwash, but she could still taste bile in her throat.

Thank goodness her housemates had both had early starts that morning, Romy reflected, crawling out of bed some time later. She couldn't make it into work. Not yet, at least. Curling up on the battered sofa in front of the radiator, still in her dressing gown, she groaned as she nursed a cup of mint tea, which was all she could stomach after the latest in a series of hectic trips to the bathroom.

She couldn't be... She absolutely couldn't be—

She wouldn't even think the word. She refused to voice it. She could not be pregnant. Kruz had always used protection.

She had obviously eaten something that disagreed with her. She must have. She had that same light-headed, bilious feeling that came after eating dodgy food.

Dodgy food at one of London's leading hotels? How likely was that? The Greasy Spoon was famously beyond reproach, and she was Mrs Disinfectant in the kitchen...

Well, *something* had made her feel this way, Romy argued stubbornly as she crunched without enthusiasm on a piece of dry toast.

A glance at the clock reminded her that she didn't have time to sit around feeling sorry for herself; she had a photoshoot with the young star of a reality show this morning, and the greedy maw of *ROCK!* magazine's picture section, infamously steered by Ronald the Remorseless, wouldn't wait.

Neither would the latest invoice for her mother's nursing care, Romy reflected with concern as she left the house. She had already planned her day around a visit to the nursing home, where she checked regularly on all those things her mother was no longer able to sort out for herself. She had no time to fret. She just had to get on and stop worrying about the improbability of two people who had undergone the same emotional bypass coming together to form a new life.

But...

Okay, so there was a chemist just shy of the *ROCK!* office block.

Dragging in the scent of clean and bright air, Romy assured herself that her visit to the chemist was essential to life, as she needed to stock up on cold and flu remedies. There was quite a lot of that about at the moment. Grabbing a basket, she absentmindedly popped in a pack of handwipes, a box of tissues, some hairgrips—which she never used—and a torch.

Well, you never know.

Making her way to the counter, she hovered in front of

the *'Do you Think you Could be Pregnant?'* section, hoping someone else might push in front of her. Finally palming a pregnancy test, with a look on her face which she hoped suggested that she was very kindly doing it for a friend, she glanced around to make sure there was no one she knew in the shop before approaching the counter. As she reached for her purse the pharmacist came over to help.

'Do you have a quick-fire cure for a stomach upset?' Romy enquired brightly, pushing her purchases towards the woman, with the telltale blue and white box well hidden beneath the other packages.

'Nausea?' the pharmacist asked pleasantly. 'You're not pregnant, are you?' she added, filleting the pile to extract the box containing the pregnancy test with all the sleight of hand of a Pick-up-Sticks champion.

'Of course not.' Romy laughed a little too loudly.

'Are you sure?' The woman's gaze was kind and steady, but her glance did keep slipping to the blue and white packet, which had somehow slithered its way to centre stage. 'I have to know before I can give you any medication...'

'Oh, that's just for a friend,' Romy said, feeling her cheeks blaze.

Meanwhile the queue behind her was growing, and several people were coughing loudly, or tutting.

'I think we'd better err on the side of caution,' the helpful young pharmacist said, reaching behind her to pick up some more packages. 'There are several brands of pregnancy test—'

'I'll take all of them,' Romy blurted.

'And will you come back for the nausea remedy?' the woman called after her. 'There are some that pregnant women can take—'

Then let those pregnant women take them, Romy thought,

gasping with relief as she shut the door of the shop behind her. How ridiculous was this? She didn't even have the courage to buy what she wanted from a chemist now.

'Someone's waiting for you in your office,' the receptionist told her as she walked back into the building.

Not Kruz. Not now. 'Who?' she said warily.

'Kruz Acosta,' the girl said brightly. 'He was here a couple of days ago, wasn't he? Aren't you the lucky one?'

'I certainly am,' Romy agreed darkly. Girding her loins, she headed for the basement.

'Weren't you with him the other night?' someone else chipped in when she stepped into the crowded elevator. 'Great shot of you on the front page of the *West End Chronicle,* Romy,' someone else chirruped. 'In fact, both you and Kruz look amazing...'

General giggling greeted this.

'Can I see?' She leaned over the shoulder of the first girl to look at the newspaper she was holding.

OMG!

'Oh, that was just a charity thing I attended,' she explained off-handedly, feeling sicker than ever now she'd seen the shot of her and Kruz, slipping not as discreetly as they had thought into the elevator. Kruz's hand on her back and the expression on her face as she stared up at him both told a very eloquent story. And now there was the type of tension in the lift that suggested the slightest comment from anyone and all the girls would burst out laughing. The banner headline hardly helped: *'Are You Ready for Your Close-Up, Ms Winner?'*

Was that libellous? Romy wondered.

Better not to make a fuss, she concluded, reading on.

'Who doesn't envy Romy Winner her close encounter with elusive billionaire bad-boy Kruz Acosta? Kruz, the only unmarried brother of the four notorious polo-playing Acostas brothers—'

Groaning, she leaned her head against the back of the lift. She didn't need to read any more to know this was almost certainly the reason Kruz was here to see her now. He must hold her wholly responsible for the press coverage. He probably thought she'd set it up. But it took two to tango, Romy reminded herself as she got out of the elevator and strode purposefully towards her cubbyhole.

Breath left her lungs in a rush when she opened the door. Would she *ever* get used to the sight of this man? 'Kruz, I'm—'

'Fantastic!' he exclaimed vigorously. 'How are you this morning, Señorita Winner? Better, I hope?'

'Er...' *Maybe pregnant...maybe not.* 'Good. Thank you,' she said firmly, as if she had to convince herself.

Slipping off her coat, she hung it on the back of the office door. Careful not to touch Kruz, she sidled round the desk. Dumping her bag on the floor at her side, she sat in her swivel chair, relieved to have a tangible barrier between them. Kruz was in jeans, a heavy jacket with the collar pulled up and workmanlike boots—a truly pleasing sight. Especially first thing in the morning...

And last thing at night.

And every other time of day.

Waving to the only other chair in the room—a hard-backed rickety number—she invited him to sit down too. And almost passed out when he was forced to swoop down and move her bag. It was one of those tote things that didn't fasten at the top, and all her purchases were bulging out—including a certain blue and white packet.

'I didn't want to knock your bag over,' he explained, frowning when he saw her expression. 'Still not feeling great?'

Clearly blue and white packets held no significance for a man. 'No...I'm fine,' she said.

'Good,' Kruz said, seeming unconvinced. 'I'm very pleased to hear it.'

So why were his lips still pressed in a frown?

And why was she staring at his mouth?

Suddenly super-conscious of her own lips, and how it felt to be kissed by Kruz, she dragged her gaze away. And then remembered the scratch of his stubble on her skin. The marks probably still showed—and she had been too distracted by hormonal stuff this morning to remember to cover them. So everyone had seen them. Double great.

'What can I do for you?' she said.

'You haven't read the article yet?' Kruz queried with surprise.

He made it impossible for her to ignore the scandal sheet as he laid it out on her desk. 'I like the way you went after publicity,' he said.

Was that a glint in his wicked black eyes? She put on a serious act. 'Good,' she said smoothly. 'That's good...'

'The article starts with the usual nonsense about you and me,' he reported, leaning over her desk to point to the relevant passage, 'but then it goes on to devote valuable column inches to the charity.' He looked up, his amused dark eyes plumbing deep. 'I'd like to compliment you on having a colleague standing by.'

'You think I *staged* this?' she exclaimed, mortified that Kruz should imagine she would go to such lengths.

'Well, didn't you?' he said.

There was a touch of hardness in his expression now, and she was acutely conscious of the pregnancy test peeping out of her bag, mocking her desire to finish this embarrassing interview and find out whether she was pregnant or not. There was also a chance that if Kruz caught sight of the test he might think she had set *him* up too. Sick of all the deception, she decided to come clean.

'I'm not sure how that photograph happened,' she admitted, 'other than to say there are always photojournalists on the look-out for a story—especially at big hotels when there's an important event on. I'm afraid I can't claim any credit for it...' She held Kruz's long, considering stare.

'Well, however it happened,' he said, 'it's done the charity no harm at all. So, well done. Hits on our website have rocketed and donations are flooding in.'

'That *is* great news,' she agreed.

'And funny?' he said.

Perhaps it was hormones making want to giggle. She'd heard it said that Romy Winner would stop at nothing to get a story. She had certainly put her back into it this time.

'So you're not offended by the headline?' she said, reverting to business again.

'It amused me,' Kruz confessed.

Well, that wasn't quite what she'd been hoping for. 'Me too,' she said, as if fun in a lift were all part of the job. 'It's all part of the job,' she said out loud, as if to convince herself it were true.

'Great job,' Kruz murmured, cocking his head with the hint of a smile on his mouth.

'Yes,' she said.

'On the strength of the publicity you've generated so far, I'm going to take you to lunch to discuss further strategy.'

Ah. 'Further strategy?' She frowned. 'Lunch at nine-thirty in the morning?'

She was going to visit her mother later. It was the highlight of her day and one she wouldn't miss for the world. It was also something she couldn't share with Kruz.

'We'll meet at one,' he said, turning for the door.

'No. I can't—'

'You have to eat and so do I,' he said.

'I've got a photoshoot,' she remembered with relief. 'And then—' And then she had finished for the day.

'And then you eat,' Kruz said firmly.

'And then I've got personal business.'

'We'll make it supper, then,' he conceded.

By which time she would know. Vivid images of losing control in the elevator flashed into her head—a telling reminder that she had enjoyed sex with Kruz not once, but many times. And it only took one time for a condom to fail.

They exchanged a few more thoughts and comments about the way forward for the charity, and then Kruz left her to plunge into a day where nothing went smoothly other than Romy's visit to her mother. That was like soothing balm after dealing with a spoiled brat who had screamed for ten types of soda and sweets with all the green ones taken out before she would even consider posing for the camera.

What a day of contrasts it had been, she reflected later. When she held her mother's soft, limp hand everything fell into place, and she gained a sense of perspective, but then it was all quickly lost when she thought about Kruz and the possibility of being pregnant.

He studied the report on Romy with interest. She was certainly good at keeping secrets. But then so was he. At least this explained why Romy lived where she did, and why she worked all hours—often forgetting to eat, according to his sources. Romy was an only child whose father had died in jail after the man had left her mother a living corpse after his final violent attack. Romy was her mother's sole provider, and had been lucky to come out of that house alive.

No wonder she was a loner. The violence she had witnessed as a child should have put her off men for life, but it certainly went some way to explaining why Romy snatched at physical relief whilst shunning anything deeper. There had been brief relationships, but nothing significant. He guessed her ability to trust hovered around zero. Which made *him* the last partner on earth for her—not that he was thinking of making his relationship with Romy anything more than it already was. His capacity for offering a woman more than physical relief was also zero.

They made a good pair, he reflected, flinging the document aside, but it wasn't a good pairing in the way Romy wanted it to be. He'd seen how she looked at him, and for the first time in his life he wished he had something to offer. But he had learned long ago it was only possible to survive, to achieve and to develop, to do any of those things, if emotion was put aside. It was far better, in his opinion, to feel nothing and move forward than look back, remember and break.

CHAPTER NINE

WHAT A CRAZY day. Up. Down. And all points in between. And it wasn't over yet. The blue and white packet was still sitting where she had left it on the bathroom shelf, and after that she had supper with Kruz to look forward to—and no way of knowing how it would go.

But her meeting with Kruz would be on neutral territory, Romy reminded herself as she soaped down in the tiny shower stall back at the house she shared with the other girls. She would be in public with him. What was the worst that could happen?

The reporter from the scandal sheet might track them down again?

Kruz had seemed to find that amusing. So why hadn't she?

The thought that Kruz meant so much to her and she didn't mean a thing to him hurt. She'd never been in this position before. She'd always been able to control her feelings. She certainly didn't waste them. She cared for her mother, and for her friends, but where men were concerned—there were no men. And now of all the men in the world she'd had to fall for Kruz Acosta, who had never pretended to be anything more than an entertaining companion with special skills—a man who treated sex like food. He needed it. He enjoyed it. But that didn't mean he remembered it beyond the last meal.

While *she* remembered every detail of what he'd said and how he'd said it, how he'd looked at her, how he'd touched her, and how he'd made her feel. It wasn't just sex for the sake of a quick fix for her. It was meaningful. And it had left her defences in tatters.

More fool her.

She was not going slinky tonight, Romy decided in the bedroom. She was going to wear her off-duty uniform of blue jeans, warm sweater and a floppy scarf draped around her neck.

Glancing at her reflection in the mirror, she was satisfied there was nothing provocative about her appearance that Kruz could possibly misinterpret. She looked as if she was going for supper with a friend, which in some ways she was, but first she had something to do—and the sooner she got it over and done with the sooner she would know.

She already knew.

He stood up and felt a thrill as Romy walked into the steak bar. She looked amazing. She always did to him.

'Romy,' he said curtly, hiding those thoughts. 'Good to see you. Please sit down. We've got a lot I'd like to get through tonight, as I'm going to be away for a while. Before I go I need to be sure we're both singing from the same hymn sheet. Red wine or white?'

She looked at him blankly.

'It's a simple question. Red or white?'

'Er—orange juice, please.'

'Whatever you like.' He let it go. Whatever was eating Romy, it couldn't be allowed to get in the way of their discussion tonight. There was a lot he wanted to set straight—like the budgets that she had to work to.

The waiter handed Romy a menu and she began to study

it, while he studied her. After reading the report on Romy he understood a lot more about her. He saw the gentleness she hid so well behind the steel, and the capacity for caring above and beyond anything he could ever have imagined. He jerked his gaze away abruptly. He needed this upcoming trip. He needed space from this woman. No one distracted him like Romy, and he had a busy life—polo, the Acosta family interests, *his* business interests. He had no time to spare for a woman.

To make the break he had arranged a tour of his offices worldwide, with a grudge match with Nero Caracas at the end of it to ease any remaining frustration. A battle between his own Band of Brothers polo team and Nero's Assassins would be more than enough to put his life back in focus, he concluded as Romy laid down the menu and stared at him.

'You're going away?' she said.

'Yes,' he confirmed briskly. 'So, if you're ready to order, let's get back to the agenda. We've got a lot to get through tonight.'

The food was good. He ate well.

Romy picked at her meal and seemed preoccupied.

'Do I?' she said when he asked her about it.

She gave a thin smile to the waiter as she accepted a dessert menu. She'd hardly eaten anything.

'Coffee and ice cream?' he suggested when the waiter returned to take their order. 'They make the best of both here. The ice cream's home-made on the premises—fresh cream and raw eggs.'

She blinked. 'Neither, thank you. I think I've got everything I need here,' she said, collecting up her things as if she couldn't wait to go.

'I'll call for the bill.' This was not the ending to the night he had envisaged. Yes, he needed space from Romy—but on his own terms, and to a timetable that suited him.

Business and pleasure don't mix, he reflected wryly as she left the table, heading for the door. When would he ever learn? But, however many miles he put between them, something told him he would never be far enough away from Romy to put her out of his head.

She guessed shock had made her sick this time. It must be shock. It was only ten o'clock in the evening and she had just brought up every scrap of her picked-over meal. Shock at Kruz going away—just like that, without a word of warning. No explanation at all.

And why would he tell her?

She was nothing to him, Romy realised, shivering as she pulled the patchwork throw off her bed to wrap around her shaking shoulders. She was simply a photographer the Acostas had tasked with providing images for their charitable activities—a photographer who had lost her moral compass on a grassy bank, a press coach and in an elevator. *Classy.* So why hadn't she spoken out tonight? Why hadn't she said something to Kruz? There had been more than one opportunity for her to be straight with him.

About this most important of topics she had to be brutally honest with herself first. This wasn't a business matter she could lightly discuss with Kruz, or even a concern she had about working for the charity. This was a child—a life. This was a new life depending on her to make the right call.

Swivelling her laptop round, she studied the shots she'd taken of Kruz. Not one of them showed a flicker of tenderness or humour. He was a hard, driven man. How would he take the news? She couldn't just blurt out, *You're going to be a daddy,* and expect him to cheer. She wouldn't do that, anyway. The fact that she was having Kruz's baby was so big, so life-changing for both of them, so precious and tender to her, she would choose her moment. She only wished things could be different between them—but wishing didn't make things happen. Actions made things happen, and right now she needed to make money more than she ever had.

As she flicked through the saleable images she hadn't yet offered on the open market, she realised there were plenty—which was a relief. And there were also several elevator shots on the net to hold interest. Thank goodness no one had been around for the grassy bank...

She studied the close-ups of her and Kruz as they had been about to get into the elevator and smiled wryly. They made a cool couple.

And now the cool couple were going to have a baby.

He ground his jaw with impatience as his sister-in-law gave him a hard time. He'd stopped over at the *estancia* in Argentina and appreciated the space. He was no closer to sorting out his feelings for Romy and would have liked more time to do so. The irony of having so many forceful women in one family had not escaped him. Glancing at his wristwatch, he toyed with the idea of inventing a meeting so he had an excuse to end the call.

'Are you still there, Kruz?'

'I'm still here, Grace,' he confirmed. 'But I have pressing engagements.'

'Well, make sure you fit Romy into them,' Grace insisted, in no way deterred.

'I might have to go away again. Can't you liaise with her?'

'And choose which photographs we want to use?'

He swore beneath his breath. 'Forgive me, Grace, but you're in London and I'm not right now.'

'I'll liaise with Romy on one condition,' his wily sister-in-law agreed.

'And that is?' he demanded.

'You see her again and sort things out between you.'

'Can't do that, Grace. Thousands of miles between us,' he pointed out.

'So send for her,' Grace said, as if this were normal practise rather than dramatic in the extreme. 'I've heard the way your voice changes when you talk about Romy. What are you afraid of, Kruz?'

'Me? Afraid?' he scoffed.

'Even men like Nacho have hang-ups—before he met me, that is,' his sister-in-law amended with warmth and humour in her voice. 'Don't let your hang-ups spoil things for you, Kruz. At least speak to her. Promise me?'

He hummed and hawed, and then agreed. What was all the rush about? Romy could just as easily have got in touch with *him.*

Maybe there were reasons?

What reasons?

Maybe her mother was ill. If that were the case he would be concerned for her. Romy's care of her mother was exemplary, according to his investigations. He hadn't thought to ask about her. Grace was right. The least he could do was call Romy and find out.

'Kruz?'

She had to stop hugging the phone as if it were a lifeline. She had to stop analysing every micro-second of his all too impersonal greeting. She had to accept the fact that Kruz was calling her because he wanted to meet for an update on the progress she was making with the banners, posters and flyers for the upcoming charity polo match. She had to get real so she could do the job she was being paid to do. This might

all be extra to her work for *ROCK!,* but she had no intention
of short-changing either the magazine or the Acosta family.
She believed in the Acosta charity and she was going to give
it everything she'd got.

'Of course we can meet—no, there's no reason why not.'
Except her heart was acting up. It was one thing being on the
other end of a phone to Kruz, but being in the same room as
him, which was what he seemed to be suggesting…

'Can you pack and come tomorrow?'

'Come where?'

'To the *estancia,* of course.'

Shock coursed through her. 'You're calling me from Argentina? When you said you were going away I had no idea
you were going to Argentina.'

'Does that make a difference?' Kruz demanded. 'I'll send
the jet—what's your problem, Romy?'

You. 'Kruz, I work—'

'You gave me to understand you were almost self-em-
ployed now and could please yourself.'

'Sort of…'

'Sort of?' he queried. 'Are you or aren't you? If your boss
at *ROCK!* acts up, check to see if you've got some holiday
owing. Just take time off and get out here.'

So speaks the wealthy man, Romy thought, flicking
quickly through the diary in her mind.

'Romy?' Kruz prompted impatiently. 'Is there a reason
why you can't come here tomorrow?'

Pregnant women were allowed to travel, weren't they?
'No,' she said bluntly. 'There's no reason why I can't travel.'

'See you tomorrow.'

She stared at the dead receiver in her hand. To be in Argentina tomorrow might sound perfectly normal to a jet-setting
polo player, but even to a newshound like Romy it sounded

reckless. And it gave her no chance to prepare her story, she realised, staring at an e-mail from Kruz containing her travel details that had already flashed up on her screen. Not that she needed a story, Romy reassured herself as she scanned the arrangements he had made for her to board his private jet. She would just tell him the truth. Yes, they had used protection, but a condom must have failed.

Sitting back, she tried to regret what had happened—was happening—and couldn't. How could she regret the tiny life inside her? Mapping her stomach with her hands, she realised that all she regretted was wasting her feelings on Kruz—a man who walked in and out of her life at will, leaving her as isolated as she had ever been.

Like countless other women who had to make do and mend with what life had dealt them.

She would just have to make do and mend *this,* Romy concluded.

Having lost patience with her maudlin meanderings, she tapped out a brief and businesslike reply to Kruz's e-mail. She didn't have to sleep with him. She could resist him. It was just a matter of being sensible. The main thing was to do a good job for the charity and leave Argentina with her pride intact. She would find the right moment to tell Kruz about the baby. They were two civilised human beings and would work it out. She would be on that flight tomorrow, she would finish the job Grace had given her, and then she would decide the way ahead as she always had. Just as she had protected her mother for as long as she could, she would now protect her unborn child. And if that meant facing up to Kruz and telling him how things were going to be from here on in, then that was exactly what she was going to do.

The flight was uneventful. In fact it was soothing compared to what awaited her, Romy suspected, resting back. She tried to soothe herself further by reflecting on all the good things that had happened. She had worked hard to establish herself as a freelance alongside her magazine work, and her photographs had featured in some of the glossies as the product of someone who was more than just a member of the paparazzi. One of her staunchest supporters had turned out to be Ronald, who had made her cry—baby-head, she realised—when he'd said that he believed in her talent and expected her to go far.

Well, she was going far now, Romy reflected, blowing out a long, thoughtful breath as she considered the journey ahead of her. And as to what lay on the other side of that flight... She could only guess that this pampering on a private jet, with freshly squeezed orange juice on tap, designer food and cream kidskin seats large enough to curl up and snooze on, would be the calm before the storm.

Tracing the curve of her stomach protectively as the jet circled before swooping down to land on the Acostas' private landing strip, Romy felt her heart bump when she spotted the *hacienda*, surrounded by endless miles of green with the mountains beyond. The scenery in this part of Argentina was ravishingly beautiful, and the *hacienda* nestled in its grassy frame in such a favoured spot. Bathed in sunlight, the old stone had turned a glinting shade of molten bronze. The pampas was only a wilderness to those who couldn't see the beauty in miles of fertile grass, or to those with no appreciation of the varied wildlife and birdlife that called this place home.

She craned her neck to catch a glimpse of thundering waterfalls crashing down from the Andes and lazy rivers moving like glittering ribbons towards the sea. It made her smile to see how many horses were grazing on the pampas, and her heart thrilled at the sight of the *gauchos* working amongst the herds of Criolla ponies. They were no more than tiny dots as the jet came in to land, and the ponies soon scattered when they heard the engines. She wondered if Kruz was among the riders chasing them…

She was pleased to be back.

The realisation surprised her. She must be mad, knowing what lay ahead of her, Romy concluded as the seatbelt sign flashed on, but against all that was logical this felt like coming home.

After flying overnight, she stepped out of the plane into dry heat on a beautifully sunny day. The sky was bright blue and decorated with clouds that looked like cotton wool balls. The scent of grass and blossom was strong, though it was spoiled a little by the tang of aviation fuel. Slipping on her sunglasses, Romy determined that nothing was going to spoil her enjoyment of this visit. This was a fabulous country, with fabulous people, and she couldn't wait to start taking pictures.

There was a *gaucho* standing next to a powerful-looking truck, which he had parked on the grass verge to one side of the airstrip, but there was no sign of Kruz. She should be relieved about that. It would give her time to settle in, Romy reasoned as the weather-beaten *gaucho* came to greet her. He introduced himself as Alessandro, explaining that Kruz was away from the *estancia*.

Would Kruz be away for a long time? Romy wondered, not liking to ask. Anyway, it was good to know that he wasn't crowding her. *But she missed him.*

Hard luck, she thought wryly as the elderly ranch-hand pointed away across the vast sea of grass. Ah, so Kruz wasn't *staying* away—he was out riding on the pampas. Her heart lifted, but then she reasoned that he must have seen the jet coming into land, yet wouldn't put himself out to come and meet her.

That was good, she told herself firmly. No pressure.

No caring, either.

She stood back as Alessandro took charge of her luggage. 'You mustn't lift anything in your condition,' he said.

She blushed furiously. Was her pregnancy so obvious? She was wearing jeans with a broad elastic panel at the front, and over the top of them a baggy T-shirt *and* a fashionable waterfall cardigan, which the salesgirl had assured Romy was guaranteed to hide her small bump. *Wrong,* Romy concluded. If Alessandro could tell she was pregnant, there would be no hiding the fact from Kruz.

Perhaps people were just super tuned-in to nature out here on the pampas, she reflected as Alessandro opened the door of the cab for her and stood back. Climbing in, she sat down. Breathing a sigh of relief as the elderly *gaucho* closed the door, she took a moment to compose herself. The interlude was short-lived. As she turned to smile at Alessandro when he climbed into the driver's seat at her side her heart lurched at the sight of Kruz, riding flat out across the pampas towards them.

It struck her as odd that she had never seen such a renowned horseman riding before, but then they actually knew very little about what made each other tick. At this distance Kruz was little more than a dark shadow, moving like an arrow towards her, but it was as if her heart had told her eyes to look for him and here he was. Her spirits rose as she watched him draw closer. Surely a man who was so at one with nature would be thrilled at the prospect of bringing new life into the world?

So why did she feel so apprehensive?

She should be apprehensive, Romy concluded, nursing her bump. This baby meant everything to her, and she would fight for the right to keep her child with her whatever a powerful man like Kruz Acosta had to say about it, but she couldn't imagine he would make things easy for her.

'And now we wait,' Alessandro said, settling back as he turned off the engine.

He had promised himself he would stay out of Romy's way until the evening, giving her a chance to settle in. He wanted her know she wasn't at the top of his list of priorities for the day. Which clearly explained why he was riding across the pampas now, with his sexual radar on red alert. No one excited him like Romy. No one intrigued him as she did. Life was boring without her, he had discovered. Other women were pallid and far too eager to please him. He had missed Romy's fiery temperament—amongst other things—and the way she never shirked from taking him on.

Reining in, he allowed his stallion to approach the truck at a high-stepping trot. Halting, he dismounted. His senses were already inflamed at the sight of her, sitting in the truck. The moment the jet had appeared in the sky, circling overhead, he had turned for home, knowing an end to his physical ache was at last in sight.

Striding over to the truck, he forgot all his good intentions about remaining cool and threw open the passenger door. 'Romy—'

'Kruz,' she said, seeming to shrink back in her seat.

This was not the reception he had anticipated. And why was she hugging herself like that? 'I'll see you at the house,' he said, speaking to Alessandro. Slamming the passenger door, he slapped the side of the truck and went back to his horse.

He could wait, he told himself as he cantered back to the *hacienda*. The house was empty. He had given the housekeepers the day off. He wanted the space to do with as he liked—to do with Romy as he liked.

He stabled the horse before returning to the house. He found Romy in the kitchen, where Alessandro was pouring her a cold drink. The old man was fussing over her like a mother hen. He had never seen that before.

'Romy is perfectly capable of looking after herself,' he said, tugging off his bandana to wipe the dust of riding from his face.

As Alessandro grunted he took another look at Romy, who was seated at the kitchen table, side on to him. She seemed small—smaller than he remembered—but her jaw was set as if for battle. So be it. After his shower he would be more than happy to accommodate her.

'Journey uncomfortable?' he guessed, knowing how restless *he* became if he was caged in for too enough.

'Not at all,' she said coolly, still without turning to face him.

'I'm going to take a shower,' he said, thinking her rude, 'and then I'll brief you on the photographs Grace wants you to take.'

'Romy needs to rest first.'

He stared at Alessandro. The old man had never spoken to him like that before—had never danced attendance on a woman in all the years he'd known him.

'I'd love a shower too,' Romy said, springing up.

'Fine. See you later at supper,' he snapped, mouthing, *What?* as Alessandro gave him a sharp look. And then, to his amazement, his elderly second-in-command took hold of Romy's bags and led the way out of the kitchen and up the stairs. 'Maria has prepared the front room overlooking the corral,' he yelled after them.

Neither one of them replied.

'What the hell is going on?' he demanded, the moment Alessandro returned.

'You had better ask Señorita Winner that question,' his old *compadre* told him, heading for the door.

'You know—*you* tell me.'

The old *gaucho* answered this with a shrug as he went out through the door.

She shouldn't have left the door to her bedroom open, Romy realised, stirring sleepily. It wasn't wide open, but it was open enough to appear inviting. She had meant to close it, but had fallen asleep on the bed after her shower. Jet-lag and baby-body, she supposed. She needed a siesta these days.

She needed more than that. Holly Acosta had warned her about this phase of pregnancy…hormones running riot…the 'sex-mad phase', Holly had dubbed it, Romy remembered, clutching her pillow as she tried to forget.

Maybe she had left the door open on purpose, Romy concluded as Kruz, still damp from his shower and clad only in a towel, strolled into the room. Maybe she had deluded herself that they could have one last hurrah and then she would tell him. But she had not expected this surge of feeling as her body warmed in greeting. She had not expected Kruz simply to walk into the room expecting sex, or that she would feel quite so ready to oblige him. What had happened to all those bold resolutions about remaining chaste until she had told him about the baby?

She didn't speak. She didn't need to. She just made room for him on the bed. She was well covered in a sheet—which was more than could be said for Kruz. Her throat felt as if it was tied in knots when the towel he had tucked around his waist dropped to the floor.

Settling down on the bed, he kept some tantalising, teasing space between them, while she covered the evidence of her pregnancy with the bedding. Resting on one elbow, he stared into her eyes, and at that moment she would have done anything for him.

Anything.

He toyed with her hair, teasing her with the delay, while she turned her face to brush her lips along his hand. Remembered pleasure was a strong driver—the strongest. She wanted him. She couldn't hide it. She didn't want to. Her body had more needs now than ever before.

'You've put on weight, Romy,' he murmured, suckling on her breasts. 'Don't,' he complained when she tried to stop him, nervous that Kruz might take his interest lower. 'The added weight suits you. I meant it as a compliment.'

Kruz was in a hurry—which was good. She wasn't even sure he noticed the distinct swell of her belly on his way to his destination. She was all sensation…all want and need… with only one goal in mind. She wasn't even sure whether Kruz pressed her legs apart or whether she opened them for him. She only knew that she was resting back on a soft bank of pillows while he held her thighs apart. And when he bent to his task he was so good… Lacing her fingers through his hair, she decided he was a master of seduction—not that she needed much persuasion. He was so skilled. His tongue… His hands… His understanding of her needs and responses was so acute, so knowing, so—

He paused to protect them both. She thought about telling him then, but it would have been ridiculous, and anyway the hunger was raging inside her now. She wanted him. He wanted her. It was a need so deep, so primal, that nothing could stop them now. She groaned as he sank deep. This was so good—it felt so right. Kruz set up a rhythm, which she followed immediately, mirroring his moves, but with more fire, more need, more urgency.

'That's right—come for me, baby.'

She didn't need any encouragement and fell blindly, violently, triumphantly, with screaming, keening, groaning relief. And Kruz kissed her all the while, his strong arms holding her safe as she tumbled fast and hard. His firm mouth softened to whisper of encouragement as he made sure she enjoyed every second of it before he even thought of taking his own pleasure. When he did it raised her erotic temperature again. Just seeing him enjoying her was enough to do that. The pleasure was never-ending, and as wave after wave after wave of almost unbearable sensation washed over her it was Kruz who kept her safe to abandon herself to this unbelievable union of body and soul.

Sensation and emotion combined had to be the most powerful force any human being could tap into, she thought, still groaning with pleasure as she slowly came down. Clinging to Kruz, nestling against his powerful body, left her experiencing feelings so strong, so beautiful, she could hardly believe they were real. She smiled as she kissed him, moving to his shoulders, to his chest, to his neck. After such brutally enjoyable pleasure this was a rare tender moment to treasure. A life-changing moment, she thought as Kruz continued to tend to her needs.

'Romy?'

She sensed the change in him immediately.

'What?' she murmured. But she already knew, and felt a chill run through her when Kruz lifted his head. The look in his eyes told her everything she needed to know. They were black with fury.

'When were you planning to tell me?' he said.

CHAPTER TEN

SHE HAD EVERY reason to hate the condemnation in Kruz's black stare. She loved her child already. Yes, cool, hard, emotionless Romy Winner had turned into a soft, blobby cocoon overnight. But still with warrior tendencies, she realised as she wriggled up the bed. If he wanted a fight she was ready.

Two of them had made this baby, and their child was a precious life she was prepared to defend with her own life. She surprised herself with how immediately her priorities could change. She wasn't alone any more. It would never be just about her again. She was a mother. In hindsight, she had been mad to think Kruz wouldn't notice she was pregnant. The swell of her belly was small, but growing bigger every day, as if the child they'd made together was as proud and strong as its parents.

She was happy to admit her guilt. She *was* guilty of backing away at the first hurdle and not telling Kruz right away. Allowing him to find out like this way was a terrible thing to do. It had been seeing him and forgetting everything in the moment…

'Are you ashamed of the baby?' he said. Springing into a sitting position, he loomed over her, a terrifying powerhouse of suppressed outrage.

Before her mouth had a chance to form words he detached

himself from her arms and swung off the bed. Striding across the room, he closed the door on the bathroom and she heard him run the shower. He was shocked and she was frantic. Her mind refused to cooperate and tell her what to do next. She'd really messed up, and now she would be caught in the whirlwind.

He'd been away, she reasoned as she listened to Kruz in the bathroom.

There was the telephone. There was the internet. There was always a way of getting hold of someone. She just hadn't tried.

They didn't have that kind of relationship.

What *did* they have?

She hadn't been prepared for pregnancy because she'd had no reason to suppose she was in line to make a baby.

You had sex, didn't you?

The brutal truth. They'd had sex vigorously and often. Two casual acquaintances coming together for no other purpose than mindless pleasure until the charity gave them a common aim. They had enjoyed each other greedily and thoughtlessly, with only a mind to that pleasure. Maybe Kruz thought she was going to hit him with a paternity suit. Holly had explained to her once that the Acostas were so close and kept the world at bay because massive wealth brought massive risk. They found it hard to trust anyone, because most people had an agenda.

'Kruz—'

She flinched as the door opened and quickly wrapped the sheet around her. Yet again she was wasting time thinking when she should be doing. She should have got dressed and then she could face him as an equal, rather than having to try and tug the sheet from the bottom of the bed so she could retain what little dignity was left to her.

'No— Wait—' Kruz had pulled on his jeans and top and was heading for the door. Somehow she managed to yank the sheet free and stumble towards him. 'Please—I realise this must be a terrible shock for you, but we really have to talk.'

'A *shock*?' he said icily, staring down at her hand on his arm.

She recoiled from him. Suddenly Kruz's arm felt like the arm of a stranger, while she felt like a hysterical woman accosting someone she didn't know.

She tried again—calmly this time. 'Please… We must talk.'

'*Now* we need to talk?' he said mildly.

She had hurt him. But it was so much more than that. Kruz was shocked—felled by the enormity of what she'd been keeping from him. His brain was scrambled. She could tell he needed space. 'Please…' she said gently, trying to appeal to a softer side of him.

'No,' he rapped, pulling away. 'No,' he said again, shaking her off. 'You can't just hit me with this and expect me to produce a ready-made plan.'

She didn't expect anything from him, but she couldn't just let him turn his back and walk away. Moving in front of him, she leaned against the door. 'Well, that's up to you. I can't stop you leaving.'

Kruz's icy expression assured her this was the case.

'I don't want anything from you,' she said, trying to subdue the tremor in her voice. 'I know a baby isn't a good enough reason for us to stay together in some sort of mismatched hook-up—'

'I wasn't aware we were *planning* to hook up,' he cut in with a quiet intensity that really scared her.

She moved away from the door. What else could she do? She felt dead inside. She should have told him long before now, but Kruz's reaction to finding out had completely thrown her. They were both responsible for a new life, but he seemed determined to shut that fact out. She would have to speak to him through lawyers when she got back to England, and somehow she would have to complete her work for the charity while she was here in Argentina—with or without Kruz Acosta's co-operation.

Needing isolation and time to think, she hurried to the bathroom and shut the door—just in time to hear Kruz close the outer door behind him.

No! No! No! This could not be happening. He micro-managed every aspect of his life to make sure something unexpected could never blindside him. So how? Why now?

Why ever?

With no answers that made sense he stalked in the direction of the stables.

A child? *His* child? His baby?

His mind was filled with wonder. But having a child was unthinkable for him. It was a gift he could never accept. He couldn't share his nightmares—not with Romy and much less with an innocent child. Who knew what he was capable of?

In the army they'd said there were three kinds of soldiers: those who were trained to kill and couldn't bring themselves to do it; those who were trained to kill and enjoyed it; and those who were trained to kill and did so because it was their duty. They did that duty on auto-pilot, without allowing themselves to think. He had always thought that last type of soldier was the most dangerous and the most damned, because they had only one choice. That was to live their lives after the army refusing to remember, refusing to feel, refusing to face what they'd done. He was that soldier.

There was only one option open to him. He would allow

Romy to complete her work here and then he would send her back. He would provide for the child and for Romy. He would write a detailed list of everything she must have and then he would hand that list over to his PA.

From the first night he had woken screaming he had vowed never to inflict his nightmares on anyone. The things he'd witnessed—the things he'd done—none of that was remotely acceptable to him in the clear light of peace. He was damned for all time. He had been claimed by the dark side, which was the best reason he knew to keep himself aloof from decent people. He could not allow himself to feel anything for Romy, or for their child—not unless he wanted to damage them both. The best, the *only* thing he could do to protect them was to step out of Romy's life.

The mechanical function of tacking up his stallion soothed him and set his decision in stone. The great beast and he would share the wild danger of a gallop across the pampas. They both needed to break free, to run, to seize life without thought or plan for what might lay ahead.

He rode as far as the river and then kicked his booted feet out of the stirrups. Throwing the reins over the stallion's head, he dismounted. All he could see wherever he looked was Romy, and all he could hear was her voice. The apprehension and concern in her eyes was as clear now as if she were standing in front of him. She was frightened she wasn't ready for a baby. *He* would never be ready. His family, who tolerated him, knew more than most people did about him, was enough.

Tipping his face to the sun, he realised this was the first time he had ever backed away from any challenge. He normally met each one head-on. But this tiny unborn child had stopped him dead in his tracks without a road map or a solution. He didn't question the fact that the child was his. The little he knew about Romy gave him absolute trust in what she told him. Whistling up his stallion, he sprang into the saddle and turned for home.

She packed her case and then left the *hacienda* to take the shots she needed for Grace. She knelt and waited silently on the riverbank for what felt like hours for the flocks of birds feeding close by to wheel and soar like ribbons in the sky. She could only marvel at their beauty. It gave her a sort of peace which she hoped would transmit to the baby.

There was no perfect world, Romy concluded. There were only perfect moments like this, populated by imperfect human beings like herself and Kruz, who were just trying to make the best of their journey through life. It was no use wishing she could share this majestic beauty with their child. She would never be invited to Argentina. She might never see the snow-capped Andes and smell the lush green grass again, but her photographs would remind her of the wild land the father of her child inhabited.

Hoisting her kitbag onto her shoulder, she started back to the *hacienda*. She had barely reached the courtyard when she saw Kruz riding towards her. She loved him. It was that simple. Turning in the opposite direction, she kept her head down and walked rapidly away. She wasn't ready for this.

Would she ever be ready for this?

She stopped and changed direction, following him round to the stables, where she found him dismounting. Without acknowledging her presence, he led the stallion past her.

He had been calm, Kruz realised. The ride had calmed him. But seeing Romy again had shaken him to the core. He wanted her—and more than in just a sexual way. He wanted to put his arm around her and share her worries and excitement, to see where the road took them. But Romy's life wasn't an experiment he could dip into. He might not be able to shake the feeling that they belonged together, but the only safe thing for Romy was to put her out of his life.

'Kruz…'

He lifted the saddle onto the fence and started taking his horse's bridle off.

'How could I go to bed with you, knowing I was pregnant,' she said, 'and yet say nothing?'

Her voice, soft and shaking slightly, touched him somewhere deep. He turned to find her frowning. 'Don't beat yourself up about it,' he said without expression. 'What's done is done.'

'And cannot be undone,' she whispered as the stallion turned a reproachful gaze on him. 'Not that I…'

As her voice faded his gaze slipped to her stomach, where the swell of pregnancy was quite evident on her slender frame. In his rutting madness he had chosen not to see it. He felt guilty now.

The stallion whickered and nuzzled him imperatively, searching for a mint. He found one and the stallion took it delicately from his hand. Clicking his tongue, he tried to move the great beast on, but his horse wasn't going anywhere. As of this moment, one small girl with her chin jutting out had half a ton of horseflesh bending to her will.

'He needs feeding,' he said without emotion as he waited for Romy to move aside.

'I have needs too,' she said, but her soft heart put the horse first, and so she moved, allowing him to lead the stallion to his stable.

'Are you going to make me wait as I made you wait?' she said as she watched him settle the horse.

He was checking its hooves, but lifted his head to look at her.

'Okay, I get it—you're not so petty,' she said. 'But we do have to talk some time, Kruz.'

He returned to what he'd been doing without a word.

She waited by the stable door, watching Kruz looking after his big Criolla. What she wouldn't do for a moment of that studied care…

So what are you standing around for?

'Can I—'

'Can you what?' he said, still keenly aware of her, apparently, even though he had his back turned to her.

'Can I come in and give him a mint?' she asked.

The few seconds' pause felt like an hour.

'Hold your hand out flat,' he said at last.

She took the mint, careful not to touch Kruz more than she had to. Her heart thundered as he stood back. There was nothing between her and the enormous horse that just stood motionless, staring at her unblinking. Her throat felt dry, and her heart was thundering, but then, as if a decision had been made, the stallion's head dropped and its velvet lips tickled her palm. Surprised by its gentleness, she stroked its muzzle. The prickle of whiskers made her smile, and she went on to stroke its sleek, shiny neck. The warmth was soothing, and the contact between them made her relax.

'You're a beauty, aren't you?' she whispered.

Conscious that Kruz was watching her, she stood back and let him take over. He made the horse quiver with pleasure as he groomed it with long, rhythmical strokes. She envied the connection between them.

She waited until Kruz straightened up before saying, 'Can we talk?'

'You're *asking* me?' he said, brushing past her to put the tack away.

His voice was still cold, and she felt as if she had blinked and opened her eyes to find the last few minutes had been a dream and now it was back to harsh reality. But her pregnancy wasn't something she could put to one side. Now it was out in the open she had to see this through, and so she followed Kruz to the tackroom and closed the door behind them. He swung around and, leaning back against the wall, with a face that was set and unfriendly, waited for her to speak.

'I would have told you sooner, if—'

'If you hadn't been climbing all over me?' he suggested in a chilly tone.

She lifted her chin. 'I didn't notice you taking a back seat at the time.'

'So when were you going to tell me that you're pregnant?'

'You seem more concerned about my faults than our child. There were so many times when I wanted to tell you—'

'But your needs were just too great?' he said, regarding her with a face she didn't recognize—a face that was closed off to any possibility of understanding between them.

'I remember my need being as great as yours,' she said. 'Anyway, I don't want to argue with you about this, Kruz. I want to discuss what has happened while we've got the chance. For God's sake, Kruz—what's wrong with you? Anyone would think you were trying to drive me away—taking *your* child with me.'

'You'll stay here until I tell you to go,' he said, snatching hold of her arm.

'Let me go,' she cried furiously.

'There's nowhere for you to go—there's just thousands of miles of nothing out there .'

'I'm leaving Argentina.'

'And then what?' he demanded.

'And then I'll make a life for me and our baby—the baby you don't care to acknowledge.'

Was that a flicker of something human in his eyes? Had she got through to him at last? His grip had relaxed on her arm.

It was a feint of which any fighter would be proud. Kruz was still hot from his ride, still unshaven and dusty, and when his mouth crashed down on hers she knew she should fight him off, but instead she battled to keep him close.

'It's that easy, isn't it?' he snarled, thrusting her away. '*You're* that easy.'

She confronted him angrily. 'You shouldn't have kissed me. You shouldn't have doubted me.' She paused a beat and shook her head. 'And I should have told you sooner than I did.'

'You kissed me back,' he said, turning for the door.

Yes, she had. And she would kiss him again, Romy realised as heat, hope and longing surged inside her. What did that make her? Deluded?

'Where are you going?' she demanded as Kruz opened the door. 'We have to talk this through.'

'I'm done talking, Romy.'

Moving ahead of him, she pressed herself against the door like a barricade. 'I'm just as scared as you are,' she admitted.

'You? Scared?' he said.

'We didn't plan this, Kruz, but however unready we are to become parents, we're no different than thousands of other couples. Whether we're ready or not, in less than a year our lives will be turned upside down by a baby.'

'*Your* life, maybe,' he snapped.

His eyes were so cold…his face was so closed off to her. 'Kruz—'

'I need time to think,' he said sharply.

'No,' she fired back. 'We need to talk about this now.'

Pressing against the door, she refused to move. She was

going to say what she had to say and then she would leave Argentina for good.

'There's nothing for you to think about,' she said firmly. 'The baby and I don't need you—and we certainly don't want your money. When I get back to England I'll speak to my lawyers and make sure you have fair access to our child. But that's it. Don't think for one moment that I can't provide everything a baby needs and more.'

The blood drained from his face. He was furious, but Kruz contained his feelings, which made him seem all the more threatening. Her hands flew to cradle her stomach. She was right to feel apprehensive. She had no lawyers, while Kruz probably had a whole team waiting on him. And she had to find somewhere decent to live. For all her brave talk she was in no way ready to welcome a baby into the world yet.

'Do you mind?' he said coldly, staring behind her at the door.

Standing aside, she let him go. What else could she do? She had no more cards to play. If Kruz didn't want any part in the life of his child then she wasn't going to beg. She couldn't pretend it didn't hurt to think he could just brush her off like this. She understood that he guarded his privacy fiercely, but the birth of a baby was a life-changing event for both of them.

But this was day one of her life as a single mother, so she had to get over it. With the lease about to run out on her rented house, she couldn't afford to be downhearted. Her priority was to find somewhere to live. So what if she couldn't afford the area she loved? She maybe never would be able to afford it. She could still find somewhere safe and respectable. She would work all hours to make that happen.

She waited in the shadowy warmth of the tackroom, breathing in the pleasant aroma of saddle soap and horse until she was sure Kruz was long gone, and then she walked out into the brilliant sunlight of the yard to find the big stallion still watching her, with his head resting over the stable door.

'I've made a mess of everything, haven't I?' she said, tugging gently on his forelock. She smoothed the palm of her hand along his pricked ears until he tossed his head and trumpeted. She imagined he was part of the herd who were still out there somewhere on the pampas.

Biting back tears, she glanced towards the *hacienda*. Kruz would be showering down after his ride, she guessed. He would be washing away the dust of the day and, judging by his reaction to her news, he would be washing away all thoughts of Romy and their baby along with it.

CHAPTER ELEVEN

HE'D SLEPT ON it, and now he knew what he was going to do. Towelling down after his shower the next morning, he could see things clearly. Romy's news had stunned him. How could it not, considering his care where contraception was concerned? It shouldn't have happened, but now it *had* happened he would take control.

Tugging on a fresh pair of jeans and a clean top, he raked his thick dark hair into some semblance of order. The future of this baby was non-negotiable. He would not be a part-time parent. He knew the effect it had had on him when his parents had been killed. It wasn't Nacho's fault that Kruz had run wild, but he did believe that a child needed both its parents. Romy could have her freedom, and they would live independent lives, but she must move here to Argentina.

The internet was amazing, Romy concluded as she settled into her narrow seat on the commercial jet. She'd used it to sell the images she didn't need to keep back for the Acosta charity, or for Grace, and had then used the proceeds to book her flight home. Alessandro had insisted on driving her to the airport and carrying her luggage as far as the check-in desk. He was a lovely man, sensitive enough not to ply her with questions. She didn't care that she wasn't flying home in style in a private jet. The staff in the cabin were polite and helpful, and before long she would be back in London on the brink of a new life.

As soon as she had taken the last shot she needed and made plans to leave Argentina she had known there would be no going back. This was the right decision—for her and for her child. She didn't need a man to help her raise her baby. She was strong and self-sufficient, she had her health, and she could earn enough money for both their needs. One thing was certain—she didn't need Kruz Acosta.

Really?

She had panicked to begin with, Romy reasoned as the big, wide jet soared high into the air. But making the break from Kruz was just what she needed. It was a major kick-start to the rest of her life. He was the one losing out if he didn't want to be part of this. She was fine with it. She could live man-free, as she had before.

Reaching for the headphones, she scrolled through the channels until she found a film she could lose herself in—or at least attempt to tune out the voice of her inner critic, who said that by turning her back on Kruz and leaving Argentina without telling him Romy had done the wrong thing yet again.

'Señorita Romily has gone,' Alessandro told him.

'What the hell do you mean, she's gone?' he demanded as Alessandro got out of the pick-up truck.

'She flew back to England this morning,' his elderly friend informed him, stretching his limbs. 'I just got back from taking her to the airport.' Alessandro levelled a challenging look at Kruz that said, *And what are you going to do about it?*

They didn't make men tame and accepting on the pampas, Kruz reflected as he met Alessandro's unflinching stare.

'She went back to England to *that* house?' he snarled, beside himself with fury.

Alessandro's shoulders lifted in a shrug. 'I don't know where she was going, exactly. "Back home" is all she told me. She talked of a lovely area by a canal in London while we were driving to the airport. She said I would love it, and that even so close to a city like London it was possible to find quiet places that are both picturesque and safe. She told me about the waterside cafés and the English pubs, and said there are plenty of places to push a pram.'

'She was stringing you along,' Kruz snapped impatiently. 'She guessed you wouldn't take her to the airport if you knew the truth about where she lived.' And when Alessandro flinched with concern at the thought that he might have led Romy into danger, Kruz lashed out with words as an injured wolf might howl in the night as the only way to express its agony. 'She lives in a terrible place, Alessandro. Even with all the operatives in my employ I cannot guarantee her safety there.'

'Then follow her,' his wise old friend advised.

Kruz shook his head, stubborn pride still ruling him. Romy was having his baby and she had left Argentina without telling him. Twisting the knife in the wound, his old friend Alessandro had helped Romy on her way. 'Why?' he demanded tensely, turning a blazing stare on his old friend's face. 'Why have you chosen to help her?

'I think you know why,' Alessandro said mildly.

'You think I'd hurt her?' he exclaimed with affront. 'You think because of everything that happened in the army I'm a danger to her?'

Alessandro looked sad. 'No,' he said quietly. 'You are the only one who thinks that. I helped Señorita Winner to go home because she's pregnant and because she needs peace now—not the anger you feel for yourself. Until you can accept that you have every right to a future, you have nothing to offer her. You have hurt her,' Alessandro said bluntly, 'and now it's up to you to make the first approach.'

'She didn't tell me she was pregnant.'

'Did you give her a chance?'

'I didn't know—'

'You didn't want to know. *I* knew,' Alessandro said quietly.

Kruz stood rigid for a moment, and then followed Alessandro to the stable, where he found the old *gaucho* preparing to groom his favourite horse.

'You drove her to the airport,' he said, still tight with indignation. '*Dios*, Alessandro, what were you thinking?'

When Alessandro didn't speak he was forced to master himself, and when he had done so he had to admit Alessandro was right. His old friend had done nothing wrong. This entire mess was of Kruz and Romy's making—mostly his.

'So she didn't tell you she was leaving?' Alessandro commented, still sweeping the grooming brush down his horse's side in rhythmical strokes.

'No, she didn't tell me,' he admitted. And why would she? He hadn't listened. He hadn't seen this coming. So the mother of his child had just upped and left the country without a word.

What now?

She wasn't *all* to blame for this, but one thing was certain. Romy might have pleased herself in the past, but now she was expecting his baby she would listen to *him*.

'No,' Romy said flatly, preparing to cut the line having refused Kruz's offer of financial help. 'And please don't call me at the office again.'

'Where the hell else am I supposed to call you?' he thundered. 'You never pick up. You can't keep on avoiding me, Romy.'

The irony of it, she thought. She knew they should meet to discuss the baby, but things had happened since she'd come back to England—big things—and now she was sick with loss and just didn't think she could take any more. Her mother had died. There—it was said…thought…so it must be true. It *was* true. She had arrived at the nursing home too late to see her mother alive. Somehow she had always imagined she would be there when the time came. The fact that her mother had slipped away peacefully in her sleep had done nothing to help ease her sense of guilt.

And none of it was Kruz's fault.

'Okay, let's meet,' she agreed, choosing an anonymous café on an anonymous road in the heart of the bustling metropolis. The café was close by both their offices, and with Kruz back in London the last thing she wanted was for them to bump into each other on the street.

'I could meet you at the house,' he said, 'if that's easier for you.'

There *was* no house. The lease was up. The house had gone. She was sleeping on a girlfriend's sofa until she found somewhere permanent.

'This can't be rushed, Romy,' Kruz remarked as she was thinking things through. 'Five minutes of your time in a crowded café won't be enough.'

He was right. In a few months' time they would be parents. It still seemed incredible. It made her heart ache to be talking to him about such a monumental event that should affect them both equally while knowing they would never be closer than this. 'I'll make it a long lunch,' she offered.

She guessed she must have sounded patronising as Kruz repeated the address and cut the line.

Without him asking her to do so she had taken a DNA test to prove that the baby was his. She had had to do it before a solicitor would represent her. Putting everything in the hands of a stranger felt like the final nail in the coffin containing their non-existent relationship. This meeting in the café with Kruz to sort out some of the practical aspects of parental custody was not much more.

Not much more? Did she really believe that? Just catching sight of Kruz through the steamed-up windows of the chic city centre café was enough to make her heart lurch. He'd already got a table, and was sipping coffee as he read the financial papers. He'd moved on with his life and so had she, Romy persuaded herself. She had suffered the loss of her mother while he'd been away—a fact she'd shared with no one. Kruz, of all people, would probably understand, but she wouldn't burden him with it. They weren't part of each other's lives in that way.

'Hey,' she murmured, dropping her bag on the seat by his side. 'Watch that for me, will you, while I get something to drink?'

Putting the newspaper down, he stood up. He stared at her without speaking for a moment. 'Let me,' he said at last, brushing past.

'No caffeine,' she called. 'And just an almond croissant, please.'

Just an almond croissant? Was that a craving or lack of funds?

He should have prepared himself for seeing Romy so obviously pregnant. He knew how far on she was, after all. He should have realised that the swell of her stomach would be more pronounced because she was so slender. If he had been prepared he might be able to control this feeling of being a frustrated protector who had effectively robbed himself of the chance to do his job.

Taking Romy's sparse lunch back to the table, he sat down. She played with the food and toyed with mint tea. *I hope you're eating properly,* he thought, watching her. There were dark circles beneath her eyes. She looked as if she wasn't sleeping. That made two of them.

'Let's get this over with,' he said, when she seemed lost in thought.

She glanced up and the focus of her navy blue eyes sharpened. 'Yes, let's get it over with,' she agreed. 'I've appointed a lawyer. I thought you'd find that easier than dealing with me directly—I know I will. I'm busy,' she said, as if that explained it.

'Business is good?' he asked carefully.

'You should know it is.' She glanced up, but her gaze quickly flickered away. 'Grace keeps me busy with the charity, and my work for that has led me on to all sorts of things.'

'That's good, isn't it?'

She smiled thinly.

'Are you still living at the same place?'

'Why do you ask?' she said defensively.

He should have remembered how combative Romy could be. He should have taken into account the fact that pregnancy hormones would accentuate this trait. But Romy's wellbeing and that of his child was his only concern now. He didn't want to fight with her. 'Just interested,' he said with a shrug.

'I don't need your money,' she said quickly. 'With money comes control, and I'm a free agent, Kruz.'

'Whoah…' He held his hands up. She was bristling to the point where he knew he had to pull her back somehow.

'I'd do anything for my child,' she went on, flashing him a warning look, 'but I won't be governed by your money and your influence. I don't need you, Kruz. I am completely capable of taking care of this.'

And completely hormonal, he supplied silently as Romy's raised voice travelled, causing people to turn and stare.

'I'm not challenging your rights,' he said gently. 'This child has changed everything for both of us. Neither of us can remain isolated in own private world any longer, Romy.'

She had expected this meeting with Kruz to be difficult, but she hadn't expected to feel quite so emotional. This was torture. If only she could reach out instead of pushing him away.

The past was a merciless taskmaster, Romy concluded, for each time she thought about the possibility of a family unit, however loosely structured, she was catapulted back into that house where her mother had been little more than a slave to her father's much stronger will.

'You don't know anything about this,' she said distractedly, not even realising she was nursing her baby bump.

'I know quite a lot about it,' Kruz argued, which only made the ache of need inside her grow. 'I grew up on an *estancia* the size of a small city. I saw birth and death as part of the natural cycle of life. I saw the effect of pregnancy on women. So I do understand what you're going through now. And I know about your mother, Romy, and I'm very sorry for your loss.'

Kruz knew everything about everything. Of course he did. It was his business to know. 'Well, thank you for your insight,' she snapped, like a frightened little girl instead of the woman she had become.

Not all men were as principled as Kruz, but he would leave her to pick up the pieces eventually. Better she pushed him away now. It wasn't much of a plan, but it was all she'd got. She just hadn't expected it to be so hard to pull off.

'When the baby's born,' she said, straightening her back

as she took refuge in practical matters, 'you will have full visiting rights.'

'That's very good of you,' Kruz remarked coldly.

She was being ridiculous. Kruz had the means to fight her through the courts until the end of time, while *her* resources were strictly limited. She might like to think she was in control, but that was a fantasy he was just humouring. 'Independence is important to me—'

'And to me too,' he assured her. 'But not at the expense of everyone around me.'

She was glad when he fell silent, because it stopped her retaliating and driving another wedge between them. 'I hope we can remain friends.'

'I'd say that's up to you,' he said, reaching for his jacket.

She wanted to say something—to reach out and touch him—but it had all gone wrong. 'I'll get the bill,' she offered, feeling she must do something.

Ignoring her, Kruz called the waitress over.

She wanted him in her life, but she couldn't live with the control that came with that. She felt like crying and banging her fists on the table with frustration. Only very reluctantly she accepted that those feelings were due to hormones. Her emotions were all over the place. She ached to share her hopes and fears about the baby with Kruz, and yet she was doing everything she could to drive him away.

'Ready to go?' he said, standing. 'My lawyers will be in touch with yours.'

'Great.'

This was it. This was the end. Everything was being brought to a close with a brusque statement that twisted in her heart like a knife. She got up too, and started to leave the table. But her belly got stuck. Kruz had to move the table for her. She felt so vulnerable. She couldn't pretend she didn't want to confide in him, share her fears with him. He stood back as she walked to the door. Somehow she managed to bang into someone's tray on one of the tables, and then she nearly sent a child flying when she turned around to see what she'd done.

'It's okay, I've got it,' Kruz said calmly, making sure everything was set to rights in his deft way, with his charisma and his smile.

'Sorry,' she said, feeling her cheeks fire up as she made her apologies to the people involved. They hardly seemed to notice her. They were so taken with Kruz. 'Sorry,' she said again when he joined her at the door. 'I'm so clumsy these days. When the baby's born we'll have another chat.'

He raised a brow at this and made no reply. Now he'd seen her he must think her ungainly and clumsy.

'I'll be in touch,' he said.

This was all happening too fast. The words wouldn't come out of her mouth quickly enough to stop him.

Pulling up the collar on his heavy jacket, he scanned the traffic and when he saw a gap dodged across the road.

Her heart was in shreds as her gaze followed him. She stayed where she was in the doorway of the café, sheltering in blasts of warm, coffee-scented air as customers arrived and left. When the door was opened and the chatter washed over her she began to wonder if a heart could break in public, while people were calling for their coffee or more ketchup on their chips.

Grace had taken her in, insisting Romy couldn't expect to keep healthy and look after her unborn child while she was sleeping on a friend's sofa. There was plenty of room in the penthouse, Grace had explained. Romy hadn't wanted to impose, but when Grace insisted that she'd welcome the company while Nacho was away on a polo tour Romy had given in. They could work together on the charity features while Romy waited for the birth of her child, Grace pointed out.

Romy had worked out that if she budgeted carefully she would have enough money to buy most of the things she needed for the baby in advance. She searched online to find bargains, and hunted tirelessly through thrift shops for the bigger items, but even with her spirit of make do and mend she couldn't resist a visit to Khalifa's department store when she noticed there was a sale on. She bought one adorable little suit at half-price but would have loved a dozen more, along with a soft blanket and a mobile to hang above the cot. But those, like the cuddly toys, were luxuries she had to pass up. The midwife at the hospital had given her a long list of essentials to buy before she gave birth.

Get over it, Romy told herself impatiently as her hormones got to work on her tear glands as she walked around the baby department. This baby was going to be born to a mother who adored it already and who would do anything for it.

A baby who would never know its grandmother and rarely see its father.

'Thanks a lot for that helpful comment,' she muttered out loud.

She could do without her inner pessimist. Emotional incontinence at this stage of pregnancy needed no encouragement. Leaning on the nearest cot, she foraged in her cluttered bag for a tissue to stem the flow of tears and ended up looking like a panda. Why did department stores have to have quite so many mirrors? So much for the cool, hard-edged photographer—she was a mess.

It had not been long since her mother's funeral, Romy reasoned as she took some steadying breaths. It had been a quiet affair, with just a few people from the care home. There was nothing sadder than an empty church, and she had felt bad because there had been no one else to invite. She felt bad now—*about everything*. Her ankles were swollen, her feet hurt, and her belly was weighing her down.

But she had a career she loved and prospects going forward, Romy told herself firmly as an assistant, noticing the state she was in, came over with a box of tissues.

'We see a lot of this in here,' the girl explained kindly. 'Don't worry about it.'

Romy took comfort from the fact that she wasn't the only pregnant woman falling to pieces during pregnancy—right up to the moment when the assistant added, 'Does the daddy know you're here? Shall I call him for you?' Only then did she notice Romy's ring-free hands. 'Oh, I'm sorry!' she exclaimed, slapping her hand over her mouth. 'I really didn't mean to make things worse for you.'

'You haven't,' Romy reassured her as a fresh flood of tears followed the first. She just wanted to be on her own so she could howl freely.

'Here—have some more tissues,' the girl insisted, thrusting a wad into Romy's hands. 'Would you like me to call you a cab?'

'Would you?' Romy managed to choke out.

'Of course. And I'll take you through the staff entrance,' the girl offered, leading the way.

Thank goodness Kruz couldn't see her like this—all bloated and blotchy, tear-stained and swollen, with her hair hanging in lank straggles round her face. Gone were the super-gelled spikes and kick-ass attitude, and in their place was…a baby.

He'd kept away from Romy, respecting her insistence that she was capable of handling things her way and that she would let him know when the baby was born. They lived in different countries, she had told him, and she didn't need his help. He was in London most of the time now, getting the new office up to speed, but he had learned not to argue with a pregnant woman. Thank goodness for Grace, who was still in London while Nacho was on a polo tour. At least she could reassure him that Romy was okay—though Grace had recently become unusually cagey about the details.

The irony of their situation wasn't lost on him, he accepted as he reversed into a space outside Khalifa's department store. He had pushed Romy away and now she was refusing to see him. She was about to give birth and he missed her. It was as simple as that.

But even though she refused his help there was nothing to say he couldn't buy a few things for their baby. Grace had said this was the best place to come—that Khalifa's carried a great range of baby goods.

The store also boasted the most enthusiastic assistants in London town, Kruz reflected wryly as they flocked around him. How the hell did he know what he wanted? He stood, thumbing his stubble, in the midst of a bewildering assortment of luxury goods for the child who must have everything.

'Just wrap it all up,' he said, eager to be gone from a place seemingly awash with happy couples.

'Everything, sir?' an assistant asked him.

'You know what a baby needs better than I do,' he pointed out. 'I'll take it all. Just charge it to my account.'

'And send it where, sir?'

He thought about the Acosta family's fabulous penthouse, and then his heart sank when he remembered Romy's tiny terrace on the wrong side of the tracks. He would respect her wish to say there for now, but after the birth...

The store manager, hurrying up at the sight of an important customer, distracted him briefly—but not enough to stop

Kruz remembering that the only births he had attended so far were of the foals he owned, all of which had been born in the fabulous custom-built facility on the *estancia*.

No one owned Romy, he reflected as the manager continued to reassure him that Khalifa's could supply anything he might need. Romy was her own woman, and he had Grace's word for the fact that she would have the best of care during the birth of their baby at a renowned teaching hospital in the centre of London. But after the birth he suspected Romy would want to make her nest in that tiny terraced house.

Another idea occurred to him. 'Gift-wrap everything you think a newborn baby might need,' he instructed the manager, 'and have it made ready for collection.'

'Collection by van, sir?' The manager glanced around the vast, well-stocked floor.

'Yes,' Kruz confirmed. 'How long will that take?'

'At least two hours, plus loading time—'

He shrugged. 'Then I will return in two hours.'

Brilliant. Women loved surprises. He'd hire a van, load it up and deliver it himself.

The thought of seeing Romy again made him smile for the first time in too long. It would be good to see her shock when he rolled up with a van full of baby supplies. She would definitely unwind. Maybe they could even make a fresh start—as friends this time. Whatever the future held for them, he suspected they could both do with some down-time before the birth of their baby threw up a whole new raft of problems.

CHAPTER TWELVE

THAT WAS NOT a phantom pain.

Bent over double in the small guest cloakroom in the penthouse while Grace was at the shops buying something for their supper was not a good place to be...

Romy sighed with relief as the pain subsided. There was no cause for panic. If it got any worse she'd call an ambulance.

For once he didn't even mind the traffic because he was in such a good mood, and by the time he pulled the hired van outside the terraced house he was feeling better than positive. They would work something out. They both had issues and they both had to get over them. They had a baby to consider now.

Springing down from the van, he stowed the keys. Relying on Grace for snippets of information about Romy wasn't nearly good enough, but he was half to blame for allowing the situation to get this bad. Both he and Romy were always on the defensive, always expecting to be let down. Raising his fist, he hammered on the door. Now he just had to hope she was in.

Oh, oh, oh... She had managed to crawl into the bathroom. *Emergency!*

They'd mentioned pressure at the antenatal classes, so she was hoping this was just a bit of pressure—

Pressure everywhere.

And no sign of Grace.

'Grace…' she called out weakly, only to have the silence of an empty apartment mock her. 'Grace, I need you,' she whimpered, knowing there was no one to hear her. 'Grace, I don't know what to do.'

Oh, for goodness' sake, pull yourself together! Of course you know what to do.

Now the pain had faded enough for her to think straight, maybe she did. Scrabbling about in her pockets, she hunted for her phone. All she had to do was dial the emergency number and tell them she was having a baby. What was so hard about that?

'Grace!' she exclaimed with relief, hearing the front door open. 'Grace? Is that you?'

'Romy?' Grace sounded as panicked as Romy felt. 'Romy, where are you?'

'On the floor in the bathroom.'

'On the floor—? Goodness—'

She heard Grace shutting her big old guide dog, Buddy, in the kitchen before moving cautiously down the hall with her stick. 'Grace, I'm in here.' There were several bathrooms in the penthouse, and Grace would find her more easily if she followed the sound of Romy's voice.

'Are you okay?' Grace called out anxiously, trying to get her bearings.

That was a matter of opinion. 'I'm fine,' Romy managed, and then the door opened and Grace was standing there. Just having someone to share this with was a help.

Grace felt around with her stick. 'What on earth are you doing under the sink?'

'I had a little accident,' Romy admitted, chucking the towel she'd been using in the bath. 'Can't move,' she managed to grind out as another contraction hit her out of nowhere. 'Stay where you are, Grace. I don't want you slipping, or tripping over me—I'll be fine in a minute.'

'I'm calling for an ambulance,' Grace said decisively, pulling out her phone.

'Tell them my waters have broken and the baby's coming—and this baby isn't waiting for anything.'

'Okay, keep calm!' Grace exclaimed, sounding more panicked than Romy had ever heard her.

He had thoughts of reconciliation and an armful of Romy firmly fixed in his head as he hammered a second time on the door of the small terraced house. Like before, the sound echoed and fell away. Shading his eyes, he peered through the window. It was hard to see anything through the voile the girls had hung to give them some privacy from the street. His spirits sank. His best guess…? The tenants of this house were long gone.

How could he not have known? He should have kept up surveillance—but if Romy had found out he was having her followed he would have lost her for good.

There was nothing more pitiful than a man standing outside an empty house with a heart full of hope and a van full of baby equipment. But he had to be sure. Glancing over his shoulder to check the street was deserted, he delved into the pocket of his jeans to pull out the everyday items that allowed him entry into most places. This, at least, was one thing he was good at.

The house was empty. Romy and her friends had packed up and gone for good. There were a few dead flowers in a milk bottle, as if the last person to turn out the lights hadn't been able to bear to throw them away and had given them one last drink of water.

That would be Romy. So where the hell was she?

Grace would know.

Grace had called the emergency services, and Romy was re-assured to hear her friend's succinct instructions on how to access the penthouse with the code at the door so she wouldn't have to leave Romy's side. But the ambulance would have to negotiate the rush hour traffic, Romy realised, starting to worry again as her baby grew ever more insistent to enter the world. Even with sirens blaring the driver would face grid-lock in this part of town.

She jumped as Grace's telephone rang. The sight of Grace's face was enough to tell her that the news was not good. 'Grace, what is it?'

'Nothing...'

But Grace's nervous laugh was less than reassuring. 'It must be something,' Romy insisted. 'What's happened, Grace?' She really hoped it wasn't bad news. She wasn't at her most comfortable with her head lodged beneath the sink.

'Seems the first ambulance can't get here for some rea-son,' Grace admitted. 'But they've told me not to worry as they're sending another—'

'Don't worry?' Romy exclaimed, then felt immediately guilty. Grace was doing everything she could. 'Can you ring them back and tell them I need someone right away? This baby won't wait.'

'I'll do that now,' Grace agreed, but the instant she started to dial her phone rang. 'Kruz?'

'No!' Romy exclaimed in dismay. 'I don't want to speak to him—there's no time to speak to him—' A contraction cut her off, leaving her panting for breath. By the time it had subsided Grace was off the phone. 'You'd better not have told him!' Romy exclaimed. 'Please tell me you didn't tell him. I couldn't bear for him to see me like this.'

'Too late. He's on his way.'

Romy groaned, and then wailed, 'I need to push!'

'Hold on—not yet,' Grace pleaded.

'I can't hold on!' She added a few colourful expletives. 'Sorry, Grace—didn't mean to shout at you—'

Kruz had heard some of this before Grace cut the line. He had called an ambulance too, but the streets were all blocked. It was rush hour, they'd told him—as if he didn't know that. Even using bus lanes and sirens the ambulance driver could only do the best he could.

'Well, for God's sake, *do* your best!' he yelled in desperation. And he never yelled. He had never lost his cool with anyone. *Other than where Romy and his child were concerned.*

The traffic was backed up half a mile away from where he needed to be. Pulling the van onto the pavement, he climbed out and began to run. Bursting into the penthouse, he followed the sound of Grace's voice to the guest cloakroom, where he found Romy wedged at an awkward angle between the sink and the door.

'Get off me,' she sobbed as he came to pick her up. 'I'm going to have a baby—'

As if he didn't know that! 'You're as weak as a kitten and you need to be strong for me, Romy,' he said firmly as he drew her limp, exhausted body into his arms. 'Grace, can you bring me all the clean towels you've got, some warm water and a cover for the baby. Do we have a cradle? Something to sponge Romy down? Ice if you've got it. Soft cloths and some water for her to sip.'

By this time he had shouldered his way into a bedroom, stripped the duvet away and laid Romy down across the width of the bed. He found a chair to support her legs. This was no time for niceties. He'd seen plenty of mares in labour and he knew the final stages. Romy's waters had broken in the cloakroom and now she was well past getting to the hospital in time.

'What are you doing?' she moaned as he started stripping off her clothes.

'You're planning to have a baby with your underwear on?'

'Stop it… Not you… I don't want you undressing me.'

'Well, Grace is busy collecting the stuff we're going to need,' he said reasonably. 'So if not me, who else do you suggest?'

'I don't want you seeing me like this—'

'Hard luck,' he said as she whimpered, carrying on with his job. 'Strong, Romy. I need strong, Romy. Don't go all floppy on me. I need you in fighting mode,' he said firmly, in a tone she couldn't ignore. 'This baby is ready to enter the world and it needs you to fight for it. This isn't about you and me any longer, Romy.'

As he was speaking he was making Romy as comfortable as he could.

'Are you listening to me, Romy?' Tenderly taking her tear-stained face between his hands, he watched with relief as her eyes cleared and the latest contraction subsided. 'That's better,' he whispered. And then, because he could, he brushed a kiss across her lips. 'We're going to do this together, Romy. You and me together,' he said, staring into her eyes. 'We're going to have a baby.'

'Mostly me,' she pointed out belligerently, and with a certain degree of sense.

'Yes, mostly you,' he confirmed. Then, seeing her eyes fill with apprehension again, he knelt on the floor at the side of the bed. 'But remember this,' he added, bringing her into his arms so he could will his strength into her, 'the harder you work, the sooner you'll be holding that baby in your arms. You've got to help him, Romy.'

'Him?'

'Or her,' he said, feeling a stab of guilt at the fact that he hadn't attended any of the scans or check-ups Romy had been to.

Yes, she'd asked him not to—but since when had he ever done anything he was told? Had she tamed the rebel? If she had, her timing was appalling. He should have been with her from the start. But this was not the best time to be analysing where their stubbornness had led them.

'Whether this baby is a boy or a girl,' he said, talking to Romy in the same calm voice he used with the horses, 'this is your first job as a mother. It's the first time your baby has asked you for help, so you have to get on it, Romy. You have to believe in your strength. And remember I'm going to be with you every step of the way.'

She pulled a funny face at that, and then she was lost to the next contraction. They were coming thick and fast now.

'How long in between?' he asked. 'Have you been keeping a check on things, Grace?' he asked Grace as she entered the room.

'Not really,' Grace admitted.

'Don't worry—you've brought everything I asked for. Could you put a cool cloth on Romy's head for me?'

'Of course,' Grace said, sounding relieved to be doing something useful as she felt her way around the situation in a hurry to do as he asked. 'I didn't realise it would all happen so quickly.'

'Neither did I,' Romy confessed ruefully, her voice muffled as she pressed her face into his chest.

'This is going really well,' he said, hoping he was right.

'It's not always this fast,' he guessed, 'but this is better for the baby.'

At least Romy seemed reassured as she braced herself against him, which was all that mattered. The speed of this baby's arrival had surprised everyone—not least him.

'Grace, could you stay here with Romy while I scrub up?'

'No, don't leave me,' Romy moaned, clinging to him.

'You're going to be all right,' he said, gently detaching himself. 'Here, Grace—I'll pull up a chair for you.' Having made Romy comfortable on the bed, he steered Grace to the chair. 'Just talk to her,' he instructed quietly. 'Hold her hand until I get back.'

'Don't go,' Romy begged him again.

'Thirty seconds,' he promised.

'Too long,' she managed, before losing herself in panting again.

'My sentiments entirely,' he called back wryly from the bathroom door.

He was back in half that time. 'I'm going to take a look now.'

'You can't look!' Romy protested, sounding shocked.

Bearing in mind the intimacy they had shared, he found her protest endearing. 'I need to,' he explained. 'So please stop arguing with me and let's all concentrate on getting this baby safely into the world.'

'How many births have you attended?' Romy ground out as he got on with the job.

'More than you can imagine—and this one is going to be a piece of cake.'

'How can you know that?' she howled.

'Just two legs, and one hell of a lot smaller than my usual deliveries? Easy,' he promised, pulling back.

'How many human births?' she ground out.

'You'll be the first to benefit from my extensive experience,' he admitted, 'so you have the additional reassurance of knowing I'm fresh to the task.'

She wailed again at this.

'Just lie back and enjoy it,' he suggested. 'There's nowhere else we have to be. And with the next contraction I need you to push. Grace, this is where you come in. Let Romy grip your hands.'

'Right,' Grace said, sounding ready for action.

'I can see the head!' he confirmed, unable keep the excitement from his voice. 'Keep pushing, Romy. Push like you've never pushed before. Give me a slow count to ten, Grace. And, Romy? You push all the time Grace is counting. I'm going to deliver the shoulders now, so I need you to pant while I'm turning the baby slightly. That's it,' he said. 'One more push and you've got a baby.'

'*We've* got a baby,' Romy argued, puce with effort as she went for broke.

Romy's baby burst into the world with the same enthusiasm with which her parents embraced life. The infant girl didn't care if her parents were cool, or independent, or stubborn. All she asked for was life and food and love.

The paramedics walked in just as she was born. A scene of joy greeted them. Grace was standing back, clasping her hands in awe as the baby gave the first of many lusty screams, while Kruz was kneeling at the side of the bed, holding his daughter safely wrapped in a blanket as he passed her over to Romy. Grace had the presence of mind to ask one of the paramedics to record the moment on Romy's phone, and from then on it was all bustle and action as the medical professionals took over.

He could hardly believe it. They had a perfect little girl. A daughter. *His* daughter. His and Romy's daughter. He didn't need to wonder if he had ever felt like this before, because he knew he never had. Nothing he had experienced came close to the first sight of his baby daughter in Romy's arms, or the look on Romy's face as she stared into the pink screwed-up face of their infant child. The baby had a real pair of lungs on her, and could make as much noise as her mother and father combined. She would probably be just as stubborn and argumentative, he concluded, feeling elated. All thoughts of him and Romy not being ready for parenthood had vanished. Of course they were ready. He would defend this child with his life—as he would defend Romy.

Once the paramedics were sure that both mother and baby were in good health, they offered him a pair of scissors to cut the cord. It was another indescribable moment, and he was deeply conscious of introducing another treasured life into the world.

'You've done well, sir,' one of the health professionals told him. 'You handled the birth beautifully.'

'Romy did that,' he said, unable to drag his gaze away from her face.

Reaching for his hand, she squeezed it tightly. 'I couldn't have done any of this without you,' she murmured.

'The first part, maybe,' he agreed wryly. 'But after that I think you should get most of the praise.'

'Don't leave me!' she exclaimed, her stare fearful and anxious on his face as they brought in a stretcher to take Romy and their baby to hospital.

As soon as the paramedics had her settled he put the baby in her arms. 'You don't get rid of me that easily,' he whispered.

And for the first time in a long time she smiled.

CHAPTER THIRTEEN

SHE WOKE TO a new day, a new life. A life with her daughter in it, and—

'Kruz?'

She felt her anxiety mount as she stared around. *Where was he?* He must have slipped out for a moment. He must have been here all night while she'd been sleeping. She'd only fallen asleep on the understanding that Kruz stayed by her side.

Expecting to feel instantly recovered, she was alarmed to find her emotions were in a worse state than ever. She couldn't bear to lose him now. She couldn't bear to be parted from him for a moment. Especially now, after all he'd done for her. He'd been incredible, and she wanted to tell him so. She wanted to hold his hand and stare into his eyes and tell him with a look, with her heart, how much he meant to her. Kruz had delivered their baby. What closer bond could they have?

Hearing their daughter making suckling sounds in her sleep, she swung cautiously out of bed. Just picking up the warm little bundle was an incredible experience. The bump was now a real person. Staring down, she scrutinised every millimetre of the baby's adorable face. She had her father's olive skin, and right now dark blue eyes, though they might change to a compelling sepia like his in time. The tiny scrap even had a frosting of jet-black hair, with some adorable kiss curls softening her tiny face. The baby hair felt downy soft against her lips, and the scent of new baby was delicious—fresh and clean and powdered after the sponge-down she had been given in the hospital.

'And you have amazing eyelashes,' Romy murmured, 'exactly like your father.'

She looked up as a nurse entered the room. 'Have you seen Señor Acosta?' she asked.

'Mr Acosta left before dawn with the instruction that you were to have everything you wanted,' the nurse explained, with the type of dreamy look in her eyes Romy was used to where Kruz was concerned.

'He left?' she said, trying and failing to hide her unease. 'Did he say when he would be back?'

'All I've been told is that Mr Acosta's sister-in-law, Grace Acosta, will be along shortly to pick you up,' the nurse informed her.

Romy frowned. 'Are you *sure* he said that?'

'I believe your sister-in-law will be driven here.'

'Ah…' Romy breathed a sigh of relief, knowing Grace would laugh if she knew Romy's churning emotions had envisaged Grace trying to walk home with Romy at her side, carrying a newly delivered baby, and with a guide dog in tow.

A chauffeur-driven car!

This was another world, one Romy had tried so hard not to become caught up in—though she could hardly blame Grace for travelling in style. She should have thought this through properly long before now. She should have realised that having Kruz's baby would have repercussions far beyond the outline for going it alone she had sketched in her mind.

'The car will soon be here to take you and the baby back to the penthouse,' the nurse was explaining to her.

'Of course,' Romy said, acting as if she were reassured. She would have felt better if Kruz had been coming to pick them up, but that wouldn't happen because she had drawn up the rules to exclude him, so she could prove her independence and go it alone with her baby.

But he couldn't just walk away.

Could he?

She shook herself as the nurse walked back in.

'It was a wonderful birth—thanks to your partner. I bet you can't wait to start your new life together as a family.' The nurse stopped and looked at her, and then passed her some tissues without a word.

Like the assistant in the department store, the nurse must have seen a lot of this, Romy guessed, scrubbing impatiently at her eyes. She was still trying to tell herself that Kruz had only gone to take a shower and grab a change of clothes when the nurse added some more information to her pot of woe.

'Mr Acosta said he had to fly as he had some urgent business to complete.'

'Fly?' Romy repeated. 'He actually said that? He said he had to *fly*?'

'Yes, that's exactly what he said,' the nurse confirmed gently. 'Get back into bed,' she added firmly as Romy started hunting for her clothes. 'You should be taking it easy. You've just given birth and the doctor hasn't discharged you yet.'

'I need my phone,' Romy insisted, padding barefoot round the room, collecting up her things.

So Kruz was just going to fly back to Argentina after delivering their baby? He was going to fly *somewhere*, anyway; the nurse had just said so. And she'd thought Kruz might have changed. The overload to her hormones could only be described as nuclear force meeting solar storm. She might just catch him before he took off, Romy concluded, trying to calm down when she found her phone.

'Mr Acosta did say you might want to take some pictures, so he had your camera couriered over.'

Of course he did, Romy thought, refusing to be placated.

The nurse gave her a shrewd and slightly amused look as a frowning Romy began to stab numbers into her phone. 'I'll leave you to it,' she mouthed.

'Kruz?' Romy was speaking in a dangerously soft voice as the call connected. 'Is that you?'

'Of course it's me. Is something wrong?'

'Where are you? If you're still on the ground get back here right away—we need to talk.'

'Romy?'

She'd cut the line. He rang back. She'd turned her phone off.

With a vicious curse he slammed his fist down on the wheel. Starting the engine, he thrust the gears into Reverse and swung the Jeep round, heading back to the hospital at speed, with his world splintering into little pieces at the thought that something might have happened to Romy or their child.

'You were going to leave us!' Romy exclaimed the moment he walked back into the room.

'Don't you *ever* do that to me again,' he said. Ignoring her protests, he took Romy in his arms and hugged her tight.

'Do what?' she said in a muffled voice.

'Don't ever frighten me like that. I thought something had happened to you or the baby. Do you have any idea how much you mean to me?'

She stared into his eyes, disbelieving, until the force of his stare convinced her.

'If they hadn't told me at Reception that you were both well I don't know what I would have done.'

'Flown to Argentina?' she suggested.

'You can't seriously think I'd do that now?'

'The nurse said you had to fly.' Romy's mouth set in a stubborn line.

'I did have to fly—I had an appointment.'

'What were you doing? I know,' she said, stopping herself. 'Sorry—none of my business.'

'It's a long story,' Kruz agreed. 'Why don't I ring Grace and give her some warning before I take you back?'

'Good idea.' It was hard to be angry with Kruz when he looked like this, as he stared down at their child, but nothing had changed. This man was still Kruz Acosta—elusive, hard and driven. A man who did what he liked, when he liked. While she was still Romy Winner—self-proclaimed battle-axe and single mother.

'Well, that's settled,' Kruz said as he cut the line. 'Grace is going back to Argentina. Nacho is coming to collect her now, so you'll have the penthouse to yourself.'

She should be grateful for the short-term loan of such a beautiful home. 'Okay,' she said brightly, worrying about how she and the baby would rattle round the vast space.

'There's plenty of staff to help you,' Kruz pointed out.

'Great,' she agreed. The company of strangers was just what she needed in her present mood. 'I'll get my things together.'

'Grace has organised everything for you, so there's nothing to worry about,' Kruz remarked as he leaned over the cradle.

She loved the way he cared about their baby, but she felt the first stirring of unease. Now the drama was over, would Kruz claim their daughter? He could provide so much more than she could for their child. Would it be selfish of her to cling on?

Of course not. There was no conflict. She kicked the rogue thought into touch. No one would part her from her baby. But would she be in constant conflict with Kruz for ever?

'You can't buy her,' she whispered, thinking out loud.

'*Buy* her?' Kruz queried with surprise. 'She's already mine.'

'Ours.'

'Romy, are you guilty of overreacting to every little comment I make, by any chance?' Before she could answer, Kruz pointed out that she *had* just given birth. 'Give yourself a break, Romy. I know how much your independence means to you, and I respect that. No one's going to take your baby away from you—least of all me.'

Biting her lip, she forced the tears back. Why did everything seem like a mountain to climb? 'I don't know what to think,' she admitted.

'Is this what I've been missing over the past few months?' Kruz asked wryly.

'I'm glad you think it's funny,' she said, knowing she *was* overreacting, but somehow unable to stop herself. 'Do you think you can house me in your glamorous penthouse and pull my strings from a distance?'

'Romy,' Kruz said with a patient sigh, 'I could never think of you as a puppet. Your strings would be permanently tangled. And if we're going to sort out arrangements for the future I don't want to be doing it in a hospital. Do you?'

She flashed a look at him. Kruz's gaze was steady, but those arrangements for the future he was talking about meant they would part.

Count to ten, she counselled herself. *Right now you're viewing everything through a baby-lens.*

She slowly calmed down—enough to pick up her camera. 'Just one shot of you and the baby,' she said.

'Why don't we ask the nurse if she'll take one of all three of us together?' Kruz suggested. 'There will never be another moment like this as we celebrate the birth of our beautiful daughter.'

'You're right,' Romy agreed quietly. 'I feel like such a fool.'

'No,' Kruz argued. 'You feel like every new mother—full of hope and fear and excitement and doubt. You're exhausted and wondering if you can cope. And I'm telling you as a close observer of Romy Winner that you can. And what's more you look pretty good to me,' he added, sending her a look that made her breath hitch.

She hesitated, not knowing whether to believe him as the nurse came in to take the shot. 'Do I look okay?' she asked, suddenly filled with horror at the thought of ruining the photo of gorgeous Kruz and his beautiful daughter—and her.

'Take the baby,' he said, putting their little girl in her arms. 'You look great. I like your hair silky and floppy,' he insisted, 'and I like your unmade-up face. But if you want gel spikes and red tips, along with tattoos in unusual places and big, black Goth eyes, that's fine by me too.'

'You're being unusually understanding,' Romy commented, trying to make a joke of it. Once a judgement was made regarding their daughter's future they would be parents, not partners, and she should never get the two mixed up.

'I'm undergoing something of an emotional upheaval myself,' Kruz confessed, putting his arm loosely around her shoulders for the happy family shot. 'I guess having a child changes you…' His voice trailed off, but his tender look spoke volumes as he glanced down at their daughter, sleeping soundly in Romy's arms.

'I've never seen you like this before,' Romy commented as Kruz straightened up.

Kruz said nothing.

'So, will you be going back to Argentina as soon as everything's settled here?' she pressed as the nurse took the baby from her and handed her to Kruz.

'I'm in no hurry,' Kruz murmured, staring intently at his daughter.

This was a *very* different side of Kruz, Romy realised, deeply conscious of his depth of feeling as she checked she had packed everything ready for leaving. He was oblivious to everything but his daughter, and that frightened her. *Would* he try to take her baby from her?

His overriding concern was that his child should grow up as part of a strong family unit as he had—thanks to Nacho. But Romy must make her own decisions and he would give her time.

'Are we ready?' he said briskly, once Romy was seated in the wheelchair in which hospital policy insisted she must be taken outside.

'Yes, I'm ready,' Romy confirmed, her gaze instantly locking onto their baby as he placed their daughter in her arms.

'Then let's go.' He was surprised by his eagerness to leave the hospital so he could begin his new life as a father. He couldn't wait to leave this sterile environment where no expressions of intimacy or emotion were possible. He longed to relax, so he could express his feelings openly.

'Kruz—'

'What?' he said, wondering if there was any more affecting sight than a woman holding her newborn child.

Romy shook her head and dropped her gaze. 'Nothing,' she said.

'It must be something.' She was exhausted, he realised,

coming to kneel by her side. 'What is it?' he prompted as the nurse discreetly left the room.

'I'm just…' She shook her head, as new to the expression of emotion as he was, he guessed. And then she firmed her jaw and looked straight at him. 'I'm just worrying about the effect of you walking in and out of our baby's life.'

'Don't look for trouble, Romy.'

Why not? her look seemed to say. He blamed the past for Romy's concerns. He blamed the past for his inability to form close relationships outside his immediate family. He guessed that the birth of this child had been a revelation for both of them. It wasn't a case of daring to love, but trying not to— if you dared. Hostage for life, he thought, staring into his daughter's eyes, and a willing one. This wealth of feeling was something both he and Romy would have to get used to and it would take time.

'Don't push me away just yet,' he said, sounding light whilst inwardly he was painfully aware of how much they both stood to lose if they handled this badly. 'I've done as you asked so far, Romy. I've kept my distance for the whole of your pregnancy, so grant me a little credit. But please don't ask me to keep my distance from my child, because that's one thing I can't do.'

'I thought you didn't want commitment,' she said.

He wanted to say, *That was then and this is now,* but he wasn't going to say anything before he was ready. He wouldn't mislead Romy in any way. He had to be sure. From a life of self-imposed isolation to this was quite a leap, and the feelings were all new to him. He wanted them to settle, so he could be cool and detached like in the old days, when he'd been able to think clearly and had always known the right thing to do.

'Grace said you've never shared your life with anyone,' she went on, still fretting.

'People change, Romy. Life changes them.'

He sprang up as the nurse returned. This wasn't the time for deep discussions. Romy had just had a baby. Her hormones were raging and her feelings were all over the place.

'Time to go,' the nurse announced with practised cheerfulness, taking charge of Romy's chair.

While the nurse was wrapping a blanket around Romy's knees and making sure the baby was warmly covered, Romy turned to him. Grabbing hold of his wrist, she made him look at her. 'So what do you want?' she asked him.

'I want to forget,' he said, so quietly it was almost a thought spoken out loud.

CHAPTER FOURTEEN

ROMY REMAINED SILENT during the journey to the penthouse. She was thinking about Kruz's words.

What did he want to forget? His time in the Special Forces, obviously. Charlie had given her the clue there. Charlie had said Kruz was a hero, but Kruz clearly didn't believe his actions could be validated by the opinion of his peers. Medals were probably just pieces of metal to him, while painful memories were all too vivid and real. She couldn't imagine there was much Kruz couldn't handle—but then she hadn't been there, hadn't seen what he'd seen or been compelled to do what he had done. She only knew him as a source of solid strength, as his men must have known him, and her heart ached to think of him in torment.

'Are you okay?' he said, glancing at her through the mirror.

'Yes,' she said softly. *But I'm worried about you...so worried about you.*

Everything had been centred around her and the baby, and that was understandable given the circumstances, but who was caring for Kruz? She wanted to...so badly; if only he'd let her. There were times for being a warrior woman and times when just staring into the face of their baby daughter and knowing Kruz was close by, like a sentinel protecting them, was enough. Knowing they were both safe because of

him had given her the sort of freedom she had never had before—odd when she had always imagined close relationships
must be confining. He'd given her that freedom. He'd given
her so much and now she wanted to help him.

He wasn't hers to help, she realised as Kruz glanced at her
again through the driving mirror. She mustn't be greedy. But
that was easier said than done when his eyes were so warm
and so full of concern for her.

'My driving okay for you?'

As he asked the question she laughed. Kruz was driving
like a chauffeur—smoothly and avoiding all the bumps. The
impatient, fiery polo-player was nowhere to be seen.

'You're doing just fine,' she said, teasing him in a mock-
serious tone. 'I'll let you know if anything changes.'

'You do that,' he said, his eyes crinkling in the mirror.
'You must be tired,' he added.

'And elated.' And worried about the future…and most worried of all about Kruz. They had no future together—none
they'd talked about, anyway—and what would happen to
him in the future? Would he spend his whole life denying
himself the chance of happiness because of what had happened in the past?

She pulled herself together, knowing she couldn't let anything spoil this homecoming when Grace and Kruz had gone
to so much trouble for her.

'I'm looking forward so much to seeing Grace,' she said,
'and being on familiar ground instead of in the hospital. It
makes everything seem….' She really was lost for words.

'Exciting,' Kruz supplied.

Her eyes cleared as she stared into his through the mirror.
'Yes, exciting,' she agreed softly.

'I can understand that. Grace has been rushing around like
crazy to get things ready in time. She's as excited as we are.'

We? He made them sound like a couple…

It was just a figure of speech, Romy reminded herself, though Kruz was right about life changing people. They had both been cold and afraid to show their feelings until the baby arrived, but now it was hard to hide their feelings. She'd been utterly determined to go it alone after the birth of their child. The baby had changed her. The baby had changed them both. She couldn't be more thrilled that Kruz would be sharing this homecoming with her.

She gazed at the back of his head, loving every inch of him—his thick dark hair, waving in disorder, and those shoulders broad enough to hoist an ox. She loved this man. She loved him with every fibre in her being and only wanted him to be happy. But first Kruz had to relearn how to enjoy life without feeling guilty because so many of his comrades were dead. She understood that now.

She had so much to be grateful for, Romy reflected as Kruz drove smoothly on. As well as meeting Kruz, and the birth of their beautiful daughter, these past few months had brought her some incredible friendships. Charlie and Alessandro—and Grace, who was more of a sister than a friend.

And Kruz.

Always Kruz.

Her heart ached with longing for him.

'Grace has been working flat out with the housekeeper to get the nursery ready,' he revealed, bringing her back to full attention.

'But I won't be staying long,' she blurted, suddenly frightened of falling into this seductive way of life when it wasn't truly hers. And Kruz wasn't her man—not really.

'We both wanted to do this for you,' Kruz insisted. 'The penthouse is your home for as long as you want it to be, Romy. You do know that, don't you?'

'Yes.' Like a lodger.

She couldn't say anything more. Her feelings were so mixed up. She was grateful—of course she was grateful—but she was still clinging to the illusion that somehow, some day, they could be a proper family. And that was just foolish. Now tears were stabbing the backs of her eyes again. Pressing her lips together, she willed herself to stop the flow. Kruz had enough on his plate without her blubbing all the time.

'I really appreciate everything you've done,' she said when she was calmer. 'It's just—'

'You don't want to feel caged,' he supplied. 'You're proud and you want to do things your way. I think I get that, Romy.'

There was an edge to his voice that told her he felt shut out. Maybe there was no solution to this—maybe she just had to accept that and move on. She could see she was pushing him away, but it was only because she didn't know what else to do without appearing to take too much for granted.

'You're very kind to let me stay at the penthouse,' she said, realising even as she spoke that she had made herself sound more like a grateful lodger thanking her landlord than ever.

Kruz didn't appear to notice, thank goodness, and as he pulled the limousine into the driveway of the Acosta family's Palladian mansion he said, 'And now you can get some well-earned rest. I'm determined you're going to be spoiled a little, so enjoy it while you can. Stay there—I'm coming round to help you out.'

She gazed out of the window as she waited for Kruz to open the door. The Acosta family owned the whole of this stately building, which was to be her home for the next few weeks. Divided into gracious apartments, it was the sort of house she would never quite get used to entering by the front door, she realised with amusement.

'This isn't a time for independence, Romy,' Kruz said,

seeing her looking as he opened the door. 'You'll be happy here—and safe. And I want you to promise me that you'll let Grace look after you while she's here. It might only be for a few more days, but it's important for Grace too. She's proving something to herself—I think you know that.'

That her blind friend could have children and care for them as well as any other mother? Yes, she knew that. The fact that Kruz knew too proved how much they'd both changed.

'Grace has been longing for this moment,' he went on. 'Everyone has been longing for this moment,' he added, taking their tiny daughter out of her arms with the utmost care.

She would have to get used to this, Romy told herself wryly as Kruz closed her door and moved round to the back of the vehicle. But not too much, she thought, gazing up at the grand old white building in front of them. This sort of life—this sort of house—was the polar opposite of what she could afford.

Every doubt she had was swept away the moment she walked inside the penthouse and saw Grace and the staff waiting to welcome her, and when she saw what they'd done, all the trouble Grace had gone to, she was instantly overwhelmed and tearful. They had transformed one of the larger bedroom suites into the most beautiful nursery, with a bathroom off.

'Thank you,' she said softly, walking back to Grace, who was standing in the doorway with her guide dog, Buddy. Touching Grace's arm, Romy whispered, 'I can't believe you've done all this for me.'

'It's for Kruz as well as for you,' Grace said gently. 'And for your baby,' she added, reaching out to find Romy and give her a hug. 'I wanted you to come home to something special for you and your new family, Romy.'

If only, Romy thought, glancing at Kruz. They weren't a proper family—not really. Kruz was doing this because he felt he should—because he was a highly principled man of duty and always had been.

Kruz caught her looking at him and stared back, so she nodded her head, smiling in a way she hoped would show him how much she appreciated everything he and Grace had done for her, whilst at the same time reassuring him that she didn't expect him to devote the rest of his life to looking out for her.

She felt even more emotional when she put their tiny daughter into the beautifully carved wooden crib. Grace had dressed it with the finest Swiss lace, and the lace was so delicate she could imagine Grace selecting this particular fabric by touch. The thought moved her immeasurably. She wanted to hug Grace so hard neither of them could breathe. She wanted to tell Grace that having friends like her made her glad to be alive. She wanted to tell her that, having been so determined to go it alone, she was happy to be wrong. She wanted to be able to express her true feelings for Kruz, to let him know how much he meant to her. But she had to remind herself that they had agreed to do this as individuals, each of them taking a full part in their daughter's life, but separately, and she couldn't go back on her word.

Damn those pregnancy hormones!

The tears were back.

How could anyone who had been such a fearless reporter, a fearless woman, be reduced to this snivelling mess? When it came to being a woman in love, she was lost, Romy realised as Grace explained that the housekeeper had helped her to put everything in place. Romy was only too glad to be called back from the brink by practical matters as Grace went on to explain that she had also hired a night nurse, so that Romy could get some rest.

'I hope you don't mind me interfering?'

'Of course not,' Romy said quickly. 'It isn't interfering. It's kindness. I can't thank you enough for all you've done.'

'You're crying?' Grace asked her with surprise when she broke off.

Grace could hear everything in a voice, Romy remembered, knowing how Grace's other senses had leapt in to compensate for her sight loss. 'Everything makes me cry right now,' she admitted. 'Hormones,' she added ruefully, conscious that Kruz was listening. 'I've been an emotional train wreck since the birth.'

She seemed to have got away with it, Romy thought as Grace and the nurse took over. Or maybe Grace was just too savvy to probe deeper into her words, and the nurse was too polite. Kruz seemed unconcerned—though he did suggest she take a break. Remembering his words about Grace wanting to help, she was quick to agree.

'Champagne?' he suggested, leading the way into the kitchen. Her heart felt too big for her chest just watching him finding glasses, opening bottles, squeezing oranges.

'What you've done for me—' Knowing if she went on she'd start crying again, she steeled herself, because there were some things that had to be said. 'What you've done for our baby—the way you helped me during the birth—'

'It was a privilege,' Kruz said quietly.

Her cheeks fired red as he stared at her. She didn't know what he expected of her. There was so much she wanted to say to him, but he had turned away.

'Drink your vitamins,' he said, handing her the perfect Buck's Fizz.

'Thanks...' She didn't look at him. Was she supposed to act as if they were just friends? How was she supposed to act like a rational human being where Kruz was involved? How could she close her heart to this man? Having Kruz deliver their baby had brought them closer than ever.

'You're very thoughtful,' he said as he topped up her glass with the freshly squeezed juice.

'I was just thinking we almost had something...' Her face took on a look of horror as she realised what she'd said. Her wistful thoughts had poured out in words.

'And now it's over?' he said.

'And now it can never be the same,' she said, making a dismissive gesture with her hand, as if all those feelings inside her had been nothing more than a passing whim.

Kruz made no comment on this. Instead he said, 'Shall we raise a glass to our daughter?'

Yes, that was something they could both do safely. And they *should* rejoice. This was a special day. 'Our daughter, who really should have a name,' she said.

'Well, you've had a few months to think about it,' Kruz pointed out. 'What ideas have you had?'

'I didn't want to decide without—' She stopped, and then settled for the truth. 'I didn't want to decide without consulting you, but I thought Elizabeth...after my mother.'

Kruz's lips pressed down with approval. 'Good idea. I've always liked the name Beth. But what about you, Romy?' he said, coming to sit beside her.

'What about me?'

She stared into her glass as if the secret of life was locked in there. There was only one place she wanted to be, and that was right here with this man. There was only one person she wanted to be, and that was Romy Winner—mother, photographer and one half of this team.

'Come on,' Kruz prompted her. 'What do you want for the future? Or is it too early to ask?'

A horrible feeling swept over her—a suspicion, really, that

Kruz was about to offer to fund whatever business venture she had in mind. 'I can't see further than now.'

'That's understandable,' he agreed. 'I just wondered if you had any ideas?'

She looked at him in bewilderment as he moved to take the glass out of her hand, and only then realised that she'd been twisting it and twisting it. She gave it up to him, and asked, 'What about you? What do *you* want, Kruz?'

'Me?' He paused and gave a long sigh, rounded off with one of those careless half-smiles he was so good at when he wanted to hide his true feelings. 'I have things to work through, Romy,' he said, his eyes turning cold.

Was this Kruz's way of saying goodbye? A chill ran through her at the thought that it might be.

For what seemed like an eternity neither of them spoke. She clung to the silence like a friend, because when he wasn't speaking and they were still sitting together like this she could pretend that nothing would change and they would always be close.

'I've seen a lot of things, Romy.'

She jerked alert as he spoke, wondering if maybe, just maybe, Kruz was going to give her the chance to help him break out of his self-imposed prison of silence. 'When you were in the army?' she guessed, prompting him.

'Let's just say I'm not the best of sleeping partners.'

He was already closing off. 'Do you have nightmares?' she pressed, feeling it was now or never if she was going to get through to him.

'I have nightmares,' Kruz confirmed.

They hadn't done a lot of sleeping together, so she wouldn't know about them, Romy realised, cursing her lust for him. She should have spent more time getting to know him. It was easy to be wise after the event, she thought as Kruz started to tell her something else—something that surprised her.

'I'm going to move in downstairs,' he said. 'There's an apartment going begging and I want to see my daughter every day.'

Part of her rejoiced at this, while another part of her felt cut out—cut off. To have Kruz living so close by—to see him every day and yet know they would never be together...

'It's better this way,' he said, drawing her full attention again. 'I'm hard to live with, Romy, and impossible to sleep with. And you need your rest, so this is the perfect solution.'

'Yes,' she said, struggling to convince herself. If Kruz was suffering she had to help him. 'Maybe if you could confide in someone—'

'You?'

She realised how ridiculous that must sound to him and her face flamed red. Romy Winner, hard-nosed photojournalist, reduced not just to a sappy, hormonal mess but to a woman who couldn't even step up to the plate and say: *Yes, me. I'm going to do it.* 'I'll try, if you'll give me the chance,' she said instead.

Pressing his lips together, Kruz shook his head. 'It's not that easy, Romy.'

'I didn't expect it would be. I just think that when you've saved so many lives—'

'Someone should save *me*?' He gave a laugh without much humour in it. 'It doesn't work that way.'

'Why not?' she asked fiercely.

'Because I've done things I'll never be able to forget,' he said quietly, and when he looked at her this time there was an expression in his eyes that said: *Just drop it.*

But she never could take good advice. 'Healing is a long process.'

'A lifetime?'

Kruz's face had turned hard, but it changed just as suddenly and gentled, as if he was remembering that she had recently given birth. 'You shouldn't be thinking about any of this, Romy. Today is a happy day and I don't want to spoil it for you.'

'Nothing you could say would spoil it,' she protested, wanting to add that she could never be truly happy until Kruz was too. But that would put unfair pressure on him. She sipped her drink to keep her mouth busy, wondering how two such prickly, complicated people had ever found each other.

'Believe me, you should be glad I'm keeping my distance,' Kruz said as he freshened their drinks. 'But if you need me I'm only downstairs.'

And that was a fact rather than an invitation, she thought—a thought borne out as Kruz stood up and moved towards the door. 'I have to go now.'

'*Go?*' The shock in her voice was all too obvious.

'I have business to attend to,' he explained.

'Of course.' And Kruz's business wasn't her business. What had she imagined? That he was going to pull her into his arms and tell her that everything would be all right—that the past could be brushed aside, just like that?

He stopped with his hand on the door. 'You believe in the absolution of time, Romy, but I'm still looking for answers.'

She couldn't stop him leaving, and she knew that Kruz could only replace his nightmares when something that made him truly happy had taken their place.

'It's good that you'll be living close by so you can see Beth,' she said. Perhaps that would be the answer. She really hoped so.

Kruz didn't answer. He didn't turn to look at her. He didn't say another word. He just opened the door and walked through it, shutting it quietly behind him, leaving her alone in the kitchen, wondering where life went from here. One step at a time, she thought, one step at a time.

She couldn't fault him as a devoted father. Kruz spent every spare moment he had with Beth. But where Romy was concerned he was distant and enigmatic. This had been going on for weeks now, and she missed him. She missed his company. She missed his warm gaze on her face. She missed his solid presence and his little kindnesses that gave her an opening to reach in to his world and pay him back with some small, silly thing of her own.

Grace had returned to Argentina with Nacho—though they were expected back in London any day soon. This was a concern for Romy, as she knew Grace had hoped a relationship might develop between Romy and Kruz. It was going to be a little bit awkward, explaining why Romy's new routine involved Beth, mother and baby groups, and learning to live life as a single mother, while the father of her baby lived downstairs.

Kruz had issues to work through, and she understood that, but she wished he'd let her help him. She had broached the subject on a few occasions, but he'd brushed her off and she'd drawn back, knowing there was nothing she could say if he wouldn't open up.

The day after Nacho and Grace arrived back in London, Kruz dropped by with some flowers he'd picked up from the market. 'I got up early and I felt like buying all you girls some flowers,' he said, before breezing out again.

This was nice—this was good, Romy told herself firmly as she arranged the colourful spray in a glittering crystal vase. She felt good about herself, and about her life here in Acosta heaven. She was already taking photographs with thoughts

of compiling a book. She treasured every moment she spent
with her baby. And watching Kruz with Beth was the best.

Crossing to the window, she smiled as she watched him
pace up and down the garden, apparently deep in conversation with their daughter. She longed to be part of it—part of
them—part of a family that was three instead of two. But she
had to stick to the unofficial rules she'd drawn up—rules that
allowed Romy to get on with her life independently of Kruz.
They both knew that at some point she would leave and move
into rented accommodation, and when she did that Kruz had
promised to set up an allowance for Beth, knowing very well
that Romy would never take money for herself.

As if the money mattered. Her eyes welled up at the
thought of parting from Kruz. What if she moved to the
other side of London and never saw him again except when
he came to collect Beth? When had such independence held
any allure? She couldn't remember when, or what that fierce
determination to go it alone had felt like. Independence at all
costs was no freedom at all.

This wasn't nice—this wasn't good. Sitting down, she buried her face in her hands, wishing her mother were still alive
so they could talk things through as they'd used to before her
father had damaged her mother's mind beyond repair. Angry
with herself, she sprang up again. She was a mother, and this
was no time for self-indulgence. It was all about Beth now.

She was used to getting out there and looking after herself.
No wonder she was frustrated, Romy reasoned. In fairness,
Kruz had suggested that a babysitter should come in now and
then, so Romy could gradually return to doing more of the
work she loved. She had resigned from *ROCK!*, of course,
but even Ronald, her picture editor, had said she shouldn't
waste her talent.

She started as the phone rang and went to answer it.

'I'm bringing Beth up.'

'Oh, okay.' She sounded casual, but in her present mood she might just cling to him like an idiot when he arrived, and burst into tears.

No. She would reassure him by pulling herself together and carrying on alone with Beth as she had always planned to do; anything less than that would be an insult to her love for Kruz.

He bumped into Nacho and Grace on his way back into the house. They were staying in the garden apartment on the ground floor, to ensure they had some privacy. It was a good arrangement, this house in London. Big enough for the whole Acosta family, it had been designed so each of them had their own space.

Nacho asked him in for a drink. Grace declined to join them, saying she would rather play with Beth while she had the chance, but he got the feeling, as Grace took charge of the stroller, that his brother's wife was giving them some time alone.

'You've made a great marriage,' he observed as Grace, her guide dog, Buddy, and baby Beth made their way along the hallway to the master suite.

'Don't I know it?' his brother murmured, gazing after his bride.

As he followed Nacho's stare he realised that for the first time in a long time he felt like a full member of the family again, rather than a ghost at the feast. It was great to see Nacho and to be able to share all his news about Romy and their daughter, and how being present at the birth of Beth had made him feel.

'Like there's hope for me,' he said, when Nacho pressed him for more.

'You've always been too hard on yourself,' Nacho ob-

served, leading the way into the drawing room. 'And a lifetime of self-denial changes nothing, my brother.'

Coming from someone whose thoughts he respected, those
straight-talking words from his brother hit home. It made
him want to draw Romy and Beth together into a family—
his family.

'Have you told Romy how you feel about her?' Nacho said.

'How I…?' Years of denying his feelings prompted him
to deny it, but Nacho knew him too well, so he shrugged instead, admitting, 'I bought her some flowers today.'

'Instead of talking to her?'

'I talk.'

Nacho looked up from the newspaper he'd been scanning
on the table.

'You talk?' he said. 'Hello? Goodbye?'

They exchanged a look.

'I'm going to find my wife,' Nacho told him, and on his
way across the room he added, 'Babies change quickly, Kruz.'

'In five minutes, brother?'

'You know what I mean. Romy will move out soon. We
both know it. She's not the type of woman to wait and see
what's going to happen next. She'll make the move.'

'She won't take Beth away from me.'

'You have to make sure of that.'

'We live cheek by jowl already.'

'What?' Nacho scoffed, pausing by the door. 'You live
downstairs—she lives upstairs with the baby. Is that what
you want out of life?'

'It seems to be what Romy wants.'

'Then if you love her change her mind. Or I'll tell you
what will happen in the future. You'll pass Beth between
you like a ping-pong ball because both of you stood on your

pride. You're not in the army now, Kruz. You're not part of that tight world. *You* make the rules.'

Kruz was still reeling when Nacho left the room. His brother had made him face the truth. He had returned to civilian life afraid to love in case he jinxed that person. He had discarded his feelings in order to protect others as he had tried to protect his men. By the time Romy turned his world on its head he hadn't even been in recovery. But she had started the process, he realised now, and there was no turning back.

The birth of Beth had accelerated everything. The nightmares had stopped. He looked forward to every day. Every moment of every day was precious and worthwhile now Romy and Beth were part of his life. That was what Romy had given him. She had given him love to a degree where not allowing himself to love her back was a bigger risk to his sanity than remembering everything in the past that had brought him to this point.

Nacho was right. He should tell Romy what she'd done for him and how he felt about her. Better still, he should show her.

CHAPTER FIFTEEN

WHEN KRUZ CALLED to explain to Romy that he and Beth were down with Grace and Nacho, so she didn't worry about Beth, he added that he wanted to take her somewhere and show her something.

She fell apart. Not crying. She was over that. Her hormones seemed to have settled at last. It was at Kruz's suggestion that Nacho and Grace should look after Beth while he took Romy out. Take her out without Beth as a buffer between them? She wasn't ready for that.

She would never be ready for that.

Her heart started racing as she heard the strand of tension in his voice that said Kruz was fired up about something. Whatever this something was, it had to be big. There was only one thing she could think of that fired the Acosta boys outside the bedroom. And the bedroom was definitely off the agenda today. In fact the bedroom hadn't been on the agenda for quite some time.

And whose fault was that?

Okay, so she'd been confused—and sore for a while after Beth's birth.

And now?

Not so sore. But still confused.

'Is it a new polo pony you want me to see?' she asked, her

heart flapping wildly in her chest at the thought of being one to one with him.

'No,' Kruz said impatiently, as if that was the furthest thing from his mind. 'I just need your opinion on something. Why all the questions, Romy? Do you want to come or not?'

'Wellies, jeans and mac?' she said patiently. 'Or smart office wear?'

'You have some?'

'Stop laughing at me,' she warned.

'Those leggings and flat boots you used wear around *ROCK!* will do just fine. Ten minutes?'

'Do you want a coffee before we go—?' Kruz was in a rush, she concluded as the line was disconnected.

Ten minutes and counting and she had discarded as many outfits before reverting reluctantly to Kruz's suggestion. It was the best idea, but that didn't mean that following anyone's suggestions but her own came easily to her. Her hair had grown much longer, so she tied it back. She didn't want to look as if she was trying too hard.

What would they talk about…?

Beth, of course, Romy concluded, adding some lips gloss to her stubborn mouth. And a touch of grey eyeshadow… And just a flick of mascara… Oh, and a spritz of scent. That really was it now. She'd make coffee to take her mind off his arrival—and when he did arrive she would sip demurely, as if she didn't have a care in the world.

While she was waiting for the coffee to brew she studied some pictures that had been taken of Kruz at a recent polo match. *She* would have done better. She would have taken him in warrior mode—restless, energetic and frustratingly sexy.

While she was restless, energetic and *frustrated*, Romy concluded wryly, leaning back in her chair.

She leapt to her feet when the doorbell rang, feeling flushed and guilty, with her head full of erotic thoughts. Kruz had his own key, but while she was staying at the penthouse he always rang first. It was a little gesture that said Kruz respected her privacy. She liked that. Why pretend? She liked everything about him.

She had to force herself to take tiny little steps on her way to the door.

Would she ever get used to the sight of this man?

As Kruz walked past her into the room he filled the space with an explosion of light. It was like having an energy source standing in front of her. Even dressed in heavy London clothes—jeans, boots, jacket with the collar pulled up—he was all muscle and tan: an incredible sight. *You look amazing,* she thought as he swept her into his arms for a disappointingly chaste kiss. Was it possible to die of frustration? If so, she was well on her way.

'I've missed you,' he said, pulling her by the hand into the kitchen. 'Do I smell coffee? Are you free for the rest of the day?'

'So many questions,' she teased him, exhaling with shock as he swung her in front of him. 'I have *some* free time,' she admitted cautiously, suddenly feeling unaccountably shy. 'Why?'

'Because I'm excited,' Kruz admitted. 'Can't you tell?'

Pressing her lips down, she pretended she couldn't.

He laughed.

Her heart was going crazy. Were they teasing each other now?

'There's something I really want to show you,' he said, turning serious.

'Okay…' She kept her expression neutral as Kruz dropped his hands from her arms. She still didn't know what to think. He was giving her no clues. 'Did you tell Nacho and Grace where we're going?' She dropped this in casually, but Kruz wasn't fooled.

'You don't get it out of me that way,' he said. 'Don't look so worried. We'll only be a few minutes away.'

All out of excuses, she poured the coffee.

'Smells good.'

Not half as good as Kruz, she thought, sipping demurely as wild, erotic thoughts raged through her head. Kruz smelled amazing—warm, clean and musky man—and he was just so damn sexy in those snug-fitting jeans, with a day's worth of stubble and that bone-melting look in his eyes.

'I could go away again if you prefer,' he said, slanting her a dangerous grin to remind her just how risky it was to let her mind wander while Kruz was around. 'Come on,' he said, easing away from the counter. 'I'm an impatient man.' Dumping the rest of his coffee down the sink, he grabbed her hand.

'Shall I bring my camera?' she said, rattling her brain cells into line.

'No,' he said. 'If you can't live without recording every moment, I'll take some shots for you.'

He said this good-humouredly, but she realised Kruz had a point. She would relax more without her camera and take more in. Whatever Kruz wanted to show her was clearly important to him, and focusing a camera lens was in itself selective. She didn't want to miss a thing.

If she could concentrate on anything but Kruz, that was, Romy concluded as he helped her into her coat. It wasn't easy to shrug off the seductive warmth as his hands brushed her neck, her shoulders and her back. Kruz was one powerful opiate—and one she mustn't succumb to until she knew what this was about.

'So what now?' she said briskly as she locked up the penthouse.

'Now you have to be patient,' he warned, holding the door.

'I have to be *patient*?' she said.

Kruz was already heading for the stairs.

'Remember the benefits of delay.'

She stopped at the top of the stairs, telling herself that it was just a careless remark. It wasn't enough to stop fireworks going off inside her, but that was only because she hadn't thought about sex in a long time.

Today it occupied all her thoughts.

She was thrilled when Kruz drove them to the area of London she loved. 'You remembered,' she said.

He had drawn to a halt outside a gorgeous little mews house in a quaint cobbled square. It was just a short walk from the picturesque canal she had told him about.

'You haven't made any secret of your preferred area,' he said, 'so I thought you might like to take a look at this.'

'Do you own it?' she asked, staring up at the perfectly proportioned red brick house.

'I've been looking it over for a friend and I'd value your opinion.'

'I'd be more than happy to give it,' she said, smiling with anticipation.

And happy to dream a little, Romy thought as Kruz opened the car door for her. There was nothing better than snooping around gorgeous houses—though she usually did it between the covers of a glossy magazine or on the internet. This was so much better. This was a dream come true. She paused for a moment to take in the cute wrought-iron Juliet balconies, with their pots of pink and white geraniums spilling over the smart brickwork. The property was south-facing, and definitely enjoyed the best position on the square.

She hadn't seen anything yet, Romy realised when Kruz opened the front door and she walked inside. 'This is gorgeous!' she gasped, struck immediately by the understated décor and abundance of light.

'The bedrooms are all on the ground floor,' he explained, 'so the upper floor can take advantage of a double aspect view over the cobbled square, and over the gardens behind the building. You don't think having bedrooms downstairs is a problem?'

'Not at all,' she said, gazing round. The floor was pale oak strip, and the bedrooms opened off a central hallway.

'There are four bedrooms and four bathrooms on this level,' Kruz explained, 'and the property opens onto a large private garden. Plus there's a garage, and off-street parking— which is a real bonus in the centre of London.'

'Your friend must be very wealthy,' Romy observed, increasingly impressed as she looked around. 'It's been beautifully furnished. I love the Scandinavian style.'

'My friend can afford it. Why don't we take a look upstairs? It's a large, open-plan space, with a kitchen and an office as well as a studio.'

'The studio must be fabulous,' she said. 'There's so much light in the house—and it feels like a happy house,' she added, following Kruz upstairs.

She gave a great sigh of pleasure when they reached the top of the stairs and the open-plan living room opened out in front of them. There were white-painted shutters on either side of the floor-to-ceiling windows, and the windows overlooked the cobbled square at one end of the room and the gardens at the other. Everywhere was decorated in clean Scandinavian shades: white, ivory and taupe, with highlights of ice-blue and a pop of colour played out in the raspberry-pink cushions on the plump, inviting sofa. Even the ornaments had been carefully chosen—a sparkling crystal clock and a cherry-red horse, even a loving couple entwined in an embrace.

'And there's a rocking horse!' she exclaimed with pleasure, catching sight of the beautifully carved dapple grey. 'Your friends are very lucky. The people who own this house have thought of everything for a family home.'

'And even if someone wanted to work from home here, they could,' Kruz pointed out, showing her the studio. 'Well?' he said. 'What do you think? Shall I tell my friend to go ahead and buy it?'

'He'd be mad not to.'

'Do you think we had better check the nursery before I tell him to close the deal?'

'Yes, perhaps we better had,' Romy agreed. 'At least I have some idea of what's needed in a nursery now.' She laughed. 'So I can offer my opinion with confidence.'

'Goodness,' she said as Kruz opened the door on a won-derland. 'Your friend must have bought out Khalifa's!' she exclaimed. Then, quite suddenly, her expression changed.

'Romy?'

Mutely, she shook her head.

'What is it?' Kruz pressed. 'What's wrong?'

'What's wrong,' she said quietly, 'is that it took me so long to work this out. But I got there eventually.'

'Got where? What do you mean?' Kruz said, frowning.

She lifted her chin. 'I mean, you got *me* wrong,' she said coldly. 'So wrong.'

'What are you talking about, Romy?'

'You bring me to a fabulous mews house in my favourite area of London because you think I can be bought—'

'No,' Kruz protested fiercely.

'No?' she said. 'You're the friend in question, aren't you? Why couldn't you just be honest with me from the start?'

'Because I knew what you'd say,' Kruz admitted tersely. '*Dios*, Romy! I already know how pig-headed you are.'

'*I'm* pig-headed?' she said. 'You'll stop at nothing to get your own way.'

All he could offer was a shrug. 'I wanted this to be a surprise for you,' he admitted. 'I've never done this sort of thing before, so I just went ahead and did what felt right to me. I'm sorry if I got it wrong—got *you* wrong,' he amended curtly.

'Tell me you haven't bought it,' she said.

'I bought it some time ago. I bought it on the day I brought you home from hospital—which is why I had to leave you. I bought it so you and Beth would always have somewhere nice to live—whatever you decide about the future. This is your independence, Romy. This is my gift to you and to our daughter. If you feel you can't take it, I'll put it in Beth's name. It really is that simple.'

For you, she thought. 'But I still don't understand. What are you saying, Kruz?'

'What I'm saying is that I'm still not sure what you want, but I know what *I* want. I've known for a long time.'

'But you don't say anything to me—'

'Because you're never listening,' he said. 'Because you haven't been ready to hear me. And because big emotional statements aren't my style.'

'Then change your style,' she said heatedly.

'We've both got a lot to learn, Romy—about loving and giving and expressing emotion, and about each other. We must start somewhere. For Beth's sake.'

'And that somewhere's here?' she demanded, opening her arms wide as she swung around to encompass the beautiful room.

'If you want it to be.'

'It's too much,' she protested.

'It isn't nearly enough,' Kruz argued quietly. Putting his big warm hands on her shoulders, he kept her still. 'Listen to me, Romy. For God's sake, listen to me. You have no idea what you and Beth have done for me. My nightmares have gone—'

'They've gone?' She stopped, knowing that nothing meant more than this. This meant they had a chance—Kruz had a chance to start living again.

'Baby-meds,' he said. 'Who'd have thought it?'

'So you can sleep at last?' she exclaimed.

'Through the night,' he confirmed.

It was a miracle. If she had nothing more in all her life this was enough. She could have kicked herself. She'd had baby-brain while Kruz had been nothing but considerate for her. The way he'd removed himself to give her space—the way he was always considerate with the keys, with Beth, with everything—the way he never hassled her in any way, or pushed her to make a decision. And had she listened to him? Had she noticed what was going on in his world?

'I'm so sorry—'

'Don't be,' he said. 'You should be glad—we should be glad. All I want is for us to be a proper family. I want it for Beth and I want it for you and me. I want us to have a proper home where we can live together and make a happy mess—not a showpiece to rattle round in like the penthouse. I don't think you want that either, Romy. I think, like me, you want to carry on what we started. I think you want us to go on healing each other. And I know I want you. I love you, and I hope you love me. I want us to give our baby the type of home you and I have always dreamed of.'

'And how will we make it work?' she asked, afraid of so much joy.

'I have no idea,' Kruz admitted honestly. 'I just know that if we give it everything we've got we'll make it work. And if you love me as much as I love you—'

'Hang on,' she said, her face softening as she dared to believe. 'What's all this talk of love?'

'I love you,' Kruz said, frowning. 'Surely you've worked that out for yourself by now?'

'It's nice to be told. I agree you're not the best when it comes to big emotional declarations, but you should have worked that out. Try telling me again,' she said, biting back a smile.

'Okay...' Pretending concentration, Kruz held her close so he stared into her eyes.

'I've loved you since that first encounter on the grassy bank—I just didn't know it then. I've loved you since you went all cold on me and had to be heated up again. I loved you very much by then.'

'Sex-fiend.'

'You bet,' he agreed, but then he turned serious again. 'And now I love you to the point where I can't imagine life without you. And whatever you want to call these feelings—' he touched his heart '—they don't go away. They get stronger each day. You're a vital part of my life now—the *most* vital part, since you're the part I can't live without.'

'And Beth?' she whispered.

'She's part of you,' Kruz said simply. 'And she's part of me too. I want you both for life, Señorita Winner. And I want you to be happy. Which is why I bought you the house—walking distance to the shops—great transport links...'

'You'd make an excellent sales agent,' she said over the thunder of her happy heart hammering.

'I must remember to add that to my CV,' Kruz teased with a curving grin. 'Plus there's an excellent nursery for Beth across the road.'

'Where you've already put her name down?' Romy guessed with amusement.

Kruz shrugged. 'I thought we'd live part of the year here and part on the pampas in Argentina. Whatever you decide the house is yours—or Beth's. But I won't let you make a final decision yet.'

'Oh?' Romy queried with concern.

'Not until you test the beds.'

'All of them?' She started to smile.

'I think we'd better,' Kruz commented as he swung her into his arms.

'Ah, well.' Romy sighed. 'I guess I'll just have to do whatever it takes…'

'I'm depending on it,' Kruz assured her as he shouldered open the door into the first bedroom.

'Let the bed trials begin,' she suggested when he joined her on the massive bed. 'But be gentle with me.'

'Do you think I've forgotten you've just had a baby?'

Taking her into his arms, Kruz made her feel so safe.

'What?' she said, when he continued to stare at her.

'I was just thinking,' he said, stretching out his powerful limbs. 'We kicked off on a mossy bank on the pampas beside a gravel path, and we've ended up on a firm mattress in your favourite part of London town. That's not so bad, is it?'

Trying to put off the warm honey flowing through her veins for a few moments was a pointless exercise, Romy concluded, exhaling shakily with anticipation. 'Are you suggesting we work our way back to the start?'

'If none of the beds here suit, I'm sure we can find a grassy bank somewhere in the heart of London…'

'So what are you saying?' she whispered, shuddering with acute sexual excitement as Kruz ran his fingertips in a very leisurely and provocative way over her breasts and down over her belly, where they showed no sign of stopping…

'I'm saying that if you can put up with me,' he murmured

as she exclaimed with delight and relief when his hand finally reached its destination, 'I can put up with you. I'm suggesting we get to know each other really, really well all over again—starting at the very beginning.'

'Now?' she said hopefully, surreptitiously easing her thighs apart.

'Maybe we should start dating first,' Kruz said, pausing just to provoke her.

'Later,' she agreed, shivering uncontrollably with lust.

'Yes, maybe we should try the beds out first, as we agreed…' Covering her hand with his, he held her off for a moment. 'I'm being serious about us living together,' he said. 'But I don't want to rush you, Romy. I don't want to make you into something you're not. I don't want to spoil you.'

'This house isn't spoiling me?' she said.

'Pocket change,' Kruz whispered, slanting her a bad-boy smile. 'But, seriously, I don't want to change anything about you, Romy Winner.'

'No. You just want to kill me with frustration,' she said. 'I can't believe you're suggesting we go out on dates.'

'Amongst other things,' he said.

'Then I'll consider your proposition,' she agreed, smiling against his mouth as Kruz moved on top of her.

'You'll do better than that,' he promised, in his most deliciously commanding voice.

'Just one thing,' she warned, holding him off briefly.

'Tell me…'

She frowned. 'I need time.'

'Does for ever suit you?' Kruz murmured, touching her in the way she liked.

'For ever doesn't really sound long enough to me,' she whispered against the mouth of the man she had been born to love.

EPILOGUE

IT WAS THE wedding of the year. Eventually.

It took five years for Kruz to persuade Romy that their daughter was longing to be a bridesmaid and that she shouldn't deny Beth that chance.

'So, for your sake,' she told her adorable quirky daughter, who was never happier than when she had straw in her hair and was wearing shredded jeans with a ripped top covered in hoof oil and horse hair, 'we're going to have that wedding you keep nagging me about, and you are going to be our chief bridesmaid.'

'Great,' Beth said, too busy taking in the intricacies of the latest bridle her father had bought her to pay much attention.

Kruz had finally managed to convince Romy that a wedding would be a wonderful chance to affirm their love, when to Romy's way of thinking she and Kruz already shared everything—with or without that piece of paper.

'But no frills,' Beth insisted, glancing up.

So she *was* listening, Romy thought with amusement. 'No frills,' she agreed—not if she wanted Beth for her bridesmaid.

And a slinky column wedding dress was out of the question for the bride as Romy was heavily pregnant for the third time. Kruz was insatiable, and so was she—more than ever now she was pregnant again. The sex-mad phase again. How lovely.

She felt that same mad rush of heat and lust when he strode into the bedroom now. Pumped from riding, in a pair of banged-up jeans and a top that had seen better times, he looked amazing—rugged and dangerous, just the way she liked him.

Who knew how many children they would have? Romy mused happily as Kruz swung Beth into the air. A polo team, at least, she decided as Kruz reminded their daughter that she was supposed to be going swimming with friends, and had better get a move on if she wasn't going to be late.

Leaving them to plan the wedding...or not, Romy concluded when he finally looked her way.

'The baby?'

She flashed a glance at the door of the nursery where their baby son was sleeping. 'With his nanny.'

She turned as Beth came by for a hug, before racing out of the room, slamming the door behind her. A glance at Kruz confirmed that he thought this was working out just fine. She did too, Romy concluded, taking in the power in his muscular forearms as Kruz propped a hip against her desk.

'Is this the guest list?' he asked, picking up the sheaf of papers Romy had been working on. 'You *do* know we only need two people and a couple of witnesses?'

'You have a big family—'

'And getting bigger all the time,' Kruz observed, hunkering down at her side.

'Who would have thought it?' Romy mused out loud.

'I would,' Kruz murmured wickedly. 'With your appeal and my super-sperm, what else did you expect?' He caressed the swell of her belly and then buried his head a little deeper still.

'I think you should lock the door,' she said, feeling the familiar heat rising.

'I think I should,' Kruz agreed, springing up.

He smiled as he looked down at her. 'I'm glad you lost those red-tipped gel spikes.'

'She frowned. 'What makes you bring those up?'

'Just saying,' Kruz commented with amusement, drawing her into the familiar shelter of his arms.

She had almost forgotten the red-tipped gel spikes. She didn't feel the need to present that hard, *stay-away-from-me* person to the world any more. And now she came to think about it losing the spikes hadn't been a conscious decision; it had been more a case of have baby, have man I love and have *so* much less time for me. And she wouldn't have it any other way.

'So, you like my natural look?' she teased as Kruz undressed her.

'I love you any way,' he said as she tugged off his top and started on his belt. 'Though the closer to nature you get, the more I like it...'

'Back to nature is best,' Romy agreed, reaching for her big, naked man as he tipped her back on the bed.

'Will I ever get enough of you?' Kruz murmured against her mouth as he trespassed at leisure on familiar territory.

'I sincerely hope not,' Romy whispered, groaning with pleasure as her nerve-endings tightened and prepared for the oh, so inevitable outcome.

'Spoon?' he suggested, moving behind her. 'So I can touch you...?'

Her favourite position—especially now she was so heavily pregnant. Arching her back, she offered herself for pleasure.

* * *

'Tell me again,' she told him much, much later, when they were lying replete on the bed.

'Tell you what again?' Kruz queried lazily, reaching for her.

'Do you *never* get enough?'

'Of you?' He laughed softly against her back. 'Never. So what do you want me to tell you?'

'Tell me that you love me.'

Shifting position, he moved so that he could see her face, and, holding her against the warmth of his body, he stared into her eyes. 'I love you, Romy Winner. I will always love you. This is for ever. You and me—we're for ever.'

'And I love you,' she said, holding Kruz's dark, compelling gaze. 'I love you more than I thought it possible to love anyone.'

'I especially love making babies with you.'

'You're bad,' she said gratefully as Kruz settled back into position behind her. 'You don't think…?'

'I don't think what?' he murmured, touching her in the way she loved.

'I'm expecting twins this time. Do you think it will be triplets next?'

'Does that worry you?'

She shrugged. 'We both love babies—just thinking we might need a bigger house.'

'Maybe…' he agreed. 'If we practise enough.'

She was going to say something, but Kruz had a sure-fire way of stopping her talking. And—*oh*… He was doing it now.

'No more questions?' he queried.

'No more questions,' she confirmed shakily as Kruz set up a steady beat.

'Then just enjoy me, use me. Have pleasure, baby,' he suggested as he gradually upped the tempo. 'And love me as I love you,' he added as she fell.

'That's easy,' she murmured when she was calmer, and could watch Kruz in the grip of pleasure as he found his own violent release. 'For ever,' she whispered as he held her close.

* * * * *

ITALIAN BOSS,
PROUD MISS PRIM

For Jenny, who is both inspired and inspiring.

CHAPTER ONE

SIX HOURS, FIFTEEN minutes in the same hard chair at the same desk, in the same cold office, in the same northern town…

She'd lost the will to live.

Almost…

Arranging a telephone conference with Signor Rigo Ruggiero in Rome was a pain, even for a young lawyer as tenacious as Katie Bannister, because first she had to get past Ruggiero's army of snooty retainers.

Let me speak to him in person, screeched inner Katie, whilst outwardly Katie was calm. Well, she had to be—she was a respected professional.

With no inner life at all.

No inner life? Hmm, wouldn't that make things easy? Unfortunately, Katie was blessed with a vivid imagination and an active fantasy life, and it was always getting her into trouble. Dumpy, plain and unprepossessing became sharp and confident in the blink of an eye—especially over the phone.

In her junior position at the small solicitor's firm, Katie wouldn't normally be expected to deal with such a high-profile client, but this was a trivial matter, according to the senior partner, and if she wanted to work her way up the profession it would be good for Katie to cut her teeth on—

'Pronto…'

At last. *At last!* 'Signor Ruggiero?'

'*Sì...?*'

The deep-pitched voice speared a shiver down her spine. But gut instinct wasn't enough. Did it prove the identity of the speaker? Spoken Italian was sexy; distractingly so. Quickly gathering her thoughts, Katie picked up her notes and went through the security checks she had drawn up.

To his credit, Signor Ruggiero answered them all accurately and politely. To her dismay her imagination insisted on working overtime as she nursed the phone—tall, dark and handsome didn't begin to cover it. Still, this was going better than she had expected after her run-in with his staff. Now it was simply a matter of informing the Italian tycoon that he was the chief beneficiary in his late brother's will.

'My late *step*brother's will,' he corrected her.

The honey-rich baritone had acquired an edge of steel. He sounded stern, cold, uninterested.

A man who was so hard to contact would hardly want chit-chat, Katie reminded herself, moving up a gear. 'My apologies, Signor Ruggiero, your late *step*brother's will...'

As the conversation continued Katie picked up more clues. If there was one thing she was good at it was reading people's voices. Time spent training to be an opera singer at one of the world's foremost music conservatoires had allowed her well-tuned ear to instantly evaluate a voice, and this one had both practised charm and a killer edge.

'Can we cut to the chase, Signorina Bannister?'

And cut out print yards of legalese? 'Certainly...'

Katie's reputation at the firm was founded on dogged persistence along with her ability to calm even the most fractious of clients, but after a long day in a cheap suit in a cold office, she was at the end of her tether. It wasn't as if she was trying to serve a writ, for goodness' sake; rather she was trying to inform Signor Ruggiero that he had come into money.

More money, Katie qualified, glancing at the magazine the girls in the office had so helpfully placed on her desk. It featured a devastatingly handsome Rigo Ruggiero on the front cover. Not that she was interested. Firming her jaw, she continued to explain to one of the richest men in Italy why she must come to see him in person. To Rome, where she had thought of going as a singer, once…

'Well, I haven't got the time to come over there—'

Katie snapped back to the present. 'Your stepbrother anticipated this…' Her heart picked up pace as she went on to read out the letter of instruction that came with the will. She was normally unflappable, but office tittle-tattle had unsettled her where Rigo Ruggiero was concerned. He was not just a successful tycoon, but a high-profile playboy who lived life in the fast lane. To say that Katie Bannister and Rigo Ruggiero were worlds apart was a massive understatement.

Everyone in the office had thought it highly amusing that the official office virgin had been appointed to deal with Italy's most notorious playboy. Katie's public face had remained unmoved through all this teasing banter, but her imagination had run riot. After her initial trepidation, she had thought, bring it on. What did she have to worry about? Rigo Ruggiero would take one look at dull little Katie Bannister and she'd be safe.

'No, I'm sorry,' she said. 'I'm afraid your late stepbrother's personal effects cannot be sent to you through the post, Signor Ruggiero.'

'Why not?'

'Because…' She took a deep, steadying breath. Forget the letter of intentions—shouldn't he care a little more? And did he have to snap like that? His stepbrother had just died, for goodness' sake. Surely he was curious to learn what he'd been left in the will? 'Your stepbrother's instructions are *most* specific, Signor Ruggiero. He appointed the firm I represent, Flintock, Gough and Coverdale, as executors to his will, and Mr Flintock has asked me to carry out the requirements therein to the letter—'

'Therein?'

Mockery now?

'Do you always speak legalese to your clients, Signorina Bannister? That must be very confusing for them.' His voice was dry and amused. 'I recommend plain-speaking myself...'

No one had ever criticised her dedication to the letter of the law before and it was becoming increasingly clear that Rigo Ruggiero couldn't care a fig for his stepbrother. She could see him now, lolling back on some easy chair as he took the call—all preposterously white teeth, inky black hair and dark, mocking eyes. Closing her eyes, she willed herself to remain calm. 'What I'm trying to explain, Signor Ruggiero—'

'Don't patronise me.'

The tone of voice both stung and acted as a warning. 'I apologise. That was not my intention.'

'Then I forgive you...'

In a voice like a caress. Was he flirting with her? Unlikely as that seemed, it appeared so, and her body definitely agreed. 'So could we fix an appointment?' she suggested, returning determinedly to the point of the call.

There was silence at the other end of the line, but somehow worldly amusement managed to travel down it anyway. 'Whenever you like,' he murmured.

The throaty drawl was enough to make her body quiver with anticipation. Katie stared out of the window at the cold, autumnal Yorkshire rain. That was the swiftest return to reality she could imagine. Beneath her conventional, even plain exterior, lurked a seam of wanderlust. She had dreamed at one time that it would be the opera houses of the world she'd be visiting. Did she have the courage to make this trip to Rome in her new guise as solicitor, or would the loss of her singing voice be a reminder that was too painful to bear?

'Well,' the deep male voice demanded, 'I don't have all day, Signorina Bannister. When would you like to meet?'

She longed for a break, and she could be in Rome tomorrow. Before she could stop herself the words tumbled out. 'What about tomorrow, Signor Ruggiero? If that's convenient for you…?'

'I'll make it so,' he said.

'Thank you for your cooperation.' She could hardly breathe her heart was thundering so fast. Talking over the phone was easy, but when Signor Ruggiero saw how plain and boring she was in person… And when she saw Rome…

'I look forward to meeting you,' he said. 'You have a lovely voice, by the way.'

A lovely voice… 'Thank you…' Playboys were expected to flirt, and Signor Ruggiero couldn't be expected to know that her voice had been reduced to husky ashes after a fire in her student lodgings. She had been overjoyed in the hospital when she found out all her friends had escaped uninjured, and devastated to discover that after inhaling too much smoke her voice had been reduced for good to a croak. Oddly enough, people who didn't know her history found that husky sound attractive. But that wasn't her only legacy from the fire. She would never sing again and had enough scars on her back to ensure no one would ever see her naked. When her singing career had crashed to a close, she had set about forging a new life as a lawyer. This was a life in the shadows rather than the spotlight, but she wasn't interested in the spotlight; it was the music she missed.

'Signorina Bannister? Are you still there?'

'I beg your pardon, Signor Ruggiero. I just knocked something off my desk.'

Or wished she had, Katie thought, staring at the magazine. A towering powerhouse of hard, tanned muscle, dressed in a sharp designer suit, stared back at her from the front cover. Rigo Ruggiero couldn't even be accused of having a smooth, rich boy's face. His verged on piratical, complete with sharp black stubble and a dangerous gleam in night-dark, emerald eyes. Add to that a shock of thick black hair and a jaw even firmer than her own—

'You haven't changed your mind about our meeting, I hope?'

There was a faint edge of challenge to his voice that her body responded to with enthusiasm. 'Not at all,' she reassured him firmly. Reaching across the desk, she was about to send the magazine flying to the floor when she paused. The cynical curve of his mouth set her teeth on edge, but she had to admit it was the perfect frame for his arrogant voice. And, as if there wasn't enough perfection in his life, the image showed him with his arm draped around the shoulders of a blonde girl so achingly lovely she looked like a doll rather than a living, breathing woman.

It would be fine, Katie told herself, straightening up. She could do this. The trip to Rome was business and no one could distract her from that.

'I have a question for you, Signorina Bannister.'

'Yes?' Tightening her grip on the phone, Katie realised she was still transfixed by the image of the girl's unblemished skin.

'Why you?' he rapped.

This was no playboy, but a merciless tycoon questioning the wisdom of sending such a young and inexperienced lawyer to meet with him. But he had a point. Why were they sending her? Because she spoke fluent Italian, thanks to her opera training, Katie reasoned, because she was plain, safe and unattached, and, as the newest recruit to the firm, she had little or no say when it came to apportioning work.

Better not let on she was so junior. 'I'm the only solicitor in the firm who could spare the time to come to Rome—'

'You're not much good, then?'

'Signor Ruggiero—'

'Piano, piano, bella...'

Piano, bella? He was telling her to calm down—and in a voice he might use with a lover.

Italian was sexy, Katie reminded herself. The language itself had a lyrical music all its own. And when you added Rigo Ruggiero to the mix—

'So,' he said, 'I'll see you in Rome tomorrow—*si?*'

See him tomorrow...

He was quicksilver to her caution, one moment stern, the next amused. But he was right to be suspicious about her credentials. She wasn't a great lawyer. She never would be a great lawyer because she didn't have the hunger for it. She sometimes wondered if the passion she'd felt for her operatic career would ever transfer to anything else. But the firm she had worked for since she had retrained as a solicitor had been good to her when her life had gone up in flames, and now she was scared a role in the background suited her.

'I'll expect you tomorrow.'

Tomorrow...

This was exactly what she'd asked for. But since she'd suggested tomorrow her confidence had been slowly seeping away. The whole idea was ridiculous. How could she go to Rome, the city where she had dreamed of being part of the musical life, only as a second-rate lawyer to deal with one of the most acute minds around?

The only reason Katie could think of was hard, economic reality. The senior partner at her firm was talking redundancies, thanks to the economic downturn, and as last into the firm she was most likely to be first out. There was no question this trip to Rome and her meeting with someone as high-profile as Rigo Ruggiero would add some much-needed colour to her CV.

It made sense—well, to everything except her self-confidence. How could Katie Bannister, dressed by the cheapest store in town, the girl who wouldn't know a fashion must-have if she fell over it, meet with the world's most notorious playboy and come out of that meeting unscathed?

The plain and simple truth was, she had to.

'I'll book a flight,' she said, thinking out loud.

'I'd recommend it,' the man in question interrupted dryly. 'Mail me with the details and I'll make sure someone is at Fiumicino Airport to meet you—'

'That's very—'

Katie stared at the dead receiver in her hands. How rude. Or look at it another way, she persuaded herself; this was a challenge, and she was hardly a stranger to that.

She had laughed when the other girls at the firm had insisted that Katie Bannister had hidden fire and would master the maverick playboy in less time than it took to say hold my briefs—maybe she had possessed that fire once, but not now—and the girls in the office hadn't spoken to him, a man so cold and heartless he could discuss a close relative's bequest without so much as a play of regret. And end a conversation without any of the usual niceties. Rigo Ruggiero was clearly an indulged and arrogant monster and the sooner her business with him was concluded the better she would like it.

It was just a shame her body disagreed.

She'd cope with that too. Palming her mouse, Katie brought up flight schedules to Rome. Could she make it there and back in one day? She would try her very best to do so.

Having replaced the receiver in its nest, Rigo settled back in his leather swivel chair. In spite of the unwelcome message Katie Bannister had delivered from a man he'd hoped never to hear from again, the young lawyer had made him smile.

Because he liked her voice?

It had certainly scored highly in several categories: it was female; it was young; it was husky; it was sexy. Very sexy. And intelligent. And...sexy. He already had an image of her in his mind.

So, he reflected, returning to the purpose of Signorina Bannister's call, his stepbrother had left him something in his will. A poisoned chalice? Shares in a crime syndicate? What? He stood up and started pacing. Why should the man who had shown him nothing but contempt and hatred since the day he had walked into his life leave him anything at all in his will? And what was it about these personal effects that made them so precious only a representative from a solicitor's firm in England could hand-deliver them?

He knew Carlo had been living in the north of England for some years, thanks to the headlines in the papers detailing his stepbrother's countless misdemeanours, and could confidently predict that if these personal effects were gold bars they'd be stolen—likewise jewellery, antiques or art. What else would Carlo care enough about not to chance it going astray? It had to be something incriminating—something that gave Carlo one last stab at him before the gates of hell closed on his stepbrother forever.

Rigo had been just fourteen when his father married again

and seventeen when he had left home for good. He had left home after a couple of years of Carlo's vicious tricks, when home became a cruel misnomer for somewhere Rigo was no longer welcome. How he had longed for his father's love, but that love had found another home. So he conquered his regret and left the countryside to pursue his dreams in Rome. He hadn't heard from Carlo, his elder by eleven years, from that day to this.

But he had a lot to thank Carlo for, Rigo reflected, standing by the floor-to-ceiling windows in his luxurious penthouse overlooking Rome. He lived in the most exclusive part of the city and this was only one of his many properties. Leaving the country all those years ago had led to success, wealth and, more important in his eyes, the chance to live life the way he believed it should be led.

These thoughts brought him back full circle to the girl from England he must somehow fit into his busy schedule tomorrow. Crossing to his desk, he scanned his diary. He'd just sacked the latest in a long line of hopeless PAs. Finding a reliable replacement was proving harder than he had anticipated.

Which left a vacancy on his staff…

If she was half as intriguing as her husky voice suggested, he would gladly clear his diary for Signorina Bannister. He would make the whole of tomorrow free just for her.

CHAPTER TWO

KATIE WAS HAVING second thoughts. Just packing a few essentials for the trip in her shabby bag proved she wasn't the right person for this job. She might have the heart to handle Rigo Ruggiero, but she lacked the panache. The firm should be sending someone sharp and polished to Rome, someone sophisticated, who spoke the same sophisticated language as him. Two new packets of tights and a clean white blouse did not a sophisticate make, but it was the best she could do. There was nothing in her wardrobe suitable for spending time in Rome with a man renowned for his sartorial elegance.

A few calming breaths later Katie had worked out that, as she couldn't compete, she shouldn't try. She should look at what she was—a competent young lawyer from a small firm in the north of England, which meant a brown suit and low-heeled brown court shoes were the perfect choice.

This wasn't a holiday, Katie reminded herself sternly, though as an afterthought she added a pair of comfortable trousers and a sweater. With the tight schedule she had planned it was unlikely there would be any off-duty time, but if there was she could dress for that too.

But everything was brown, even her bag, Katie noticed as she prepared to close the door on her small terraced house. A life in the shadows was one thing, but she hadn't noticed the colour seeping from it. Perhaps it had gone with the music...

She shook herself round determinedly. She was going to Rome—not as a singer as she had always hoped, but as a representative of a respectable legal firm. How many people got a second chance like that?

Locking the door, she tested the handle and picked up her bag. Tipping her chin at a confident angle, she walked briskly down the path. She was going to Italy to meet one of the most exciting men of his day. She didn't expect to be part of Rigo Ruggiero's life but, for a few short and hopefully thrilling hours, she would be an observer. At the very least she could report back to the girls in the office and brighten up their coffee breaks for the foreseeable future.

Signor Ruggiero had lied. Clutching her sensible bag like a comfort blanket, Katie stood bewildered amongst the crowds on the pavement outside Fiumicino Airport in Rome. The sun was beating down like an unrelenting spotlight and the heat was overpowering. She stared this way and that, but it only confirmed what she already knew, which was, no one had come to meet her. Plus everyone else seemed to know where they were going. She was the only country bumpkin who appeared to be cast adrift in the big city.

And was fervently wishing she'd handled her own transport arrangements into Rome.

What was wrong with her? She had the address...

Having found it in her bag, she looked for a taxi. Was she going to be defeated before she even started this adventure? But each time she stepped forward to claim an empty cab, someone taller, slicker and more confident than Katie stepped in front of her—

'Signorina Bannister?'

The voice reached into her chest and squeezed her heart tight before she even had chance to look around, and when she did she almost stumbled into the arms of a man who put his photographs to shame. Her heart drummed an immediate tattoo. Rigo Ruggiero in the hard, tanned flesh was infinitely better-looking than his air-brushed images—so hot you wouldn't touch him without protective clothing. He was the type of man Katie had spent her whole life dreaming about and wishing would notice her, but who, of course, never would—other than today, when he had no alternative.

'Sorry…sorry.' She righted herself quickly before he was brought into contact with her cheap polyester suit. 'Signorina Bannister? That's me.'

'Are you sure?'

Her cheeks flamed. 'Of course I'm sure…'

Thrusting her serviceable bag beneath her arm, she held out her free hand in greeting. 'This is very good of you, sir—' She braced herself for contact.

Contact there was none.

Startlingly green and uncomfortably shrewd eyes refused to share Signor Ruggiero's practised smile. He was not the man in the magazine photograph. That man was a playboy with pleasure on his mind. The man in front of her was a realist, a thinker, a business tycoon, and he took no prisoners. The hand she had extended dropped back to her side. 'I didn't think you would come to meet me in person—'

'It is my pleasure to do so.'

He even bowed slightly, but his tone suggested it was anything but a pleasure for him.

Katie's worst fears were confirmed. Rigo Ruggiero was hiding disappointment. Having heard her husky voice over the phone, he had imagined he had come to the airport to meet a siren. They had both been misled, Katie reflected wryly.

Now this was not business for her; it had become personal. Rigo Ruggiero had shadows behind his eyes she couldn't resist and wanted to understand, and he was so handsome he made her heart ache.

'You had a good journey, I hope.'

'Very good, thank you.' She registered the fact that he had spoken to her in a tone of voice she imagined he might use with a maiden aunt. He was so much taller, bigger and had a more powerful aura than her imagination had allowed and was far more rugged. He was the type of man who could look dangerous even in tailored clothes. The dark trousers complemented his athletic figure and the crisp blue shirt was open a couple of buttons at the neck, revealing a hard, tanned chest, shaded with black hair. The sight of this gave parts of her that were largely unused a vigorous workout. If this wasn't lust at first sight, it was the closest Katie Bannister had ever come to it.

But what she needed now, Katie reasoned with her sensible head on, was some form of identification to prove to Rigo Ruggiero she was who she said she was. On plundering her bag she managed to spill the contents all over his designer-clad feet.

'Allow me, Signorina Bannister...'

To his credit, he immediately dipped to rescue her passport, tickets, toffees, tissues and all the other embarrassing detritus she had accumulated during the flight.

'Why don't I take your bag?' he suggested, staring her straight in the eyes as he straightened up.

My shabby, disreputable-looking bag? 'That's very kind of you. And here's my passport for purposes of identification.'

'I don't think we'll need that,' he said, lips pressing down in an unfeasibly attractive way. And then, in a final cataclysmic put-down, he suggested, 'Why don't you put your passport somewhere safe before you lose it?'

So she wasn't a maiden aunt, she was a child.

She'd made a great first impression. He even held the bag steady for her as she stuffed her possessions back inside. She glanced at him apologetically. He had no need to flag it up. Her clothes, her gaucheness, her red cheeks and clumsiness, all told a story Rigo Ruggiero had no interest in reading.

'And my stepbrother's personal effects?' he pressed, gazing past her.

She wondered if he expected a packing case to be following on. 'Your stepbrother's effects are right here.' She patted the breast pocket of her jacket to reassure him.

'That doesn't look like very much.'

'Well, it is a very small package.' She blushed violently to see him conceal a smile.

'OK,' he said, neither agreeing nor disagreeing, 'I'll get the car.'

'Honestly, I'm quite happy to take a cab—'

'So we arrive at my penthouse in convoy?' he suggested, shooting her a look.

How much better could this get? 'See your point,' she murmured with a nervous laugh.

How much better? A lot better, Katie realised as a blood-red sports car drew up at the kerb. She didn't need to remember the blonde in the magazine to know she was hardly in this class. A sick, heavy feeling was building in her stomach as an admiring crowd gathered around the high-performance vehicle and its elegant driver. They had recognised Rigo, of course, and now they were eager to find out who he was meeting at the airport.

That was what she had to walk through to get to the car.

'I don't bite, Signorina Bannister.'

The throaty drawl drew her attention to the man leaning over the roof of the low-slung sex-machine.

A laugh rippled through the crowd as she locked gazes with him. Everyone was staring at her and she could feel their disappointment. She was not some famous beauty or a supermodel. She was about the furthest thing from that you could get. Steeling herself, she took the half-dozen steps required to close the distance between herself and the car. Signor Ruggiero had already stowed her bag, and so all she had to do was get in—but that meant she had to slot herself into an impossibly narrow-looking opening.

'When you're ready,' he drawled.

She had already anticipated that folding her inelegant body into such an elegant car was a skill she didn't possess. She was right and, to her horror, she got stuck.

What made it worse was that Signor Ruggiero came to help her, and all but lifted her into the formed seat, which she now discovered had been moulded around a fairy's bottom.

But at least she was out of sight of the crowd, Katie reasoned as he slid into the driver's seat beside her.

'Comfortable?' He glanced at her to check.

'Perfectly.' On edge.

Now she had to convince herself that you couldn't die from the shock of meeting a man like this in person, and that the air in the confined cabin hadn't changed with an overload of ions and his delicious scent. But it had. And it was charged with something else…sex, Katie realised, primly tugging down her skirt. Rigo Ruggiero radiated sex.

'You can understand my impatience, I'm sure,' he said.

She gripped the seat as the engine roared like a jet.

'This bequest from such an unexpected quarter has intrigued me,' he went on.

This was business, she told herself in a silent shout, but that reassurance was growing a little thin.

'I ask myself,' he said, 'what can be so important that only a personal delivery of the documents would do?'

As he glanced at her, Katie thought: And by a girl like this? She shrank beneath a gaze that took in every stitch of man-made fibre until finally it came to rest on her sensible, low-heeled shoes. She quickly tucked her feet away, out of sight. 'I'm sorry if I kept you waiting.'

He shrugged. 'I must have missed you, somehow.'

Searching for that husky-voiced siren would do it every time.

'But never mind,' he added dryly, flashing that wolf smile of his. 'I've got you now.'

'Indeed you do.'

He shrugged as he released the brake and pulled away. *The adventure begins,* Katie thought, hoping she was up to it. She didn't need Signor Ruggiero to spell it out. Katie Bannister was hardly the type of woman he would normally put himself out for.

She held on tightly to the seat as he steered smoothly away from the kerb. 'Ten kilometres an hour OK for you?' he murmured as they joined a crawling stream of traffic.

'Sorry, I'm just not used to…'

How many people were used to driving in a sports car? Katie asked herself sensibly. She had entered a world that was completely alien to her, and it would take a while to adjust. Closing her eyes and wishing herself a million miles away wouldn't work this time, because this time she really was living the fantasy.

She didn't realise how tense she had become until she heard Signor Ruggiero say, 'Don't worry, Signorina Bannister. I shall strive to achieve a balance between my impatience and your obvious lack of confidence in my driving ability—'

'Oh, I'm not—' Her mouth slammed shut when she realised too late he was mocking her. And now the set of his jaw did nothing to encourage conversation.

He was hardly her typical client, but this sort of impatience was universal. The reading of a will was notoriously full of surprises and, whether those surprises turned out to be bad or good, human nature demanded answers fast.

Katie's hand crept to the breast pocket of her suit, where she wished fervently for some last small legacy of love for him contained within the envelope she was carrying—though, if past experience was any guide, she was wasting her time.

OK, so meeting Katie Bannister had been a shock, but he was growing used to her unique vibe. She was as different from the women he was used to mixing with as it was possible to imagine, but that wasn't necessarily a bad thing, only different. He didn't need false breasts and false smiles—but neither did he need complications. Signorina Bannister was a quiet little mouse and awkward, which meant he would have to spend more time with her than he had anticipated, but how could he throw her to the wolves in Rome? She was out of her comfort zone and had anticipated more time to prepare before meeting him. She found herself in a much bigger, faster world than her comfortable country cocoon and would have to adapt quickly. Meanwhile they had a forty-five minute journey ahead of them and he couldn't stand this uncomfortable silence. 'I'd like you to call me Rigo.'

She bit her lip. Her pale cheeks blazed. She said precisely nothing.

Ducking his head, he checked the road before steering north-east to Rome. It gave him an excuse to flash a glance at her. 'Try it,' he said, thinking she looked like a rabbit trapped in headlights. 'Rrr...igo...'

She pressed back in her seat. He felt instinctively that this was someone to whom life had not always been kind. Did he have time to be a social worker? OK, so she brought out his protective instinct, but he was no bleeding heart. Perhaps it would help if he let her know he was no threat to her—absolutely no threat at all. 'You don't even have to say my name in Italian,' he said dryly. 'English will do.'

She said his name—a little reluctantly, he thought. *'Bene,'* he said. 'That was very good.'

'And you can call me Signorina Bannister,' she said.

He laughed. And for the first time that day, he relaxed. 'Very well, Signorina Bannister,' he agreed. 'Your wish is my command...' At least on the subject of names.

CHAPTER THREE

MAYBE THE CLIENT was always right, but she was going to keep this formal. She would never get used to a man like Rigo Ruggiero in the short time available as he seemed to think she could, and so it was better not to try.

But that didn't mean she couldn't enjoy this quietly. This tasty slice of *la dolce vita* was her first real adventure. Rigo Ruggiero—Roma, Italia—a real-life Italian playboy driving a blood-red sports car with Katie Bannister sitting next to him. The closest she had ever come to this before was in her fantasy world.

The view from the tinted window was extraordinary. They had cleared the boring industrial places and were driving into Rome. It was like entering the pages of a living history book—if one with a serious traffic problem, traffic Rigo Ruggiero had no problem negotiating. Her confidence had grown, Katie realised, noting how relaxed she had become. She could get used to this—the Colosseum here…Trajan's Market there. The only place she dared not look was to her left, in case Signor Ruggiero thought she was staring at him. But she didn't need to stare to know he was built like a gladiator and had the commanding face of a Roman general. She could feel that in every part of her.

'Trajan's Market has recently been reopened to the public.'

She refocused as he spoke. This conversational tone was not what she expected from the gladiator in her head, but then she hadn't expected him to speak at all. Signor Ruggiero was being kind by entering into conversation with her—and at least it gave her an excuse to stare at him. 'Really?'

She knew her eager gaze was gauche, but he was perfection, which made it hard not to stare. If she could have designed a man, this would be him. Even her imagination couldn't have mapped a face so perfect or a body made for uninterrupted sin—

'Even in AD 113,' he went on, 'these large shopping malls were in demand.'

As he smiled, a flash of strong white teeth against his tan made her think even more wicked thoughts. She could think of a better use for those firm, mobile lips and those wolf teeth, and when he angled that rough, stubble-shaded chin towards the remarkably well-preserved Roman buildings she felt a pulse begin to throb where it had absolutely no business doing so. Did he know the effect he was having on her? Katie wondered, blushing when he looked at her for her opinion. Hopefully not.

'I read somewhere that Trajan's Market was the experiment in bringing shops together under one roof,' she said, trying to seem gripped by Roman history when the only thing she wanted to be gripped by was him.

His face creased in an attractive smile. 'It was the first— unless you know of one dating from earlier times, of course?'

She shook her head. Obviously he knew more than she did about his own city, but she remained silent, because she thought it was safer to keep things formal rather than to chat. And she had only visited one shopping mall in her whole life. The girls from the office had persuaded her to accompany them and she had vowed, never again! The lights, the crowds jostling her, the shops full of things she didn't need or want. Give her the wide-open spaces in the country any day…

'I think Rome is going to be quite an eye-opener for you.'

You could say that again, Katie thought as Rigo steered the sports car down a fashionable shopping street with more glitz and glamour than her poor fantasies could hope to conjure up.

Katie's head was still spinning with all the lavish things she'd seen when she sat down in Rigo's vast, ultra-modern study. Light flooded in, revealing every flaw—or would have done had there been any, but, as she might have imagined, Rigo lived in unimaginable luxury. His penthouse was immaculate, and his study boasted every conceivable high-tech man-toy. She found it starkly beautiful, with its colour scheme of steel and white. There was glass everywhere and vibrant modern art on the walls. Incredibly, the roof could be open to the sky, which it was. Her jaw dropped as she stared up to watch birds wheeling overhead in a flawless cobalt sky. So this was how the rich lived. After the chaos and bustle of the city streets, Rigo's eyrie at the very top of an ancient palazzo was a haven of quiet. She could even hear the birds singing if she held her breath.

Katie forced her attention away from the aerial display as Rigo came to sit across the desk from her. He sprawled in such a relaxed fashion, while she was anxiously perching on the very edge of one of his divine cream leather chairs. It was showroom-new, like the huge glass desk in front of her—and that was another concern. What if she left a smudge on its pristine surface?

'Do you like the view?' he prompted.

'I love it.' There were windows to three sides overlooking the rooftops of Rome, but Rigo's husky baritone attracted her more. Her heart squeezed tight as he looked out of the window and she looked at him. He was so perfect. And she would never know him, not properly. But she would never forget today, or how attractive he was, or how polite to her—though how that would affect her future when it came to men remained to be seen. They would all fall short if she compared them to Rigo.

For his part, Rigo seemed to have got over the shock of meeting her and was treating her with indulgence like a young relative recently arrived from the country.

'There's the Colosseum,' he said, pointing it out. 'Can you see it?'

And was that St Peter's Basilica? She wanted to ask, but realised he would only think her more gauche and awkward than ever. Signor Ruggiero's home in Rome was in one of the most fashionable squares and had a panoramic view of so much of the beautiful city.

'I'll draw the blinds,' he said when she impulsively shaded her eyes to take another look. He pressed a button and it was done. He pressed another button and a tinted glass roof closed over their heads. 'Thank you,' she murmured, glad to be in the shadows again.

And now it was down to business—no more time wasted on wishing Signor Ruggiero could look at her and see her differently, someone with more class and polish than she possessed…and no flaws.

'Are you cold, Signorina Bannister?'

Try frigid.

'You're trembling,' he said.

'Just travel-weary, I expect.' By then he had pressed yet another button on the console on his desk, activating some invisible heat source.

'Travel-weary?' he murmured, and there was a faintly amused look in his eyes. 'I forgot—you've had such a long flight.'

And it would be the same short flight home, Katie thought, knowing she would have to sharpen up with this man or be made a complete fool of. She started by putting a professional smile on her lips. 'Shall we begin?'

'Whenever you're ready,' he said, still looking at her with faint amusement.

Reaching for the thick manila envelope she had put in front of her on the desk, Katie opened it. But concern for its contents washed over her and she stopped. She had heard so many unkind things expressed in wills, and was well aware they could be used like a weapon to hurt those left behind. She hoped she wasn't the bearer of some last bitter note from Rigo Ruggiero's stepbrother.

'What are you waiting for, Signorina Bannister?'

Yes, why should she care what was in the will? She fumbled the sheets and finally managed to spread the document out in front of her. 'This is the last will and testament of—'

'Cut to the chase—we both know whose will this is.'

Rigo Ruggiero's charm had evaporated. He could change in an instant, she had discovered. It would be a foolish person who underestimated him. He had charm only when he chose to have charm.

'My time is short, Signorina Bannister.'

And you are handling this badly, his expression clearly said. She wasn't supposed to get involved. She had received this same criticism at work. It was her only failing, the senior partner had told her at her annual assessment. Deal with the facts, Ms Bannister. We are not employed to dole out tea and sympathy—and make sure you keep an accurate time sheet of every moment you spend with the client.

Even at times like these when she could be revealing anything to Signor Ruggiero? Was she supposed to close her heart and send the bill? She had never managed to do so before, and now she stood less chance than ever. Her clock wasn't running. They should have sent a more experienced member of the firm if they wanted her to account for every second of compassion in her.

'Please move on.'

She did so with a dry throat. Even her so-called sexy voice sounded strained. There was clearly no love lost between Rigo and his stepbrother. Didn't he feel any nostalgia for his childhood? His darkening expression suggested not. She was out of place, out of step here…

Reminding herself she was merely a servant of the firm, she pulled herself together and got on with it, only to have Rigo explode with, *'Tcha!'* as the phone rang. He made her jump as he banged the table. Obviously he didn't want to be interrupted at a time like this, and as he reached for the telephone she spoke up.

'If I answer it I can put them off for you. I can say I'm your PA…'

Briefly, she thought she saw something light in his eyes, and then with a curt nod of agreement he withdrew his hand, leaving her to pick up the phone.

'Pronto?' She shot Rigo a glance. People had different ways of expressing emotion when someone close to them died. Carlo Ruggiero had been part of Rigo Ruggiero's life once—he must be feeling something, though he was hiding it well.

Refocusing on the call, Katie continued to talk in fluent Italian, and only slowly realised that Rigo was staring at her in astonishment.

'Why didn't you tell me you spoke Italian?' he said accusingly as she ended the call.

'I didn't realise it would be of any interest to you.'

He looked taken aback, but quickly recovered. 'No, you're right. Well?' he said impatiently. 'Are you going to tell me who it was?'

She managed her feelings. This was none of her business. 'It appears you have forgotten a rather important engagement...'

He jumped up immediately when she explained. Extracting a phone from his pocket, he placed a call and began to pace.

He would only break off this meeting before he found out everything for one reason and this was it. The scheme he had set up to fulfil children's dreams came ahead of his personal concerns. If taking a child around the track in his sports car was being brought forward then there must be a very good reason for it. 'Of course he can come right away,' he told his friend.

Moving out of earshot so Katie Bannister couldn't hear, he explained his schedule for the day had been thrown thanks to missing the solicitor he was due to meet at the airport—and, yes, he had found the young woman, eventually.

'A young woman?' his friend murmured with a knowing air.

'A very quiet and respectable young woman,' he emphasised, staring at the back of Katie Bannister's head. She had thick, glossy hair the same shade of honey as her eyes, but she wore it scraped back cruelly in a way that did her no favours. He refocused on his conversation and shut her out. His friend brought her back in again.

'What a disappointment for you, Rigo,' he drawled, 'but no doubt you have a plan in mind to change this young woman's way of thinking?'

Actually, no, he had no plan, and his friend's comment had left him feeling vaguely irritated. 'I'm leaving now.' He ended the call. This was not the moment to be discussing such things, and something about Signorina Bannister called for the role of protector, rather than seducer. She was far too young for him, and almost certainly a virgin—or at least incredibly inexperienced; ergo, she was not his type at all. He stowed the phone in his shirt pocket and turned back to her. 'You'll have to keep this reading on hold. I've been called away. We'll reschedule—'

'But my flight home…' she said anxiously.

'I can only apologise.'

Katie frowned. It wasn't up to her to judge the client, but this was unforgivable. Rigo Ruggiero intended to leave something as important as the reading of his stepbrother's will to race his sports car around a track. Couldn't he do that some other time? His equally arrogant friend hadn't been prepared to tell her much more, but she gathered that was the plan. 'There's no need to apologise,' she said coldly, remembering the senior partner's words. 'After all, you're paying for my time—'

'Plus ça change,' he interrupted and his expression registered nothing more than resigned acceptance of the way of things.

Now she was insulted. Her motive in coming to Rome had not been money. The fact that she had come here to fulfil his stepbrother's last request didn't matter to him at all, apparently.

He saw this change in her and emphasized, 'This is something I cannot miss—'

'And I cannot miss my flight,' she said, standing up.

'You can change it—'

'I'm not sure I can—'

'Why not?'

Because she would have to buy a new ticket—an expense that would mean nothing to this man and that in their present parlous state her firm probably wouldn't reimburse. She had bills to pay—and the prospect of no job to return to ahead of her.

She had tried so hard to strike the right tone and be professional, but she was growing increasingly agitated as she faced Rigo Ruggiero across the desk. Like it or not, they were in conflict now. 'Couldn't you change your appointment?' she suggested hesitantly.

'No.'

'But you are eager to get this over with?' she reminded him. And not put off by a drive around the racetrack with the boys.

'I assure you I am every bit as eager as I was before, but now I must go—'

'Shall I wait for you?'

Already halfway to the door, he spun around. 'Make yourself at home.'

Tension had propelled her to breaking point. She might be a small-town solicitor, and dull as ditchwater if you compared her to the blistering glamour of a man like this, but she wasn't anyone's doormat. 'Signor Ruggiero, please,' she called, chasing after him. 'This just can't wait—'

'And neither can my appointment,' he called back to her from the door. 'You must be content—'

Content?

As he spoke one strong, tanned hand flexed impatiently on the door handle. 'I will return as quickly as I can—'

'But my flight—'

'Book another flight.'

The next sound she heard was the sound of the door slamming on his private quarters.

Great, Katie thought, subsiding. She was going to miss her flight.

So what would she do? She would have to stay in Rome. But since the fire privacy was all-important. She'd never stayed away from home since the fire. She had never risked anyone seeing her scars. What if a hotel maid or a porter walked in on her by accident? The thought of it made her blood run cold.

She wasn't ready for this—maybe she never would be. And where would she stay? Could she even afford to stay in a city as expensive as Rome on her limited budget?

'Ciao, bella.'

On the point of tears, she swung around clumsily, almost crashing into the fabulous desk as Rigo Ruggiero stormed out of the apartment in a cloud of testosterone and expensive cologne. *Ciao, bella?* He must have mistaken her for someone else.

But her nipples were impressed, Katie realised with astonishment. Well, she could dream, couldn't she? *Ciao, bella...*

Her sensible self lost no time telling her she should be concerned at these unmistakeable signs of arousal, because Rigo Ruggiero roused more than awe inside her, he roused lust.

And frustration.

And anger.

He inspired that too, because this just wasn't fair. How long did it take to race around a track? Was she supposed to sit here waiting indefinitely for him?

She would go and find a cheap hotel, Katie concluded, putting the will back in its envelope. Wandering to the window, she took a last look out, debating whether to book a flight today, tomorrow—or next week, maybe? Who the hell knew? She was of no importance to Signor Ruggiero and had been dismissed. Far from being impatient to know the contents of his stepbrother's will, as he had told her, he had proved himself all too easily distracted. The words *play* and *boy* had never made more sense to her. Rigo Ruggiero was like a film star—all top show. He was a man with too much money and not enough to occupy his time.

Staring down at the road a dizzying distance below, she watched his sleek red car pull out smoothly into the chaos of Roman traffic. Everyone gave way for him, of course. But not her, Katie determined, firming her jaw. Not that she'd ever get the chance. But then her dreamy self came to the fore and she wondered, if she had looked different—more glamorous, more appealing—would Rigo have taken her to the track with him?

And why should she care? It was time to stop daydreaming and start making plans.

An open ticket home was the best thing, Katie decided, and then the moment this business was concluded she could fly home. Rigo Ruggiero might have consigned her to the pigeonhole marked miscellaneous, along with all the other women who, for reasons of age, or inferior looks, had failed to meet his exacting standards, but even in her dreams she didn't want to spend any more time than she had to with a man so self-absorbed he'd put a drive around a racetrack ahead of the reading of his stepbrother's will.

Which naturally accounted for her heart trying to beat its way out of her chest. Who was she trying to fool? Katie wondered as the phone rang again. She looked across the room. Where were the snooty staff she'd had to get past at his office? Had he sacked them all? Surely a man like Rigo Ruggiero had a PA who could sort out his appointments and answer his phone? But if he had, there was no sign of him or her.

The phone continued to peal until finally she gave in and picked it up. *'Pronto?'*

'Signorina Bannister?'

No. A Hollywood film star, she felt like telling Rigo Ruggiero at that moment. *'Sì,'* she said instead, forcing an agreeable note into her voice.

'I feel bad.'

Oh, no! She pulled a face and somehow managed to sound pleasantly surprised at the same time. 'Oh…?'

'You should make the most of your time in Rome.'

Really? 'But I'll be leaving shortly,' she pointed out, waiting in vain for the surge of relief those words should bring.

'Have you booked another flight yet?'

Ah, so he couldn't wait to get rid of her. 'I was about to—'

'Well, don't. Not until I get back.'

Commands now? Did she work for him? 'But, Signor Ruggiero, I'm not equipped to stay over—'

'Not equipped? What's your problem? Buy whatever you need and charge it to me.'

What? 'I couldn't possibly!' Katie exclaimed with affront—though she did allow her imagination a five-second trolley dash through Rome's most expensive store with Rigo Ruggiero's credit card clutched tightly in her hand. 'I don't have a hotel.'

'A hotel? Don't be ridiculous. I have seven bedrooms.'

Now she really was too shocked to speak.

'Signorina Bannister? Are you still there?'

'Yes,' Katie managed hoarsely.

'Don't forget we still have business to conclude, you and I. I expect you there on my return. How hard can it be?' he added in a more soothing tone. 'My penthouse has a roof garden accessed through the staircase in the hallway, as well as an outdoor pool with the finest views over Rome you'll ever see. There's a resident chef on call at the press of a button, and an entertainment centre with a gym attached to the spa. Use the place like your own. And don't forget—be there when I return. Oh, and in the meantime—answer any incoming calls and make a note of them, would you?'

Katie was still choking out words of protest when Rigo cut the line.

CHAPTER FOUR

THE TELEPHONE RECEIVER was in serious danger of connecting with the plate-glass window. And she thought she knew everything there was to know about controlling feelings? Did Rigo seriously expect her to remain on standby at his command? He must think everyone lived the same racy billionaire lifestyle he did. Some people had work to do.

Yes…like answering his phone, Katie concluded as it rang again. Glaring at the receiver, she walked over to the cradle, pressed a few buttons and switched it to record. Now she could take stock. She could fret all she liked, but she *was* going to miss her plane, meaning she *would* have to stay another night in Rome. But not here. Not with Rigo Ruggiero. Not in a million years.

She didn't want to panic anyone, so her first call must be to the office. She would give them a carefully edited version of events. That done, she would book into a reasonably priced hotel—if she could find such a thing in Rome. Then she must do some shopping—toiletries and nightclothes, if nothing else. And if Rigo Ruggiero wanted to hear the reading of his stepbrother's will and receive the package she had brought with her, he could damn well come and find her.

Katie booked into a respectable hotel, taking a compact room on the fourth floor with a view of the air-conditioning units.

But she had everything she needed: a clean bed and a functioning bathroom, as well as a desk, an easy chair and a television. Best of all, there were quiet spaces in the lobby where she could meet up with Rigo when he found her. She was confident he would find her; that was what men like him were good at.

And now what?

She had paced the three strides by six it took to mark out the floor of her room, and was left facing the fact that she was alone in the raciest and most fashionable city on earth...a city she longed to explore. So, she could sit here in her hotel room, or be really adventurous and sit in the lobby.

She could always watch TV...

In Rome?

What about her shopping? There had to be a chain store close to the hotel.

Katie asked the concierge, who directed her to the Via del Corso, which he said was one of the busiest shopping streets in town. It certainly was, she discovered, though it bore no resemblance to any shopping street back home. It was so glamorous and buzzy she just stood and stared when she found it, until people jostled her and she was forced to move along.

So now what? Now she was a tourist, and she was enjoying every minute of it. Work seemed a million miles away...

After a moment's hesitation, she took a deep breath and plunged right in.

To Katie's surprise she loved every moment of the chaotic bustle, and hearing the lyrical Italian language being spoken all around her more than made up for the mayhem of the crowded streets. She had learned to love Italian at the music conservatoire she had attended, in what seemed to her like another lifetime now. Determined to brush all melancholy thoughts away, she told herself that she would never get another opportunity like this and should be savouring every moment so she could store away the memories to share with the girls in the office.

She began with some serious window shopping, which involved frantically trying to work out how many fantasy purchases she could fit into her fantasy wardrobe, not to mention how much fantasy designer luggage would be required to transport all these fantasy purchases home. But there was one adventure she could afford, Katie realised as she walked along, and that was drinking coffee at a pavement café like a real Roman.

She would be mad not to enjoy the shade of late afternoon, Katie convinced herself, feeling a little nervous as she eyed up a likely café. There were a few free seats, and, with all the new scents and sounds around her and the clear blue sky like an umbrella overhead, the temptation to linger and soak it all in was irresistible.

If she didn't do it now she never would. Everyone had their shoulders thrown back in the warmth of the sun, and were talking loudly—as much with gestures as with their voices. This way of life intrigued her. It was so different from seeing people with their backs hunched against an icy wind and she wanted to be part of it, even if it was only for an afternoon. She wanted to let her hair down and be as uninhibited as all the other girls her age, who looked so fashionable and sassy in their street clothes.

Let her hair down? Yes. She might even unbutton her jacket, Katie decided in a wry moment of abandon. Spotting an empty table in a prime position, she targeted it. Why not? Shouldn't she make the most of this short trip and live a little while she had the chance?

The handsome, dark-eyed waiter who brought Katie the menu was quite a flirt. He repeated the old cliché that while she was in Rome she must do as the Romans did—though the look in his eyes suggested that might be a step too far for her. When her cheeks pinked up he pursued a different line, suggesting *gelato alla vaniglia* as an alternative—making vanilla ice cream sound like the most decadent food on earth. He advised that this should be accompanied by a strong black coffee and some iced water to help the sweetness down.

Katie thanked him in Italian. *'Ringrazie molto, signore.'*

'Ah, you speak Italian…!' Elaborate gestures accompanied this exclamation, and then he continued to stare at her with deep pools of longing in his puppy-dog eyes. 'Are you quite sure that's *all* I can help you with, *signorina*?' he murmured passionately.

'Quite sure, thank you.'

Katie smiled. She knew the waiter was only joking but, looking around, she had gathered that was the Roman way—every man was duty-bound to flirt. 'However,' she said, deciding to play the waiter at his own game, 'there is one thing…'

'Sì…?' Hope revived, the man dipped lower.

'May I have my coffee now, please?'

'Certamente, signorina,' he said, affecting disappointment, but as he left he gave Katie a wink as if to say he'd recognised a fellow tease.

She was really beginning to enjoy herself, Katie realised, eyes sparkling with fun as the waiter walked away. She hadn't flirted with a man since before the accident and then never seriously. In fact, this was the most excitement she'd ever had. Rome was proving to be everything it was reputed to be—magical, romantic, awe-inspiring…a city of adventure, and it had unleashed something in her.

Let's just hope it wasn't her reckless, inner self, Katie mused, because that fantasy Katie was far safer locked away. Thinking of Rigo—which she was doing rather a lot lately—it wouldn't be wise to push the boundaries too far on this first attempt to live her dream.

A shadow fell over her table. A ripple of awareness ran down her spine.

No.

It couldn't be—

'Signorina Bannister.'

'Rigo!' Lurching to her feet, she quickly sat down again. Why should she feel so guilty? But she did. 'You're the last person I expected to see—'

'Clearly.'

Tipping designer shades down his nose, he shot a glance at the waiter. Had he heard something of their conversation? Well, if he had he'd got the wrong idea. Rigo's hackles were so far up he was practically snarling. 'So, this is what you get up to while I'm away?' he demanded when the waiter disappeared inside the café.

'Did you enjoy your drive around the track?' she countered pleasantly.

'I thought I asked you to wait for me at the penthouse?'

'I didn't know how long you would be—'

'I also thought you had a plane to catch,' he interrupted. 'You were in a tearing hurry to leave, as I remember—'

'But how can I before I've read the will? And I missed my plane.' She resisted the temptation to add, thanks to you. Leaning on her hand, she stared up and from somewhere found the courage to hold his stare.

Rigo visibly bridled again as the waiter returned with her coffee. What was the poor waiter supposed to do? She'd ordered coffee and he was perfectly within his rights to bring it. And how dared Rigo question her actions when he had left her on the flimsiest of pretexts and for an unspecified length of time?

But as they still had business to complete her reasonable self conceded that it might be better to build bridges. 'Would you like to join me?' She pointed to an empty chair.

Rigo pulled out two chairs. 'As you can see, I am not alone…'

Now she noticed his companion was the beautiful young blonde in the magazine. The girl had been shopping and was making her way towards them, weighed down by countless carrier bags. The café was obviously a prearranged meeting place.

Every man turned to watch as the young girl threaded her way through the tables. Katie couldn't blame them, the girl was gorgeous—especially when she lifted the carrier bags on high to avoid hitting anyone with them, revealing even more perfectly toned thigh.

Composing her face, Katie determined to love this young woman for the short time she would have to know her—if only so as not to appear small-minded and deadly jealous, though this resolution took a nosedive when the girl draped herself over Rigo.

'Rigo, il mio amore,' she pouted, tugging at his resistant arm, *'sì sara lunga?'*

Having asked whether he would be much longer, she turned her luminous stare on Katie.

Katie smiled, or tried her very hardest to.

After taking full inventory of Katie, Rigo's companion appeared satisfied and risked a sultry smile.

No doubt having concluded I'm no threat, Katie reasoned.

'Antonia,' Rigo protested in a weary voice, 'please try to remember that Signorina Bannister is here in Rome on business.'

Rigo was defending her? She *had* gone up in the world,

Katie thought wryly, trying not to mind when Rigo settled his young companion into the chair next to her own.

'Don't worry, I know when I'm not wanted,' Antonia responded sulkily, refusing to sit down now she had deposited her bags. 'I don't want to be here while you're talking business—'

'Oh, please, don't go on account of me…' Katie seized the opportunity to stand up. 'I was just going anyway—'

'No, you weren't,' Rigo argued. 'You've barely started your coffee.'

Katie's instinctive reaction was to look down at Rigo's hand on her arm. Could he feel her trembling beneath his touch?

'And you sit down too,' he instructed Antonia, lifting his hand away from Katie. 'What's wrong with you both?'

Where to begin? Katie thought, feeling like the poor relation. But Rigo had made it impossible for her to leave without appearing rude, and so reluctantly she sat down again.

Only Rigo appeared relaxed as silence stretched between them. With Antonia sulking and Rigo paying neither of them much attention, this was uncomfortable. 'So…you found me?' Katie mumbled self-consciously. She wasn't the best conversationalist at the best of times—and this was hardly that. As Rigo turned to her she was vaguely aware that the waiter was serving more coffee, as well as a soda and a piece of delicious ice-cream cake known as *semifredo* for Antonia.

'Found you?' Rigo's sexy lips pressed down. 'It appears so,' he agreed, lowering a fringe of jet-black lashes over his emerald eyes. 'I guess it must be fate.'

His direct stare made her hand shake and she quickly replaced her coffee-cup in the saucer before she spilled it.

'Of course,' he added, 'if you will choose to walk down the most popular shopping street in Rome…'

His wry look plus Antonia's raspberry and vanilla scent was a lethal combination, Katie realised, finding her gaze drawn to his sexy mouth. 'Er—yes...'

'And here was I, thinking you were back at the penthouse answering my calls—' his lips pressed down '—while all the time you were out shopping.'

By now her cheeks must be luminous crimson, Katie realised, glancing at Antonia, who, having decided to stay, was wolfing down cake as if calories never stuck to her thighs. 'I awarded myself a break—'

'I applaud your initiative, Signorina Bannister.'

A bone-melting stare over the rim of his coffee-cup accompanied this assurance.

Play with fire and you are likely to get burned, Katie reminded herself, managing to slop her own coffee over the table.

She reached for a wad of paper napkins, but Signor Ruggiero got there first.

'Allow me,' he insisted. 'Tell me, Signorina Bannister,' he said, angling his stubble-shaded chin to slant a stare directly into her eyes, 'should I want to employ you, do you think I could trust you to resist the lure of shopping in Rome?'

Was he serious? Did he think she could endure this level of tension every day? '*If* you wanted to employ me, Signor Ruggiero, I should have to warn you, I'm not free—'

'Rigo,' he reminded her. 'Ah, well,' he murmured, lips pressing down in mock-regret, 'I shall just have to find a way to live with the disappointment.' He glanced at his watch. 'We should be getting back to finish our business. What have you done about your flight?'

'I've bought an open ticket.'

'Ah, good,' he said, relaxing back. 'In that case we're in

no hurry, and you have no excuse not to join me and Antonia for dinner tonight.'

Dinner? Tonight? With Antonia and Rigo? It would take too long to list all her objections. To give herself time to come up with a watertight excuse, she smiled as she pretended to consider the offer. While she was doing that, and with exquisitely bad timing, the same testosterone-fuelled waiter placed an enormous dish of ice cream in front of her.

'Or perhaps you would prefer to eat something less wholesome tonight?' Rigo challenged, flashing a vicious stare on the hapless man. 'Ice cream, for instance?'

This was ridiculous, Katie concluded. Men were ridiculous. The waiter was still pulling those funny faces at her, while Rigo was taking the man's interest in her for real. And now both men were glaring at each other.

Because of her?

How preposterous!

CHAPTER FIVE

THIS COULD ONLY happen in Rome, Katie concluded. She knew the waiter would run a mile if she so much as showed the slightest interest in him. As far as Rigo was concerned, it was slightly different. He was the leader of the pack and brooked no competition, whether false or genuine. No one looked at a woman when Rigo Ruggiero was with her; that was Rigo's law. But he had to understand she wasn't his possession. She was an independent woman of independent means—even if those means were somewhat slim compared to his—and she was trying to enjoy her short time in Rome…or she had been up to a few minutes ago. 'Thank you for the offer of dinner,' she said, standing up, 'but I have decided to have a lazy evening by myself at the hotel—'

'The Russie?' Rigo frowned as he mentioned arguably the most exclusive hotel in Rome and probably the only one that registered on his radar.

Katie had to curb her smile when she mentioned the name of the hotel where she was actually staying. 'I can assure you, it's perfectly respectable,' she said, seeing Rigo's and Antonia's reaction to the name.

'I have no doubt,' Rigo said, looking less than convinced.

When Antonia yawned and said she might as well go home if Rigo was going to ignore her Katie seized the opportunity to suggest they reschedule their meeting for the following morning at nine. There was still plenty of sightseeing she wanted to do. 'If nine isn't too early for you?' She tried very hard not to look at Antonia.

'Nine o'clock is perfect for me,' Rigo assured her, 'but at my penthouse, not your hotel.'

As he stared at her she found the way he had seized back control arousing. But as she had never experienced this sort of power play before…

Slipping on the designer shades, he stood up so that now he was towering over her. 'And this time you shall have my undivided attention.'

Why did that sound like such a threat?

It took her entirely by surprise when he brought her hand to his lips and kissed the back of it. The touch of those warm, firm lips was an incendiary device sending streams of sensation to invade her body and blank her mind.

'Before you go, Signorina Bannister—'

She snatched her hand away. 'Yes?' She tried prim. She tried haughty. And failed miserably with both. Haughty was so foreign to her and, with those wicked eyes staring deep into her own eyes, how on earth was she supposed to fake prim?

'This is most remiss of me,' Rigo said, turning to Antonia and indicating that she should stand up too.

'What is?' Katie tensed, immediately on guard.

'I should have introduced you two to each other—'

'Which I made impossible,' Antonia cut across him to Katie's surprise, 'because I had to guzzle that delicious cake before I did another thing.'

Cake she could understand, but introductions?

'Indeed,' Rigo agreed patiently, brushing a strand of errant blonde hair out of Antonia's eyes. 'Signorina Bannister, I would like to introduce you to my spoiled little sister, Antonia...'

Losing her pout, the girl bounded round the table to give Katie a hug. 'Welcome to Rome, Signorina Bannister.' And then she found her pout again. 'Rigo never lets me meet anyone interesting.'

Interesting? Katie was so shocked she remained unresponsive for a moment. Well, this was something to report back to the girls in the office, as was the hug, and the kiss on both cheeks from Antonia. Having hugged the young girl back, she thought this had to be the perfect example of the attraction of opposites. Katie couldn't imagine there were many quiet, country secretaries in the world Antonia inhabited, and there certainly weren't any vivacious little pop-star look-alikes in hers.

Now that the barrier of believing Antonia was Rigo's girl-friend had been removed, Katie was surprised to find that conversation between them flowed easily and Antonia soon persuaded her to sit down again. Being a willowy blonde, Antonia didn't look a bit like her tough, dark-haired brother, which meant she must be the child born when Rigo's father had married Carlo's mother. He had no trouble with this relationship, so why did he hate his stepbrother? She really should pay more attention to the editorial in gossip magazines.

'So, do you really have everything you need?' Antonia prompted, giving Katie a meaningful look. 'Now that my wicked brother has kept you here in Rome, you must need to go shopping. It never occurs to you, Rigo,' she added, turning to him, 'that other people don't have a home in every city.' And when he shrugged carelessly, Antonia added, 'I bet poor Katie doesn't even have a decent toothbrush with her—'

'Well, as it happens,' Katie interrupted wryly, getting the

gist of this conversation, 'I do need to do some shopping for…essentials.'

'Lucky for you, then, that you have an expert on hand!' Antonia exclaimed, satisfied that her ruse had worked. 'You'll definitely need toothpaste and a hairbrush, and all sorts of boring stuff…'

Katie was relieved Rigo hadn't seen Antonia's theatrical wink.

'Are you offering to take Katie shopping?' he said, frowning.

'Could you spare your sister?' Katie suggested, thinking what fun it could be.

'Anyone who can keep Antonia entertained for an hour or two…' His voice faded when he noticed Antonia looking at him and Katie thought Antonia's smile had faded too. 'I'd love to go shopping with you,' she said, taking pity on the young girl, at which point Antonia quickly brightened.

'But don't forget—dinner at eight,' Rigo reminded them as the two girls collected up their things.

'Really, I'm perfectly happy eating in my room at the hotel,' Katie assured him, sending an apologetic smile Antonia's way.

'I wouldn't hear of it,' Rigo insisted with a decisive shake of his head. 'Antonia is right. You must allow me to make up for leaving you so abruptly this afternoon—'

'I *must*?' The challenge flew from Katie's blunt mouth before she could stop it, which made Antonia laugh.

'It seems to me, you have met your match, Rigo,' she told her brother in Italian.

Rigo didn't look nearly so pleased and Katie took note of the cold look in his eyes. Fortunately, she had the perfect excuse. 'It's very kind of you, but I don't have anything to wear.'

'Antonia is taking you shopping.'

'Yes, for a toothbrush.'

And now Antonia was looking at her as if she had gone completely mad.

'I really don't need anything special to wear for a night in at my hotel…' Seeing Antonia's disappointment, Katie knew she had to backtrack. 'But I do need a really good toothbrush…'

'And I know every toothbrush shop in Rome,' Antonia assured her, smiling again now she had got her shopping companion back onto the right track.

It was easy to see why Antonia was spoiled, Katie concluded. Antonia had her brother's charm, only with Antonia that charm didn't have an off switch. But there was another look in Antonia's eyes—a defensive look, almost as if the young girl was used to being let down.

'And if we should see some lovely dresses on the way?' Antonia pressed, glancing anxiously at her brother.

Katie tensed. Shopping for clothes was an absolute no. What if Antonia saw her scars? What if, in her enthusiasm, Antonia burst into the changing room and screamed? She couldn't do that to such a vulnerable young girl. She couldn't risk it. She had to renege on her promise, even with Antonia smiling hopefully at her.

She would have to tread very carefully here, Katie realised with concern.

She was barely given time to worry before Rigo offered her a way out. 'Buy something nice for both of you,' he said, glancing at Katie as he pressed a pile of money into Antonia's hand.

'Oh, no.' Katie held up her hands. This was something she drew the line at. 'I couldn't possibly accept your money—'

'But I can,' Antonia said, quickly securing the wad in her super-sized handbag.

'Please,' Rigo insisted. 'It's the very least I can do after treating you so badly, Signorina Bannister—'

'The very least,' Antonia assured him with a frown.

'So…dinner at eight?' he said, turning to Katie. 'Don't forget—I'll pick you up at your hotel.'

This was a man to whom no one had ever dared to say no, Katie concluded. 'I'll be eating in my room tonight,' she reminded him pleasantly.

'After you go shopping with me,' Antonia insisted.

'Of course,' Katie reassured Antonia with a smile. She was beginning to feel like the bland filling in a particularly glamorous sandwich. 'I can't wait to go shopping…for a really good toothbrush,' she added for Rigo's benefit, 'and I look forward to concluding our business tomorrow morning,' she finished with absolute honesty. How much more of this high-octane challenge could she take? To make the point that she wasn't the type to take advantage, as the waiter threaded nimbly past she picked up their bill from his tray.

Which Rigo stole from her hand with a warning glance.

The shopping trip with Antonia exceeded Katie's wildest expectations.

Did it come any wilder? She had no idea how to rein in Antonia's enthusiasm—this was shopping on a heroic scale. Just as she had anticipated, Antonia ignored her insistence that Katie only needed a toothbrush and, as everything in the shops was so stylishly arranged…

But Katie knew she'd reached her boundary when Antonia called her over to look in one particular window. Katie had never seen so many exclusive boutiques in one place and had been lagging behind. The specialist shops they were browsing now sold everything under the sun and more besides—

things that should only come out at night, like garments of a frilly nature, for example…

Katie stood awestruck, taking in the breathtaking display. Cobweb-fine lace and slinky satin vied with cotton so delicate you could see through it—and many of the items were trimmed with eye-catching diamanté and pearl. 'Oh, no, I couldn't,' she said when Antonia tried to persuade her to go with her into the shop. 'You go in if you want to,' Katie said, hanging back.

'Not without you,' Antonia insisted, taking hold of Katie's arm. And before Katie knew what was happening Antonia had marched her into the shop, announcing, 'It's time you spoiled yourself.'

Antonia immediately summoned assistants over to help them. 'Not with Rigo's money,' Katie said, determined to resist Antonia's enthusiasm.

'But you've got your own money, haven't you?'

How to say, yes, but I need it for bills? Though she could do with some pyjamas for tonight, Katie conceded, mouth agape as she stared around. Did people wear these things?

'Well, that's a start,' Antonia approved when Katie suggested that perhaps pyjama trousers and a vest to sleep in that night might be a good idea.

What the assistants brought them was the furthest thing from Katie's mind, but as she handled the delicate garments her longing for them grew. They were in such glorious colours—turquoise, cerise, lemon and lavender trimmed with baby-pink. It went without saying that she would never find anything like this at home.

Did she have to wear winceyette all the time? Katie wondered, staring at her plain face in the mirror. As no one else was going to see the satin shorts and revealing strappy top she liked, surely it wouldn't hurt to buy a set…or two?

Giving herself the excuse she wouldn't risk offending Antonia, she asked the assistant to wrap them up.

'And what about these?' Antonia cut in, pointing out some racy underwear.

'Oh, no…' Shaking her head, Katie blushed furiously, knowing she would never have the opportunity to wear it. She had only seen underwear like that in magazines before.

'You can't wear white cotton all your life,' Antonia observed, staring frankly into Katie's eyes.

'How do you…' Katie's words froze on her lips. Was she that obvious?

'They are expensive,' Antonia continued thoughtfully as she studied the set, 'so you really should try them on before you buy them.'

Alarm bells rang in Katie's head. She had pushed all her hang-ups to the back of her mind, she realised as Antonia waited for her to do the obvious and ask to use the changing room. 'No,' she said firmly, knowing she had to get out of this somehow. She'd say she'd changed her mind. 'There's no need…'

'Oh, well, if you're sure,' Antonia said, completely misunderstanding her. 'We'll take these too, please—'

Katie didn't speak up quickly enough and as she watched Antonia handing the racy garments to the assistant they were being wrapped up before she knew it.

She could have stopped this at any time, Katie admitted to herself, but the bare truth was, she didn't want to stop it. She wanted to take the underwear back to her hotel where she could try it on with no one seeing her scars, and pretend.

To make matters worse, the assistant, having secured Katie's purchases in fuchsia-pink tissue paper, was lowering them reverently into a pale pink carrier bag decorated with the logo of a naked woman seated in a champagne glass.

'Very subtle,' Katie commented wryly as the two girls left the shop. She loved the bag, but part of her wished the logo didn't have to be on both sides.

Linking arms with her, Antonia gave Katie a squeeze. 'We're going to buy a few more things for you, and then I'm under strict instructions from Rigo to put you in a taxi back to your hotel— Oh, look,' she broke off excitedly, 'there he is now…'

Katie gasped to see Rigo coming out of a menswear shop across the street. He was just pushing his sunglasses back on his nose and spotted them right away. He came over. How could she hide the carrier bag?

He stood in front of them, making every part of her sing with awareness. But worst of all he was staring at the brazen proof that her latest purchase had not been a toothbrush.

'I trust you girls found everything you needed in the shops?' he said, straight-faced.

She could read the subtext and blushed violently. 'Yes, thank you,' she said, raising her head to meet his gaze. 'And, as you can see, I'm carrying some of Antonia's bags for her.'

Rigo's amused stare called her a liar.

CHAPTER SIX

When Rigo left them Katie and Antonia continued their shopping, but there was a frisson of understanding between them now. Neither girl commented on the change Rigo had made to their day, but they were aware of how profoundly he affected them, each in their own way. It brought them closer, though it took a little time when he'd gone to recapture the rhythm of easy friendship they had established. When they did Katie almost forgot to buy her toothbrush.

The fun of being with someone as non-judgemental and as warm as Antonia was so unexpected Katie threw herself into the expedition with enthusiasm, and by the time she returned to her small hotel room there were lots more packages. Antonia had shown Katie the best shopping in Rome—small boutiques hidden in side-streets around the Piazza Navona and Campo di Fiori, and other places that were well off the regular tourist beat, and when they both finally admitted defeat, they had more coffee and ice cream at a café on Via Acaia, where Katie thought the lemon cream or *crema al limone* and the scrunchy chocolate *stracciatella* were to die for. She insisted before they parted on buying Antonia a special little gift to say thank-you to Rigo's sister for being so kind to her.

It was obvious Antonia adored her brother. To hear Antonia talk you would think Rigo was a saint—but, as Antonia appeared to be the chief recipient of Rigo's generosity, Antonia could hardly be called impartial.

Katie smiled, remembering Antonia's pleasure when Katie bought her a small aqua leather-backed journal. To prove the point, Antonia had started scribbling in it right away, and when she secured the small gilt lock she had exclaimed, 'Thank you so much for today, Katie…'

And when it was she who had everything to thank Antonia for…

Katie's heart went out to the teenager, who on the face of it appeared to have everything a girl of Antonia's age could possibly want, but she suspected all Antonia really wanted was a little of her brother's time.

Time. That was what so many rich and successful people lacked, Katie mused, moving the faded curtain back to stare out of the window. They had none to spare when it came to those closest to them.

'We are friends, aren't we?' Antonia had demanded fiercely when they parted. Whatever she thought of Antonia's brother Katie had put to one side, promising Antonia they would be friends forever.

After a rocky start it had been a good day, Katie reflected, turning back to look at her purchases spread out on the bed. Now her smile was one of disbelief. What on earth had possessed her? Antonia was the simple answer. Thanks to Rigo's sister, it was goodbye brown, hello colour! And in the open-air market Katie had spotted a silk dress swinging on its hanger in the breeze. In a bright gypsy-rose print, it had long sleeves and a short, flirty skirt, and there was a sexy cut-out panel at the midriff—one of the few places where she could afford to show some skin. With the option of trying it on taken away from her, she hadn't been able to resist. She had added a couple of tops and a shawl to her haul, as well as a pair of jeans—something she had never owned before.

'And trainers,' Antonia had insisted, determined that Katie should update her image. 'For someone who is only twenty-five, you dress too old,' she had commented with all the blunt assurance of a teenager.

And that was me told, Katie reflected, smiling as she left the bedroom to enter her small *ensuite* bathroom. She had treated herself to some foam bath too. It was a cheap way to turn even the most basic of bathrooms into a better place. And now there was nothing more for her to do but soak and dream until she felt like ringing downstairs for Room Service.

Bliss.

Now he remembered why it was so long since he had treated Antonia to dinner. Nothing was quite right for his teenage sister. Their table could have been better—it was too near the door. Their fellow diners were too stuffy—meaning most of them were over twenty-five and had brushed their hair before coming out. She sniffed everything that arrived at their table with suspicion as if three Michelin stars was no guarantee at all, and to top it off she ordered chips with ketchup on the side, leaving everything else on her plate.

But his worst crime, apparently, was *abandoning* Katie in Rome on her first night in the eternal city.

'Katie?'

'Signorina Bannister insisted I call her Katie,' his sister informed him smugly as he raised a brow.

'May I remind you that Signorina Bannister is on a business trip and will shortly be returning home? She was invited to join us tonight, but she refused. And that's an end of it, Antonia.'

And might well have been, had he not felt his conscience prick.

His sister lost no time in turning that scratch into an open wound. 'Do you know where she's staying?' Antonia demanded with her customary dramatic emphasis. '*How* can you leave Katie in a place like that? Can you *imagine* what the restaurant is *like*?'

Yes, he could, unfortunately.

And so the rant went on until he couldn't face another mouthful. Laying down his cutlery, he demanded, 'What do you suggest I do, Antonia?'

Antonia appeared to be studying the menu, and he imagined she was choosing a pudding until she exclaimed, 'A picnic!'

Before he could stop her she called a waiter over.

'Take it to Katie—deliver it,' she begged him, clutching his wrist in her excitement as the waiter hurried away with the order.

'Don't be so ridiculous—'

'You don't even have to see her—'

'I have no time for this nonsense, Antonia,' he snapped impatiently, shaking her off.

'You never have time,' she flared. 'Katie gave me a whole afternoon of her time, which is more than you ever do.' Her voice was rising and people were staring at the small drama as it unfolded. 'Why can't you do something different, for once?'

'I do something different every day, Antonia. It's called business. It's what keeps you in the style to which you're accustomed.'

Thrusting back her chair, his sister took her performance to its ultimate conclusion: The Dramatic Exit. 'Well, if you won't take the picnic to Katie, I will,' she declared, storming off.

They had the attention of the whole restaurant now. As Antonia stalked away he stood up, politely murmuring an apology to those people closest to him. They should be glad of the free entertainment, he concluded as strangers exchanged knowing looks.

He caught up with Antonia at the door. 'Stop this, Antonia. You're drawing attention to yourself—'

'Oh, no!' she gasped theatrically, clutching her chest.

'I will not allow you to walk the streets of Rome alone at night—'

'That's why you must take the picnic to Katie.'

The waiter chose this moment to bring out the hamper—to a touching soundtrack of Antonia's inconsolable sobs. 'Have you no shame?' Rigo murmured, realising this was a ploy Antonia had contrived to get her own way.

'None,' his sister whispered back triumphantly.

Pressing money into the man's hand, he thanked him for his trouble. Then he escorted Antonia outside. Bringing out a handkerchief, he mopped her eyes. 'Stop crying immediately,' he insisted. 'Acting or not, you know I cannot bear to see you cry. If you're so concerned about Signorina Bannister's diet, I *will* deliver this hamper. But not before I see you safely home.'

He thought his voice had been quite stern, but he could have sworn there was a smile on Antonia's face as he helped her into the car.

Katie had put on her new dress, and after examining it from every angle in the full-length mirror had reassured herself that everything she might want to hide was hidden. It was the perfect dress for the perfect night out in Rome. Not that she was going anywhere, but there was no limit to her dream. In fact the dream was so real she had put her shawl and bag on the bed, as if all she had to do was snatch them up last minute before leaving the room.

In reality her skin prickled with apprehension just at the thought. She might be wearing her new dress, but she was frightened to leave the room wearing it.

She performed an experimental twirl, loving the way the silk felt against her skin. There wasn't room for much of a twirl, because the hotel room was very small. She had no complaints—it was functional and clean, which was all she needed.

But Rome was waiting for her outside—and tomorrow she was going home...

Moving back to the window, she stood a little to one side, staring out at the busy street scene far below. There was an open-topped tour bus that stopped right outside the hotel, and she could see people chatting to each other as they waited to board. Across the road was a family-oriented pizzeria with a neon sign. That looked fun too. Perhaps they would have room for one later...

Stop, Katie told herself firmly, pressing back against the wall. It was one thing buying into the pretence of going out and something else when she started to believe it might happen. But pretending had been fun. She had even styled her hair a number of different ways—up and down—but she had forgotten how thick and glossy even boring brown hair could be when it was washed, conditioned and blown dry with more than her usual care and even for a fantasy night out she wouldn't want to look too obvious. Her everyday style was safest, she had concluded. Over the years she had perfected the technique of brushing her hair straight back before twisting it tightly and securing it with a single tortoiseshell pin.

But she wouldn't change a thing about the dress, Katie mused, smoothing her palms over the cool silk. She eased her neck, imagining Rigo at her side…or perhaps behind her with his hands resting on her shoulders. She would lean against him…relax against him, until he dipped his head and kissed her neck as he murmured that he loved her…

She held the image in her heart for a moment, before opening her eyes and facing reality. Rigo was eating dinner with Antonia, after which he would go home to bed.

Antonia had so much to give, Katie reflected, but her brother had no time to take anything from anyone, because Rigo was too busy driving forward…

Rigo…

Leaning back against the wall again, she closed her eyes. He would look like a god tonight. She imagined him wearing a dark tailored suit with a crisp white shirt and discreet gold cuff-links. The elegant look would show off his tan, his rugged strength and the power of his commanding personality. His hair would be freshly washed with thick, inky black waves lapping his brow and his cheekbones. He had the thickest, strongest hair she had ever seen, and though Rigo's grooming would be impeccable he would still carry that air of danger that made him irresistible, and like a magnet he would draw the gaze of every person in the room.

And she still wasn't going out, Katie told herself bluntly, opening her eyes as she pulled away from the wall. And whichever way she looked at it dreams could never compete with the reality of Rigo.

No, but dreams were safe, Katie's sensible self reminded her. With dreams there were no complications, no embarrassing moments, no…

Nothing.

But…

The mini-bar was full of chocolate, so it wasn't all bad.

* * *

He'd taken Antonia home and then gone back to the pent-house to change into jeans and a casual shirt before setting off again to Katie Bannister's hotel. He felt tense. Wishing-he-didn't-have-to-do-this tense? Expectant tense? He couldn't tell. He only knew they hadn't got off to the best of starts and Katie Bannister was alone in Rome. He wanted her to relax. He wanted to relax.

No, he didn't, Rigo conceded as he shouldered open the door of the small, dingy hotel. Relaxing was the last thing on his mind. He didn't have anything half so worthy in mind for Katie Bannister. His hunting instincts had brought him here. He couldn't get her out of his head, the contradictions—the primness, weighed against the logo on a shopping bag from one of the sexiest lingerie stores in Rome. Her excuse that it belonged to Antonia was a lie. He'd driven Antonia home and unless his little sister had eaten the bag she certainly didn't have it with her. Since then his imagination had dressed Signorina Bannister in lace and silk—which, bearing in mind he'd only seen her in an ugly brown suit before, had been quite a startling revelation.

He approached the reception desk with his package and made his request.

'*Mi dispiace*, I'm sorry, Signor Ruggiero, but there is no reply from Signorina Bannister's room.' The man behind the desk shrugged as he replaced the telephone receiver.

He should have known he would be recognised. It couldn't be helped. 'Could Signorina Bannister be in your restaurant?' He stared across into an uninviting and markedly empty dining room.

'We have no reservations tonight, Signor Ruggiero.'

No surprise there. 'Her room number?'

The man barely paused a beat—something to do with the

money he had just pressed into his hand, no doubt, before telling him, 'Room one hundred and ten, Signor Ruggiero.'

There was no answer when he knocked on the door. He used the house phone to ring the hotel kitchen and ask them to put Antonia's picnic in their cold room. Someone would be up right away to collect it, he was told. He waited until the porter arrived, and then he returned to room one hundred and ten. Where would Katie Bannister go this time of night?

He knocked and waited. He heard sounds from the room and knocked again.

She answered the door cautiously, leaving the security lever in place.

'How many times do I have to tell you I don't bite?'

'Rigo?' Her voice rose at least an octave when she gasped his name.

'Unless I have a double...' He leaned back against the wall. The corridor was narrow and they were agreeably close. Signorina Prim's sexy voice had done it again, he registered, enjoying the sensation.

'What do you want?' she whispered nervously through the gap.

Admittedly this wasn't the type of reception he had anticipated, or was used to, but then Katie Bannister wasn't his usual type of date. 'We had a dinner engagement, if you remember?'

'I told you I'd be eating dinner in my room.'

And he had chosen to ignore that. 'You haven't eaten yet?' he said with surprise. 'It's nine o'clock.' As if anyone in Rome ate before nine.

'I didn't say I haven't eaten.' She opened the door a little wider and bit her lip.

She looked cute. 'You didn't say you have eaten,' he pointed out. 'Open the door, Katie. I can't stand here all night.'

The bar slid back and the door opened, but instead of standing to one side to let him in, she retreated into the shadows at the far end of the room.

CHAPTER SEVEN

'GOOD EVENING, SIGNORINA Bannister. I trust I find you well?'

'Good evening, Rigo,' she said shyly, remaining pressed back against the wall.

'You look nice.' He closed the door softly behind him. Nice? She looked beautiful, which raised a number of questions. But taking things at face value to begin with, he knew her taste in lingerie and had already dallied with erotic images, but seeing this new, softer side had unexpectedly brought out the best in him. Until his suspicions raced to the fore. 'I beg your pardon for calling so late.'

She glanced at her wristwatch.

'And it seems you were going out?' After refusing his dinner invitation, was it possible the waiter won her over?

'I wasn't going anywhere.'

Was that a wistful note in her voice? 'But the dress?'

'I was just trying it on.' Raising her chin, she looked at him steadily. 'I bought it today. I don't know what I was thinking—'

'That it suited you?' he suggested.

'Do you really think so?'

In that moment she was like a child, and as pleasure flashed across her face she touched his heart, something that hadn't happened in a long time. 'Yes, I do. You look great.'

Fragile, proud and womanly he didn't say. Even her profile with her hair scraped back so tightly was delicately appealing.

'I was going to return it—'

'Don't you dare—I mean, do as you like,' he said casually as she looked at him in surprise. She wasn't the only one to be surprised by the force of his reaction. 'So…you're not going out, but you'd like to?'

'Not really…' She made a little hand gesture. 'I'm fine right here—'

'But a dress like that is meant to be worn by a beautiful woman on a warm evening in Rome.'

She all but said, that rules me out.

'An evening just like this…'

She laughed nervously as he gestured towards the mean little window. 'It's very kind of you, Rigo—'

'I don't do kind. I'm hungry.'

'But you just ate with Antonia—'

'Fiddly food?' He dismissed the gourmet feast he'd enjoyed with an airy gesture. 'And, as you can see—' he ran a hand down his casual shirt and jeans '—I'm off-duty now.'

She risked a laugh.

'I'm thinking pizza—though Antonia sent a picnic for you, if you prefer?'

'I love your sister!' she exclaimed impulsively. 'Only Antonia would think of a picnic.'

He gave her a wry look. He couldn't deny Antonia held the record for delivering the unexpected, and doing it well. 'The hotel has it in their cold room—but I'm thinking real Roman pizza.'

He could see she was tempted.

'I'd have to get changed.'

'Into what?'

Her warning look told him not to make light of this because she hadn't made up her mind yet.

'You'd have to leave the room while I get changed.'

'I'm not going anywhere. And you're not getting changed. You're fine as you are. Here, grab this.' Snatching up a shawl from the bed, he tossed it to her.

She caught it.

'Now throw it round your shoulders and let's get out of here.'

He gave her no chance to change her mind. Opening the door, he ushered her through.

This wasn't a walk on the wild side—it was absolute lunacy. The moment they left the hotel she felt naked. She never went out in a flimsy summer dress. To do so with Rigo made her feel more vulnerable than ever.

And to think of all the things she could have done to get out of this—she could have played the tiredness card, the headache, the work to finish, the phone call to make, but instead she had fallen under Rigo's spell. It didn't help that he looked like a man from the pages of myth and legend. In casual clothes he was more aggressively virile than she had ever seen him and fitted perfectly into the template of ancient Rome. With his stern features and rugged, fighting form, he could have been a gladiator; the best.

As Rigo eased his pace to accommodate her shorter stride Katie wondered how safe her heart was. As he glanced at her with eyes like back-lit emerald that promised all the danger she could take, she concluded it was her chastity she should be concerned about. Could she trust herself to behave?

Did she want to behave?

If she was ever going to experience lovemaking, wouldn't it be better to do so under the tutelage of an expert?

'I'm not moving too fast for you, am I?'

Her cheeks flushed pink with guilty thoughts. 'Not at all...' Not as fast as my fantasies would have you move.

The dangerous smile creased his cheeks and fired every nerve in her body. She was transfixed by lips that curved in a firm and knowing smile. He knew how to walk close but not touching. He must know how that made her long to touch him—

And right on cue her scars shouted a stinging hello. They might be covered by the prettiest silk fabric, but they hadn't gone away and were as ugly as ever. And now the doubts crept in. What if Rigo put his arm round her shoulders? What if his hand strayed down her back? What if he pressed those long, lean fingers against her? He couldn't help but feel the ridges. And her final thought? What if he was repulsed by them?

Breathe deeply and stay calm, Katie's sensible self advised. Rigo hadn't made any attempt to touch her and was unlikely to do so. She might be dressed up by her own small-town standards, but she was hardly a femme fatale. This outing was merely a courtesy Signor Rigo Ruggiero was extending to a representative of the legal firm handling his brother's will.

To prove it, they were walking alongside each other like a couple of friends—

Friends?

Friends looked at each other's crotch, did they?

Katie wished her inner voice would shut up and stop acting as her conscience. Rigo's gaze might never stray, but she hadn't perfected the technique of not looking at something so prominently displayed.

What else was he supposed to do with it? her inner voice piped up again.

OK, so he was blessed in every department, but she didn't

have to fixate, did she? Hadn't she worked out yet how acute his senses were? Did she want him to know she had a crush?

They had reached a crossing and he stared down at her. 'Are you OK?'

'Perfectly.' But she flinched when he put his hand in the small of her back to steer her across the road.

'Relax.'

Yes, relax. What did she think? That he had X-ray vision now?

'You really are tense...'

She gasped as he caught hold of her hand and quickly concealed it in a cough. Was this supposed to help?

'What are you doing?' he said as she broke free. 'The traffic is dangerous and unpredictable—'

Like Rigo. 'Sorry—I promise to be more careful.'

'I'll make sure of it.' He locked his arm around her shoulder.

For a moment she didn't breathe. Surely he must feel her trembling? And then he walked her straight past the pizza place.

'That's for tourists,' he said as she turned her head.

She had to scurry along to keep up with his easy, loping stride. That wasn't easy on legs that felt like jelly. For the first time in her life she longed for her cheap suit. It might be ugly, but both the fabric and the shape were concealing. 'So where *are* we going?'

'First, we take a bus—'

'A bus?' He really was the master of surprises, she registered silently.

'Unless a tour bus isn't grand enough for you, Signorina Bannister?'

'It's fine by me.' And was what she had wanted to do all along. 'I'm just surprised you take buses...'

'You mean, a man like me?' he said. Rigo's face creased in a smile. 'I know every way there is to get around Rome.' He helped her onto the running board. 'I haven't always travelled by private jet.' He broke off to dig in the pocket of his jeans for some money to pay their fare.

A curtain lifted. She saw him clearly as the youth who had come to Rome with nothing and had made his fortune here. She only realised she was still frowning as she thought about it when Rigo dipped his head to stare her in the eyes. Her heart thundered a warning. 'It's only a bus trip costing a few euros,' he said. 'You can deduct it from your fee, if that makes you feel better?'

Better he misunderstood than read every thought in her head too clearly. 'I'm good—'

'Please allow me to reassure you that I have no intention of compromising your professional duties in any way, Signorina Bannister.'

He made her laugh. His humour was more dangerous than she knew.

And then the self-doubt crept in. Was that what he thought of her? She was all duty and no fun? That equalled dull in any language.

He chivvied her up the stairs. 'The view is better up here.'

He persuaded her to take a seat at the front. She checked her skirt was pulled down as she sat. No wonder Rigo thought her dull. He was easygoing, charming and, even in denim jeans and a fitted casual shirt clinging tenaciously to every hard-wired inch of his impressive torso, he was sex on two strong muscled legs. While she was—

'Dolcezza.'

'What?' He was paying her a compliment. Why couldn't she just accept it?

Maybe because, having sprawled across the seat next to her, Rigo was looking at her in a way that made her cheeks burn.

'I like the new look, Katie; keep it.'

Before she could reprimand him for using her first name he draped an arm around her shoulder and drew her close. 'Though I think you should be tempted to let your hair down.'

The murmured words sent her senses haywire as his warm breath connected with her ear. That must be why it took her a moment to realise what he meant to do, and by then it was too late. As he removed the single tortoiseshell pin from her hair it cascaded around her shoulders.

'*Bene,*' he said, sitting back.

'My hair ornament, please.' She held out her hand.

'You can have it back later,' he said, putting it in his pocket. 'Now concentrate on the view.'

As he spoke, what might well be his ancestral home hove into view. The Colosseum—the ancient amphitheatre with its pitted archways glowing eerily with honeyed light.

But as Rigo related the history of the building she was gripped. Discovering the man beneath the public face was a non-stop revelation. His depth aroused her to the point where it was no longer possible to concentrate. She had to shift position to ease the ache inside her. She wanted to remain immune to him and soon realised what a pointless exercise that was. What she really wanted was for Rigo to touch her intimately. All this she accepted whilst maintaining a serious conversation about ancient Rome.

CHAPTER EIGHT

EXPANDING HER FANTASIES as the tour bus drove on into the night allowed for Rigo touching her skilfully and persistently, rhythmically and expertly, until she found release. It didn't stop there. They might experiment in the Colosseum—before a concert, maybe. As her gaze slipped to his lips while he talked she indulged in another image—one that stirred her more than most: she was being held down by Rigo while he subjected her to a lengthy feast of pleasure. She wanted sex with him. Which meant it was time to put a stop to such a dangerous fantasy.

Thankfully, Rigo provided the exit she had been looking for, when he thanked her for giving Antonia such a good day.

'It was my pleasure. Your sister is wonderful—and in fairness, it was Antonia who went out of her way to give me a good time.'

'Well, my little sister sees it another way. Come on, we get off here,' he said, standing up.

'But we're not back at the hotel.' She looked in vain for a landmark she recognised.

'Pizza?' Rigo reminded her.

But they seemed to be in the middle of nowhere. Katie frowned.

'I asked the bus driver to drop us here. Come on.' Rigo indicated that she must go ahead of him.

She disembarked onto a dimly lit street. Could this be right? Her skin prickled with apprehension.

'I don't have a clue where I am,' Rigo murmured.

But when she glanced at him in alarm, he smiled.

'You're teasing me—'

'Would I?'

She refused to hold that gaze, and stared instead at the bus as it drove away.

'I haven't always lived in the best part of Rome.'

She couldn't resist the hook and followed him.

'When I left my home in Tuscany and came to Rome I found myself in the Monti—all narrow lanes and steep inclines. It's where craftsmen ply their trade and there was always plenty of casual work for a strong boy from the country.'

By now she was consumed with curiosity. To learn about this other side of Rigo was irresistible.

'Is this our destination?' she said when he stopped walking on the high point of a bridge spanning the River Tiber. As she stared into Rigo's dazzlingly handsome face, waiting for his reply, she got another feeling—he enjoyed showing off his city to someone who wouldn't mock him for how poor he'd been. He still liked these offbeat trails to places that held no appeal for the fashionistas.

He was resting his hands on the stone balustrade, staring out across the river. Her heart picked up pace as he turned to look at her. Suddenly it didn't matter where they were going, and as crazy as it might seem they had reached at least one erotic destination, which was enough for her.

He broke the spell. 'Come on.' Straightening up, he reached for her hand and this time she didn't resist him. She even managed to persuade herself that it made perfect sense for Rigo to take her hand if they had to cross a busy main road. What did she know about Roman traffic? What did anyone know? Even the Romans didn't know. No one on earth could predict the unpredictable.

She shrank against him, glad of his protection as cars and scooters buzzed around them like angry bees. This contact with Rigo was the most foreplay she'd ever had. On that short journey to safety on the other side tiny darts of pleasure raced up her arm and spread...everywhere.

Rigo led her way up some stone steps that curved steeply around the outside of an ancient lookout tower. A pair of these towers marked either end of the bridge. 'This is the best place in Rome to watch the fireworks,' he explained, 'and it's free.'

She saw the boy he must have been—a boy who hadn't wasted time wailing about his fate, but who had squeezed the last drop of enjoyment out of his new life. And the way her heart swelled in admiration was a very worrying development indeed.

At the top of the tower she had to stop to catch her breath and, resting her arms on the warm stone, she leaned over the battlements.

'Since when can you fly?' Rigo demanded, pulling her back.

Having someone look out for her felt so good and as he stared down even breathing was difficult. He was close enough now for her to feel his body heat warming her.

She turned away. She wasn't sure how to deal with her feelings or this situation. She was going home tomorrow. They were complete opposites. This was one casual night in Rigo's life, but her life could be changed for good—

'Open your eyes, Katie, or you'll miss the fireworks.'

There was so much sensation dancing through her veins she barely registered the first fantastic plumes of sparkling colour. And then Rigo reached over her shoulder to point out some more, and as he did so he brushed her cheek. It made her turn and now their faces were only millimetres apart.

She looked away, but not quickly enough. A darkly amused stare was her reward. He must know how strongly she was attracted to him. Did he also know how frustrated she was? Or what agony it was for her to be this close to him? Or that he made her body ache with need and longing?

He pulled back when the fireworks were over, allowing her to breathe freely again. She gulped in air enough to say, 'Thank you for bringing me here.'

'It isn't finished yet.' Spanning her waist with his hands, Rigo turned her to face the river.

There was no way to express her feelings towards what she could see, or what she could sense. Fireworks were falling from the sky, replacing the streamers of moonlight on the river with a dancing veil of fire. And there was fire in her heart.

Leaving the bridge, they walked deeper into the old part of the city. 'Ancient palaces!' Katie exclaimed with pleasure, staring about.

'Once this was a very grand area indeed,' Rigo confirmed, 'and now I have another surprise for you.' As he spoke he opened a street door and a blaze of light and heat burst out.

And good cooking smells, Katie registered, inhaling appreciatively as Rigo held the door open for her. He had brought her to a small, packed pizzeria where the noise of people enjoying themselves was all-enveloping.

'Don't worry,' he said, dipping his head to speak to her when he saw her hesitation, 'you'll be safe with me.'

He had also guessed correctly that she rarely went out, Katie thought wryly. She was glad of Rigo's encouragement.

There was a tiny dance floor on which a number of couples were entwined and a small group of musicians tucked away in a corner. Surrounding this, tables with bright red gingham cloths were lit by dripping candles rammed into old wine bottles.

'Do you like it?' Rigo shouted to her above the noise.

'I love it.' And she loved the feel of his arm around her shoulders.

The party atmosphere was infectious, but she was shy. Without Rigo she would never have ventured into a place like this. But when she took a proper look around and re-alised that all the other customers were as down-to-earth as she was, she relaxed. This certainly wasn't the type of night-life she had imagined Rigo would indulge in. And she liked him all the better for it.

'Will you stop trying to tuck your hair behind your ears?' he said as they waited for a seat.

'I'm just not used to it hanging loose—'

'Then you should be. You have lovely hair. Leave it alone,' he insisted. 'You look fine. Ah—' he stepped forward as a portly man dressed in chefs trousers bustled over to them '—I'd like you to meet my friend Gino.'

Katie gathered Gino was the patron.

'Rigo! Brigante!' he exclaimed, clapping the much taller man on the back. 'Why is it I can't get rid of you?'

Katie suspected that both men knew the answer to that, judg-ing from the warmth in their eyes as they stared at each other.

'And who is this?' Gino demanded, turning his shrewd, raisin-black stare Katie's way.

'This is Signorina Bannister…an associate of mine.'

'An associate?' Gino gave Katie an appreciative once-over before shaking hands with her. 'You must think a lot of your associate to bring Signorina Bannister to meet me?' He looked at Rigo questioningly, but Rigo's shrug admitted nothing.

'Signorina Bannister is in need of real Italian pizza be-fore she leaves Rome. Where else would I take her, Gino?'

'Where else indeed?' Gino agreed. 'And for such a beautiful *signorina* I have reserved the best table in the house.'

'But you're full,' Katie observed worriedly. She didn't want to cause anyone any trouble. 'And how could you know we were coming?'

'I don't need to know,' Gino informed her, touching his finger to his nose. 'I keep my own special table ready at all times for my *speciale* guests…'

Before she could stop him Gino had whisked away her shawl. 'Oh, no!' Katie exclaimed, reaching for it, feeling suddenly naked again.

'You won't need a shawl here,' Gino assured her. 'It's always too hot in my restaurant—'

'But I…'

Feeling exposed and self-conscious beneath Rigo's amused gaze, Katie could only stand and watch helplessly as the burly restaurateur disappeared into the cloakroom with her prized piece of camouflage equipment.

'Don't worry,' Rigo soothed. 'Gino will keep your shawl safe.'

Rigo saw her comfortably settled and then took the seat opposite, while Katie sat demurely, taking stock of her fellow diners. Every other woman around them had stripped down to bare arms and shoulders.

But they all had flawless skin—

'Do you mind if I roll back my sleeves?' Rigo said, misinterpreting her look.

He was halfway through the process and hardly needed her permission. 'Go ahead.' She tried very hard not to stare at his massively powerful forearms and concentrated instead on a formidable steel watch that could probably pinpoint their position in relation to the moon. One thing was sure—Gino was right: it was hot in here. Steaming.

'Ten o'clock.'

'I beg your pardon?' Katie swiftly refocused as Rigo spoke.

'I said it's ten o'clock. I noticed you looking at my watch.'

'I was—'

'Not because you want to go home, I hope?'

Gino saved her further embarrassment, bringing them the pizzas they had ordered. They were delicious. A thin, crispy crust baked just the way she liked it was loaded with succulent vegetables and slicked with chilli oil. Beneath that a yummy layer of zesty tomato sauce was crowned with fat globs of melted cheese. She only realised how hungry she was when she took her first bite—and there was no polite way to eat pizza when you were this hungry.

'Now you see why Gino and I became such good friends,' Rigo said, leaning forward to mop her chin. 'There was always something he needed doing—and I always needed feeding after a hard day of manual labour.'

She could understand how their friendship had been forged. 'You found a mutual need,' she said. And could have bitten off her tongue as Rigo's gaze lingered. 'Indeed,' he agreed, sitting back. 'Napkin?' he suggested.

'Good idea…' Drool was not a good look. She returned her attention determinedly to her food.

'This is only the first course, to whet your appetite.'

'Oh, no. I really couldn't eat another thing…'

'If you lived in Italy you would soon develop a healthy appetite.'

She had no doubt. But was that wise?

Katie sensibly avoided Rigo's gaze, reminding herself she was going home tomorrow.

So? Didn't that mean she should make the most of today?

There was such a festival air in the small bistro Katie was soon tapping her foot in time to the music. Gino had insisted she must try his home-made wine—how right he was. Picking up her glass, she drank the delicious ruby-red liquid down. It was so moreish. Who needed brand names when the house wine tasted like this? She immediately craved more and held out her glass for a refill. 'It tastes just like cranberry juice—'

'And packs a kick like a mule,' Rigo warned. 'So drink it slowly…'

He really did think of her as a kid sister—that, or an ancient aunt. Of course she would drink it slowly.

Well, she had meant to, but it tasted so fruity and innocent, and one more glass couldn't hurt her surely?

'And now you must dance,' Gino insisted, waltzing past with an armful of plates.

'I don't dance.' She announced this to Rigo, who didn't seem to care whether she danced or not.

'Do what you like,' he said, leaning back in his chair.

It seemed to Katie that the young women at the pizzeria had no inhibitions at all, and that their sole reason for being here was to shimmy into Rigo's eye line. Something tight curled in her stomach as she watched them flash lascivious glances at him.

'Well, *signorina*,' Gino said on his return, 'will you make an old man happy?'

It took longer than Katie had expected to focus her eyes on Gino's face, and even longer to register surprise that he was serious. Gino did want to dance with her. Suddenly Rigo's warning about the wine made sense. Her head was on straight, but the room was tilting—and now Gino was opening his arms to her.

'Go ahead,' Rigo said helpfully as the band launched into a wild tarantella.

Having stumbled to her feet, she barely had chance to exclaim, as Gino, quite literally, whisked her off her feet.

CHAPTER NINE

RIGO CUT IN.

By the time he cut in Katie was happy to forget her reservations and fall into his arms.

Gino melted away.

Had she been set up? Katie wondered. A bleary glance into Rigo's totally sober face told her precisely nothing—at least, not in her present state. This was great. She couldn't dance. She could barely stand up. And Signor Superior had been proven right. The wine had gone to her head. And now she was in danger of making a complete fool of herself.

There was nothing for it, Katie concluded. Before she fell over she had to appeal to Rigo's better nature—that was, supposing he had one. 'If you could just get me back to our table...' When cast adrift in a storm of flying heels and elbows, it didn't do to stand on your pride.

But Rigo didn't lead her off the dance floor. Couldn't he understand? Hadn't he heard her? 'I don't dance,' she complained.

She got a reaction this time. One inky brow rose in elegant disbelief but, rather than leading her to safety, he tightened his grip on her arms. 'Everyone can dance, Signorina Bannister.'

'I absolutely don't dance.' And, taking that as her cue, she broke free and attempted to totter back to their table unaided.

Thankfully, Rigo caught her in his arms just as she was on the point of lurching into a waiter. 'I'm fine.' She flapped her arms around to demonstrate this.

'Well, clearly, you're not.' So saying, he banded her arms firmly to her body.

'Let me go.' Her breath caught in her throat as she stared into Rigo's amused gaze. 'I did warn you about the wine,' he pointed out, keeping a firm hold of her.

Right now the wine was the least of her worries.

And then at Rigo's signal the music changed abruptly. From jigging up and down like frantic monkeys the couples all around them eased effortlessly into the sinuous rhythm of the rumba.

'What did I tell you?' he soothed, murmuring in her ear. 'You dance beautifully...'

How could she not when Rigo had somehow managed to mould her clumsy body to his? And Rigo could dance.

Oh, yes, he could...

By some miracle she stopped wobbling, and began to move her feet in some sort of recognisable pattern. As long as he didn't hold her too close she'd be all right. As long as his hands didn't wander to the scars on her back she could do this.

And now she was even beginning to relax, it felt so safe and good...

Not so her fantasies. They weren't safe at all. Dancing close to Rigo with all the other couples masking them gave Katie's imagination all the excuse it needed. She had everything to learn about a man's body and this was her opportunity.

As the music filled her, her senses grew ever more acute. Her body was like molten honey curling round him until Rigo changed position and her fantasies flew away.

'What's wrong?' he said as she grew tense.

'Nothing...' She took a deep breath and tried to relax, but

the magic had vanished. Rigo's hand had slipped into the hollow in the small of her back as they danced and then his fingers had eased a little higher. Good manners for him not to touch her anywhere remotely intimate, but a danger signal for her, and her head had cleared at once. There was no possibility she could relax now. Even her deepest longings stood no chance against her greatest fear. She wanted Rigo to hold her—she also wanted to be perfect. She wanted to rest unresisting in his arms, and dance and dream, and enjoy herself, but how could she with her scars?

'Katie?' Dipping his head, Rigo stared into her troubled eyes. 'If you concentrate on dancing the rest will follow.'

He couldn't know how wrong he was. But as he drew her to him there was something reassuring about him. The power of his command and the fact that she didn't want to make a scene…

His hands slipped lower. Theoretically she should be hearing more warning signals—and this time they wouldn't be connected with her scars, but her body was clamouring and she didn't want to fight it. This was like skirting the fringes of a hurricane and, instead of running as fast as she should in the opposite direction, hoping to be swept away by it.

'Let go,' Rigo murmured, encouraging her to relax.

But the damage was done and now she could think of nothing but securing her mate in the most primitive way possible. 'I'm trying to.'

If only she dared.

He was enjoying this far more than he had expected. His initial impulse had been to rescue Katie from the risk of being trampled by Gino's enthusiasm, but that was before he discovered how she felt beneath his hands. Timid, yet eager, she had everything to learn, and that in itself was irresistible.

He had to remind himself that she was going home tomorrow and there was no time for the style of initiation he had in mind. Resting his chin on her hair, he smiled as he dragged in her light, wildflower scent. It was a revelation to him to feel how Katie trembled beneath his intentionally light touch. He knew she wanted more. She proved it by moving closer, seeking contact, seeking pressure between their bodies, seeking sex.

So was Signorina Prim strait-laced and just a little drunk, or was she a dam waiting to burst? Perhaps Katie Bannister was the best actress he had ever met. She was certainly a storm loosely contained in a cage of inexperience. He knew that he should take her back to the table and call for the bill, prior to taking her back to sleep alone in her chaste, maidenly bed.

And he would…soon.

If Rigo's hands should slip lower…

Katie gulped. She was relieved that he was nowhere near her scars, of course, but he was almost cupping her bottom, which had set off a chain reaction in parts of her he mustn't know about. But how could she hide her response to him? She didn't have the experience to know. She arched her back. She couldn't help herself. She wanted to feel those big, strong hands holding her. She wanted to read all the subliminal messages that could pass between a man and a woman through the merest adjustment of a finger…

As the sultry beat of the slow, Latin American dance thrilled through her Katie found herself angling her buttocks ever more towards Rigo's controlling hands. It was a signal as old as time and one he couldn't help but read.

She exhaled raggedly as he confirmed this by adjusting the position of his hands once again. His fingertips were dangerously close now and, rather than feeling alarm, she felt small and safe, and violently aroused. She had never done anything as bold as this before, but here in the wholesome surroundings of the simple pizzeria, hidden in a mass of dancing couples, she felt free from the usual constraints. Gazing up, she met with eyes as dark and watchful as the night. Lower still she saw the sardonic smile playing around the corners of Rigo's mouth, and realised he knew.

He knew.

She closed her eyes and tried to steady her breathing, when what she really wanted to do was whisper, make love to me. But, other than in her wildest and most erotic fantasy, she would never find the courage to do that.

His senses were on fire. For the first time in his life he didn't want a dance to end. The sexual chemistry between them had surprised him. He had enjoyed teasing Katie Bannister, the girl he thought of as Signorina Prim, but now his thoughts were taking the direct route to seduction. He wasn't alone in feeling the power of this erotic spell. The other couples on the dance floor were drawn to them like moths to immolate on erotic flame. Even the musicians were swept up in this inferno of desire and, with a key change like a sigh, had re-inforced the mood.

But he didn't do one-night stands, or complications. Usually.

'You're quite a surprise to me,' he murmured, feeling her tremble as his breath brushed her ear.

'I wasn't always so dull…'

He wasn't going to argue about Katie's interpretation of dull. Sensing there was more to come, he remained silent.

'I trained to be an opera singer once.'

'Did you?' He couldn't have been more surprised and pulled back to stare into her eyes. 'What went wrong?'

He knew at once he shouldn't have asked. He hadn't meant to spoil the evening for her. Drawing her back into his arms, he held her gently and securely until she relaxed.

She'd tell him if she wanted to tell him, he reasoned. But the revelation had intrigued him. There was obviously so much more to uncover in this woman who favoured dull brown suits—perhaps an artistic diva waiting to break out. But as far as he was concerned, she must remain a shy, brown mouse who was under his protection while she was in Rome. Katie Bannister might be many things, but she was not a seductress—and even if in this sultry setting she appeared to be, it was up to him to keep things light between them and send her home as innocent as the day she had arrived in Italy.' Reluctantly he disentangled himself from her arms. *'Andiamo, piccolo topo—'*

'I am not your little mouse,' she slurred.

And then he realised that three glasses of wine was probably her annual quota back home and she had drunk Gino's firewater as if it were cordial—which almost certainly accounted for her openness about her opera training too.

'You must learn to call me Signorina Bannister,' she insisted, drawing her taupe brows together in her approximation of a fierce stare.

'Bene,' he said, happy to indulge her—at least on that one point.

'It's much better if we keep it…' She frowned as she searched for the right word.

'Formal between us?' he suggested. 'I think it's time I took you home now,' he said firmly, holding her away from him at arm's length.

* * *

Rigo's sudden change of mood from sexy to serious was so unexpected Katie blanked for a moment. Only when she finally managed to refocus did she wonder how she had ever wasted a moment thinking Rigo Ruggiero uncomplicated and fun. He was a playboy who lived every moment for the pleasure it brought him before moving on to the next distraction. Gino's genuine warmth and the restaurateur's homely restaurant must have clouded her thinking.

OK, that and the wine.

Common sense should have warned her Rigo was not the youth who had pitched up in Rome hoping to make his fortune. Rigo enjoyed these nostalgic visits but that didn't mean he was the same uncomplicated youth he'd been then.

As he frogmarched her back to the table she faced the ugly truth. She was as naïve as she had ever been and Rigo was the same playboy for whom the main attraction on tonight's menu of amusement had been an impressionable out-of-towner. He'd played the game for a while, but had soon tired of her lack of sophistication. She felt bad, because she never put herself in the way of rejection, knowing the outcome was a foregone conclusion. And the one time she had...

Katie smiled as she thanked Gino for her shawl. Rigo was already standing by the door, waiting for her. He couldn't wait to bring the evening to a close. It was up to her to pull herself together and leave with enough pride to be able to deal with him on a professional level tomorrow morning.

Taking a shower in cold reality was the swiftest antidote to male pride he knew. As he held the restaurant door for Katie her cool gaze assured him—don't worry, you won't get the chance. Tipping her chin, she walked proudly past him into the night. Even that amused him. Most women with one eye on his fortune tried harder. Katie wasn't that sort. In her eyes he was a man who preferred racing his sports car to keeping an appointment. Shallow? He was barely puddle-deep. Yes, all this he could see in Katie Bannister's cool, topaz-coloured gaze.

He only had to raise his hand and a limousine drew up in front of them at the kerb. 'Your chariot awaits, *signorina*. I plan ahead,' he said when she looked at him in surprise. 'Don't worry,' he added when her gaze flickered with alarm. 'I'll see you safely back to your hotel.'

He let his driver help her into the car, which appeared to reassure her. He took his seat in the back, ensuring he kept a good space between them. She didn't risk further conversation; neither did he. It seemed the most sensible course of action after the fire they'd ignited at Gino's. He glanced at his wristwatch and was surprised by the way time had flown. 'If you'd like to make our meeting a little later—'

'Not at all,' she interrupted in a way that drew his attention to her lips. She had beautifully formed plump pink lips. The thought of pressing his mouth against them while his tongue teased them apart stirred him. He could imagine how she would taste, and how it would feel when she wound her arms around his neck. 'In that case, I suggest we have lunch immediately afterwards—'

'Immediately after our meeting tomorrow I'll be on a plane home, Signor Ruggiero.'

He awarded her more than one brownie point for that swift riposte. 'I thought we'd agreed you'd call me Rigo?'

She didn't answer, and as she turned away to stare out of the window he found the chill between them erotic. He liked a challenge. And, even if he had decided to take her home and treat her chastity with the respect it deserved, he was a man.

She spoiled the mood by asking for her hair clip.

He shrugged and gave it to her, and then had to watch as she scraped her hair back as tightly and as primly as it would go. She only relaxed when she had completed the transformation from lovely young woman to maiden aunt.

But the obvious had always bored him, which was why Katie Bannister intrigued him. So much passion so tightly controlled could only end one way. And remembering her visit to his favourite shop—what a contrast that style of underwear would be to her precisely ordered hair. When did she intend on wearing it? Was she wearing it? What had provoked Signorina Prim into that walk on the wild side? And what would persuade her to take another walk on the wild side with him?

As if sensing the path his thoughts were taking, she looked at him shyly, but, shy or not, that look plainly said he shouldn't imagine everything had been put on this earth for his amusement.

'In another thirty-six hours,' she said, and with rather too much relish, he thought, 'I'll be back at my desk in Yorkshire—'

'In that case we'll have to work quickly,' he said.

She flashed him a concerned glance.

'I'll take you to the airport immediately after the reading of the will.'

He felt sure she would refuse this offer, but instead she said, 'Thank you, Signor Ruggiero, that will save me taking a cab.'

Katie was on tenterhooks until they reached the hotel. She couldn't wait to bury her head under a pillow and wish the night away so it could be morning and she could gabble out the contents of the will and go home to her dull, quiet, safe life. To her disappointment, for the remainder of the journey home Rigo had no trouble keeping things on a business footing and didn't speak to her at all. By the time they reached the hotel she was tied up in knots.

He escorted her across the lobby and even insisted on pressing the elevator button. When the lift doors slid open he kept his finger on that button as he said, 'Goodnight, Signorina Bannister. I hope you sleep well. And don't worry about calling a cab in the morning—I will send a car for you.'

She said thank you for the evening and then got into the lift. She wished, hoped, prayed, Rigo would step in after her. Of course, he didn't. Something she had every cause to be grateful for, Katie reasoned sensibly as the elevator door closed.

After that everything felt flat and a restless night followed. There was only one face in her dreams, which explained why her eyes were red the next morning. Her face was washed-out too, and as for her hair…

Better not to dwell on that disaster, she decided, scraping it back neatly into the customary bun before securing the severe style with the whole of a packet of hair grips.

Job done, she stared at her reflection in the mirror. Unfortunately, the image hadn't changed. She was the same ordinary person. The next task was automatic. Angling her head to stare at her naked back in the mirror, she checked her scars. Nothing had changed there either. They were still as livid, the sight of them just as stomach-churning.

What had she expected? Did she think she could wish them away?

Impatient with herself for this moment of weakness, she turned away to dress in modest brown. There was only one thing out of sync in this neat brown package, she concluded after slipping on her sensible brown court shoes, and that was some rather striking underwear, purchased from a luxury

boutique in Rome. Well, if she waited for a suitable opportunity to wear it the moths would have a feast.

Before leaving the room she slicked on some lip gloss.
Mashing her lips together experimentally, she decided to wipe
it off again. Did she want to draw attention? As no other delaying tactics sprang to mind, she drew in a deep, steadying
breath and picked up her bag.

CHAPTER TEN

HE SETTLED HIS shades in place. Zapping the lock, he swung into the car. Resting the phone in its nest, he was still talking, grim-faced and tight-lipped as he pulled away from the kerb outside the imposing hospital building. 'Yes, of course, do everything you can—whatever it takes—and please keep me informed.'

He stopped and drew breath as he cut the line. Now it was business as usual. This was his life—swinging from the charity that meant so much to him to the business that sustained it. The only difference today was that he was going to be late again for a meeting with Katie Bannister.

It couldn't be helped and he wouldn't explain the delay. He didn't want the world knowing what he did in his private time and only a very few individuals knew he was behind the charitable foundation. His only concern was ensuring confidentiality for anyone helped by the foundation. Today it had provided life-saving surgery; tomorrow he might be taking a teenager around the track in his sports car. Whatever was required he made time for—and sometimes Antonia suffered; he knew that and felt bad about it, but there were never enough hours in a day.

Antonia knew nothing about this other life. She was too young. He would never put the burden of silence on her shoulders.

Resting his unshaven chin on his arm, he waited for a gap in the traffic. Before he could placate Antonia he must meet with Signorina Prim, and learn what last thought Carlo had sent his way. Katie Bannister would be cooling her sensible heels at the penthouse, feeling justly affronted because he was late by more than an hour.

In spite of the rush-hour traffic he made it back in record time. Leaving the sports car where it was sure to be clamped and in all probability towed away, he raced into the building. He stabbed impatiently at the elevator button and barged inside the steel cage before the doors were properly open. Throwing himself back against the wall, he watched the floor numbers changing—more slowly, surely, than they had ever changed before.

Edgy didn't even begin to describe his condition. Impatience steaming out of every pore. He used the few seconds remaining to compartmentalise his thinking. He couldn't take so much anger and concern into this meeting—it wasn't fair to Katie. She didn't know about his day, or the fact that Carlo was trying to stab him one last time from the grave—how could she?

He liked her. She was a quiet little mouse, but the way she stood up to him suggested there was a spine of steel in there somewhere—who wouldn't like that? Maybe if things had been different…

But things weren't different and the elevator had just reached his floor.

She found it hard to believe Rigo would be late again. Surely, not even he could be this inconsiderate—this rude? It proved how little he thought of her professionally; in every way. She was an inconvenience and nothing more. Staring down at the busy main road framed by exquisite palaces and gardens,

Katie tried to make herself believe it didn't matter Rigo was late again. Why should she care? This was business. Lots of clients were late for business meetings—some even forgot about them entirely. Why should this be any different?

Because this appointment was with Rigo.

Because of the ache in her heart.

Because she wanted him to treat her better than the average client would treat her, and because she had allowed herself to commit the cardinal sin of becoming emotionally involved with a client—a one-sided arrangement that left her feeling daft and stupid. As she continued to beat herself up her attention was drawn to one of the large Roman car-towing vehicles. No doubt someone else's day was about to be spoiled—

'Katie.'

She whirled around as Rigo's husky voice broke the silence.

'I'm so sorry.' He strode towards her. Having burst in like a whirlwind, he spread his arms wide in a gesture of regret. 'Please accept my apologies.'

She took him in at a glance—the unshaven face, the rumpled clothes, the less than brilliant eyes. A horrible thought occurred to her, making her feel sick inside. Had he come here straight from someone's bed?

And why should she care? Was his sex life her business now?

But she did care. She cared a great deal too much. 'Rigo,' she said, extending a cool hand in greeting. 'I had almost given you up.'

'You've been well looked after, I hope?' He glanced around and relaxed when he saw her coffee.

'I've been looked after very well, thank you, and while I was waiting—'

'Yes?'

His eyes were warmer now. 'I took down some messages for you.'

'*Bene*...good.'

She crossed to the desk to pick up the notes she had made. 'One was from the PA you just sacked,' she said, turning. 'Signorina Partilora was most disappointed that you weren't here for her to deliver her message to you in person. Perhaps you'd like me to read it to you—'

'No,' he interrupted. 'That's OK. I can imagine...'

'If you're sure?' Her eyes glinted.

'Signorina Bannister,' Rigo growled, 'if I am any judge, I cannot imagine that such words would ever cross your lips.'

Then I might surprise you, Katie thought, flashing her innocent look. 'I think it's safe to say Signorina Partilora will not be working for you again,' she told him mildly.

Rigo laughed. 'What a relief. I have your cast-iron guarantee on that, do I?'

He was close enough to touch and her senses were ignited by his delicious man scent. If she could bottle that warm, clean, spicy aroma she'd make a fortune, Katie concluded. And then she would be able to walk away from a job she had no passion for.

'The will?' Rigo prompted.

'Yes, of course.' Her eyes stung with tears as she walked to the desk.

Because this was the end, Katie realised. It was the end of her Roman fantasy and the end of her fantasy life with Rigo—except she had no life with Rigo and she'd be going home after this.

Instead of sitting across from her Rigo came up behind her and put his hands on her shoulders. His touch was electric. Had he seen her eyes fill with tears? She couldn't bear the humiliation.

'I understand why you are upset and short tempered,' he said, keeping his hands in place, 'and you have every right to be angry with me. Please be assured my delay was necessary.'

She let her breath out slowly as he lifted his hands away and walked to the other side of the desk. She found it even harder to control her feelings when Rigo was nice to her, and now her nose was having a seizure, while her throat felt as if someone was standing on it. 'Shall we start?' she managed hoarsely.

'Of course,' he said.

She focused her attention on the legal documents in front of her, but the imprint of Rigo's fingers on her shoulders remained. She had to remind herself Rigo was Italian and caresses came easily to him. Such shows of emotion were practically unheard of in Katie's world—except perhaps under the office mistletoe at Christmas, when the ancient caretaker made sure she wasn't left out and always gave her a peck on the cheek.

Rigo made a sign for her to begin.

Must he sprawl across the seat? Must he look quite so sexy even in repose?

In the best acting scene of her life, she began.

Grim-faced, he listened. Carlo had left him everything? His mouth curved with distaste. He couldn't wait to find out what 'everything' entailed. He guessed debt would play some part in it. Katie caught sight of his expression and gave him a troubled glance.

Getting up from the desk, he turned his back on her. Today he could have used her soothing presence and common sense.

Today he wanted nothing more than to have this sordid business over with so he could ring the hospital. *If they didn't ring him first...*

'There's also a private letter from your stepbrother, Rigo, as well as a small package.'

Katie's soft voice cut through his thoughts and he heard her push back her chair, get up and walk across the room towards him.

'Grazie.' He turned.

'I'll leave you, shall I?' she offered, hovering uncertainly.

'No.' He held out his hand, palm up. 'Stay. Please,' he added, when her steady gaze called him to account for his brusque manner.

He walked some distance away before opening Carlo's letter. Katie could have no idea of the depths of depravity to which his stepbrother had sunk and the disgrace Carlo had brought on the family. He didn't want her to know. Why give her that as a parting gift to take home? Like his visit to the hospital earlier, none of this was Katie's responsibility. Let her return to England with her presumptions about his glittering life intact. Just so long as she left Rome as carefree as she arrived he was fine with that.

After years of practice he thought he was immune to feeling, but the sight of Carlo's familiar hand gave him a punch in the gut he hadn't expected. He glanced at Katie, who discreetly looked away. He had shut himself off emotionally years back when his father had chosen a woman and that woman's son over him. The same loneliness and isolation he'd felt then swept over him now.

He tensed, hearing Katie ask him softly, 'Are you all right?'

He nodded curtly and turned back to Carlo's letter. His heart was closed.

Wasn't it?

Dragging the usual mental armour round him, he began to read.

Rigo—

There is nothing I can say to make up for the years I stole from you, but I want to make my peace with you before I die. I'm not giving you anything that isn't rightfully yours.

Carlo.

Cryptic to the end, he thought, ripping open the small package.

The keys of the family *palazzo* in Tuscany tumbled into his hands, followed by his father's ring. He slipped on the ring and felt both the weight of responsibility it carried and an agonising longing. He had waited so long for contact with his father, and that it should come like this...

And to see his home again...his beautiful home...

He lowered the letter to his side as a well of emotion threatened to drown him.

The here and now fell away as his mind travelled back to the past. He had lived a blissful country existence at the *palazzo*, ignorant of pomp and pretension until his father fell in love and brought Carlo and his stepmother home. He had welcomed Carlo with open arms, thinking he would have a brother to share things with, only to have his youthful naïvety thrown back in his face. Carlo hadn't had time to spare for a boy much younger than him, and one who stood in the way of easy money.

'Shall I get you a drink?'

He glanced up, still a little disorientated as Katie spoke to him. 'No. Yes...a glass of water...please.'

SUSAN STEPHENS   293

'I'll go and get it for you.'

Her expression told him she understood something of what he was going through, and for the briefest of moments there was a real connection between them.

Everything had come full circle, he realised as Katie left him to pace. She was going home. He was going home. He could hardly take it in. He would have liked a bit longer to get used to the idea, but there was no time.

Katie returned a little later with a tray of coffee, hot and strong. She brought him some iced water too. He guessed she had wanted to leave him alone with his thoughts for a while.

'That's very good of you, Signorina Bannister,' he said as she laid everything out for him, 'but I should take you to the airport now.' He glanced at his watch, feeling his head must explode from everything he'd learned.

'There's time enough for that.' She busied herself making sure his coffee was poured the way he liked it.

'I thought you were in a hurry to get back to England.'

'I can't leave you like this—'

'Like what?' he demanded sharply. He didn't need her pity. What business was it of hers how he felt?

She raised her steady gaze to his and as if a veil had lifted a torrent of impassioned words poured out. 'I do this all the time, Rigo—I see this all the time. I can't stand it. I can't stand how cruel people can be to each other.'

'Then you should toughen up.'

'Or get out of the job,' she said thoughtfully.

'There is that,' he agreed, watching her as he sipped the hot, aromatic liquid.

She calmed him. Against all the odds, Katie Bannister calmed him. Dread at what the contents of the will might reveal had been replaced by shock when he'd learned that Carlo had left him the only place he cared about. The *palazzo* had been in the Ruggiero family for centuries and Carlo must have recognised this at the end, so there was some good in him after all. The question now was, could he live with the guilt of knowing the past could never be mended?

Turning away from Katie, he passed a hand over his eyes. Too much emotion.

But he was going home…

Home…

Growing elation was threatening to leave him on the biggest high he'd ever known. He wanted someone to share that feeling with. He wanted Katie to share it with him, but she was already packing up her things, a little hesitantly, he thought. 'What's on your mind?' She looked as if she was struggling with a decision.

'Oh…you know…' She flapped her hand, dismissing his concern.

'No, I don't know. I want you to tell me. What's wrong?' He was feeling increasing concern for this quiet girl who made everyone else's problems her own and yet seemed so isolated, somehow.

'You have your own problems.'

As always she made light of her own concerns. 'I just inherited an estate and a *palazzo* in Tuscany,' he pointed out. 'How bad can it be?'

'That must mean a lot to you.' All her focus was on him now.

'My birthright? Oh, you know…' He dismissed the home of his dreams, his childhood and his heart with an airy gesture.

'Don't, Rigo. You make it sound so flippant, when anyone with half an ounce of sense can see how much this means to you.'

'You can tell, maybe…' It was a turning point. He wanted the moment to last, but the best thing for Katie was for him to let his driver take her to the airport. A more unworthy part of him was reacting in the age-old way in the face of death. He wanted sex. The urge to make new life was an imperative inborn command. He wanted to have sex with Katie Bannister.

CHAPTER ELEVEN

WHAT WAS WRONG with him? After years of emotional absti-
nence, why this sudden roller-coaster ride? He'd had huge
and fantastic coups in business many times and hadn't felt a
thing. He'd learned long ago to turn his back on an inheritance he thought he'd never see again. So it wasn't the just the
palazzo in Tuscany gnawing at his gut. Was it possible this
shy, innocent girl was slowly melting his resolve and bringing emotion into his life?

He watched Katie cross the room to the desk in her neat,
precise way. Her feelings were bound up tight just like his.
He would like to see her respond to life and all its opportu-
nities, and with abandon.

'Before I go, here is the list of phone messages I took for
you,' she said in her strait-laced way. 'And don't be offended,
but while I was waiting for you I tidied up that pile of documents by your chair on the floor—'

'I meant to get round to that.'

'How many PAs have you sacked?' she asked him bluntly.

Many, but did he want to frighten her off with an idea
being born in his head? 'I'm not the easiest man to work
for,' he admitted with monumental understatement. 'I need
someone who can use their initiative and do more than answer the phone—'

'Well, lucky for you,' she cut in dryly, 'I made a list of all the written messages I found lying around.'

'Most of them written on the back of envelopes,' he said, remembering his latest PA's failure to grasp the simple fact that a desk diary could be quite a useful office tool if she remembered to use it.

'Your diary is in quite a mess,' Katie added, levelling a stare on him.

'And has been for some time,' he agreed.

'And the staff at your office…'

Could be called obnoxious; he'd admit that. 'Go on,' he prompted, feeling there was something more to come.

'Have no manners at all,' she told him frankly. 'And that's not good for your image.'

'What image?'

'Exactly.'

He missed a beat. 'Why, Signorina Bannister, I think you just revealed another side to your character.'

'Really?'

'PA—'

'Oh, no.' Shaking her head, she laughed at the thought of him offering her a job.

'Pain in the ass?'

She stared at him and then laughed again. 'For a moment there I thought you were offering me a job—'

'Do you think I'm mad?' he teased her, watching closely for a reaction. Then he told himself the idea of employing her was mad; a momentary lapse of judgement. Did he want a woman who cared so much around him?

His phone rang, bringing these thoughts to an end.

He had a brief conversation before cutting the line.

He swung around, elated. 'Now I could kiss you—'

'Let's not get carried away,' she said awkwardly, losing

no time putting the desk between them. 'I don't like to rush you, but my flight leaves at four o' clock. You've had good news, I take it?'

'The best—'

It must have been one heck of a deal, Katie concluded. 'Congratulations—'

'Congratulate the doctors, not me—'

'The doctors?'

'A friend of mine has had an operation,' Rigo told her vaguely, ruffling his thick black hair. His glance was evasive and he gave her the impression that he thought he'd said too much already.

'I hope your friend's okay?'

'The operation went really well, apparently.'

'Then that's the best news you could have.'

'And it frees me to go to Tuscany right away.'

'Don't let me keep you. I can take a cab—'

'I wouldn't hear of it. I'll arrange a driver—'

And that would be the end of everything.

Katie froze as Rigo continued chatting about flight schedules. He'd been equally matter-of-fact when they had returned from their amazing evening together, when she'd felt anything but matter-of-fact. She'd been frightened by the strength of her feelings for him—out of her depth and bewildered that feelings could be so one-sided. She had longed to return to her safe, quiet life in Yorkshire, but now the opportunity to do so had arrived she didn't want the adventure to end. She wanted to stay until she knew the secret of Carlo's will, because something told her the contents would hurt Rigo. She had to be there for him, because she cared for him, she cared for him desperately.

There was an alternative, Katie's inner voice suggested—if she was brave enough.

'I could go back now,' she blurted, clumsily interrupting him, 'or…'

'Or?' Rigo echoed.

Would her mind re-engage in time to speak with clarity, when all this man had to do to melt every bone in her body was to turn and give her that look? 'Or I could come with you…' By now she was hyperventilating to the point where she thought she might faint.

'Come with me? I thought you couldn't wait to leave Rome?'

She would have to share at least part of her reason for wanting this, Katie realised. 'Can I tell you the truth?'

'I would expect nothing less of a lawyer,' Rigo responded dryly.

'I'm not even sure I'll have a job when I get home. You see, my firm's cutting back—'

'A failing firm doesn't mean you can't get a job elsewhere.'

'I'd take my chances,' she agreed, 'but I'm not sure I even want to be a lawyer.'

Rigo's brows shot up.

'I get too involved,' she explained. 'Everyone has to constantly remind me I'm not a social worker and should concentrate on the facts—'

'But you still care.'

'Yes, I do.'

'Is that something to be ashamed of?'

'No, but it might mean I'm in the wrong job.'

He laughed. It was a short, very masculine sound. 'And you think you'd be happier working for me? I don't think so, Signorina Bannister.'

'Oh, well…' Raising her arms a little, she dropped them to

her sides. Of course Rigo didn't want her working for him. He wanted someone slick and polished at his side. But a longing inside her stirred—a longing so strong she couldn't ignore it. This might be her one chance to embrace change and adventure and, yes, see him sometimes. She drew a deep breath. 'You can't keep a PA—'

'That's true.'

'I might not have the makings of a good lawyer, but I am incredibly organized.'

'And you care too much about people—'

'Not you,' she quickly assured him.

Pressing his hand against his chest, he gave her a mock-serious look. 'Of course not.'

'How about you take me on for a trial period?'

'Are you serious?'

'Absolutely.' She held his gaze. 'Your stepbrother has left you the family estate in Tuscany, but you haven't been there since you were a boy and you don't know what to expect when you get there. I could come with you and take notes—make suggestions. I have a passion for historical design—only a hobby,' she added quickly, cheeks flushing, knowing she was the last person on earth Rigo would turn to for advice. 'And I speak fluent Italian.' Her trump card.

'OK, OK,' he said, halting the flow of her enthusiasm with raised hands. 'Let's stop this fantasy right now. Do you have any idea what the drop-out rate is for my staff?'

'No, but I can imagine. Maybe you need an office manager too.'

'Are you creating a role for yourself, Signorina Bannister?'

'No, I'm identifying a need,' Katie argued. 'A mutual need.' She bit her lip as she came to the crux of it all. 'I need a change and you need a second string.'

'A second string?' Rigo's face creased in his trademark

smile, but his eyes were steadily assessing her. 'Do you really think you can walk in here and, after five minutes' exposure to my world, be ready to work alongside me and understand my business? I don't think so—'

'No, of course I don't think that, but we'd both be new to this project—'

'Tuscany is not a project,' Rigo cut across her. 'The Palazzo Farnese is the past and, though I loved it once, I intend to sell it on. There are too many unhappy memories—'

'Good ones too—'

'Leave it,' he warned. 'You don't know me that well.'

Katie braced herself. 'But you are going to see it before you sell it on?'

'I said so, didn't I?'

'That's good.' She believed it was crucial he did. She'd seen the mixture of emotions pass behind Rigo's eyes when he realised Carlo had left him the *palazzo*—elation being one of them. 'Remedial work might be necessary before the *palazzo* goes on the market. You should make time—'

'Oh, should I?' His gaze turned cold. 'You're an expert, suddenly?'

No, but she knew one thing—Rigo mustn't treat this bequest like a cold-blooded business deal or he would regret it all his life. She knew it would be a difficult pilgrimage for him to make and his look warned her to drop it, but she couldn't; she'd gone too far. 'I wouldn't get in your way. I'd just be there to take notes—act as your go-between. I could even help you source people to handle any necessary restoration work. You wouldn't have time for all that with all your other interests.'

'You seem to know a lot about me, Signorina Bannister.'

'I know you don't have a PA right now.'

Everything inside her tensed as Rigo went silent. The road

out of her small town in Yorkshire was littered with return-
ees who had tried the big city and hurried back to the safety
of home. Perhaps she should be doing that too, but she'd tried
the big city—admittedly Rome with Rigo Ruggiero in it—
and was in no hurry to return home.

'And you're telling me you can start immediately—without giving notice to anyone?'

Yes, she was burning her bridges. 'I have called the office
and warned them I might not be back right away.'

'That's not a very good recommendation to a prospec-
tive employer, is it?' The look in Rigo's eyes told her how
crazy this idea was, but then he added, 'I guess neither of
us comes highly recommended where longevity of employment is concerned.'

He appeared to be battling with a decision, while her hands
had balled into fists, Katie realised, slowly releasing them.
Where had this crazy idea sprung from? She had never come
across anyone like Rigo Ruggiero before, she reminded herself. He was still thinking. She had to interpret that as a maybe
and, having taken the first step, found the second was much
easier. Better to get things out in the open now. 'I do have
one condition.'

'You're making conditions?'

Rigo's look pierced her confidence, but this was an all-important step in rebuilding her life. Yes, she was a small-town
girl who was scarred comprehensively inside and out—and she
should know her place—but retiring into the shadows would
be a step back into the dark place she'd inhabited after the fire.

'Go on,' Rigo prompted impatiently.

'If we stay over in Tuscany—'

'I haven't agreed to you coming with me yet.'

'But you will,' she said, crossing her fingers behind her back.

'*If* we stay over?' he prompted.

'I'll need a place to stay.'

'Of course you will.'

'A separate place to stay…' Her face was growing hotter every second.

'Separate from me, do you mean?'

She heard the faint derision in his voice. 'That is correct,' she said tightly, feeling like that certain someone had come back to stand on her throat.

Rigo barked a laugh. 'Why?' he demanded. 'Don't you trust yourself alone with me, Signorina Prim?'

He was a busy man. Why was he making this hard for her? He needed a PA. And as he stared into Katie's pale, passionate face, he knew he wanted her to go with him. 'Well? What are you waiting for?' he snapped, frowning impatiently. 'Grab your bag, and let's go.'

Katie hadn't realised Rigo's idea of a trip to Tuscany would include a sleek white executive jet, which he piloted into Pisa Airport. Scurrying alongside him as he strolled through the terminal building without any of the usual formalities was another eye-opener. Next he introduced her to what seemed like an acre of cream calfskin in the back of a limousine. His chauffeur did the rest, driving them seamlessly through the exquisite Tuscan countryside, while she felt her thigh ping with the proximity of Rigo's thigh and fretted about sleeping arrangements.

Was she mad suggesting this? Dull little Katie Bannister off on a jolly with her drop-dead-gorgeous boss? What surprised her even more was that Rigo had accepted her offer to work for him—temporarily, of course. And now he was sending her senses haywire. She risked a glance his way as the car swept round a bend.

'Look, Katie…that palace on the hill is the Palazzo Farnese.'

Katie looked, but what she saw did not match Rigo's tone of voice. One of the ice-cream-cone-shaped towers looked as if it had been attacked with a battering ram, and to her eyes Rigo's inheritance looked more like a fat toad squatting on the top of the hill than a fairy-tale *palazzo*.

'It's a jewel, isn't it?' he breathed.

Katie hummed, trying not to sound too noncommittal. True, the hill the *palazzo* stood upon was lush and green, and had it been in good order the *palazzo* would indeed be set on the brow of that hill like a jewel. She set her imagination to work. It wasn't so hard. In some places where the passage of time had been kind the ancient stone glowed a soft rose-pink in the late-afternoon sunlight, and there were tiny salt-white houses clustered around the crumbling walls. Yes, it could be called beautiful—if you squinted up your eyes and tried to picture how the *palazzo* might look after a world of renovation—but oh, my goodness, how would Rigo react when they finally arrived?

'My family home…' Rigo's voice betrayed his excitement. 'I haven't been back for years…'

And years and years, Katie thought, trying not to imagine Rigo's disappointment when he moved past this nostalgia for a childhood that had ended with Carlo's arrival on the scene. Strangely, though she had no emotional involvement with the *palazzo*, it called to her too. She was bewitched and could already picture the rooms, which she imagined to have high vaulted ceilings, when they were loved and cared for. She knew instinctively the *palazzo* was worth saving. Monuments to another time were rare and precious and she could never dismiss one out of hand. How she would love to take a hand in restoring it…

And with her sensible head on she had an open ticket home if the job didn't work out.

Having driven up to the grounds, they entered through some ornate gates. A little shabby perhaps but that only added to their charm. They would need checking, of course, to make sure they were safe. She made a note. A gracious drive lay ahead of them, lined with stately sentinels of blue-green cypress. Well, at least those wouldn't need trimming, she thought, noting the overgrown flower beds and thinking of the work needed there. As the limousine swept on she could see it was all very grand—or had been at one time. Crenellated battlements scraped a cloudless cobalt sky and each conical tower, damaged or not, wore a coronet of cloud. 'It's magical,' she murmured.

'Let's hope so.'

Rigo's tone of voice suggested he had ditched the rose-coloured spectacles, and for that she was glad. And the setting was perfect. A limpid silver lake lay behind the *palazzo*, while the ghost of a formal garden could still be seen at the front amongst the weeds. To reach the main entrance they crossed a vast cobbled courtyard, which fortunately had survived intact, and as they passed beneath a stone arch she noticed a royal crest carved into the stone. Her heart juddered to see the same rampant lion engraved on Rigo's father's ring. That royal seal only put another wedge between them.

Rigo saw her interest and dismissed it. 'Everyone's son's a prince in Italy,' he said. 'Look on it as a benefit,' he added dryly. 'You can have a whole royal apartment to yourself.'

She smiled thinly and gave a little laugh. That was what she'd wanted, wasn't it?

CHAPTER TWELVE

ONCE UPON A time she had believed in fairy tales, but that was before the fire. She knew Rigo only wanted her for her organised mind with the same certainty she knew this visit would be a disappointment for him. She was in serious danger of falling in love with him, Katie realised as the chauffeur slowed the car.

A group of uniformed staff was waiting for them at the top of the steps. They looked a little anxious, Katie thought, hoping Rigo would reassure them. Her heart was thundering as the limousine slowed to a halt. This was awful. She couldn't bear to think of Rigo disappointed or the staff let down. From start to finish this whole business was proving more disturbing than she could possibly have dreamed.

But Rigo seemed to have come to terms with the damage to the palazzo and put his disappointment behind him. 'I'm home,' he said, seizing hold of her hands.

He quickly let them go.

She followed him out of the car, registering more alarm now she could see how many twinkling windows were broken. She was still calculating the damage when she heard Rigo groan. Following his gaze, she felt like groaning too. A crowd of squealing fashionistas had started pouring out of the doors, pushing the hapless staff aside as they fought to be the first to greet Carlo's brother. These must be Carlo's friends, Katie realised, only now they were anxious to transfer their affections to Rigo.

'Hold this, will you?'

Thrusting a suitcase-sized handbag into Katie's arms, one of the older, immaculately groomed women elbowed her way through the scrum to reach Rigo, who was handling everyone with charm and patience, but as the woman reached his side and launched herself at him he frowned and turned around to look for Katie.

'You should have waited for me,' he said, coming immediately to her side. 'And whose is this?' he demanded. Removing the handbag from Katie's grasp, he dumped it on the ground. Putting his arm around Katie's shoulders, he shepherded her up the steps.

It didn't mean a thing, Katie told herself as her heart raced. Rigo was a very physical man for whom touching and embracing were second nature—a man who radiated command. Seeing her on the outside of the group had simply stirred his protective instincts.

She stood by his side at the top of the steps as he gave an ultimatum. His Press office would issue a further statement, he said, and in the meantime he was sure everyone would respect his grief and go home.

Smiles faded rapidly. People looked at each other. Then they looked at Katie and a buzz of comment swept through the group. Katie's cheeks reddened as she imagined what everyone must be saying—it ran along the lines of, what was a man like Rigo Ruggiero doing with a woman like her? She didn't have a clue either, if that helped them.

Rigo didn't appear to care what anyone thought, and chose to neither explain nor to excuse her presence.

Everyone saw a different side of him, Katie realised, from

the Press, who loved to photograph him, to the hangers-on, who hoped to gain something by being here. She had seen his fun side and wondered how many people had seen that. Right now he was all steel and unforgiving. And if she'd only stopped to think—if these people had only stopped to think—they would all have known that a playboy could never have built up the empire Rigo had. She was as guilty as they were of being distracted by his dazzling good looks and his charm, but she had learned that to underestimate him was a very dangerous pastime indeed.

He went straight from this announcement to introduce himself to the staff and to reassure them. He insisted Katie accompany him for this and he introduced her as his assistant. No one seemed to think this the slightest bit odd and she received some friendly smiles.

Rigo looked magnificent, Katie thought as he returned to the top of the steps to be sure his orders were being carried out to his satisfaction. A Roman general couldn't have had better effect. Hope was already blossoming on the faces of his staff, and a very different look had come over the faces of Carlo's friends.

'We have to be a little patient,' Rigo confided in her, leaning close. 'Everyone has yet to learn that I am a very different man from my brother.'

'I think they may have guessed that,' Katie ventured.

'Your luggage and belongings will be packed and brought out to you,' Rigo announced to those who still refused to believe the gravy train had reached the station. 'Meanwhile, please feel free to enjoy the beauty of the grounds.'

But not the *palazzo*, Katie guessed as a groan went up.

'Come—' his face was set and hard as he turned to her '—we have work to do.'

The power emanating from Rigo was both thrilling and

concerning. Even as Katie's hand strayed to trace the pattern of Rigo's breath on her cheek she could not shake the feeling that the inside of the *palazzo* was going to be worse than the outside. Wouldn't he need time alone to deal with his feelings? 'Maybe you'd like space?' she suggested.

'Space?' He looked at her as if she were mad.

'Some time alone? I'm sure I'll have no trouble finding somewhere to stay in town—'

'I thought you worked for me?'

'Of course—'

'Then why would you stay in town? This isn't a holiday, Signorina Bannister.'

'I didn't—'

'Did you bring a notebook?'

This was another side of Rigo—ruthless and without the playboy mask. He walked straight in while she hesitated on the threshold. Beneath her boxy jacket the tight skin on her back had begun stinging with apprehension, but for the first time in a long time she ignored it and started jotting notes: 'Replace damaged architrave…sand down and re-polish entrance doors…replace broken tile just inside the door. Replace all floor tiles,' Katie amended, feeling a chill grow inside her. At her side Rigo had gone quite still.

He swore in Italian. 'This is bad. And if you're still worrying about sleeping arrangements, don't.'

Rigo was in a furious temper, Katie realised, as well he might be, considering the abuse of his ancestral home.

'Whatever the state of this building,' he assured her in a snarl, 'you'll have a lock on your door and at least a mile of corridor between us.' And I wouldn't touch you with a barge-pole, his expression added viciously.

She held her ground and Rigo's stare. She had to believe

his anger wasn't directed at her. So her precious chastity would remain intact—that was what she wanted, wasn't it?

Yes, but not like this, not with Rigo treating her like the enemy.

Standing in the centre of what must once have been a gracious vaulted hall was heartbreaking, even for Katie. They had moved from the seductive heat of Tuscany, from air drenched in sunlight and laced with the heady scent of honeysuckle and roses, into a dank, dark space that reeked of decay. Spilled wine marked what must have once been an elegant marble floor and there were even cigarette butts trodden carelessly into the tiles.

'*Dio,*' Rigo murmured softly at her side.

If he had been anyone else, she would have reached out and grasped his hand to show her support, but she knew he didn't want that. His rigid form forbade all human contact. How would she feel if the beautiful home she remembered from her childhood and had longed to see again turned out to be a crumbling ruin that Carlo's friends had treated like an ashtray?

But a lot of the damage was superficial, Katie concluded as she stared around. She guessed there must have been one heck of a party in anticipation of Rigo's arrival, which made everything look so much worse. But there was some structural work to do as well… She made a note.

Rigo's face reflected both his anger and his agony. He looked on the point of walking out. She could sympathise with that. There had been many times when she had wanted to give up after the fire, and here in the *palazzo* it must seem as if the last remnants of Rigo's childhood had gone up in flames.

'*Vero*…I knew it was too good to be true,' he murmured. 'Now you can see my stepbrother's true nature and his legacy to me.'

As he raked his hair with stiff, angry fingers she could no longer resist the impulse to reach out. 'Rigo, I'm so sorry—'

'I don't need your pity,' he snapped. 'We're going back to Rome. I'm going to put the *palazzo* on the market—'

'And turn your back on it?' She was acutely aware that members of staff were hovering uncertainly in the background.

'I'll do what I have to do.'

'Rigo.' She chased him to the door. 'Don't you think you should—?'

'What?' he demanded furiously. 'Why can't you leave me alone?' He lifted his arm, shunning her concern, but the murmur of a worried staff was still ringing in her ears. 'No— wait,' she said, seizing his arm.

Rigo stared coldly at her hand on his arm. She slowly removed it. Here in this derelict *palazzo*, surrounded by old memories and faded glory with a battalion of servants watching them, she was more out of place than she had ever been, but someone had to try and reach Rigo. 'So Carlo wins—'

'He's already won.' Slamming his fist against the ruined door, Rigo leaned his face on his arm and fought to control his feelings. A long moment passed before he raised his head again. 'Call a meeting of the staff.' He sucked in a steadying breath before adding, 'Tell them I'll meet them here in the hall in two hours' time. And please reassure them,' he continued in a voice that was devoid of all expression, 'that before I go back to Rome they will all be taken care of.'

But who would take care of Rigo? Katie wondered. Seeing his childhood home reduced to a ruin had ripped his heart out. She knew how that felt too. 'Where will you go now?' she said, unconsciously clutching her throat.

'To find my driver. To make certain he has some rest and refreshment before we return to Pisa—'

'To fly to Rome?'

'Yes.' Distractedly he wiped a hand across his face.

'Don't you have to draw up a flight plan?' He needed time to get over this shock before he piloted a plane—before he decided what to do. She was looking for something, anything that would give him time to think.

Rigo shook his head as if to say, don't concern yourself with such things, and his next words proved to be the final nail in the coffin of her dreams. 'There's no job for you here, as I'm sure you've worked out. Please accept my apologies for a wasted journey,' he added stiffly. 'My driver will, of course, take you to the airport so you can catch the next flight home.'

Home…

The sound of the battered door slamming heavily into place behind him brought more plaster off the walls, but even as Katie turned to look around and saw the group of people waiting for her to reassure them she experienced something she couldn't put a name to. It was uncanny, almost like a sixth sense, but she felt as if she was already home.

CHAPTER THIRTEEN

THE SERVANTS WERE whispering and casting anxious glances Katie's way. Tears stung her eyes when she realised many of them were armed with sweeping brushes, buckets and mops. She crossed the hall, intending only to deliver Rigo's instructions about the meeting, but seeing all those worried faces triggered something inside her. 'Do you have a spare brush?' she said instead to the housekeeper. 'If we all pitch in,' she explained in Italian, 'this won't take so long…'

There was no need for words—no time for conversation from that moment on. There was just concentrated effort from a small team of people including Katie, all of whom were determined to give the grand old *palazzo* a second chance. The Palazzo Farnese might have been brought to its knees by Carlo Ruggiero's lack of investment and care and his friends' rough treatment of it, but everyone sensed this could be a turning point if they worked hard enough.

When the old hall smelled fresh and clean Katie made some discreet enquiries about where Rigo had gone.

'After speaking to his driver he went to the leisure suite,' the housekeeper told her. 'I took the precaution of locking it,' the older woman added, touching her finger to her nose as Gino had. This brought the first smile of the day to Katie's face. 'Very sensible,' she agreed.

Rigo's concern for his driver had obviously delayed their departure, so this was her chance.

'I would not allow those people near the swimming pools,' the housekeeper confided in Katie, 'and the new master has chosen to swim in the indoor pool today.'

The new master? Katie thought of the crest on the arch and on the ring. Here, Rigo wasn't Signor Ruggiero, the infamous international playboy, but someone else entirely. 'The new master?' she prompted.

'Sì,' the housekeeper said with pride. '*Principe Ruggiero. Principe Arrigo Ruggiero.*'

Arrigo? Prince Arrigo? 'Ah, yes, of course,' she said. The housekeeper might think her a little slow on the uptake, but it was better to be sure of her facts. And never mind that he was a prince, it was Rigo's state of mind Katie was most concerned about.

Thanking the housekeeper and the rest of the staff for all their help, she left the hall in search of him. She had to know he was all right. She had to let Rigo know he wasn't alone and that she'd stay by his side until he sorted this mess out.

Katie stood in the shadows, watching Rigo power down the length of the pool. He had dropped his clothes on the side and hadn't even stopped to turn on the light, though there was lighting in the pool. The luminous ice-blue water was a perfect frame for the dark shape slicing through it and she was fascinated by Rigo's strength and by his magnificent body. His powerful legs pounded the water into foam, while his sculpted shoulders gleamed bronze as they broke the surface. They were the powerhouse for his punishing freestyle stroke, though every part of him was involved.

And every part of him was naked.

She should turn and walk away, but she couldn't; she didn't

want to. She remained motionless, watching, until Rigo finally cruised to the end of the pool.

Now she really must go…

But the moment came and went and she still hadn't moved.

Rigo sprang out. Water fell away from his hard-muscled frame. Every inch of him was in gleaming, spectacular focus. She remained riveted, staring, learning more about a man's body than she could have imagined. Rigo naked was even more perfect than Rigo clothed…so perfect Katie's scars tingled a reminder that she was not.

'Signorina Bannister?'

His husky voice surrounded her. She shrank as he padded towards her. She couldn't move. She was trapped in the beam of his stare.

'What are you doing here?' he demanded.

She lacked the guile to lie. 'Watching you.' She was careful to stare straight into his eyes, but she could feel his sexual energy invading her. She wasn't afraid. If he had caught her without her clothes she would have been terrified, Katie realised. But shouldn't Rigo be making some attempt to cover up? Was it possible to lack all inhibition? Her body thrilled to think all things were possible for him. But not for her, the scars on her back gave her a stinging reminder.

'Forgive me,' he mocked softly as he came to stand in front of her. 'I would have worn swimming shorts had I expected a visitor.'

'I'm sorry to intrude…'

She was about as sincere as he was. She would never forget these few minutes at the side of an unlit swimming pool. Every craving nerve she had was on fire. She would try to store that feeling. Before this she hadn't understood that such levels of arousal were even possible. The pool lights were reflected in Rigo's eyes, casting forbidding shadows on his rugged face. 'I was worried about you,' she confessed awkwardly.

'Worried about me?'

He sounded amused. Heat grew inside her as he continued to stare at her. Why didn't he walk away? Why didn't she?

Because her bones had turned to honey...

She was slow to react when he moved and her heart drummed a warning, but all he wanted was the towel he'd left on a chair. Relief coursed through her when he snatched it up, but he only used it to wipe his face and left his naked body on full view.

Having dried his face, he drew the towel back over his hair and rubbed it with fluid, lazy strokes. Water-heavy hair caught on his stubble and meshed with his eyelashes, and it seemed forever before he looped the towel around his waist.

'You were watching me for quite some time, worried *signorina*,' he murmured. 'Did you learn anything?'

His eyes were challenging and amused. It came home to her then how much older Rigo was, and how much more experienced and sophisticated. She was little more than a trembling wreck, and had no idea how to behave in these circumstances. 'You swim well,' she ventured.

His short laugh displayed strong white teeth and one inky black brow peaked, but his mouth remained hard and his eyes were watchful. He was fresh from the shock of discovering what had happened to his childhood home, she reminded herself, and had been swimming to exorcise those demons.

But he still had energy to burn...

'You're blushing,' he said.

'How can you see in this light?'

Reaching out, he traced the line of her cheek. 'I can feel the heat coming off you...'

Her swift intake of breath sounded unnaturally loud. 'It is

very warm in here…' She gazed about in a pathetic attempt to distract him.

Rigo's low voice pulsed with intent. 'I don't think it's that sort of heat I can feel. Well, *signorina*?' he pressed. 'There must be something other than my swimming technique that kept you fascinated…'

Mutely, she shook her head. It was blood heat in the leisure suite and almost dark. Just the pool lights shimmering behind her like dots of moonlight on a lake. She felt cornered by a powerful predator, a predator she had sought out, and now her reward was to be wrapped in a cloak of arousal as she waited to see what would happen next.

The darkness concealed her flaws, and with Rigo's powerful body changed to shadowy imprecision in that darkness they could almost be two equals meeting here. It was a compelling fantasy in which she longed to lose herself, and as the pool room shrank around them she swayed towards him.

'Careful,' he murmured, putting warm palms on her upper arms, but only in a steadying gesture, 'you're very close to the edge of the pool…'

Still the child. Ever the innocent. Would he never see her any other way?

And shouldn't she be relieved about that?

She made light of it. 'Sorry…I didn't realise—I can hardly see anything in this light.'

Lies. All of it. She had seen every part of him, including the tattoo on his hip. 'I only came because I'm worried about you,' she said again. 'I called the meeting.'

'Good,' Rigo murmured.

His concentration on her hadn't wavered and his watchful eyes bathed her in heat. As he eased onto one hip she was consumed by the longing to touch him.

'Why don't you—?'

'Why don't I what?' she blurted guiltily.

'Why don't you tell me the real reason you came here?'

She heard the faint amusement in his voice. If only he would stop staring down at her. 'I already said—you had a shock…the will—'

'My brother and I were practically strangers.'

Katie's mouth felt dry as Rigo continued to stare down at her. 'The *palazzo*…' She was grasping at straws, they both knew it. She gasped as Rigo coiled a long hank of her hair around his finger. It must have escaped her bun while she was cleaning.

'The only distress I feel,' he assured her, 'is knowing my stepbrother wasted his life—'

'It doesn't have to be a wasted life.' She gazed up. 'You could change that.'

He laughed and let her go. 'You will learn that it is pointless looking back and wishing things might have been different. They are as they are.'

She had not expected him to move so fast, or to slip his hand into her hair again, and to make the next move cupping her head. 'The knack is in learning to move on, Katie…'

Their faces were very close and he was staring at her intently. 'Rigo…'

'What?' he murmured, drawing her gaze to his lips.

'You could stay here at the *palazzo* and make things right for everyone…' She couldn't forget the faces of the servants waiting hopefully for news.

'Delaying tactics,' he breathed with his mouth only a whisper from her lips.

Perhaps, Katie admitted silently, though her concerns for the people who lived here were real enough. And now they had reached the point she had longed for she was frightened—frightened she would disappoint him. How could she not when Rigo was perfection—when he had taken one look at the flawed *palazzo* and turned his back on it? 'You don't strike me as the sort of man who walks away from problems.'

The mood changed as she spoke. The heavy, erotic beat fell silent and was replaced by humour, at least in Rigo's eyes.

'I thought I told you, no counselling?' he said.

'Sorry...' She eased her neck as he stepped back. Would she ever forget his touch? 'I wouldn't dream of advising you—'

'I think you would,' he argued. 'I think you do a lot of dreaming, Signorina Bannister. I think you dream and want and need as much as anyone else.'

Breath shot from her lungs as Rigo seized hold of her.

He wanted her. Wanted her? He wanted to lose himself in Katie Bannister. He wanted to bask in her goodness and have it heal him. To begin with he'd been amused by the fact that Katie had worried about him enough to come and seek him out, but now he remembered that no one had ever done that for him before. And then he saw the hunger in her eyes matched his own and the time for restraint had passed.

There was no subtlety. As he slammed her against his hard warmth and his towel hit the floor he made no attempt to retrieve it.

Katie's senses had sharpened in the darkness to the point where she could smell the water on Rigo. She pressed against him, believing she was someone else—someone flawless, bold and hungry. She might be falling deeper into the rabbit hole and leaving reality behind—and maybe she should try to pull things back, but she didn't want to, and her body wouldn't cooperate, anyway. It was swollen with need, moist and ready, and so instead of pulling away from Rigo, she raised her face to his.

'Needs are nothing to be ashamed of, Katie. Even I have them. I understand you, Katie,' he assured her. 'I know everything you feel.'

In that case he'd be ready to catch her when her legs buckled. Did he have any idea how hungry she was for this—how desperate for his touch? Did he know where and exactly how she wanted him to touch her? Her eyes were shut. She was barely breathing. She was suspended in an erotic net, and was totally unprepared when he pulled away.

The ache morphed into real physical pain. It took her a moment to realise Rigo's actions were so fluid he hadn't left her, but was kneeling on the hard tiles in front of her.

'No.' Her voice clearly said yes. As he lifted her skirt she clutched his shoulders for support.

'Yes,' Rigo murmured, burying his face.

An excited whimper ripped the silence as she unashamedly edged her legs apart. She was greedy for sensation, for experience, for him. Having taken the first step, she was ready to fly.

'Relax, worried *signorina*,' Rigo murmured, 'there's no rush.'

She could hear him smiling in the darkness.

CHAPTER FOURTEEN

HER HEART WAS pounding so hard she couldn't breathe. Her wildest fantasy was coming true. Held firmly by Rigo, she was trapped, not by his grasp, but by her own overwhelming need. She didn't move, couldn't move, because she didn't want to. She craved fulfilment and satisfaction and a door into that world that had always been closed to her. She wanted everything Rigo was prepared to give her. She wanted to climax—and not once, but many times. She wanted this erotic dream to last forever and for reality to fade away. Closing her eyes, she bathed in darkness where there were no scars and only sensation registered. Consequences? What were they?

She sighed with disappointment as he started to stand up, but he took his time as if imbibing her scent on the way up. It thrilled her—aroused her even more. His face was only millimetres distant from her own, and her body was crying out for more contact between them. Swinging her into his arms, he lowered her down onto one of the recliners facing the pool, where silence enveloped them.

She blinked as he switched on the lamp by the chair.

'I want to see you come—'

'No.' She wasn't ready for that.

'Yes,' he argued steadily.

She was painfully self-conscious as he pressed her back against the cushions.

'Relax,' he said.

She was out of the dream and back to reality. This was embarrassing and wrong. She would regret it in the morning.

In the time it took to think that, he had pushed her skirt back to her waist, removed her underwear and lifted her legs to rest them on his shoulders.

She was completely exposed. Cool air brushed her most heated self as Rigo cupped her bottom in warm, strong hands, and instead of pulling away she settled down. Moments later he found her with his tongue and with his lips and with his fingers, rough stubble scratching the insides of her thighs, pleasure and pain intermingling. She hit a wall of pleasure and that wall gave way, drawing her deeper into a world of the senses where reality could not intrude. She bucked wildly. He held her in place. She screamed with abandon as he tipped her into the abyss, and while she was moaning with amazed contentment he kept her safe in his arms until the last flicker of sensation had subsided.

'Greedy girl,' he murmured.

With some satisfied sounds she was ready to fall silent. Language was a civilised pursuit and there was nothing civilised about her feelings for him. She was spent, exhausted, satiated—

And then she noticed the fire in Rigo's eyes. He was neither spent, exhausted nor satiated.

She jerked away as a hot stream of panic filled her. He didn't attempt to follow as she clambered awkwardly away from him. 'I'm sorry—'

'So am I. What are you ashamed of, Katie?'

'Nothing.' She spoke too fast and Rigo's eyes narrowed with suspicion. 'Sorry,' she said again, backing away. 'I don't know what I was thinking—'

'That we were two consenting adults, maybe?' he suggested in a voice that was calm while the expression in his eyes was anything but.

And who could blame him? Katie thought. She had led him to this point and then pulled away. 'I know what you must think of me—'

'You have no idea,' he assured her. Springing lightly to his feet, he collected his robe from the back of a chair and shrugged it on, belting it securely. 'So, Signorina Prim?' His voice had lost all warmth. 'What do you hope to get out of this?'

Rigo's expression frightened her. 'Nothing.'

'Nothing? So you haven't been leading me on in the hope of landing a greater prize?'

He wasn't talking to her, she felt instinctively, but to the woman who had taken his father from him, and to the many women who saw Rigo as the ultimate prize. 'No, of course I haven't been leading you on. Rigo, you're upset—you're not thinking straight—'

'Don't mistake me for one of your hard-luck causes—' dipping down, he scooped up her underwear from the floor. '—and don't forget these.'

He threw them at her, only for her to fumble and drop the dainty briefs she had bought in Rome.

'Pick them up,' he snarled. 'You might need them when you identify your next target.'

And with that he turned his back on her and stalked away.

He took the private staircase from the leisure suite to his rooms. The episode with Katie Bannister had sickened him. He knew who and what she was, just as he knew himself. This will, this so-called legacy, had undermined the man he had become and had left him feeling tainted by everything he had vowed to leave behind. Seeing his childhood home desecrated had done exactly what Katie said. It had rocked his world and he wasn't thinking straight.

Shouldering his way through the door, he entered his room pacing and didn't stop until he had reasoned his motives through on every point. He had encountered just about every ruse to capture his interest and reel him in and was always on his guard. Katie had reaped the whirlwind. Her appetite was undeniable, but when he weighed that appetite against her naïvety, or the shock on her face when she realised the road they were on led to penetrative sex, he knew she was innocent. So she had splurged on some decorative underwear. Did he begrudge her even that small luxury?

Anger, regret and frustration had coagulated into one ugly mass, he concluded. Seeing the *palazzo* brought to ruin hadn't just shaken him to his foundations, it had filled him with unnatural energy—or just plain fury, maybe. Whatever the cause, he had needed an outlet for that energy and had chosen badly. He should have stuck to swimming, he mused, smiling bleakly. He could never give Katie Bannister what she wanted and deserved, which was a loving husband and babies, a home, romance, a happy-ever-after ending. Thanks to him she had lost her innocence tonight. But perhaps it would keep her safe from men with fewer scruples than he.

Stripping off his clothes, he took a long, cold shower before swinging naked into bed. He wasn't going anywhere. He was staying until this mess was sorted out. As Katie hoped, he had embraced his legacy. He would take a negative and make it positive. He would drink from Carlo's poisoned chalice—but Principe Arrigo Ruggiero Farnese would not be making any more mistakes.

He woke at dawn after a restless night. One face had held sway in his mind, but she would hate him now. He turned his thoughts to practical matters he could do something about and went straight to examine the north tower, where he found the roof caved in. But it could be fixed. Having survived centuries, the old place would stand a few more knocks before it surrendered.

It wouldn't be easy to restore the *palazzo*, he concluded after further investigation, and it would take many years and a lot of money. Money he had, and he had the determination to set it right. He would oversee this project personally. He'd handled many major building works in the past, but they had been investments for his money rather than his heart. He consulted with architects who sent teams in, but he wasn't prepared to do that here. He would be the main point of contact. He couldn't allow anyone to interfere with the *palazzo* who didn't remember it as he did.

Swinging across a beam, he dropped lightly to the floor. It was time to persuade Katie Bannister to stay. He needed her clear thinking and organisational skills. She could coordinate the various teams—if she had the courage to stay after what had happened last night.

He went to the window in his room and pushed the rotten frame with the heel of his hand until it yielded. He had to breathe some fresh air. He looked down, searching for Katie. Something told him she'd be outside. Birds were singing— the sun was shining; it was Katie's kind of morning. Resting his hands on the cool stone, he looked in vain. Pulling back, he felt the wear of time. Like everything else the stonework required expert attention. He would ask her to find the best team of stonemasons to begin work right away—if she still worked for him.

She must work for him.

Last night he had been infected by a maelstrom of emotion, but today he could see clearly that it was an assistant he needed, not a lover. And if Signorina Bannister didn't work

out he could always sack her like the rest. Meanwhile, he'd
take a shower and get rid of this dust.

Last night the choice had seemed clear. She was going home.
She had proved conclusively she wasn't cut out for this any
more than she was cut out for her dead-end job in Yorkshire.
Her encounter with Rigo had proved to be the worst humiliation of her life.

But the best sex.

Better than anything she could dream up, Katie conceded.
But deeply humiliating; she'd never get past it. And as for
Rigo? Trying to imagine what he must think of her made
her shudder.

But, when she came down to breakfast and discovered a
new mood of optimism sweeping the staff, she immediately
put her own feelings on the back burner.

'You have to stay,' the housekeeper protested when Katie
explained she was leaving. 'It's such a lovely morning,' the
older woman pressed her. 'The best of the year so far.' And
then the clincher. 'We have cleaned the outdoor swimming
pool especially for you.'

Bare skin. Scars. More humiliation. 'But I don't—'

One of the maids stepped forward. 'We are about the same
size, *signorina*,' she said shyly, 'and I have a new swimming
costume I have never worn.'

As the young girl held it out to her Katie knew she couldn't
refuse.

'You'd be quite alone, *signorina*,' the housekeeper quickly
reassured her. 'I'll make sure everyone is kept away—'

'You're very kind—'

'And you're the first person to come here and give us hope,'
the woman told her frankly.

Was she going to show her weakness now? She had to be strong for these people all the time, not just selectively.

'It would be such a shame to waste the day,' the maid said as the housekeeper nodded agreement.

The damaged skin on Katie's back tightened, but she would feel more than shame if she refused this kind gesture. 'If… if I was alone—'

'You have my word on it,' the housekeeper assured her.

The cool water felt like satin on her heated skin, and as sunshine warmed her shoulders any remaining cares she had floated away. This was the first time since the fire that she had stripped off outside the privacy of her own home and she was surprised to find the costume the young maid had lent her fitted her so well. She had Rigo's staff to thank for making this possible.

Submerging her face in the fresh, clean water, Katie basked in the unaccustomed luxury of having a whole swimming pool to herself. And what a swimming pool it was—if she had thought the *palazzo*'s leisure complex was like something out of a film, this outdoor pool was far more beautiful. Stern Doric columns marked the perimeter, while mosaics tempted her to look beneath the water to where a kaleidoscope of images told a story of ancient Rome, complete with gladiators and graceful beauties clad in flattering flowing robes. I want one of those glorious gowns, Katie thought, buying into the dream. She was beginning to believe she could forget anything swimming here.

The housekeeper had opened the shutters and folded them back, allowing him a clear view of the gardens and swimming pool. Drawn by the particular brilliance of the sunlight that day, he walked over to the window after his shower and stared out. His gaze was immediately drawn to the activity in the pool, where someone was preparing to dive in…

Katie…

She had already been swimming and her hair was slicked back. Her honey-blush skin gleamed like an impossibly perfect sculpture in the brilliant light. She had surprised him once again. He had always suspected she was concealing a stunning figure beneath her dowdy clothes—just how stunning had eluded him, he realised now. He already knew her legs were beautiful, but… A whisper from last night intruded on his thoughts. Could he forget? He had to forget—he had a pressing need for a PA and she'd make a great PA. But with her hair drawn back and her elegant profile raised towards the sky, there was no doubt she was one of the loveliest sights he had ever seen. He remembered their first telephone conversation, when her sexy voice had revealed so much about her. You could hear beauty in a voice. Why she dressed down almost to the point of disguise was Katie's business, but he couldn't deny he was curious. Pulling away from the window, he stretched his limbs. Even an hour without activity was an hour too long for him. He was restless with last night playing on his mind again. Katie's responses to him…her soft whimpers…her tremulous, yet passionate plunge into abandonment and pleasure—

Maybe a swim was what he needed too.

'No, Rigo, no…'

He stopped dead in his tracks. He had only walked halfway down the pool, but she was recoiling from him as if he meant her harm. The last thing he had intended was to frighten Katie, but the moment she caught sight of him she had catapulted out of the pool and now she was stumbling backwards with a towel clutched tightly to her chest.

'I didn't see you, Rigo,' she gasped.

Was he such a terrifying sight? It was certainly terror in her eyes. He took a step back with his hands raised, signalling his intention to come no closer. Still she backed away. If she didn't stop soon she'd fall over the sunbed—

He breathed a sigh of relief when she felt the bed behind her knees and stopped, but now she was feeling awkwardly behind her for a wrap she'd left there earlier, and only he could see she was in real danger of tumbling into the pool.

'No! Stay back!' she shouted in alarm when he moved to save her.

'What the hell's wrong with you? I'm not going to touch you.'

Ever again, he added silently. If this was Katie Bannister's reaction to him, imagine if they'd had sex.

None of this made sense. She'd seen him naked. She'd held him. He'd let her go without once trying to stop her. He was respectably attired this morning in swimming shorts with a towel slung around his neck. He couldn't understand her bizarre behaviour and was growing increasingly resentful. But still her safety was uppermost in his mind. 'Stay where you are before you fall in. I'm going to reach for your robe,' he told her firmly, 'while you don't move a single muscle. Do you understand me?'

He wasn't even sure she could hear him, so he put his promise into action, moving slowly and deliberately. 'And now I'm going to hand it to you.'

Part of him said this was ridiculous, while another part of him was too busy seeking an answer to the mystery to walk away. Katie, meanwhile, remained stock-still, staring at him in wide-eyed dread.

He held out her wrap at arm's length. She took it from him.

Dragging it on, she belted it tightly, tweaking the edges as if not a single part of her could be on view.

Had last night done this to her? He would never forgive himself if that was the case, though he could fathom no reason why it should. She had been a willing partner all along, up to the point where a natural conclusion was facing them both, and then, because she for whatever reason had drawn back, he had let her go.

'When you've showered and dressed I'd like to see you in the library,' he said evenly. 'Anyone will tell you where that is. Say, twenty minutes—half an hour?' His look also added, if you still work for me? But he didn't labour the point.

He didn't stop walking until he reached the entrance to the *palazzo*, when he turned to see Katie still standing where he'd left her. He wondered if he would ever forget the look on her face. You would have thought she had been in danger of her life.

CHAPTER FIFTEEN

WHEN RIGO LEFT her at the poolside it took her a long time to settle, mentally and physically. Since the fire she had longed to be invisible and had almost achieved that goal—until this trip to Rome, when Rigo had forced her to face reality again. Deep down, she was grateful to him. There was still such a lot of life to be lived. Even before the fire her appearance had placed her in the pigeonhole marked good girl, plain girl, quiet girl, studious girl, which did nothing to douse the fires inside her. Last night Rigo had been right to point out she had needs like everyone else. Her needs were exactly the same as all the pretty, vivacious girls with great figures and unblemished skin.

There had been one short interlude when she had found an outlet for her passion in training to be an opera singer. Music had given her a means of expression until the fire stole her voice away. She had never thought to experience passion again until Rigo proved her wrong. And now she was at another crossroads, Katie realised. She could go back to Yorkshire and pick up her old life, or she could stay on in Italy as Rigo's PA.

When she had buried her face in the hospital pillows and cried the first time she saw the scars on her back the doctors had told her she would have to be brave. Take it one step at a time, they had advised. Life was a series of steps, she had discovered since then. You could take them bravely, or you could refuse to take them at all.

So the past had got the better of her?

She wouldn't let it.

Twenty minutes after leaving Katie at the pool, he was tapping a pen on the table, wondering if she was going to turn up—and if she did, was he about to make the biggest mistake of his life? He hadn't imagined taking Katie out of her comfort zone would throw her so badly. Forget the sex—that was never going to happen. But where the job was concerned he had to know if she was up to working alongside him in Italy.

The door opened and he put down his pen as she walked in.

'I know this is a business meeting,' she said when his face registered surprise, 'but I thought—if we needed to scramble round the building…'

His surprise that she had come at all was instantly replaced by relief and admiration. It took some guts to climb back to a position of composure and responsibility when you had lowered your guard to the point where you appeared a gibbering wreck. 'Sensible outfit,' he agreed, wishing she wouldn't always wear everything so big.

Camouflage, he realised, remembering the voluptuous figure she'd revealed at the pool. But why did Katie always feel this overwhelming need to cover up? The plain tailored trousers and simple jumper were a great improvement on the boxy suit, but they were hardly flattering. Thinking of the PAs he'd hired in the past made him want to shake his head in bemusement—when he would have preferred them to keep their clothes on they couldn't wait to whip them off. 'Don't you have any other clothes with you? Jeans?' he suggested.

'Just one pair I bought when I went shopping with Antonia. I didn't want to spoil them.'

He curbed a smile. That simple comment touched him somewhere deep. He'd become a stranger to having one of anything years ago. He turned determinedly back to business. He was already dressed in off-duty jeans and a casual top and was ready for the dirty work ahead of them. 'So you're ready to start work?'

'Yes, I am,' she said, staring straight into his eyes.

He came around the desk to shake her hand. 'Welcome to the team.'

She liked the way Rigo could be strong and unemotional. She also didn't like it—and for his sake more than anything else. A man so easily divorced from emotion could end up lonely. But she wanted this job and Rigo's grip was firm and compelling. She wished with all her heart things could have been different between them, but they weren't different. She had to hold her nerve now so he would understand she had drawn a line under everything that had happened between them. 'I hope I don't disappoint you,' she said, noting that Rigo held her hand for precisely the right length of time an employer should hold the hand of an employee.

He smiled slightly. 'I don't think there's the slightest danger of that.'

When roused, don't stand in his way. Rigo waited for no one, Katie concluded as he strode off. Even her embarrassment had been refused time to ferment. He was out of the library and across the hall before she had pulled a pen out of her bag, and now her heels were rattling across the floor in hot pursuit. They were surrounded by priceless antiques and frescoes that wouldn't have looked out of place in the Sistine Chapel, and the scent of history competed with the strong smell of disinfectant from the recently cleaned floor and was a dizzyin~

combination. Or was that the Rigo effect? She was going to work for him. She did work for him. She ran faster and almost collided with him at the foot of the stairs. He gave her no time to recover. Seizing her shoulders, he swung her around. 'Tell me what you make of this.'

Breath shot out of her lungs in a gasp as she followed his gaze up the stairs to take in the garish stair carpet. Truth? Or diplomatic lie?

'Come on, come on,' he pressed. 'I want a reaction—'

'It stinks.'

'That's what I think. What should we put in its place?'

A runner at most. Or, depending on what they found underneath, the naked steps. She told him. He agreed.

'Make a note.'

She did so.

Oh, this job was fun. She raced after him. Who else had a boss so big and hard and sexy, a boss who only had to look at her to fill her body with the zest for life—along with other things? She didn't mind running to keep up with Rigo's easy, loping stride, because if he stopped suddenly she had discovered that crashing into him was like crashing into a padded wall—and who wouldn't want to rest against that, and even writhe a little, given half a chance?

'Well?' he demanded, thumping the wall with his meaty fist. 'What do you think of this?'

'They've plastered over stone that might have been better left exposed.' She pressed her lips together as their eyes met briefly. Images of other things—more interesting, but just as hard as stone—made her cheeks blaze.

'Exactly,' he rapped, striding off again.

e sucked in a breath and refocused determinedly before
ing after him.

'This is a recent addition too.' He disdainfully flicked a hand at some dismal curtains and strode on again.

She made a note to replace the hangings.

'This is a disgrace,' he snapped, moving her aside to examine a sleazy mural more closely.

'Sandblast it?'

He almost smiled.

'We'll need a historical architect to advise us on renovations,' he said, walking on. 'Take a note.'

Something in the tone of that voice doused her enthusiasm. He was beginning to take her for granted. '*You'll* need one,' she said. 'I don't know how long I'm going to be here—trial period,' she reminded him, chasing after him down some stairs. This wasn't turning out as she had expected. She wanted more out of life than taking notes. She wanted to be listened to, at the very least, even if her thoughts were later discarded. But had Rigo even heard her?

She was ready to renege on their deal, Katie realised. She had been invited to become part of a team, not a dictatorship. She would stay until Rigo found a replacement for her, but then she would go home and find some other, safer way to spread her wings.

'This is more like a casino than a valuable historical site,' he remarked, opening one door and slamming it shut with a bang. 'Make a note—'

'You make a note.' She shoved her notebook in his hand. 'You know what you want. Presumably you can write it down.'

She'd never thrown a temper tantrum in her life. Rigo paused to look at her. He let one beat pass, and then another. He made no attempt to take the pen and paper she was offering him. 'What do you think of the room?' he said mildly then.

She gritted her teeth. 'I think it looks more like a casino than a site of historical importance,' she ground out.

His lips tugged. Her body yearned. They walked on.

'This used to be a slate floor,' he observed, sounding more relaxed.

The mood was catching and, in spite of her reservations, she relaxed too; enough to carry out her own investigations. They had entered a second, dimly lit corridor leading off from the first and once again it was lavishly carpeted in hotel style. 'I think we'd better add a stone-floor specialist to the list.'

'I agree,' he murmured in her ear. There was humour in his gaze that did considerable damage to her composure. He walked on. 'It wouldn't surprise me to find a nightclub and a spa down here.'

'Could this be it?' Katie wondered, peering into a stale-smelling cavern. Judging by the heaped ashtrays and the litter of drinks, this was the room in which Carlo's friends had chosen to wait for them. 'I'll get round to clearing it up as soon as I can—'

'*You'll* get round to it?' He swung towards her. 'That's not your problem. Katie.'

Signorina Prim, Signorina Dull, had had enough. The demon temper had been roused and was still very close to the surface. She only had to remember working alongside Rigo's staff the previous evening for that temper to erupt into words. 'I might not be stylish and rich like you, but if there's one thing I do know about, it's cleanliness and order. Who do you think cleaned the hall? You have a wonderful staff if you chose to notice them.'

To her surprise Rigo didn't respond to her attack, and instead granted her a mocking bow. 'I can assure you my wonderful staff has already told me what you did here yesterday.'

'They did most of it—'

'You claim no credit?'

'Why should I?'

He gave her a look. 'Why didn't you ask me to help?'

Her only thought had been to start getting things in a better state for him. 'I didn't want to trouble you last night.' Blushing now, she quickly changed the subject, having convinced herself she neither needed nor wanted Rigo's praise. 'You were upset and so—'

'You're making excuses for me?' he suggested mildly.

There was that flash of humour again in his intense green gaze and she hungered for more of it. There was silence while they studied each other's faces with new understanding. It was no longer Rigo Ruggiero, infamous playboy confronting Katie Bannister, poorly paid messenger girl with a hopeless taste in suits, but a man and a woman who each had the same goal.

But don't get too carried away, Katie warned herself, breaking eye contact first. A leopard doesn't change its spots that easily. A maxim that could apply to both of them, she conceded as Rigo resumed his inspection.

'This room will have to be gutted…'

And with that the spell that had so briefly held them was broken.

'In fact,' he added, 'all the rooms will have to be gutted— make a note.'

She did so, but this time there was a smile hovering round her lips. No wonder he couldn't keep his staff. 'It's only cleaning and redecoration,' she pointed out, but by the time she looked up from her notebook Rigo was out of sight.

Had he forgotten she was with him? Katie wondered when she found Rigo examining an electrical circuit box. 'Electrician?'

'Full check,' he confirmed. 'Our first goal must be safety

for everyone, and then we must concentrate on bringing the *palazzo* back to its authentic state.'

'No earth closets, I hope?' she couldn't resist murmuring as he cast an eye over her notes.

'State-of-the-art plumbing. There's nothing better than a long, hot shower.'

As he looked to her for agreement she blushed again.

Opening a door at the far end of the corridor, he stepped outside. She followed, desperate to be free of all the conflicting emotions bottled up indoors. Gulping in the fresh, clean air, she exclaimed with pleasure and relief.

Rigo turned to look at her. 'How do you like the job so far?' he demanded.

She saw the irony in his eyes. 'I'm only here until you find a replacement.'

'Or I sack you.'

There was another of those long moments where they stared into each other's eyes. A breeze had whipped Rigo's hair into a fury, but his eyes were full of laughter as he raked it back.

She'd asked for this and she'd got it. Mad for him or not, she was under no illusion: Rigo wanted someone with an organised mind to take notes for him, just as he said. He needed her—not for all the reasons she'd like, but because she could keep life organised. She was a convenient choice, Katie reasoned as he dropped onto one hip. 'Are you coming or not?' he said.

'I'm right here.'

'Of course, you do realise if you prove satisfactory this could become a permanent position.'

'*If* I decide I want it.' She looked away so he didn't see her disappointment. Her dreams extended further than being his PA in a suit.

They spent the rest of the morning checking and discussing and formulating an initial plan of action, while she filled her notebook with notes. By lunchtime Katie could only conclude Rigo had some magic dust that had wiped the previous night's debacle from her mind. The incident at the pool also appeared to have been forgotten. It was better this way for both of them, Katie concluded; no tension, no agenda, purely business.

They joined the staff for lunch, all of whom were keen to put Rigo's plan for them into action right away. 'But run everything past me,' Rigo reminded Katie as he left her in charge. 'I've had enough surprises for one visit.'

She didn't doubt it.

CHAPTER SIXTEEN

KATIE'S FACE BURNED as she saw knowing smiles exchanged between the staff. Rigo had come back into the kitchen to tell her that two teams of men were waiting and he needed her right away.

'To take notes?' she suggested, avoiding his gaze.

'You're quick,' he murmured, ushering her out. 'One team is here to start work on the heavy cleaning,' he explained, 'so we don't put unnecessary pressure on the staff.'

'Good idea. And the other?'

'They're here to sort you out—'

'Sort me out?' Katie exclaimed.

Taking the pad from her hand, Rigo stuck it in the back pocket of his jeans. 'You won't need to take notes for this.'

'For what?' Katie's heart leaped into her throat as Rigo took her by the hand.

'If you're going to be working for me you'll need a new wardrobe of clothes—'

'To go rooting round the cellars with mice and spiders?'

'Your clothes are giving me eye-ache.'

'Well, I'm sorry if I—'

'You might be in Italy, but you don't have to dress like a *nonna*.'

Katie was too shocked to speak. A maiden aunt was one

thing, but a grannie? Freeing her hand, she stood her ground. 'I'm hardly on show. And as I'm only here until you find a—'

'Think of it as your uniform,' Rigo interrupted, 'though, of course, I expect you to set a good example to the servants when you're off duty too—'

'And will you be buying them clothes?'

'I will, as it happens. It's about time they had something new, don't you think?'

He'd put her in an impossible position, but then Rigo was good at that.

'Rigo, wait—'

He stopped suddenly in the middle of the hall. Catching hold of her, he steadied her on her feet and stood back. Two groups of men were waiting at the far end of the hall—one team wearing overalls, the other in flamboyant suits. The overalls looked more appealing right now. She freed herself as discreetly as she could, conscious that even in a space as big as this sound travelled. As did sexual chemistry between two people. 'Even if I did work for you on a permanent basis, which I don't,' she told Rigo in an impassioned whisper, 'I have a perfectly serviceable suit—'

'That brown thing? Chuck it. Or, if I find it first, I'll chuck it out.'

'Fortunately it's already packed in my suitcase.'

'So you've decided not to stay?'

'I was ready to leave last night,' she admitted. 'I asked your driver if he would take me to the airport today.'

'Well, lucky for you I spoke to him too. And next time please do me the courtesy of speaking to me before you instruct my staff. Now, let's get on. None of these people want to be kept waiting. I can't think of a woman in the world who would turn down the chance to have the designers I have chosen create a look for her.'

'A mistress in the world, maybe.'

It was only a mutter but he heard her.

'Don't flatter yourself.'

Ouch.

'I'm merely extending the same courtesy to you I show to all the people who work for me—'

'And you can't keep any of them.'

She could always call a cab, Katie reasoned as Rigo's expression darkened.

'Those I don't want leave my employ.'

'So I have to earn the right to work for you?'

'You have to do the job you're paid for. That's reasonable, isn't it? There's a wonderful opportunity here if you want to be part of it. With the right team I can take Carlo's poisoned chalice and turn it into something wonderful—and that's all I'm prepared to say at the moment.'

'You're talking about something more than renovating the *palazzo*?'

'When my ideas are fully formed I'll let you know.'

'So you don't trust me, but you want me to work for you?'

'I'm saying confidentiality is an issue.'

'I'd need to know more.'

'When I'm ready.' And, when she still looked doubtful, his lips curved in a dangerous smile. 'Do you really need more time to get used to the thrill of working for me?'

Rigo's arrogance she could deal with, even his impossible behaviour she was getting used to, but when he played the humour card she was lost.

Just about. 'I can't afford to deal in riddles where my career is concerned,' she prompted, only to have Rigo close the matter with a decisive gesture. 'This will have to wait until you've seen your team. Come and show me when you've made your selection.'

'At most I need one plain and simple suit.'

Rigo shrugged. 'Your loss.'

And with that he left her to negotiate plain and simple with men for whom Katie guessed plain and simple was an abomination.

Katie was forced to admit she was wrong. As the designers discussed their ideas she realised their taste wasn't so far distant from her own—just in monetary terms. Unlike some men she could mention they were prepared to listen. When she asked for plain and simple they called it stylish and smiled. Once they had reassured her that all the measurements they needed could be taken over her clothes, she relaxed. They agreed on one tailored suit with both skirt and trousers to ring the changes, as well as three sharp shirts. They could dress her from stock, they admitted, to which she agreed immediately. It was both cheaper, and…well, truthfully, she couldn't wait to see what they had in mind.

So she did have a figure, Katie realised as she performed a twirl later in the privacy of her own room. It was a surprise to find she was a stock size and didn't even need an alteration, but then breasts were most definitely 'in' in Italy, where clothes made allowances for women with generous curves.

Left to her own devices she might have chosen something concealing, but the designers had insisted the jacket would hang off her shoulders if she chose a larger size. The elegant navy-blue tapered pencil skirt and matching short jacket with a sexy nipped-in waist made her look, well, if not glamorous—she could never be that—then, at least, something the right side of presentable. It was such a thrill to have some smart new clothes—and, as uniforms went, she conceded wryly, staring at the label in awe, this wasn't half bad.

The accommodation the housekeeper had chosen for her

was another delight. It had survived the worst excesses of Rigo's brother and was the most beautiful suite of rooms Katie could imagine. The silks might be faded, as was the counterpane on the bed, but Katie had always loved shabby chic and this was the perfect example of it. She wouldn't change a thing in the room. Having everything pristine and new would take away from the *palazzo*'s charm. Any renovations would have to be carried out with the utmost sensitivity—though she had no doubt Rigo was more than capable of that. He was very different from his public face. The Press might think him a playboy, but that only showed how little they knew him.

She sighed as she gazed out across the formal gardens. She was more than a little in love with him even though much of Rigo was hidden behind whichever mask he had chosen to suit his purpose. She wondered what he was hiding and why—and what were these plans of his? He had decided to keep the *palazzo* and renovate it, but then he was going to use it for something he wouldn't tell her about. Would he ever trust her enough to tell her? And could she stay until he did?

He'd have to tell her if she was going to work for him, Katie reasoned, pulling back from the window. No employer could hide much from his PA. Was that why he'd sacked so many? Rigo was asking them to give blind loyalty to a man they knew to be ruthless and who would only tell them what he thought they should know. Would she put up with that?

Glancing at her watch, Katie realised it was time to show Rigo the outfits she had selected. Outfit, she corrected herself, smoothing the skirt of her new suit. So that shouldn't take up too much of his time—though what he would think of the sexy shoes the designers had insisted she must wear with the severely cut two-piece, she couldn't imagine. Well, she could. He would think her frivolous and extravagant and with very good reason. Lifting up a heel, she stared rapturously at the luscious crimson sole. The contrast with the black patent court shoe was both subtle and fabulous. She had never owned shoes like these in her life before and would have to pay Rigo back from her wages, which meant staying on—for a time. The shoes were worth it, Katie concluded.

Katie Bannister in high heels and designer labels—who'd have thought it? Katie Bannister, whose heart was beating like a jack-hammer, because she was going to see the man she loved, though Rigo must never guess how she felt about him.

He stood watching her as she walked across the hallway towards him. He noticed the way her hips swayed as if she had only recently become aware of her femininity. She loved her new suit. He loved to see her wearing it. He could tell she liked it by the way she moved. It was so good to see her standing straight, walking tall, hiding nothing.

He wanted her.

She hadn't seen him yet and so she knocked on the door of the library, where she expected to find him. Hearing no reply, she moved on towards the entrance to the leisure suite. He walked up behind her, hoping to surprise her, but something flashed between them and she turned. 'You look beautiful,' he murmured.

He heard her swift intake of breath. She remained quite still. 'Really beautiful…' He didn't touch her. He didn't want to spoil the moment as it shimmered between them. And then he noticed she was trembling.

'Do you really like it?' she said.

'More than you know…' He was sick of the pretence. He was sick of Katie's lack of self-belief. He wanted the chance to help her rebuild it. He wanted her in his bed. She wanted him. She couldn't have made it more obvious. Her honey-coloured eyes had darkened to sepia and her parted lips offered him a challenge he couldn't ignore. Katie Bannister was changing faster than any woman he had ever known and the look of question, of adventure in her eyes mirrored his own. 'Now you've got the uniform,' he teased her, 'be sure you obey all my commands.'

'Until you sack me?' She refused to see the joke. 'I'll work in a team as you first suggested, Rigo, but I refuse to be the next in a long line of disposable dollies dressed for your amusement—'

'Is that what you think this is?' He gave the suit ensemble an appreciative once-over. 'And I thought you'd like it.'

'I do,' she admitted. Her eyes were wide and innocent, but there was a riot of activity behind them.

'Rome *and* Tuscany,' he tempted, sure that was an offer she couldn't refuse.

'I'll stick with the trial period we agreed on, thank you.'

'I need your organised brain on board.'

'I'm flattered,' she said dryly.

'I mean it. You're quiet, organised, discreet, quick-witted—'

'Biddable, do you mean?' she interrupted. 'Or just plain dull?'

'Dull? Who said quick-witted was dull?' Had the definition changed since the last time he used it? 'Work *with* me,' he tempered, keeping the bigger picture at the forefront of his mind.

'As what, Rigo? The perfect back-room girl?'

'You want to run the show?' he demanded with exasperation, planting his fist on the door above her head.

'Before I agree to anything I'd have to know exactly what's involved. That's reasonable, isn't it?'

Their lips were inches apart and he was tempted to take advantage of that and then tell her everything. But he was still developing the idea and his kids' club wasn't up for negotiation. It was and always would remain confidential—not for his sake, but for theirs. He wouldn't go out on a limb where that was concerned and he wouldn't put unfair pressure on Katie. 'I can't tell you yet—'

'But you expect me to throw up everything I have in England and move to Italy to work with you on a permanent basis on this…secret project?'

'I'm asking you to take a chance.'

'With you?'

He stared into her eyes and wondered how he had ever thought Katie Bannister a quiet little mouse. Passion lurked so close to the surface in both of them and her sweet wild-flower scent was driving him crazy.

But he was not as innocent as she was.

'No, you're quite right,' he said, 'this would never work. I can't imagine what I was thinking.'

Rigo enjoyed provoking her. She knew that. Even so she was tempted to go along with his plan. He had injected danger into her life and she was addicted to it now. But could she work for him and feel like this? Could she do anything with a clear head until he finished what he had started last night? Sexual desire did not play by the usual rules. Clear thinking could vanish in an instant, leaving only the danger of desire.

'Shall we take this somewhere more private?' Reaching past her, he opened the door.

The door swung to, enclosing them in the sensual cocoon of the luxury spa. Rigo locked the door and handed her the key. Neither of them spoke; they didn't need to. Heat spread through her body until it came to a pulsing halt. Her lips were parted and her eyelids were heavy. She was ready and so was he. She could feel Rigo's breath on her face, on her neck, on her ear, his lips only millimetres away. They stood facing each other, staring into each other's eyes. When she was certain she could stand it no longer he drew her close. The relief was such she cried with pleasure. Her body was pressed hard against his and she could feel his erection throb and thicken as it strained against the fabric of his jeans. The more she tried to fight this Katie registered dizzily, the more she wanted him.

'So what would it take to bend you to my will?' he suggested wickedly.

'A miracle?' she countered, deliberately provoking him.

'A miracle?' he murmured. 'Or this...'

He claimed her mouth, teasing her lips apart—punishing her with kisses. As she responded he cupped her bottom and memories of sensation came streaming back. Was it only last night? How could she be so hungry? This wasn't decent—she would go mad. She was composed of sensation and need, she was all hunger, all mindless, searching, craving, desire. 'Oh, please...'

Briefly, he lifted his head to stare down at her.

'Please, touch me...' She was so swollen and aching. Winding her fingers through his hair, she dragged him close, demanding more, demanding everything he had to give her.

'Is this any way to behave?' he whispered with amusement.

'Now...' She cried out with frustration. 'Don't tease me...' Edging her legs apart, she gave him the most brazen invitation yet. She had to have him. She had to draw him deep inside her. It was a primitive imperative she had no will to resist. Her inhibitions were cancelled out by the demands of a body that craved his touch. She needed more contact, more touching and stroking, more pleasure. Memories from last night were too vivid for her to ignore this opportunity.

'Tell me what you want,' he taunted her softly. 'Direct me…'

'I want all of you now…'

'Explain.' His voice was stern. He held back.

'I want you to touch me again.' She said this in a clear and lucid voice. 'I want you to touch me exactly as you did before…'

'Exactly?'

'But this time I don't want you to stop.'

There were no more words spoken between them. Rigo undid the fastening on her skirt and let it drop to the floor. Her new lace briefs followed. She closed her eyes as he enclosed the luscious swell between her legs. The touch of him there was indescribable.

'More,' she insisted in a groan, clinging helplessly to him. 'Give me more—'

'Like this?'

'Oh, yes…'

But he was teasing her with almost touches. He would stroke her deliberately the way she liked and then return to a touch that was far too light.

'Don't tease me,' she begged, and as her legs buckled he took her weight.

Somehow her legs were locked around his waist, and as he freed himself and protected them both, he insisted, 'Use me.'

She gasped with shock as if the idea had never occurred to her. Rigo had given her the key to a new world, and one she had been longing to open since the moment they met. Taking him in her hands while he supported her, she touched him to her swollen flesh.

'Again,' he commanded.

CHAPTER SEVENTEEN

SHE USED RIGO for her pleasure, not once, but many times, although there came a point where using him that way wasn't enough. As her hunger rose Rigo backed her against the wall. 'Yes,' she groaned, clinging to him. 'Yes,' she husked gratefully on a long note of satisfaction as he eased inside her. Still cupping her buttocks with one hand, he added to her pleasure with the other and as he thrust deeper, faster, she arced towards him, urging him on with impassioned pleas. She had never thought, dreamed anything could feel so good, but this was more than a craving; for the first time in her life she felt complete.

He had never known sex like it. She was insatiable. She was passionate. She was perfect. But for him this was only the appetiser and now he wanted the feast. He wanted to take Katie to bed and make love to her all night.

He had lost count of how many times she had climaxed by the time he withdrew. He did so carefully, making sure she was steady on her feet when he lowered her to the ground. Embracing her, once, twice, his heart throbbed with unexplored feelings. The next step had to be bed, but to his astonishment when he suggested it she pushed him away. 'Not again.' He shook his head, refusing to believe she could do this a second time.

'I can't—'

'What do you mean, you can't?' Drawing her close, he kissed her passionately, tenderly, but she wouldn't or couldn't respond. It made no sense. Anger grew inside him. She wanted him for sex—for instant gratification, but when it came to something deeper, more meaningful...

He had been used. A surge of disgust swept over him. Had he misjudged this? Was it all an act? Was Katie Bannister in love with someone else? He stepped back. Seeing his expression change, she reached out to him. 'Rigo, please—you have to believe me when I say there's a very good reason—'

'For sating yourself and moving on?' He shook his head in disbelief. He had only felt this level of betrayal once before, as a child whose pure love had been wasted on a man whose lust for a woman had taken precedence over love for his only son. 'Give me the key.'

Fumbling through her pockets, she finally found the door key and gave it to him.

Clutching it in his fist, he left the spa without a second glance.

As the door slammed behind Rigo Katie slowly crumpled to the floor. Burying her head, she sobbed in a way she hadn't been able to cry since the fire. She had never grieved for what she'd lost. She had never let the feelings inside her come out. Only her love for Rigo could open those floodgates. She had never felt anything as life-changing as this before—or directed so much loathing at her scars. She was crying because they could never be together and because sometimes it was easier to be strong than to break down, because being strong meant putting on an act, but when the mask dropped and there was just Katie Bannister facing up to her new life Katie wondered if she was strong enough or if too much had been lost.

Strong enough? Dry your eyes this minute, Katie's inner voice commanded.

Picking herself up from the cold tiles, she rebuilt herself breath by ragged breath. There was no reprieve, no easy way, because deep inside her was a determined little light that kept on shining however hard she tried to put it out. She would get over this. She would get over Rigo. She would go on living. Scarred or not, she knew there would always be problems. She could sit here on a hard floor in an empty spa, wailing for a past that had whistled away, or she could pick up her mental armour and go back into battle.

Which was it to be—wailing or winning?

She would do more than survive; she would make a difference.

'What's this?' Rigo stared at the letter Katie had just placed in his hand. They were in the library where she had found him pacing.

After what had happened in the spa she had no option but to do this. 'It's my resignation… You don't have to accept it, but I'll understand if you do.'

'That's very good of you.' He eyed her brown suit with distaste. 'So, are we right back where we started, Signorina Bannister?'

'Hardly.' She had barely finished the denial when Rigo's look communicated all he thought of her in wounding detail.

'I don't accept your resignation.' He handed the letter back. 'You agreed to stay until I could find a replacement.'

'That was before—'

'Before what?' he snapped.

She looked away, unable to meet his gaze.

'As you may be aware, I haven't had time to find a replacement for you yet. So I'd be grateful if you'd stay.'

He sounded so cold, so distant and, yes, so contemptuous. She flinched as he threw himself from his chair and stalked to the window, where he remained with his back turned to her, staring out. 'If I weren't so pushed…' he grated out, leaving Katie in no doubt that he would get rid of her the moment he could.

'I could resign. I still have my open ticket home—'

'You can do what the hell you want—and seem to do just that, from what I've observed.' Rigo's eyes were narrowed with fury and suspicion as he looked at her.

'I'm sorry—'

'Don't even go there.'

'You don't make it easy, Rigo.'

'I don't make it easy?' he demanded incredulously. 'You're guilty on that count too—and if it's easy you've come for you might as well leave now.'

Turn her back on him for ever? Face life with no possibility of seeing Rigo again? 'Is there any way we can work together now?'

'You tell me.'

Could he sound any more hostile? 'If we kept it on a strictly business footing?'

'Let me assure you right away there's no chance of anything else.'

Less than an hour ago there had been fire in those eyes. And now…

Digging her nails into her palms, she agreed to stay on. 'If you tell me what the job entails.'

'That's very good of you.'

'Rigo, please…I've said I'm sorry—'

'You're always sorry—maybe once too often.'

'I understand why you're angry with me—'

As she said this he made a sharp sound of disbelief. 'You understand nothing,' Rigo assured her. 'You're a child.'

And he, with all his Roman passion in full flood, was a formidable sight. She had never wanted him more or felt so distanced from him. Feet braced against the floor, fists planted on his tightly muscled hips, Rigo Ruggiero was a force she should run from as fast as she could before her heart was lost for good. 'If you won't accept my resignation—'

'Which I won't. We have an agreement,' he reminded her.

'Then will you tell me what you plan for the *palazzo*?'

'Do you really think I should trust you after what happened between us—not once, but twice?'

If they couldn't move past the sex there was no hope of a working relationship and if she was going to stay she had to do so with her head held high. The only way to do this was not to blush and shrink, but to challenge Rigo as he had challenged her. 'You threw down the gauntlet when you dared me to take a risk. I'm throwing that same gauntlet at your feet. Take a chance on me.'

Where had she come from, this female virago? Had he created her or were they equally guilty? Did they rouse such powerful feelings in each other that neither of them were capable of behaving as they should? He pointed to a chair. She sat while he paced. He was weighing up the potential of the *palazzo* for the scheme he had in mind—a scheme that would benefit his foundation—against his obligation to secrecy. Should he trust this woman? Could he trust her? What did his instinct tell him? 'I'm going to outline your contract,' he said, 'so if you would like to take a note…'

She hid a smile. He let it go. He dictated a letter to his legal team asking them to draw up a contract for Katie Bannister that gave her cast-iron guarantees.

She turned to look at him halfway through. 'I can't sign anything until I—'

He swore viciously in Italian. 'Must you argue every point? I want you to send the letter exactly as I have dictated it—'

'Don't I have any say in my own contract of employment?'

'Yes.' He was tired of playing softball. 'You can sign it or not. You can go back to Yorkshire and look for another job, if that's what you want, but I don't think it is. Am I right?'

She ground her jaw and came right back at him. 'I want a clause that allows for a time limit and fair notice to be given on either side—'

'A quick fix?' he suggested coldly. 'Is that the type of thing you deal in, Signorina Bannister?'

'Please don't turn me down out of hand. Try to see this from my point of view—'

His hackles stood on end. 'From your point of view? Isn't all this from your point of view? And what do you mean, don't turn you down out of hand. *Caro Dio*, what is this? I'm the one making the offer—'

'And making no allowance for my feelings—'

'You have too many feelings,' he roared, only to realise she was in tears. 'Don't play that card with me,' he warned, shaken to his core. 'I know your type—'

'My *type*?' she exploded, rallying faster than he could ever have expected. 'And what type would that be, Rigo?'

They were facing each other like combatants in a ring, but indignation gave way to amusement when it occurred to him that to any outsider Katie would appear by far the more dangerous of the two. With her hands balled into fists, her jaw jutting and mouth firm, her eyes blazing with the light of battle she was a magnificent sight, this woman of his—

His woman?

His woman.

The only woman he could ever want.

But his woman hadn't finished with him yet. Not by a long way.

'So I'm the type who can see you naked in a pool and make the mistake of thinking we could share something special—' She broke off. 'Oh, no, I forgot.' She held up her hand as if to silence him, though he had no intention of saying a word. He was content to let her continue this one-way argument with herself and by herself.

'I'm the woman who had sex up against a wall, and felt nothing, presumably? I'm a robot—an automaton.' Her voice was rising. 'I'm a frigid, sexless, boring spinster—'

'Hardly frigid,' he cut in mildly.

She made a sound like an angry bear, which made it all the harder for him to hide his smile.

Forget all things sexual? That had been her plan. She should have known Rigo would make this hard for her. His confidence was obvious in the way his lips tugged in anticipation of victory, as if nothing she could say would have the slightest effect on his arrogant assumption that she would sign his wretched contract without alteration or complaint. How dared he look at her and smile? How dared he use that look to stir erotic thoughts?

But—and it was a big but—he was offering her the chance to do something exciting and different. Living in Italy was that, even if she didn't know the precise details yet. Had she come all this way in attitude and distance only to wimp out now? She'd pin him down and then she'd decide. Drawing herself up, which brought her—well, almost to his shoulder, she suggested, 'Can we sit down and talk?'

Could they? He kept his expression carefully neutral.

A negotiation beckoned. Now that he'd woken the tiger inside Katie Bannister, there was no way he wanted to see her vulnerable again. This was his type of woman. The type of woman he would like working alongside him, he amended. Katie Bannister had passed the interview process with flying colours and was definitely the type of feisty, focused individual his foundation needed on the board.

She was sitting at the desk, waiting for him. He leaned his hip against it and looked down. She looked too, but not into his eyes. Not that he was any measure of propriety and chaste thought. 'I'm going to tell you everything,' he said, reclaiming her attention. 'The club I run—'

'The club?' she interrupted, snapping into attack mode. 'I would never leave England for Italy to work in a club, Rigo. I'm sorry,' she said, standing up, 'but I really don't think there's any point in continuing this conversation—'

He cut her off at the door, one fist pressed against it. 'Now you listen to me.' His gaze dropped to her lips.

'And if I won't?'

He might kiss her?

Mild eyes flashed fire. 'Let me go, Rigo…' She rattled the door handle.

'Not until you tell me what you're hiding.'

'What I'm hiding?'

But her eyes told him clearly that she was. 'I know you're hiding something; you're not leaving here until I know what it is.'

'I'm your prisoner?'

He allowed himself a smile. 'If you like.'

Her jaw worked and then she said, 'All right—but not here, not now. Please, Rigo, let's sort out one thing at a time.'

He ground his jaw as she stared unflinchingly into his eyes. Questions competed in his mind. Why the pretence? Why had she pulled back, not once, but twice when they were so heavily into pleasure? Katie had no difficulty enjoying sex.

It was anything deeper she shied away from. So what was Katie Bannister hiding from? Him? Men in general? Everyone? He had to remind himself how much she would benefit his foundation if he kept this rigidly confined to business. 'Please sit down again,' he said.

She still looked unsure. He could hear her thinking, work in a club? 'Before you jump ship you should make sure you're not jumping to conclusions. I'm going to tell you about my club and I'm asking you to hear me out. I think you'll be glad if you do—'

'So you trust me now?'

'As much as you trust me. Shall we?' He angled his chin towards the chair at the opposite side of the desk. He didn't turn to see if she was following; something told him she would be. Katie couldn't resist a challenge any more than he could and her curiosity was fully roused.

She walked towards him with her head held high until there was just the desk between them. Resting her fingertips on the edge, she remained standing. Leaning forward to make her point, she said, 'When I was a girl saving up to go to music college I checked coats and served drinks and I considered myself lucky to have a job in a club, but that was then and, at the risk of sounding ungrateful, I don't want to—'

'Pole dance?' he suggested dryly. 'Why don't you sit down, listen to what I have to say first and then give me the lecture?'

'On one condition—'

'Name it.'

'You take me seriously?'

'Believe me, I do take you seriously.' He would like to take her very seriously indeed and the only reason he hadn't taken the relationship to the next level was that Katie was holding him off.

Pulling out the chair, she sat down. 'I promise to hear you out.'

He ignored the rush of interest in his groin and concentrated on the scrapbook in front of him. He spun it round so it was facing her. 'This is my club…'

She went very still as she turned the pages and then she looked at him.

He shrugged. What could he say? This was his life's work, and had been the only thing he cared about and worked for… up to now. The fact that he had never forgotten his roots, or that by assisting these children he was not only helping them but also somehow healing the child he had once been, was his concern, and his alone. The fact that he was sharing this with Katie was a measure of his respect for her. She must stay, and not because revealing this had bared his soul. He knew his secret would be safe with her, but he wanted her to stay because he couldn't imagine life without her. She was a remarkable woman, this self-effacing, quiet, kind girl, and he knew he would never meet anyone like her again.

Katie studied the image on the first page. Rigo was standing in the middle of a small group of men dressed in motor-racing red. They all looked tanned and fit and wealthy, and they all had their arms casually draped across each other's shoulders. At that point she was still thinking the worst of him, but then she moved on to the second page and everything inside her went still. As misjudgements went, hers had been enormous. 'I don't understand…'

'What's to understand?' he said, frowning. 'How can you look at those photographs and tell me you don't want to become involved?'

Rigo's organisation fulfilled as many of the dreams of sick and disadvantaged children as it could. 'So that's why you were racing round the track when I arrived?' Each of the photographs was dated, and as she traced the image for that day lightly with her fingertips her heart filled with admiration and love for him. 'And your friend—the one who was in hospital having the life-saving operation…'

Rigo didn't answer and his expression didn't flicker. He took no credit for any of this, she realised, and even now he wouldn't reveal the identities of any of the families he helped. Now she understood that it wasn't his privacy he guarded so assiduously, but that of the children and their families and his friends.

'The children do occasionally make me late for appointments,' he admitted, smiling faintly.

One glance into Rigo's eyes told a world of stories and, while some of them were happy, many were sad.

'As far as I'm concerned,' he said, 'the children come first. Well, Katie? Now I've explained why I need someone to help me with the expansion of the scheme, how do you feel?'

Rigo would stop at nothing to continue this work. Even his much vaunted pride counted for nothing in Rigo's mind compared to these children. How did that make her feel? Her heart was aching with love for him. She wanted the job. It was a job she could devote her life to willingly and without question. She could feel passion for the job, a passion that would never falter, but—

'I should warn you,' Rigo said, interrupting Katie's thoughts with a condemning glance at her dull brown suit, 'that everyone involved in the scheme is under orders to inject fun and colour into the lives of those we help—'

'And must embrace a more extensive palette than brown, I take it?' she suggested in the same dry tone.

A half-smile creased his face in the attractive way she loved. 'As you can see from the scrapbook,' he said, looking at it, 'you must wear whatever is appropriate for the activity you're taking part in.'

'I draw the line at a yellow jumpsuit.' She was remembering one of the most hair-raising photographs with one part of her brain, and longing for something that could never be with the other part.

'If you do a tandem parachute jump with me, Katie, the yellow jumpsuit is required equipment.'

Bizarrely, as he spoke a wedding dress flashed into her mind. She smiled it away, thinking of the children and the wonderful opportunity Rigo had put in front of her.

'We have to do anything that's asked of us.'

'I understand,' she said.

'Are you ready to give me your answer?' he said. 'Will you join us?'

CHAPTER EIGHTEEN

SHE WOULD DO ANYTHING for him right now.

Don't give up, Katie's inner voice begged, while common sense told her she could have the job of her dreams, but not the man. Maybe Rigo was playing with her in the sexual sense, Katie reasoned, but she knew he was wholly sincere about his scheme. Perhaps she should choose the security of home over the freedom and romance she had always longed for—at least if she did that her heart wouldn't ache constantly.

She smiled. She knew. There'd never been any doubt what she would do. 'I'll go and put on my new suit, shall I?'

Rigo relaxed. He understood the code. He had offered her the chance to make the difference she had longed to make and she was saying yes.

And now they were both on their feet.

'I can't tell you how pleased I am!' Rigo exclaimed as he came around the desk. 'Thank you so much for agreeing to join us, Katie. I'm going to turn Carlo's legacy into something wonderful. I've already decided I'll keep a small apartment here, but the Palazzo Farnese is going to become Carlo's Kids' Club—'

'So your stepbrother will be remembered for all the right reasons...'

'He will.'

'It's a great name—fun and friendly.' Could hearts explode? Katie wondered as hers pounded violently in her chest.

'I'm already talking to my team of doctors to make sure the centre is everything it needs to be and I'll build their suggestions into my plans—'

'I'll do anything you ask,' she interrupted. 'I mean it, Rigo. I want to be part of this.'

'Welcome to the team, Katie.'

He grasped her hand and let it go. 'This is a big ask.' He stared directly into her eyes. 'I need more than a personal assistant.'

She didn't breathe.

'I need someone like you to speak independently on the steering committee.'

She pulled herself together. 'Of course.'

This was so much more than she had hoped for, Katie told herself firmly. 'I only wish I'd understood all this from the start.'

'Would it have made a difference?'

Rigo's eyes searched hers relentlessly and they both knew he wasn't talking about business now. She knew she looked uncomfortable, but it couldn't be helped. She'd lost the art of masking her feelings the day Rigo had kissed her.

She was thankful when he let it go.

'People's lives are precious,' he said, referring to his scheme, 'and they are entitled to discretion from us.'

'You have my word,' she said, knowing Rigo's foundation was infinitely more important than her own small world of doubt and negative self-image issues.

'The last thing the families need is the media spotlight focused on them—and my friends aren't too happy about it either,' he confessed with a wry smile. 'It's better for everyone if we keep it low-profile.'

'Everything you have told me will remain between you and me,' she promised him. 'The details of your foundation are safe with me.'

'I never doubted it.'

But there was a question in his eyes. And that question was: why couldn't she be as open with him?

And then with an effortless switch of tempo, he became her boss again. 'I can't wait to get started. I'm so glad you're joining us, Katie.'

In his enthusiasm he caught hold of her arms and spun her round. They were both on a high. And Rigo was an impulsive man. Still, the last thing she had expected was that he would kiss her on the mouth...

The kiss was like no other they'd shared. The impulse and joy that caused it changed instantly to something more. Once reignited that fire raged unabated. She couldn't press herself close enough or hard enough. She had to taste him and feel him in every part of her. She could barely drag in enough air to sustain life...

Rigo swung her into his arms and strode out of the room. He didn't walk up the stairs, he ran.

Closing her eyes, she nuzzled her face into his chest. She was hiding from reality and intended doing so until the last bubble burst. Having mounted the stairs, he shouldered his way into his apartment. It was as shabby as her own, but to Katie's eyes it was equally charming and comfortable. Thanks to the attentions of a reinvigorated staff, it was also spotlessly clean, and as Rigo launched them both onto the super-sized bed she inhaled the faint scent of sunshine and lavender contained in crisp white bedlinen.

'Are you happy?' he demanded, drawing her into his arms.

She could never express how she felt. There was such joy in the air, such exuberance and laughter, and for every nanosecond left to her she was going to live this out to the full. While he was kissing her Rigo removed her jacket and tossed it away. 'Remind me to make a bonfire for that old suit,' he said, raising his head to look into her eyes, and while she was laughing her skirt followed the same trajectory. All that remained now between Rigo and her scars were her underwear and a blouse. The last bubble was about to be burst. She turned her face away. It was wrong to allow this. She would not cause him any more pain.

He searched for her lips with his.

She pushed him away. His eyes flickered and changed. She'd hurt him. There was no way not to hurt him. It broke her heart to do this, but it would destroy them both if she let him see her scars. Rigo would turn away from her in disgust, believing he'd been betrayed again.

But she should have known he wouldn't be so easily dissuaded. She let him kiss her one last time and felt her heart soar. When he released her she stared at him to imprint every atom of his features on her mind. Reaching up, she wove her fingers into his thick black hair, loving the way it sprang, glossy and strong, beneath her palm. She needed that sensation branded on her mind to sustain her in a future without him. In Katie's world love was a cause for concern. Whatever she felt for Rigo must be rigorously controlled so it never reached past the bedroom door.

Yes, and look where she was now...

Touching his fingers to her chin, Rigo made her look at him. 'What are you frightened of, Katie?'

Instead of answering, she traced the line of his beloved face with her fingertips until he captured her hands and kissed each fingertip in turn. Her skin was still prickling from contact with Rigo's sharp black stubble. Tears welled in her eyes as the thought, sharp and dark, like the end of this romance, rose in her mind; there could be no happy ending.

'So, *signorina*,' he murmured against her lips, 'have you no answer for me? Will you not tell me what is wrong, so I can help you?'

What is wrong? I love you with all my heart, she thought, and always will. My love for you fills every part of me with happiness… But she would never speak of this to Rigo. He was so confident and so happy. He was still at the top of the mountain, while she was rapidly slithering down it—though his sexy, slumberous eyes had begun to gain an edge of suspicion. In that brief moment she saw the same vulnerability everyone felt when they had bared their soul to another. And right on cue her scars stung a reminder of why this love for Rigo must go no further.

She pulled away. He dragged her close, kissing her until her soul was as bare as his. He tasted her tears and pulled back. 'What aren't you telling me? Is there someone else?'

'No!' she exclaimed; the idea was abhorrent to her. But Rigo's voice had turned cold and everything had changed. Their brief idyll was over.

'Katie?'

Someone else? No. Something else.

'I knew it.' He thrust her away. 'I can see it in your eyes.'

Could he? Could he see the ridged skin—the ugly, ruined skin? Those foul red shiny scars stood between them as surely as another person—

'Why don't you just admit it?' He launched himself from the bed.

Because she had wanted this too much.

But she had forgotten Rigo was not the tame, civilised man he appeared to the wider world, but a man who had survived life on the streets, fighting for every piece of bread he put in his mouth. Rigo had never stopped fighting, whether for his foundation or for his company and employees, or anyone else he believed needed someone to champion them, and he wasn't about to lose this fight. Whirling round, he seized her wrists and tumbled her back onto the pillows. Holding her firmly in place, he cursed viciously in her face. 'Not again! Do you understand me, Katie? Tell me the truth. Tell me why you have such a problem with commitment.'

'There's no one else—'

'And I should believe you?'

But his grip had loosened fractionally.

'I swear, Rigo—there's only you.'

He let her go and sank down on the bed with his head in his hands.

'You're my world,' she said. 'You fill my mind every waking moment and my dreams are full of you when I'm asleep—'

'Then I don't understand,' he said, looking up. 'What's standing between us? Tell me, Katie. I have to know. Maybe I can help you.'

This big, strong, powerful man, this man who was so confident he could make everything right for her if she only wanted it badly enough. But her voice would never come back and her scars would never go away. Could she burden him with that? Shaking her head, she clung to the edges of her blouse.

Rigo's gaze followed her movement. 'Oh, Katie,' he murmured and, gently disentangling her hands, he brought them to his lips. Letting her go at last, he stood in front of her, stripping off his clothes. When he was completely naked he lay on the bed and drew her into his arms. 'Why couldn't you tell me the truth? Do you think my feelings for you are so fragile?'

As understanding flooded her brain shame suffused her. 'It's not my breasts.'

'What, then?' He went still.

Moments passed and then Rigo drew her to him. 'You have to tell me, Katie. You can't live like this.'

He was right. Without him she was only half-alive.

'I'm going to take your blouse off.' He started unfastening it. He shared his courage, staring into her eyes. He lifted her up into a place he inhabited, a place where problems were dealt with and not pushed aside. He slid the blouse from her shoulders and embraced her back. His hands explored and his expression never wavered. 'Come to me, *cara*,' he said, drawing her closer. 'Trust me…'

And so at last she lay with her face pressed into the pillows while he looked at her back. Hot shame coursed through her. She felt dirty and ugly. She was repulsive. That was how she'd felt when she'd left the hospital and taken a long, hard look at herself in the mirror. Squeezing her eyes shut now, she pictured Rigo recoiling in horror. How could he not? He only had to measure his perfection against her flaws to know jokes didn't come this bad.

But she waited in vain for his exclamation of disgust, and felt the bed yield as he lay down at her side. And then, incredibly, she felt him kiss her back…all down the length of the scars. And when he'd finished, he said softly, 'Tell me—how do you think this changes you?'

'Isn't it obvious?' she mumbled, her voice muffled by the pillows.

'Not to me. Is this what you were hiding from me?'

She turned her head to look at him.

'I can't believe it,' Rigo murmured. 'I can't believe you would think me so shallow—'

'I don't. I think you're perfect—so perfect, how can you not be disgusted?'

'By you holding out on me, perhaps that might disgust me, but by these? You said you'd trained as an opera singer when we were at Gino's, and the letter of introduction sent to me by your firm mentioned it, but it said nothing about a fire—'

'I didn't put it on my CV. I didn't think it relevant to my new life.'

'So you shut it out and tried to forget you were in a fire that left you badly scarred and stole your voice away? And every day you were reminded of what you'd lost each time you spoke or when you took your clothes off.'

'It's not so bad—'

'Not so bad? You lost the future you'd planned. That's big—huge, Katie. Who did you confide in? No one!' he exclaimed when she remained silent. 'And you've been hiding your feelings ever since?'

'I had to hide my scars from you—'

'Because you thought I would throw up my hands in alarm?'

'Because I thought they would sicken you. I thought if you saw them they would take any feelings you might have for me and turn them sour and ugly.'

'So how do you feel now when I tell you that I love you?'

'You—'

'Sì, ti amo, Katie. I will always love you. I can't imagine life without you. You're my life now.'

He stopped her saying anything with a kiss so deep and tender, she felt cherished and knew the nightmare that had mastered her for so long didn't exist in Rigo's mind. Bottling things up, just as he had said, had allowed the consequences of the fire to ferment and expand in her imagination until they ruled her life. And now he was kissing her in a way that sealed the lid on those insecurities. There was no need for words; this was the ultimate reassurance.

Rigo made love to her all night and they woke in the morning with their limbs entwined, when he made love to her again while she was still half-asleep. To wake and be loved was the miracle she had always dreamed of, only it was so much better in reality. 'I love you, Rigo.' She said this, kneeling in front of him, naked. 'You've made me strong.'

'You've always been strong,' Rigo argued. Taking hold of her hands, he drew her to him. 'You just needed reminding how strong you are. If you weren't strong you wouldn't have chosen such a challenging path through life—first music, and now me.'

She laughed. How could she not? 'I love you so much,' she whispered, staring into his eyes.

'You're sure?'

'You made it possible for me to love.'

'So now the world is your oyster?' he teased in his sexy drawl.

'My world is you—'

'Brava,' he murmured with one of his killer smiles. Lowering her onto the bank of pillows beside him, he added, 'Just remember, I love every part of you—not just this leg, or that finger, or these ears. I love the whole Katie.'

And the fierce pledge in his eyes said that as far as Rigo was concerned her scars did not exist. 'I love every part of you that goes to make you the woman I love now and always.'

And to prove it he moved down the bed.

As she cried out with pleasure he took her again, and this time when they were one her heart sang.

They had a leisurely breakfast in bed, planning the future. They had already discussed the possibility of Katie seeing a plastic surgeon, should she want to, but for some reason the one thing that had obsessed her since the fire seemed unimportant to her now. Rigo had made it so. He had taken her internal compass and pointed it towards the future—a future they would enjoy together. 'But we will have to leave the room sometime,' she pointed out when Rigo's eyes darkened in a way she recognised.

'But not yet,' he insisted, drawing her down beside him.

'No, not yet,' she agreed.

And when he finally released her, she admitted, 'I fell in love with you the first hair-raising moment we met.'

'I was a brute.'

'You were challenging.'

'And you were very patient with me.'

'And just look at my reward…'

'Ah, there is that.'

Modest to the last, Katie thought, recognising the wicked smile.

'And, Katie—'

'Yes?' she whispered as Rigo drew her beneath him.

'Have you never considered singing again?'

'Now?'

'Later, perhaps,' he suggested, easing into her. 'But just think how the public would love your sexy, breathy voice. If I can fall in love with that voice over the phone—'

'But that's you…'

'Are you daring to suggest there's something wrong with my judgement?'

He was making it very hard to think at all. 'If I did that I would have to question your love for me,' she managed on a shaky breath.

'And you won't, so have some confidence, Katie. There

is more than one popular style of music. You can still sing in tune, can't you?'

She was supposed to answer while he was making every part of her sing? 'Well, yes, but I can't sing as I used to—' She gasped as he moved up a gear.

'Your new public wouldn't want you to—'

'My? Oh…' She conceded defeat. No thought possible.

'Have you forgotten that one of my passions is making dreams come true? And I have a keen nose for business.'

She could only groan her agreement.

'You're going to record a track—an album—' he picked up pace '—and who knows? I might even make some money out of you.'

'Rigo, you're impossible,' she shrieked, recognising his game now. Rigo distracted himself while he concentrated on her pleasure.

'I try my very best,' he admitted, still moving as she quietened.

She had no doubt that he would.

CHAPTER NINETEEN

SUMMER CAME AND went in a flurry of love and activity. It was almost Christmas before Katie knew it. The renovations to the *palazzo* were well under way, and she was fully involved in Carlo's Kids' Club. She had started this sunny December day in the kitchen at the Palazzo Farnese, where she was helping to prepare a special lunch for Antonia, who was travelling to see them on one of her regular visits from Rome. Katie was closer than ever to Antonia, having persuaded Rigo that, if she wanted to, his sister must play a full part in his scheme. She had pointed out that Antonia wasn't too young to face up to life and that, if Rigo insisted on shielding his little sister and sent her shopping all the time, Antonia would never grow up. Antonia had embraced this idea with the enthusiasm only Antonia could, and even Rigo had admitted then his sister had been brushed aside for far too long, both by his father and her mother, and then by him. Antonia had seized the opportunity to prove herself and had more than repaid Katie's faith in her, and now they were not just friends but soon to be sisters—

'Hey, *tesoro.*'

Katie's heart bounced with happiness as Rigo walked into the room. She would never lose the sense of excitement she felt each time she saw him.

Walking up to her, he swung her round to face the staff and, leaning his disreputable stubble-shaded chin on the top of the shiny tumble of hair she always wore down now, he announced, 'I have a surprise for you, *tesoro*—'

'Another surprise?' Katie exclaimed.

There had been nothing but surprises from Rigo since the day she moved in—not just to the *palazzo*, or the penthouse, but into Rigo's life. The wardrobe of clothes she had initially refused had miraculously appeared in her dressing room. And when she had asked him where they came from, he said, 'They must have been brought by fairies.' And when she finally stopped laughing, he admitted that he had given most of her measurements to the designers, and that her short audience with them when she first arrived had been a ruse.

'How did you do that?' she demanded.

'I have a good eye,' he admitted.

'Two good eyes,' she remembered telling him with a scolding look. Goodness knew where Rigo gained that sort of experience—and, frankly, she didn't want to know. 'You mentioned a surprise?' she reminded him now.

'Just a little something,' he said, delving into the pocket of his jeans. 'It's something for the wedding. See what you think. I got the colour scheme right, didn't I? White and ivory with a garnish of red roses…?'

Their wedding… She could hardly believe it. Two more days and they would be married at the cathedral in Farnese. 'You know you did,' she rebuked him playfully, wondering what could be in the beautifully wrapped box, with its iridescent ivory wrapping paper and rose-red ribbon.

'Well, open it,' Rigo prompted.

It must be a lacy garter, Katie thought, ripping the paper in her excitement. As the ribbon fluttered to the ground, Rigo caught it and handed it to her. 'Open the box,' he said.

She did so and gasped.

Everyone gasped.

Rigo affected a frown. 'Is blue-white straying too far from your original scheme?'

A huge blue-white diamond solitaire winked at her from its velvet nest.

Katie collected herself. 'Blue-white,' she said, lips pressing down as she pretended to think about it. 'I think it will tone quite nicely.' She turned to him, a smile blooming on her face.

'Is it big enough?' Rigo demanded.

Did Rigo ever do small? 'It's absolutely perfect,' she breathed, 'but you really didn't have to—'

'But I wanted to.'

'Then that's different.'

'Let me put it on your finger.'

He stared deep into her eyes as he did so, and all the staff gave them a round of applause.

'So you finally did it!'

Everyone turned as Antonia bounded into the room. A haze of vanilla and raspberry perfume accompanied her. Antonia's first hug was for Katie. 'My new sister!' she exclaimed. 'At least, you will be in two days' time.' She turned to Rigo. 'You took long enough,' she accused him. 'I thought you would never get round to asking Katie to marry you.'

'A week is too long?' He exchanged a glance with Katie.

'In my world it's forever!' Antonia exclaimed with a sigh. 'And now it's almost four months later, so you have no excuse—there's only me to sort out now—'

'Some day your prince will come,' Rigo interrupted, handing Antonia another box.

'I thought you didn't like shopping?' she accused him, staring at the gorgeous box with wide, excited eyes.

'For my wife-to-be and for my sister, I made an exception

to that rule. I bought your gift with Katie along to guide me to thank you for being our chief bridesmaid.'

'There would have been trouble if I hadn't been your chief bridesmaid,' Antonia assured him.

Another amused glance was exchanged between Katie and Rigo. They didn't doubt it.

Antonia's fingers trembled as she held up the slim white-gold chain. 'Rigo, it's *favoloso*!' she exclaimed.

There were two charms hanging from Antonia's chain. The first was a diamond set into a sundial to remind them all to make time for each other, while the second charm was a tiny Cinderella slipper to remind Antonia that her prince would come one day—if she could only be a little patient.

'I love you, Katie!' Antonia exclaimed, throwing her arms around Katie's neck. 'And I have something for you.'

'For me?'

'I have bought you your own journal,' Antonia explained. 'Would you like to see what I wrote in mine that first day we met?'

'Only if you want to show it to me,' Katie said as Antonia delved into her industrial-sized bag.

Antonia extracted the small aqua leather-bound book with a flourish and opened it at the appropriate page. '"I want Katie to marry my brother,"' she announced. 'Well? Am I good at predictions or not?' she demanded, staring at Rigo.

'You're the best,' he admitted, 'and for once we were in absolute harmony, though I fell in love with Katie when I heard her voice on the phone before she even came to Italy. I heard the inner beauty when she spoke, and when I met her I fell in love with her all over again.'

Everyone sighed and it took a moment for life to take on its regular beat. When it did, Rigo turned to Katie. 'I have another surprise for you, *cara*, which will be revealed over lunch.'

* * *

Music was playing as they walked into the sun-drenched orangerie and it took Katie a good few moments to recognise her own husky voice. It sounded quite different when she was singing sultry love songs rather than opera.

'Your first album,' Rigo said, embracing her. 'I hope you like it...'

'As long as you love me, I don't need anything more.'

'Can I have your ring?' Antonia piped up.

'Find your own prince,' Rigo told her as they all laughed.

'I love you,' Katie whispered, staring into the eyes of the man without whom her life might have remained unrelieved brown.

'And I love you,' Rigo murmured, with a darkening look they both recognised, 'for...'

'For?' Katie prompted softly, her gaze slipping to his mouth.

'For allowing me to make a bonfire of that suit—'

'Yay!' Antonia exclaimed, discreetly leaving them to it. 'I love a happy ending...'

EPILOGUE

THE CATHEDRAL IN Farnese was lit entirely by candlelight. The soft glow brought out the colours of the stained-glass windows and created jewel-coloured garlands on the white marble floor. The scent of the red roses Rigo had insisted on was everywhere, and the angelic voices of a children's choir provided the only fitting soundtrack for a bride and groom who had dedicated their lives not only to each other, but also to their children's foundation. Each ancient wooden pew was decorated with roses secured by a cascade of cream lace, which echoed the glorious floral arrangements throughout the cathedral supervised by the housekeeper and staff of the newly opened children's centre at the Palazzo Farnese. Guests had come from all over the world to celebrate this wedding, but the place of honour was given to Katie's friends from the office and to Gino and his wife from the pizzeria in Rome, while the young maid who had first lent Katie a swimming costume was now a bridesmaid.

Everyone applauded as the Principe and Principessa Farnese walked down the aisle. Rigo had never looked sexier in the dark, full dress uniform of a prince of the line, with a wide crimson sash across his powerful chest, while his bride wore a cream velvet cloak lined with ivory silk satin and, beneath that, a fitted guipure lace dress, frosted with diamonds.

There were more diamonds in Katie's hair and on the diaphanous veil that billowed behind her. In fact, there was only one anomaly in Katie's modest outfit—her crimson shoes. 'It doesn't do to be too predictable,' she warned Rigo, smiling when he spotted them.

'I love your shoes,' he murmured, bringing Katie into the sunlight so the crowd could see their new princess. 'Life could be so bland and boring without any surprises—though something tells me life will never be that with you around, Signorina Prim.'

As he spoke the cathedral organ swelled with uplifting chords and mellow tonal resolutions in celebration of a true love story between Prince Arrigo Ruggiero Farnese and Katie Bannister, and as the crowd cheered them to their horse-drawn carriage Rigo squeezed Katie's hand and asked her, 'Happy?'

'How could I not be happy?'

His face creased in his attractive curving smile as he helped her into the golden carriage. 'I guess you must like the fact that we Italians laugh, cry and make love on a grand scale.'

Amen to that, Katie thought as she embraced her new world.

* * * * *

COMING NEXT MONTH from Harlequin Presents®

AVAILABLE MARCH 19, 2013

#3129 MASTER OF HER VIRTUE
Miranda Lee

Shy, cautious Violet has had enough of living life in the shadows. She resolves to experience all that life has to offer, starting with internationally renowned film director Leo Wolfe. But is Violet ready for where he wants to take her?

#3130 A TASTE OF THE FORBIDDEN
Buenos Aires Nights
Carole Mortimer

Argentinian tycoon Cesar Navarro has his sexy little chef, Grace Blake, right where he wants her—in his penthouse, at his command! She should be off-limits, but Grace has tantalized his jaded palette, and Cesar finds himself ordering something new from the menu!

#3131 THE MERCILESS TRAVIS WILDE
The Wilde Brothers
Sandra Marton

Travis Wilde would never turn down a willing woman in a king-size bed! Normally innocence like Jennie Cooper's would have the same effect as a cold shower, yet her determination and mouth-watering curves have him burning up all over!

#3132 A GAME WITH ONE WINNER
Scandal in the Spotlight
Lynn Raye Harris

Paparazzi darling Caroline Sullivan hides a secret behind her dazzling smile. Her ex-flame, Russian businessman Roman Kazarov, is back on the scene—is he seeking revenge for her humiliating rejection or wanting to take possession of her troubled business?

You can find more information on upcoming Harlequin® titles, free excerpts and more at www.Harlequin.com.

HPCNM0313RA

#3133 HEIR TO A DESERT LEGACY
Secret Heirs of Powerful Men
Maisey Yates

When recently and reluctantly crowned Sheikh Sayid discovers his country's true heir, he'll do anything to protect him—even marry the child's aunt. It may appease his kingdom, but will it release the blistering chemistry between them...?

#3134 THE COST OF HER INNOCENCE
Jacqueline Baird

Newly free Beth Lazenby has closed the door on her past, until she encounters lawyer Dante Cannavaro who is still convinced of her guilt. But when anger boils over into passion, will the consequences forever bind her to her enemy?

#3135 COUNT VALIERI'S PRISONER
Sara Craven

Kidnapped and held for ransom... His price? Her innocence! Things like this just don't happen to Maddie Lang, but held under lock and key, the only deal Count Valieri will strike is one with an *unconventional* method of payment!

#3136 THE SINFUL ART OF REVENGE
Maya Blake

Reiko has two things art dealer Damion Fortier wants; a priceless Fortier heirloom and her seriously off-limits body! And she has no intention of giving him access to either. So Damion turns up lethal charm to ensure he gets *exactly* he wants....

HPCNM0313RB

REQUEST YOUR
FREE BOOKS!

2 FREE NOVELS PLUS
2 FREE GIFTS!

PASSION GUARANTEED SEDUCTION

YES! Please send me 2 FREE Harlequin Presents® novels and my 2 FREE gifts (gifts are worth about $10). After receiving them, if I don't wish to receive any more books, I can return the shipping statement marked "cancel." If I don't cancel, I will receive 6 brand-new novels every month and be billed just $4.30 per book in the U.S. or $4.99 per book in Canada. That's a saving of at least 14% off the cover price! It's quite a bargain! Shipping and handling is just 50¢ per book in the U.S. and 75¢ per book in Canada.* I understand that accepting the 2 free books and gifts places me under no obligation to buy anything. I can always return a shipment and cancel at any time. Even if I never buy another book, the two free books and gifts are mine to keep forever.

106/306 HDN FVRK

Name	(PLEASE PRINT)	

Address		Apt. #

City	State/Prov.	Zip/Postal Code

Signature (if under 18, a parent or guardian must sign)

Mail to the **Harlequin® Reader Service:**
IN U.S.A.: P.O. Box 1867, Buffalo, NY 14240-1867
IN CANADA: P.O. Box 609, Fort Erie, Ontario L2A 5X3

**Are you a current subscriber to Harlequin Presents books
and want to receive the larger-print edition?
Call 1-800-873-8635 or visit www.ReaderService.com.**

* Terms and prices subject to change without notice. Prices do not include applicable taxes. Sales tax applicable in N.Y. Canadian residents will be charged applicable taxes. Offer not valid in Quebec. This offer is limited to one order per household. Not valid for current subscribers to Harlequin Presents books. All orders subject to credit approval. Credit or debit balances in a customer's account(s) may be offset by any other outstanding balance owed by or to the customer. Please allow 4 to 6 weeks for delivery. Offer available while quantities last.

Your Privacy—The Harlequin® Reader Service is committed to protecting your privacy. Our Privacy Policy is available online at www.ReaderService.com or upon request from the Harlequin Reader Service.

We make a portion of our mailing list available to reputable third parties that offer products we believe may interest you. If you prefer that we not exchange your name with third parties, or if you wish to clarify or modify your communication preferences, please visit us at www.ReaderService.com/consumerschoice or write to us at Harlequin Reader Service Preference Service, P.O. Box 9062, Buffalo, NY 14269. Include your complete name and address.

*These two men have fought battles, waged wars and won.
But when their command—their legacy—is challenged by
the very women they desire the most…who will win?*

*Enjoy a sneak peek from HEIR TO A DESERT LEGACY,
the first tale in the potent new duet,*
SECRET HEIRS OF POWERFUL MEN,
by USA TODAY bestselling author Maisey Yates.

* * *

CHLOE stood up quickly, her chair tilting and knocking into
the chair next to it, the sound loud in the cavernous room.
"Sorry, sorry." She tried to straighten them, her cheeks
burning, her heart pounding. "I have to go."

Sayid was faster than she was, his movements smoother.
He crossed to her side of the table and caught her arm, drawing her to him, his expression dark. "Why are you running
from me?" he asked, dipping his face lower, his expression
fierce. "It's because you know, isn't it? You feel it?"

"Feel what?" she asked.

"This…need between us. How everything in me is demanding that I reach out and pull you hard against me. And
how everything in you is begging me to."

"I don't know what you're talking about," she said.

"I think you do." He lowered his hand and traced her
collarbone with his fingertip, sliding it slowly up the side of
her neck, along her jawbone.

She shook her head, pulling away from him, from his touch. "No," she lied, "I don't."

She didn't understand what was happening with her body, why it was betraying her like this. She'd never felt this kind of wild, overpowering attraction for anyone in her life. But if she was going to, it would have been for a nice scientist who had a large collection of dry-erase pens and looked good in a lab coat.

It would not be for this rough, uncivilized man who believed he could move people around at his whim. This man who sought to control everything and everyone around him.

Unfortunately, her body hadn't asked her opinion on who she should find attractive. Because that was most definitely what this was. Scientific, irrefutable evidence of arousal.

* * *

Will Chloe give in to temptation? And will she ever be able to tame the wild warrior?

Find out in HEIR TO A DESERT LEGACY, available March 19, 2013.

HPEXP0213-2